STAR WARS™

SURVIVOR'S QUEST

Also by Timothy Zahn

STAR WARS™
SURVIVOR'S QUEST

TIMOTHY ZAHN

arrow books

Published by Arrow Books in 2005

1 3 5 7 9 0 8 6 4 2

Arrow Books Limited
The Random House Group Limited
20 Vauxhall Bridge Road, London, SW1V 2SA

Random House Australia (Pty) Limited
20 Alfred Street, Milsons Point, Sydney,
New South Wales 2061, Australia

Random House New Zealand Limited
18 Poland Road, Glenfield
Auckland 10, New Zealand

Random House (Pty) Limited
Endulini, 5a Jubilee Road, Parktown 2193, South Africa

The Random House Group Limited Reg. No. 954009

www.randomhouse.co.uk
www.starwars.com
www.starwarskids.com

A CIP catalogue record for this book
is available from the British Library

Papers used by Random House are natural, recyclable products made from wood grown
in sustainable forests. The manufacturing processes conform to the environmental
regulations of the country of origin

ISBN 0 099 47263 5

Printed and bound in Great Britain by
Bookmarque Ltd, Croydon, Surrey

For Vader's Fist:
The Fighting 501st

THE STAR WARS NOVELS TIMELINE

6.5-7.5 YEARS AFTER
STAR WARS: A New Hope

X-Wing:

Rogue Squadron
Wedge's Gamble
The Krytos Trap
The Bacta War
Wraith Squadron
Iron Fist
Solo Command

8 YEARS AFTER STAR WARS: A New Hope

The Courtship of Princess Leia
A Forest Apart*
Tatooine Ghost

9 YEARS AFTER STAR WARS: A New Hope

The Thrawn Trilogy:

Heir to the Empire
Dark Force Rising
The Last Command

X-Wing: Isard's Revenge

11 YEARS AFTER STAR WARS: A New Hope

I, Jedi

The Jedi Academy Trilogy:

Jedi Search
Dark Apprentice
Champions of the Force

12-13 YEARS AFTER STAR WARS: A New Hope

Children of the Jedi
Darksaber
Planet of Twilight
X-Wing: Starfighters of Adumar

14 YEARS AFTER STAR WARS: A New Hope

The Crystal Star

16-17 YEARS AFTER STAR WARS: A New Hope

The Black Fleet Crisis Trilogy:

Before the Storm
Shield of Lies
Tyrant's Test

17 YEARS AFTER STAR WARS: A New Hope

The New Rebellion

18 YEARS AFTER STAR WARS: A New Hope

The Corellian Trilogy:

Ambush at Corellia
Assault at Selonia
Showdown at Centerpoint

19 YEARS AFTER STAR WARS: A New Hope

The Hand of Thrawn Duology:

Specter of the Past
Vision of the Future

22 YEARS AFTER STAR WARS: A New Hope

Junior Jedi Knights series

Friendly Fire*
Survivor's Quest

23-24 YEARS AFTER STAR WARS: A New Hope

Young Jedi Knights series

25-30 YEARS AFTER
STAR WARS: A New Hope

The New Jedi Order:

Vector Prime
Dark Tide I: Onslaught
Dark Tide II: Ruin
Agents of Chaos I: Hero's Trial
Agents of Chaos II: Jedi Eclipse
Balance Point
Recovery*
Edge of Victory I: Conquest
Edge of Victory II: Rebirth
Star by Star
Dark Journey
Enemy Lines I: Rebel Dream
Enemy Lines II: Rebel Stand
Traitor
Destiny's Way
Ylesia*
Force Heretic I: Remnant
Force Heretic II: Refugee
Force Heretic III: Reunion
The Final Prophecy
The Unifying Force

*An ebook novella

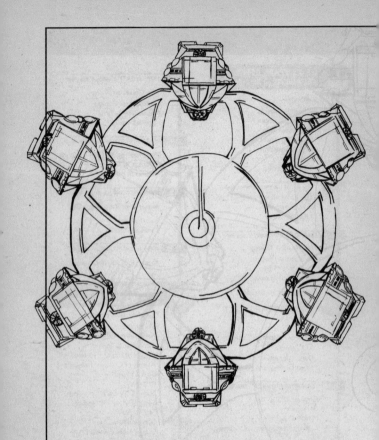

OUTBOUND FLIGHT:

Dreadnaughts and core,

front view

OUTBOUND FLIGHT:

Six Dreadnaughts arranged

around a central core.

CHAPTER 1

THE IMPERIAL STAR DESTROYER MOVED SILENTLY THROUGH the blackness of space, its lights dimmed, its huge sublight engines blazing with the urgency of its mission.

The man standing on the command walkway could feel the rumble of those engines through his boots as he listened to the muttered conversation from the crew pits below him. The conversation sounded worried, too, as worried as he himself felt.

Though for entirely different reasons. For him, this was a personal matter, the frustration of a professional dealing with fallible beings and the capriciousness of a universe that refused to always live up to one's preconceived notions as to what was fitting and proper. An error had been made, possibly a very serious error. And as with all errors, there would likely be unpleasant consequences riding in its wake.

From the starboard crew pit came a muffled curse, and he stifled a grimace. None of that mattered to the Star Destroyer's crew. Their worries stemmed solely from their performance, and whether they would be facing a pat on the back or a boot in the rear at journey's end.

Or possibly they were merely worried about the sublight engines blowing up. On this ship, one never knew.

He shifted his attention downward, his gaze leaving the grandeur of the starscape and coming to rest on the bow of the Star Destroyer stretching out more than a kilometer in front of him. He could remember the days when the mere sight of one of these ships would send shivers up the spines of the bravest of fighters and the most arrogant of smugglers.

1

But those days were gone, hopefully forever. The Empire had been rehabilitated, though of course many within the New Republic still refused to believe that. Under Supreme Commander Pellaeon's firm guidance, the Empire had signed a treaty with the New Republic, and was no longer any more threatening than the Bothans or the Corporate Sector or anyone else.

Almost unwillingly, he smiled as he gazed along the Star Destroyer's long prow. Of course, even in the old days of the Empire, this particular ship would probably have inspired more bewilderment than fear.

It was, after all, hard to take a bright red Star Destroyer very seriously.

From behind him, audible even over the rumble of the engines, came the sound of clumping boots. "Okay, Karrde," Booster Terrik grunted as he came to a halt at his side. "The comm's finally fixed. You can transmit whenever you want."

"Thank you," Talon Karrde said, turning back toward the crew pits and trying hard not to blame Booster for the state his equipment was in. An Imperial Star Destroyer was a huge amount of ship to take care of, and Booster never had nearly enough personnel to do the job right. "H'sishi?" he called. "Go."

[Yes, Chieftain,] the Togorian called back from the comm board, her fur fluffing slightly as her clawed fingers touched the keys. [Transmission complete. Shall I begin alerting the rest of the network now?]

"Yes," Karrde said. "Thank you."

H'sishi nodded and returned her attention to the board.

With that, Karrde knew, he'd done all he could for the moment. Turning again to face the stars, he folded his arms across his chest and tried hard to cultivate his patience. "It'll be all right," Booster murmured from beside him. "We'll be around this star in half an hour and be able to jump to lightspeed. We can be in the Domgrin system in two standard days, tops."

"Assuming the hyperdrive doesn't break down again." Karrde waved a hand. "Sorry. I'm just—you understand."

"Sure," Booster said. "But relax, all right? This is Luke and Mara we're talking about, not some fresh-hatched Neimoidian grubs. Whatever's going on, they're not going to be caught flat-footed."

"Maybe," Karrde said. "Though even Jedi can be surprised." He shook his head. "But that's not the point, is it? The point is that I messed up. I don't like it when that happens."

Booster shrugged his massive shoulders. "Like any of the rest of us do?" he asked pointedly. "You have to face the facts, Karrde, and Fact Number One is that you simply can't know everyone who works for you anymore."

Karrde glared out at the mockingly cheerful red ship stretched out in front of him. But Booster was right. This whole thing had gotten completely out of hand.

He'd started out modestly enough, merely offering to provide timely information to the leaders of the New Republic and Empire so that both sides could be assured that the other wasn't plotting against them. And for the first couple of years everything had gone just fine.

The trouble had come when the various planetary and sector governments within the New Republic had woken up to the benefits of this handy service and decided they wanted aboard, too. After the near civil war that had broken out over the Caamas Document, Karrde hadn't really felt like turning them down, and with permission from his clients on Coruscant and Bastion he'd gone ahead and expanded his operations.

Which naturally meant expanding his personnel as well. In retrospect, he supposed, it had only been a matter of time before something like this happened. He just wished it hadn't happened to Luke and Mara. "Maybe not," he told Booster. "But even if I can't handle everything personally, it's still my responsibility."

"Ah," Booster said knowingly. "So it's your pride that's hurt, is it?"

Karrde eyed his old friend. "Tell me, Booster. Has anyone ever told you you're truly irritating when you try to be sympathetic?"

"Yeah, the subject's come up once or twice," Booster said, grinning. He slapped Karrde's back. "Come on. Let's go down to the Transis Corridor and I'll buy you a drink."

"Assuming the drink dispensers are working today," Karrde murmured as they headed back along the command walkway.

"Well, yeah," Booster conceded. "Always assuming that."

As CANTINAS WENT, MARA JADE SKYWALKER THOUGHT AS SHE sipped her drink, this was definitely one of the strangest she'd ever been in.

Part of that might simply have been due to the locale. Here in the Outer Rim, culture and style weren't exactly up to the standards of Coruscant and the rest of the Core Worlds. That might explain the gaudy wall hangings juxtaposed with ancient plumbing woven around modern drink dispensers, all of it set against a background decor consisting mainly of polished droid parts dating back to before the Clone Wars.

As for the unbreakable mugs and the heavy, stone-topped table she was seated at, the smoothed-over blaster scars in the walls and ceiling were more than enough explanation. When the patrons dived under the tables in the middle of a firefight, they would want those tables to afford them some protection. And they wouldn't want to find themselves sitting on bits of broken crockery, either.

There was no rationale at all, of course, for the very loud, very off-key music.

A brush of air touched her shoulder, and a heavyset man appeared from behind her, pushing his way through the milling crowd. "Sorry," he huffed as he circled the table and landed his bulk back in the seat across from her. "Business, business, business. Never lets up for a minute."

"I suppose not," Mara agreed. He didn't fool her for a second; even without Force sensitivity she would have spotted the furtiveness hidden behind the noise and bustle. Jerf Huxley, master smuggler and minor terror of the Outer Rim, was up to something unpleasant.

The only question was how unpleasant he was planning for that something to be.

"Yeah, it's crazy out here," Huxley went on, taking a noisy swallow of the drink he'd left behind when he hurried off on the mysterious errand that had taken him away from their table. " 'Course, you know all that. Or at least you used to." He eyed her over the rim of his mug. "What's so funny?"

"Oh, nothing," Mara said, not bothering to erase the smile that had caught the other's attention. "I was just thinking about what a trusting person you are."

"What do you mean?" he asked, frowning.

"Your drink," Mara said, gesturing to his mug. "You go away and leave it alone with me, and then you just come back and toss it down without even wondering if I've put something in it."

Huxley's lips puckered, and through the Force Mara caught a hint of his chagrin. He hadn't worried about his drink, of course, because he'd had her under close surveillance the whole time he was gone. He also hadn't intended for her to know that. "All right, fine," he said, banging the mug back onto the table. "Enough with the games. Let's hear it. Why are you here?"

With a man like this, Mara knew, there was no point in glaze-coating it. "I'm here on behalf of Talon Karrde," she said. "He wanted me to thank you for your assistance and that of your organization over the past ten years, and to inform you that your services will no longer be required."

Huxley's face didn't even twitch. Clearly, he'd already suspected this was coming. "Starting when?" he asked.

"Starting now," Mara said. "Thanks for the drink, and I'll be on my way."

"Not so fast," Huxley said, lifting a hand.

Mara froze halfway to her feet. Behind Huxley, blasters had abruptly appeared in the hands of three of the men who had hitherto been minding their own business at the bar. Blasters that were, not surprisingly, pointed at her. "Sit down," he ordered.

Carefully, Mara eased back into her chair. "Was there something else?" she asked mildly.

Huxley gestured again, more emphatically this time, and the off-key background music shut off. As did all conversation. "So that's it, is it?" Huxley demanded quietly. In the sudden silence, even a soft voice seemed to ring against the battered walls. "Karrde's going to toss us aside, just like that?"

"I presume you read the news," Mara said, keeping her voice calm. All around her, she could sense the single-minded animosity of the crowd. Huxley had apparently stocked the place with his friends and associates. "Karrde's getting out of the smuggling business. Has been, for the past three years. He doesn't need your services anymore."

"Yeah, *he* doesn't need," Huxley said with a sniff. "What about what *we* need?"

"I don't know," Mara said. "What *do* you need?"

"Maybe you don't remember what it's like in the Outer Rim, Jade," Huxley said, leaning over the table toward her. "But out here, you don't split things three ways against the ends. You work for one group, period, or you don't work at all. We burned our skyarches behind us years ago when we started working for Karrde. If he pulls out, what are we supposed to do?"

"I expect you'll have to make new arrangements," Mara said. "Look, you had to have known this was coming. Karrde's made no secret of the direction he's been taking."

"Yeah, right," Huxley said contemptuously. "Like anyone believed he'd really go straight."

He drew himself up. "So you want to know what we need? Fine. What we need is something to tide us over until we can get back in the business with someone else."

So there it was: a simple and straightforward pocket-shake. Nothing subtle from this bunch. "How much?" she asked.

"Five hundred thousand." His lip twisted slightly. "In cash credits."

Mara kept her face expressionless. She'd come here prepared for something like this, but that number was way beyond reason. "And where exactly do you expect me to get this little tide-me-over?" she asked. "I don't carry that much spending money on me."

"Don't get cute," Huxley growled. "You know as well as I do that Karrde's got a sector clearinghouse over on Gonmore. They'll have all the credits there we need."

He dug into a pocket and produced a hold-out blaster. "You're going to call and tell them to bring it to us," he said, leveling the weapon at her face across the table. "Half a million. Now."

"Really." Casually, keeping her hands visible, Mara turned her head to look behind her. Most of the cantina's nonsmuggler patrons had already made a quiet exit, she noted, or else had gathered into groups on either side of the confrontation, staying well out of the potential lines of fire. Of more immediate concern was the group of about twenty humans and aliens who had spread themselves out in a semicircle directly behind her, all of them with weapons trained on her back.

All of them also showing varying degrees of wariness, she noted with a certain malicious amusement. Her reputation had apparently preceded her. "You throw an interesting party, Huxley," she said, turning back to face the smuggler chief. "But you don't really think you're equipped to deal with a Jedi, do you?"

Huxley smiled. A very evil smile. A surprisingly evil smile, actually, given the circumstances. "Matter of fact, yeah, I do." He raised his voice. "Bats?"

There was a brief pause. Mara reached out with the Force, but all she could sense was a sudden heightened anticipation from the crowd.

Then, from across the room ahead and to her right came the creak of machinery. A section of floor in a poorly lit area at the far end of the bar began to rise ponderously toward the ceiling, revealing an open-sided keg lift coming up from the storage cellar below. As it rose, something metallic came into view, its shine muted by the patina of age.

Mara frowned, trying to pierce the gloom. The thing was

tall and slender, with a pair of arms jutting out from the sides that gave it a not-quite-humanoid silhouette for all its obvious mechanical origins. The design looked vaguely familiar, but for those first few seconds she couldn't place it. The lift continued to rise, revealing hip-bone-like protrusions at the base of the object's long torso and a trio of curved legs extending outward beneath them.

And then, suddenly, it clicked.

The thing was a pre–Clone Wars droideka—one of the destroyer droids that had once been the pride of the Trade Federation army.

She looked back at Huxley, to find that his smile had widened into a grin. "That's right, Jade," he gloated. "My very own combat droideka, guaranteed to blast the stuffing out of even a Jedi. Bet you never expected to see one of *those* here."

"Not really, no," Mara conceded, running a practiced eye over the droideka as the lift reached the top and wheezed to a halt. It had arrived fully open in combat stance, she noted, instead of rolled into the more compact wheel form used to move into position. That could mean it wasn't able to maneuver anymore.

Did that mean its guns wouldn't track, either? Experimentally, she leaned back in her seat.

For a moment nothing happened. Then the droideka's left arm twitched, its twin blasters shifting angle to match her movement.

So the weapons could indeed track, though they appeared to be under someone's manual control instead of a central computer's or anything on board the droideka itself. In the dim lighting, she couldn't tell whether or not its built-in deflector shield was functioning, but it almost didn't matter. The thing was armed, armored, and pointed straight at her.

Huxley was right. Even the Jedi of that era had gone out of their way to avoid fighting these things.

"But of course I should have," she continued, turning to face Huxley again. "This place is littered with old droid parts. Stands to reason someone would have scraped together enough pieces to make a reasonable copy of a droideka to scare people with."

Huxley's eyes hardened. "You try something cute and you'll see how good a copy it is." He looked over at the group of casual observers to his right, and his eyes locked on someone in the crowd. "You—Sinker!"

A kid maybe sixteen years old stepped out from a knot of older men. "Yes, sir?"

Huxley gestured toward Mara. "Get her lightsaber."

The kid goggled at Mara. "Get—uh—?"

"You deaf?" Huxley bit out. "What are you afraid of?"

Sinker made as if to speak, looked furtively at Mara, swallowed visibly, then stepped hesitantly forward. Mara kept her face expressionless as she watched him approach, his nervousness increasing with each step, until he was visibly shaking as he stopped beside her. "Uh . . . I'm—I'm sorry, ma'am, but—"

"Just take it!" Huxley bellowed.

In a single desperate motion Sinker ducked down, unhooked her lightsaber from her belt, and scampered backward with it. "There," Huxley said sarcastically. "That wasn't so hard, now, was it?"

"Wasn't so useful, either," Mara said. "You think that's all it takes to stop a Jedi? Taking her lightsaber?"

"It's a start," Huxley said.

Mara shook her head. "It's not even that." Looking over at Sinker, she reached out with the Force.

Abruptly, the lightsaber ignited in his hand.

Sinker's startled squeak was mostly lost in the *snap-hiss* as the brilliant blue blade blazed into existence. Rather to her surprise, he didn't drop the weapon and run, but held gamely on to it. "Sinker, what the frost are you doing?" Huxley snapped. "That's not a toy."

"I'm not doing it," Sinker protested, his voice running about an octave higher than it had been before.

"He's right," Mara confirmed as Huxley drew in another bellow's worth of air. "He's not doing this, either."

She reached out to the lightsaber again, making it weave

back and forth in Sinker's grip. The kid wove back and forth with it, hanging on with the grim air of someone who's found himself astride an angry acklay with no idea how to get off.

The rest of the crowd was probably feeling much the same way. For those first few seconds there had been a mad scramble by everyone near Sinker to get out of range of the weapon bobbing in his hands like a drunken crewer. They had mostly stopped moving now, though a few of the smarter ones had decided it was time to get out entirely and were making tracks for the exits. The rest were watching Sinker warily, ready to move again if necessary.

"Knock it off, Jade," Huxley snarled. He wasn't smiling anymore. "You hear me? Knock it *off*."

"And what do you plan to do if I don't?" Mara countered, continuing to swing the lightsaber even as she kept an eye on Huxley's blaster. The others wouldn't shoot her without orders or an immediate threat, she knew, but Huxley himself might forget what his goals and priorities were here.

It was a risk worth taking. With every eye in the cantina on Sinker and his disobedient lightsaber, no one was paying the slightest attention to the droideka standing stolid guard across the room.

Not the droideka, and certainly not the barely visible tip of brilliant green light stealthily slicing a circle through the lift floor around its curved tripod feet.

"I'll blast you into a million soggy pieces, that's what I'll do," Huxley shot back. "Now, let him go, or I'll—"

He never finished the threat. Across the room, with a sudden creaking of stressed metal, the lift floor collapsed, dropping the droideka with a crash back into the cellar.

Huxley spun around, screeching something vicious.

The screech died in midcurse. From the direction the droideka had disappeared, a black-clad figure now appeared, leaping up from the cellar to land on the edge of the newly carved hole. He lifted the short cylinder in his hand to salute position, and with another *snap-hiss*, a green lightsaber blade blazed.

Huxley reacted instantly, and in exactly the way Mara would

have expected. "Get him!" he shouted, stabbing a finger back toward the newcomer.

He didn't have to give the order twice. From the semicircle of gunners behind Mara erupted a blistering staccato of blasterfire. "And *you*—" Huxley added over the noise. He lifted his blaster toward Mara, his finger tightening on the firing stud.

Mara was already in motion. Rising halfway out of her chair, she grabbed the edge of the stone-topped table and heaved it upward. A fraction of a second later Huxley's shot ricocheted off the tabletop now angled toward him, passing harmlessly over Mara's head to gouge yet another hole in the ceiling behind her. Mara heaved the table a little higher, and Huxley's eyes abruptly widened as he realized she intended to drop its full weight squarely into his lap, pinning him helplessly into his chair and then crushing him to the floor.

He was wrong. Even as he scrambled madly to get out of his chair and away from the falling table before it was too late, Mara kicked her own chair back out of her way. Using her grip on the table edge as a pivot point, she lifted her feet and swung herself forward and downward.

With a lighter table, the trick wouldn't have worked, and she would have simply landed on her rear in front of her chair with the table in her lap. But this one was so massive, with so much inertia, that she was able to swing under the edge now falling backward toward her, land on the floor beneath where it had been standing, and get her hands clear before the edge crashed into the floor behind her.

This put the heavy tabletop neatly between her and the twenty-odd blasters that had been trained on her back.

Huxley, still completely off stride, had time for a single yelp before Mara lunged forward, slapped his gun hand aside with her left hand, and then grabbed a fistful of his shirt and hauled him down into cover with her. Her right hand snaked up her left sleeve, snatched her small sleeve gun from its arm holster, and jammed the muzzle up under his chin. "You know the drill," she said. "Let's hear it."

Huxley, his eyes on the edge of terror, filled his lungs. "Huxlings! Cease fire! Cease fire!"

There was a second of apparent indecision. Then, around the room, the blasters fell quiet. "Very good," Mara said. "What's part two?"

Huxley's lip twisted. "Drop your weapons," he growled, opening his hand and letting his own blaster fall to the floor. "You hear me? Drop 'em."

There was another brief pause, then a dull clatter as the others followed suit. Mara stretched out with the Force, but she could sense no duplicity. Huxley had caved completely, and his gang knew better than to try to second-guess his decisions. Keeping her blaster pressed under his chin, she got to her feet, hauling Huxley up with her. She gave each of the half-sullen, half-terrified gang members a quick look, just to make it clear what rash heroics would cost, then turned to the man in black as he walked up to her. "So didn't you see that droideka before Huxley lifted it up here?" she asked.

"Oh, I saw it," Luke Skywalker acknowledged, closing down his lightsaber but keeping it ready in his hand.

"And?"

Luke shrugged. "I was curious to see whether it still worked. Did it?"

"We didn't get a complete field test," Mara said. "It didn't look very mobile, and I'd guess its tracking is on manual instead of automatic. But it probably fires just fine."

"Fired," Luke corrected. "It's going to need a little reworking."

"That's okay," Mara assured him, sliding her sleeve gun back into its concealed holster. "Huxley's people will have some time on their hands."

She gave Huxley a push away from her, letting go of his shirt. He staggered slightly but managed to maintain his balance. "Here's the deal. Before I leave, I'll credit twenty thousand to your account. Not because Karrde owes you anything at all, but simply as a thanks for your years of service to his organization."

"Karrde's a little softhearted that way," Luke added.

"Yes, he is," Mara agreed. "I, on the other hand, am not. You'll take it, you'll be happy with it, and you will never even *think* about making trouble for any of us again. Clear?"

Huxley had the look of a man chewing droid parts, but he nodded. "Clear," he muttered.

"Good." Mara turned to Sinker and held out her hand. "My lightsaber, please?"

Bracing himself, Sinker walked toward her, the lightsaber still humming in his grasp. He offered it to her at arm's length; taking it, she closed down the blade and hung it back on her belt. "Thank you," she said.

Across the room, the door slid open, and a young man darted in. He got two steps before everything seemed to register, and he faltered to a confused halt. "Uh . . . Chief?" he called, looking at Huxley.

"This better be important, Fisk," Huxley warned.

"Uh . . ." Fisk looked around uncertainly. "It's—I just got a signal in for someone named Mara. It was from—"

"It was from Talon Karrde," Luke cut in. "He wants Mara to contact him aboard the *Errant Venture* as soon as possible at—" He narrowed his eyes as he gazed across the room at the boy. "—in the Domgrin system."

Fisk's mouth was hanging slightly open. "Uh . . . yeah," he breathed. "That's right."

"Yes," Luke said, almost offhandedly. "Oh, and it came in under the Paspro-five encrypt. That's the one that starts out usk-herf-enth—well, you know the rest."

The kid's jaw was hanging even lower now. Blinking once, he nodded.

"We'd better get going then," Mara said. She started to step around the table, then paused. "Oh, and by the way," she added, looking back at Huxley. "It's not *Jade* anymore. It's *Jade Skywalker*. This is my husband, Luke Skywalker. The Jedi Master. He's even better at this stuff than I am."

"Yeah," Huxley muttered, eyeing Luke. "Yeah, I got the message."

"Good," Mara said. "Good-bye, Huxley."

She and Luke headed toward the door through a wide path that magically opened up for them through the crowd. A moment later, they were out in the cool evening air.

"Very impressive," she commented as they headed down the street toward the spaceport and the waiting *Jade Sabre*. "When did you start being able to pull details like that out of other people's minds?"

"It's easy enough when you know how," Luke said with a straight face.

"Uh-huh," Mara said. "Let me guess. Karrde sent you the same message?"

Luke nodded. "I got it in relay from the ship while I was poking around the storage cellar."

"That's what I thought," Mara said. "And so when the opportunity presented itself, you couldn't resist playing the Omniscient Jedi trick."

Luke shrugged. "It never hurts for these fringe types to have a little healthy fear of Jedi."

"I suppose not," Mara agreed hesitantly.

Luke looked sideways at her. "You don't agree?"

"I don't know," she said. "Something about it bothers me. Maybe because Palpatine always ruled through fear."

"I see your point," Luke admitted. "But this isn't quite the same. It's more like putting the fear of justice into them. And of course, I would never pull anything like this with regular people."

"I know," Mara said. "And it should help keep Huxley in line. I suppose that's what counts."

She waved an impatient hand. "Never mind. I'm just feeling the weight of my past, I guess. So what exactly *was* this message from Karrde?"

"Basically just what I said in there," Luke told her. "We're to meet him and Booster at Domgrin as quickly as we can get there."

"And he sent it to the *Sabre* and Huxley's people both?"

"Apparently so." Luke shook his head. "He must really be anxious to talk to us if he's doubling up messages this way."

"I was just thinking that," Mara said. "And that's not like him. Unless," she added thoughtfully, "there's some crisis brewing."

"Isn't there always?" Luke asked dryly. "Come on, let's get these funds of yours transferred and get out of here."

CHAPTER 2

THE BRIGHT RED STAR DESTROYER WAS WAITING SILENTLY IN the distance as Luke brought the *Jade Sabre* out of hyperspace. "There it is," he said, nodding at the curved forward canopy. "What do you think?"

"I'm picking up some mining and transport ships in the area," Mara said, peering at the long-range scanner. "We'd better get a little closer if we don't want eavesdroppers."

"You want to take us in, or shall I?"

"I'll do it," Mara said. Taking a quick look at the monitors, she got a grip on the control stick and pushed it forward. Luke leaned back in his seat, hunching his shoulders once to stretch tired muscles, and watched his wife work.

Wife. For a moment he listened to the word as it bounced around his brain, marveling at the sound of it. Even after nearly three years of marriage there was something that felt strange and awesome about the whole concept.

Of course, it had hardly been three years the way normal couples counted time. Even Han and Leia, who'd dealt with crisis after crisis early in their marriage, had at least been fighting those battles at each other's side. In Luke and Mara's case, his responsibilities at the Jedi academy and her need to disengage herself in an orderly fashion from the intricate workings of Talon Karrde's organization had kept them apart almost as much as they'd been before their wedding. Their moments together had been few and precious, and they'd had only a handful of the longer periods of togetherness that Han had once privately referred to as the breaking-in period.

That was in fact one of the reasons Luke had suggested he

accompany Mara on this particular trip. She would still be working, of course, meeting with groups of Karrde's current and former associates. But between meetings he'd hoped they would be able to spend some decent stretches of time together.

It had actually worked pretty well. Up until now.

"I trust you've already noticed how strange this is," Mara said into his musings. "Even if we push the *Sabre* for all she's worth, we're at least a week away from Coruscant. Whatever this new crisis is, we're too far away to be of any use to anyone."

"Especially since I made it clear to Leia at the start that we weren't supposed to be disturbed unless it was a flat-out invasion," Luke agreed. "Of course, if this isn't Leia, it only leaves one possibility."

"Two, actually," Mara corrected. "And I'd certainly hope Karrde knows better by now than to flag us for anything trivial."

"Leia and Karrde make two," Luke said. "Who's this third option?"

She threw him a sideways look. "We're meeting Karrde aboard the *Errant Venture*, remember?"

Luke made a face. "Booster."

"Right," Mara said. "And Booster might *not* know better. If he doesn't, shall we make a pact right now to make sure he does before we leave this system?"

"Deal."

She threw him a slightly evil smile and returned to her piloting.

Luke turned back to the canopy, smiling out at the stars. Despite all the time they'd spent apart, he and Mara had a distinct advantage: They were both Jedi. And because of that, they shared a mental and emotional bond that was far deeper than most couples were able to forge in an entire lifetime together. Deeper and stronger even than anything Luke had experienced in his doomed relationships with Gaeriel Captison or the long-departed Callista.

He still remembered vividly the moment that bond had

first appeared, hammered into existence as the two of them fought those combat droids deep under the fortress their old adversary Grand Admiral Thrawn had set up on the planet Nirauan. At the time Luke had thought it was nothing more than a temporary melding of their minds created by the heat and pressure of a life-and-death situation. It was only afterward, when the battle was over but the bond remained, that he'd realized it had become a permanent part of their lives.

Even then, he hadn't completely understood it. He'd assumed that it had sprung forth complete; that in those few hours it had brought the two of them into as deep an understanding of each other as it was possible to have. But in the three years since then, he'd come to realize that he had just barely scratched the surface. Mara was far more complex a human being than he'd ever suspected. As, in fact, he himself was.

Which meant that, Jedi or not, Force-bond or not, there was going to be more for them to learn about each other for a long time to come. In all likelihood, a lifetime's worth of time. He was very much looking forward to the journey.

And yet, at the same time, he couldn't help but feel a small twinge of uncertainty. His marriage to Mara felt *right* to him, in every respect . . . but hovering in the background behind all their happiness and success was the distant echo of Yoda's stories of the old Jedi Order during Luke's training on Dagobah.

Specifically, the part about Jedi keeping themselves out of precisely this kind of love relationship.

He hadn't given those teachings much weight at the time. The Empire was in control of the known galaxy, Darth Vader was breathing down the Rebel Alliance's collective neck, and all his thoughts were focused on his own survival and the survival of his friends. When Han and Leia had gotten married, Leia having Force skills hadn't seemed like a big deal. She was certainly strong in the Force, but she hadn't progressed nearly far enough in her training to call herself a Jedi.

But it was different with Luke. He *had* been a Jedi when

he'd asked Mara to marry him. True, their chances of survival at the time had been somewhat uncertain, but that hadn't affected the sincerity of his proposal or the depth of his feelings toward her. And despite these occasional twinges, he'd certainly found peace in his decision and in their subsequent marriage.

Could Yoda have been wrong about how Jedi relationships were supposed to work? That was the easiest answer. But that would mean the entire Jedi Order had been wrong about it. That didn't seem likely, unless on some level all of them had lost the ability to hear the Force clearly.

Could that particular dictum have ended with the fall of that particular group, then? Yoda had also said something about the Force having been brought back into balance, though he'd been somewhat vague about the details. Could this have rendered that part of the Jedi Code no longer applicable?

He didn't have the answers. He wondered if he ever would.

"Okay, they're on us," Mara announced, leaning back in her seat. "Got an antenna swiveling for a tight beam. I've been wondering how far away a Star Destroyer's sensors could pick us up."

Luke forced his thoughts back to the situation at hand. "Though with the *Errant Venture* you always have to allow for malfunctions," he reminded her.

"True," she agreed. "Sometimes I think of that ship as one massive red warning light."

"It's certainly bright enough." Luke shook his head. "I am never, *ever,* going to get used to that color."

"I kind of like it," Mara said. "Especially given where it came from."

"You mean Booster strong-arming General Bel Iblis to refit and repaint?"

"I was thinking of the paint itself," Mara said. "Did you know the New Republic bought all of it from Karrde?"

Luke blinked. "You're kidding. Did Bel Iblis know?"

"Don't be silly," Mara said with a lopsided smile. "You know Bel Iblis. He'd have had a fit on general principles if he'd known Karrde had made any money on this deal. No, Karrde played it all very cool and through at least three intermediaries and a dummy corporation. I don't think even Booster knows."

"Trust me, he doesn't," Luke said. "Corran once told me that one of Booster's great joys in life these days is telling people how he managed this whole thing without any help or interference from the great Talon Karrde. I wonder what he'd say if he knew that was Karrde's paint on his hull."

"I know what *Karrde* would say," Mara warned. "Both before *and* after he nailed my hide to the hull. One of *his* great joys is watching Booster strut around blissfully unaware of the ways he's dipped in and out of the old pirate's life over the years."

Luke shook his head. "They're a matched pair. You know that?"

"Don't tell them that, either," Mara said. There was a beep from the board. "Okay, here we go. Encrypt Paspro-nine . . ."

She touched a few keys. There was a second beep, and suddenly the comm display lit up with Karrde's familiar face.

He wasn't smiling.

"Mara; Luke," he greeted them, his voice as grim as he looked. "Thank you for coming so promptly. I'm sorry I had to drag you out here like this, away from your schedule. Especially you, Luke; I know how much you went through to free up time for this."

"Don't worry about it," Mara said for both of them. "The trip was getting a little routine anyway. What's up?"

"What's up is that I've lost a message," Karrde said bluntly. "Four days ago my sector relay post at Comra picked up a transmission, marked urgent, and addressed to you, Luke."

Luke frowned. "Me?"

"So the chief of the station says," Karrde replied. "But that was about all he got. Before he or anyone else could pass it on down the line, it vanished."

"You think it was stolen?" Luke asked.

Karrde's lips compressed briefly. "I know it was stolen," he said. "We even know the name of the man who stole it, because when the message disappeared from the station, so did he. Have you ever heard of anyone by the name of Dean Jinzler?"

"Doesn't sound familiar," Luke said, searching his memory. "Mara?"

"No," Mara said. "Who is he?"

Karrde shook his head. "Unfortunately, I don't know, either."

"Wait a second," Mara said. "This is one of *your* people, and you don't know everything there is to know about him?"

The corner of Karrde's lip twitched. "I didn't know everything about *you* when I hired you, either," he pointed out.

"Sure, but I was a special case," Mara countered. "I thought you knew better with everyone else. Do we have any idea where the message originated or who sent it?"

"Actually, we have both," Karrde said, his voice going even darker. "The planet of origin was Nirauan." He paused. "The sender was an Admiral Voss Parck."

Luke felt his forehead creasing, a strange sensation trickling through him. Nirauan: Thrawn's private base, full of Imperials and warriors of Thrawn's own people, the Chiss. The fortress he and Mara had escaped from by the skin of their teeth three years before.

And Admiral Voss Parck, the onetime Imperial captain whom Thrawn had left in command of that base before his death. They'd had a brief run-in with Parck during their time on Nirauan, too, right after the admiral had tried to recruit Mara to their side.

"I see that name *is* familiar to both of you," Karrde said. "I've always had the feeling I didn't get the complete story of your little visit out that way."

Luke could sense Mara's sudden discomfort. "That was my doing," he said. "I insisted we keep most of the details from everyone except the highest-ranking New Republic officials."

"I quite understand," Karrde said calmly. "Actually, with

Parck's name I think I can probably re-create most of the missing pieces myself. He was a close associate of Grand Admiral Thrawn's, wasn't he?"

"Actually, he was the *Victory*-class Star Destroyer captain who found Thrawn at the edge of the Unknown Regions after he'd been exiled by the rest of his people forty-odd years ago," Mara said. "He was so impressed with Thrawn's tactical skill that he took a chance and brought him to Palpatine. When Palpatine himself later exiled Thrawn back to the Unknown Regions, Parck was one of the officers who was sent out there with him."

"Exiled," Karrde murmured. "Yes. And I take it whatever Thrawn's true mission was, Parck stayed behind to complete it?"

"Basically," Luke conceded. So much for the clever little cover story Palpatine had created to explain Thrawn's departure from the Empire. But then, Karrde had always been good at reading between the lines. "I wish I could be more specific."

"That's all right." Karrde smiled. "I suppose the New Republic has to have *some* secrets."

"Not that they have very many from you anymore," Mara said. "So what's the story on this Dean Jinzler?"

Karrde shrugged. "He's a middle-age man, somewhere in his sixties. Quite intelligent, though he's apparently never made much of a name for himself in any profession or system. He traveled around quite a bit during the Clone Wars, though the details of his activities are sketchy. He joined the organization about a year ago with certificates in comm tech, droid maintenance, and hyperdrive tech."

"Impressive credentials," Mara commented. "Doesn't sound like the sort of person you'd stick in an Outer Rim Dead Zone station."

"Well, that's where it gets interesting," Karrde said heavily. "When I pulled up his file, I discovered that about eight weeks ago he himself asked for a transfer to that particular post."

Luke and Mara exchanged looks. "Now, that *is* interesting," Mara said. "Eight weeks, you say?"

"Yes," Karrde said. "I don't know if it means anything, but that was just about the time my researchers finished pulling together the material I'd asked for on Nirauan, Thrawn, and associated topics."

"Sounds like our boy Jinzler may have a certificate in creative eavesdropping, too," Mara said. "I presume we have someone digging up everything we can on him?"

"We do," Karrde said. "Unfortunately, it's going to take time. In the meantime, Admiral Parck has apparently sent you a message important enough for Jinzler to consider worth stealing. The question is what exactly we do about it."

"I don't see that we have any choice," Luke said. "Until we know what the message says, we can't even begin to guess what Jinzler might want with it." He shrugged. "So I guess we're off to Nirauan."

Beside him, Mara stirred in her chair, and he sensed her sudden tension. But she remained silent. "I was afraid you'd say that," Karrde said heavily. "Given all I don't know about your last trip there, I *do* know that you were chased out of the system. True?"

"Not exactly *chased* out," Luke said. "On the other hand, I'll admit I've never felt we'd be especially welcome if we went back. But the situation's changed. If Parck has a message for us, I assume he'll at least wait until he's delivered it before he tries to shoot us out of the sky."

"Not funny," Mara muttered.

"Sorry," Luke apologized. "I'm open to other suggestions."

"Why can't you just signal him from here?" Karrde asked. "Between the *Venture* and the HoloNet, we should be able to boost a signal that far."

Luke shook his head. "No. He sent the signal through your station, not the regular HoloNet. *And* he addressed it to me, not the Senate or anyone else on Coruscant. That implies it's something he doesn't want leaking out."

"A little late for that," Karrde murmured.

"Even so, we can't risk running any of this through regular communications channels," Luke said. "And under the circumstances, we'd better not trust your network with it, either. Jinzler may have left friends behind in case of follow-up messages."

"I suppose that makes sense," Karrde said reluctantly. "Mara? Thoughts or comments?"

"Only that if we're going, we'd better do it," she said, her voice under careful control. "Thanks for the heads-up."

"Under the circumstances, it seemed the least I could do," Karrde said. "It also occurred to me that if you went, you might prefer to use that alien ship you brought back from there. I've sent Shada and *Wild Karrde* to go pick it up."

"A nice thought," Luke said. "But I don't think we've got time to wait for it."

"Definitely not," Mara agreed. "Thanks anyway. How many people have you told about that ship, by the way?"

"Just Shada," Karrde said. "No one else."

"Good," Mara said. "I'd like to keep it a secret a little longer, if we can."

"No problem," Karrde assured her. "If and when we dig out information on Jinzler, shall I send a courier to Nirauan to meet you?"

"Don't bother," Luke said. "Chances are we'll be heading straight back to Coruscant within a couple of days anyway."

"And never mind Jinzler's history," Mara added. "You just concentrate on tracking down the man himself. The last time secret information slipped through our fingers, we nearly ended up with a civil war."

Karrde winced. "Yes; the Caamas Document," he said. "Don't worry, we'll find him."

"Good," Luke said. "We'll talk to you when we get back to civilization."

"Right," Karrde said. "Good luck."

"And happy hunting to you," Luke said.

He touched the comm switch, and Karrde's face vanished. "Well, like you said, the trip was starting to get routine," he commented.

Mara didn't answer. "I take it you're not happy about all this?" Luke suggested as he punched for the nav computer.

"You mean about going to Nirauan?" Mara asked, her voice thick with sarcasm. "Nirauan, where I single-handedly destroyed their whole docking bay deck for them? I'm sure Parck's just dying to see *me* again."

"Oh, come on," Luke soothed. "I'm sure he's gotten over that by now. Anyway, it's really Baron Fel you should be worried about. He was probably the one in charge of the fighters you wrecked."

She turned a high-voltage glare on him. "You're just dripping with cheer and good humor today, aren't you?"

"*Somebody* has to be," Luke said, giving her a totally innocent look.

Mara held the glare another moment. Then her face softened. "You're as worried as I am, aren't you?" she asked quietly.

Luke sighed. "I can think of only one reason Parck would suddenly want to talk to us," he admitted. "Probably the same reason that's already occurred to you."

Mara nodded. "The unidentified enemy he told me was coming this direction," she said. "The one that had both him and Fel seriously concerned."

"Unless they were lying about that," Luke suggested. "They *were* trying to talk you into joining them, remember."

Mara turned to look out at the canopy. "No," she said. "No, they were convinced. They might have been wrong, but they were sincerely wrong."

"You're probably right," Luke agreed. "I wish now we'd brought Artoo with us. He came in pretty handy the last time we were there."

"We're not going down to the planet itself," Mara said firmly. "Besides, I know Leia is a lot more comfortable having him aboard during this stage of Jaina's flight training."

Behind Luke, the computer beeped completion of its task. "Here we go," he said, feeding the course setting into the helm.

"It's almost funny, you know," Mara commented thoughtfully. "You actually called it, not fifteen minutes ago. Remember?"

Luke grimaced. *Especially since I made it clear to Leia at the start that we weren't supposed to be disturbed unless it was a flat-out invasion.* "The Force is strong in my family," he murmured.

"So I've heard," Mara said. "Let's just hope that was you talking and not the Force. Come on; let's get this over with."

TWO DAYS LATER, THEY REACHED THE NIRAUAN SYSTEM.

"Looks quiet enough," Luke said as they flew through space toward the battle-scarred planet itself. "No fighter patrols or anything else I can pick up."

Mara was silent a moment, and Luke could sense her reaching out with the Force. "I'm not getting anything, either," she said. "I get the bad feeling Parck wasn't expecting us."

Luke frowned at her. "I thought you *didn't* want him waiting for us."

"I didn't want his *fighters* waiting for us," Mara corrected. "But the complete lack of a welcoming committee implies that the message he sent was complete in and of itself. He may be annoyed to find he has visitors."

"Well, there's one way to find out," Luke said, adjusting the comm for one of the frequencies the Imperials and Chiss had been using the last time they were here. "Let's knock and see if anyone's home."

He tapped the key. "This is Luke Skywalker, Jedi Master of the New Republic, to Admiral Voss Parck. Repeat; this is Luke Skywalker calling Admiral Parck. Please respond."

He leaned back in his seat. "Now, I guess we wait until—"

Abruptly, the comm display came on, revealing the blue face and glowing red eyes of a Chiss. "Hello, Skywalker," the alien said. His eyes seemed to burn into Luke's face. "And Jade is here, too, I see," he added, his face turning slightly to gaze at Mara. "This is Kres'ten'tarthi, commander of Mitth'raw'nuruodo's household phalanx for the Empire of the Hand. This is certainly a surprise."

"I don't know why it should be," Luke said evenly. "Or didn't you know Admiral Parck had sent me a message?"

"Yes, I knew," Kres'ten'tarthi said. "The admiral will be here in a moment. In the meantime, would you care to land and join us?" His face seemed to tighten slightly. "Don't worry, the docking bay has been completely repaired since your last visit."

"Thanks for your hospitality," Mara said before Luke could answer. "I think we'll stay here."

The Chiss inclined his head. "As you wish."

The display blanked. "You know him?" Luke asked.

"Yes, though I'd only heard his core name, Stent," Mara said. "He was one of the Chiss on guard duty when Parck and Fel were talking to me. I think he took it personally when you came charging to the rescue."

Luke shook his head. "We have friends all over this planet, don't we?"

"We have friends all over this whole region of space," Mara retorted. "Don't forget, the rest of Thrawn's people are out there somewhere. Whole star systems full of Chiss, whom I notice haven't exactly been eager to make their presence known to the New Republic."

"Maybe they've got enough troubles of their own, and figure they don't need to share ours," Luke offered.

"Maybe," Mara said. "Interesting term Stent used. Did you notice?"

"Empire of the Hand," Luke said, nodding. "Probably relates to the Hand of Thrawn."

"Obviously," Mara said. "I was wondering more about the *Empire* part. You and your Rebel friends certainly had plenty of trouble with Palpatine's Empire. You suppose the Chiss might be having similar problems with Thrawn's?"

"Could be," Luke said doubtfully. Grand Admiral Thrawn— *Mitth'raw'nuruodo,* to give his full Chiss name—had been arguably the greatest military genius the galaxy had ever known, certainly the greatest the Empire had ever had in its ranks. Palpatine had sent him and a task force out into the Unknown Regions before the Rebel Alliance had been formed, ostensibly in punishment for a breach of palace politics, but in reality with the secret mission of exploring and conquering new systems for future Imperial expansion.

On their last visit to Nirauan, Luke and Mara had learned just how well he had succeeded at that task. In just those few short years he had opened up huge expanses of territory, putting them under the control of his Imperial forces and the handful of Chiss such as Stent who had remained loyal to him. The original secrecy of the project had also been maintained, with the leaders of the Imperial Remnant on Bastion having never even heard of the project up to that point.

Now, three years later, Supreme Commander Pellaeon and a handful of trusted advisers had had some limited contact with Parck and the Nirauan offshoot of their former regime. Leia and some of the other top people in the New Republic also knew of its existence, though Luke suspected neither government had any idea how extensive the new territory actually was. Only he and Mara knew that, and for the moment they had decided to keep it private.

The designation *Empire of the Hand* for the region, however, was a new one on them. "I can't see Thrawn becoming that kind of tyrant, though," he went on, thinking back over the New Republic's own struggles against the Grand Admiral. "He never struck me as the sort to rule by terror or suppression."

"Doesn't mean he couldn't have learned," Mara pointed out. "Palpatine was an excellent teacher. Or if not Thrawn himself, maybe those who succeeded him went in that direction. Happens all the time."

"I suppose," Luke conceded. "Still—"

He broke off as the comm display came on again, this time revealing a gray-haired human with a lined face and quick, shrewd eyes. "Hello, Mara," he said. "Master Skywalker. This is a surprise, I must say. I assumed you'd be well on your way to Crustai by now."

Luke frowned. "Crustai?"

"The rendezvous point," Parck said, his forehead furrowing as he frowned in turn. "Didn't you get my message?"

"Unfortunately, it took a wrong turn," Mara told him. "Someone named Dean Jinzler made off with it before anyone else could see the contents."

"Really," Parck murmured, looking back and forth between them. "You know this man?"

"Never heard of him before," Mara said. "I take it this message was worth stealing?"

"In the proper hands, it could very well be," Parck said, his lips compressing briefly. "This is not good at all."

"Yes, that's basically the conclusion we came to," Mara agreed. "You want to fill us in?"

"Of course," Parck said, his thoughts clearly still on the wayward message. "Though if the Chiss . . ." He seemed to shake himself. "Well, what's done is done," he said briskly. "Reality must always be dealt with, whether we like it or not. Tell me, Skywalker, have you ever heard of something called Outbound Flight?"

"Yes, I think so," Luke said slowly, thinking hard. "I came across a reference to it when I was searching for information on Jorus C'baoth, back when his clone was working with— was trying to kidnap Leia's twins," he corrected himself quickly. C'baoth's former connection with Thrawn, and especially his connection with Thrawn's death, might not be a wise subject to bring up. "Wasn't it some grand effort a few years before the Clone Wars to send an expedition to another galaxy?"

"Very good," Parck said. "Yes, that was basically it. The project consisted of six brand-new Dreadnaughts, clustered together in a hexagonal pattern around a central storage core. The personnel consisted of six Jedi Masters and a dozen Jedi Knights, including C'baoth himself, plus some fifty thousand others, crewers and their families."

Luke blinked. "And their *families*?"

"Traveling to another galaxy would take time," Parck reminded him. "Especially at the low speeds Dreadnaughts were capable of making. In addition, since they would be passing through the Unknown Regions on the way, there was some suggestion of planting a few colonies as they went."

"Ah," Luke said, nodding. "Hence the design."

"Correct," Parck said. "If a colony was indeed formed, one of the Dreadnaughts could be easily detached from the cluster to provide the colonists with protection and mobility."

"Yes," Luke said. "Aside from that, about all I know is that the expedition never returned. Did they make it to another galaxy?"

Beside him, Mara stirred. "They didn't even make it out of ours," she said quietly. "Thrawn intercepted the mission at the edge of Chiss space and destroyed it."

"Yes," Parck said. "The rest of the Chiss were not pleased, to say the least. Thrawn was nearly exiled on the spot, though he apparently was able to talk his way out of it somehow."

"Yes, I remember the history lesson from the last time I was here," Mara said. "The Chiss are fanatics on the topic of preemptive strikes. So what does a fifty-year-old tragedy have to do with us?"

"Just this." Parck's eyes bored into hers. "The Chiss have found the remains of Outbound Flight. And they want to give it back."

FOR A LONG MOMENT, MARA JUST STARED AT THE SCREEN, a hundred different thoughts and emotions twisting themselves through her mind. "No," she said, the word popping out without conscious effort. "That's impossible. It has to be a trick."

Parck shrugged. "I agree it sounds odd. But Aristocra Formbi seemed sincere when he contacted me."

"It's impossible," Mara insisted again. "You told me Thrawn destroyed Outbound Flight. When Thrawn destroys something, he does a very thorough job of it."

"Which I would know far better than you," Parck returned pointedly. "The fact remains that the Chiss say they've found Outbound Flight. The description Formbi gave certainly fits the design, and there's no other reason I can think of why even a single Dreadnaught should be out this far."

He lifted an eyebrow. "The hows and whys are questions

none of us can answer right now. The only question you have to deal with is what you're going to do about it."

"What *we're* going to do?" Luke asked. "It seems to me this is something for the entire New Republic leadership, not a couple of Jedi."

"Perhaps," Parck said. "But perhaps not. Outbound Flight *was* a brainchild of the Jedi, after all, not the Old Republic Senate or even Palpatine. That's why Formbi asked that you be contacted and invited to join the official expedition to the site of the remains."

"He asked for *Luke*?" Mara asked.

"Specifically," Parck confirmed, turning to look toward a screen to his right. "Here's the entire message: 'To Luke Skywalker, Jedi Master, Jedi academy, Yavin Four; from Chaf'orm'bintrano, Aristocra of the Fifth Ruling Family, Sarvchi. A patrol from the Chiss Expansionary Defense Fleet has located what appears to be the remnants of the expeditionary mission known to you as Outbound Flight deep inside Chiss territory. As a token of respect, and with deep regret for Chiss involvement in its destruction, we offer you the opportunity to join the official examination of the vessel. I will await you at the world Crustai'—here he gave the coordinates—'for the next fifteen days, at which time we will travel together to Outbound Flight's location. I urge you to attend, so that through you we may discuss arrangements for the return of the remains to your people.' End of message."

"And this all came from this Chaf'orm'whatever?" Mara asked. "The address and everything?"

"Chaf'orm'bintrano," Parck supplied. "Call him Formbi. Obviously, I supplied the location of the Jedi academy for him. The Chiss know virtually nothing about the New Republic, and certainly nothing about its worlds."

"Yet he knew Luke's name?"

"Well, no, not exactly," Parck said. "Formbi asked for the name of the New Republic's most prominent Jedi. That would of course be Master Skywalker."

"So you and Formbi are on good speaking terms?" Mara pressed.

"I wouldn't say we're on *good* speaking terms," Parck hedged. "Official Chiss policy is still that Thrawn was a renegade who brought nothing but dishonor on the rest of his people."

"Tell that to Stent," Luke murmured.

Parck shrugged. "I didn't say all the Chiss agreed. I simply said that was the official line. But Formbi and I have spoken on occasion, and the conversations have been reasonably civil."

He glanced somewhere offscreen. "I've run the numbers on travel to the Crustai system. Assuming you can make at least point three in that ship, you should have just enough time to get there before Formbi's fifteen days are up."

"Thank you," Luke said. "If you don't mind, we'll discuss it and get back to you."

"As you wish," Parck said. "I hope to speak with you again soon."

He was still sitting there, gazing at them, when Luke switched off the comm.

Mara kept her eyes on the planet, feeling Luke's unspoken question hanging in the air between them. "What do you think?" she asked instead.

"It's an intriguing offer," Luke said. "As far as I could tell, the whole Outbound Flight Project was wrapped in secrecy. There was hardly anything even in the Coruscant archives that I could find."

"There's a lot we don't know anymore about that whole era," Mara said. "The Clone Wars and Palpatine's purge saw to that."

"That's my point," Luke said. "If even a part of Outbound Flight survived, there's a chance that some of its records survived with it. This could be the kind of glimpse into the past that we've always wanted."

"That *we've* always wanted?" Mara countered, looking at him. "Or that *you've* always wanted?"

"All right, fine," Luke said, clearly puzzled by her reaction. "I admit it: I'd like to know more about the Jedi of that time. Wouldn't you?"

"That's also when Palpatine came to power," she reminded him darkly, turning back to the canopy. "Personally, there's a lot about that era that I *don't* want to know."

"I understand," Luke said gently. "But on the other hand, we can't ignore the potential of this offer."

"What potential?" Mara scoffed. "The chance for the Chiss to assuage their guilt over letting Thrawn run wild as long as they did?"

"I'm sure that's part of it," Luke said. "The Chiss claim to be an honorable people. Even Thrawn made a point of not killing or destroying more than he thought was necessary. But I have a strong feeling that there's more to this than just a simple act of atonement."

"Such as?"

Luke shrugged. "I don't know. It may be that the Chiss are looking to open diplomatic relations with the New Republic, and finding Outbound Flight has given them the opening they needed to do so."

"Really," Mara said. "Well, in that case, my dear, they're going about it in an awfully strange way. I've been running some numbers, too, and even if that message had been delivered when it was supposed to be, we'd barely have had time to alert Coruscant before we flash-tailed it out to the Unknown Regions. And *they* wouldn't have had time to even organize a diplomatic mission, let alone get it in space in time. Face it, Luke: Formbi doesn't *want* the New Republic involved, at least not on any official level."

"I can't argue with that," Luke conceded. "Still, if the Chiss consider Outbound Flight to have been a Jedi project, it makes sense for them to ask for me instead of someone from the Senate."

"*If* Parck's telling the truth," Mara said. "It also could be that he's lying through his teeth."

"There's one way to find out," Luke pointed out. "I doubt he could hide that massive a deception from both of us in person."

"We're not going down there," Mara said flatly. "The last time I sat in the same room with him he first tried to recruit me, then almost had me shot with those wonderful little charric fire guns the Chiss carry. Thanks, but I can hear him just fine from up here."

"Okay, don't get excited," Luke said. "I'm not in any rush to go down there again, either. Just bear in mind that in that case all we've got to go on is what he says."

"I know," Mara muttered. "I just don't like it."

Luke shrugged. "It's a gamble," he said. "But I think it's worth taking." He cocked his head to the side, and again Mara could feel his mind pressing at hers. "Unless you have something more solid to go on, one way or the other?"

"You mean am I getting something from the Force?" Mara grimaced. "I wish I was. But all I've got is my own natural suspicion."

"No, it's not just that," Luke corrected her thoughtfully. "There's something else there, something deeper than just caution or suspicion. It feels a little like the way I felt when Yoda told me I would have to face my father before I would truly be a Jedi."

"But I've already been through that," Mara protested. "You told me that that transition had to do with sacrifice. I made mine." She jabbed a finger toward the planet in front of them. "Right down there."

"I know," Luke said, and Mara felt a new warmth flow into his concern. That sacrifice, after all, was what had finally made this whole relationship possible. "But it wasn't the sacrifice aspect I was thinking of. It was more the—I don't know. Call it the need to face the past."

Mara snorted. "I've never even been to Chiss space. How can going out there possibly have anything to do with my past?"

"I don't know," Luke said. "I just said that was what it felt like, that's all."

Mara sighed. "You want to go, don't you?"

Luke reached over and took her hand. "I think we have to," he said. "If Parck was right about an enemy moving in toward us, we're going to need all the allies we can get. If there's even a chance of getting the Chiss on our side, we need to take it."

"Yes," Mara said, a shiver running up her back. "Unless Parck was lying about that, too. Well, if we're going to go, we'd better go."

Squeezing Luke's hand once, she let go and reached for the comm switch. "Let's contact Parck and get those coordinates."

CHAPTER 3

THE *JADE SABRE* WAS CAPABLE OF SOMEWHAT BETTER THAN 0.3 past lightspeed, and they made it to Crustai with nearly a day to spare. Here, unlike the apparently more casual situation they'd found at Nirauan, there *was* a welcoming committee waiting.

There were five of them, in fact: alien fighters, midway in size between an X-wing and a Skipray blastboat, moving up behind the *Sabre* as Luke brought the ship out of hyperspace. "Identify yourself," a hard voice snapped from the comm in passable Basic.

"Jedi Master Luke Skywalker and Jedi Knight Mara Jade Skywalker," Luke replied, glancing at the tactical plot Mara had pulled up. The fighters had moved neatly into flanking positions around the *Jade Sabre*, a move that could easily be justified as an innocent escort formation, but which would serve equally well for attack if necessary. "We're here at the request of Aristocra Chaf'orm'bintrano of the Fifth Ruling Family."

"Welcome, Master Skywalker," the voice said. "We will escort you to the Aristocra's diplomatic courier vessel. You will dock there and go aboard."

"Thank you," Luke said.

One of the fighters broke formation and moved out in front of the group, angling off to the left toward the edge of the planet directly ahead. Taking the cue, Luke shifted course to follow. "What do you think?" he asked.

"If they've borrowed any of our technology, it sure doesn't show," Mara said, leaning over the sensor scan she'd done of the fighters. "Most of the weapons are registering as unknowns, but they seem to be mainly energy and projectile types, with a couple of small missiles racked together on the underside."

"Proton torpedoes?" Luke suggested, studying the schematic the sensors had drawn for them.

"Seem a bit big for that, but I can't tell for sure," Mara said. "I definitely wouldn't want to go up against one of these things in combat, though, let alone five of them."

"We'll do our best to avoid that," Luke agreed. "Seems odd that they haven't used any of our stuff, though, considering Thrawn's relationship with the Empire."

"You heard Parck," Mara reminded him. "They don't think much of Thrawn out here."

"Yes, but you'd think they'd at least swallow their pride where useful technology is concerned," Luke said. "Most people's principles don't extend *that* far."

Mara shrugged. "Maybe we've finally found a society of people where they do."

The courier ship the fighter pilot had mentioned, like the fighters themselves, turned out to be something of a surprise. It was bigger than Luke had expected, for one thing, nearly half again as big as the Corellian corvettes that the New Republic routinely used for such tasks. In addition, instead of the corvette's smooth lines, the Chiss ship seemed to be all planes and corners and sharply defined angles, rather like a Mon Calamari star cruiser roughly carved out of stone before the sculptor began smoothing the surface into the proper curves.

"Interesting design," Mara commented as they flew toward it. "It would be great for hiding in asteroid fields."

"It *would* blend in pretty well, wouldn't it?" Luke said, nodding. "I was just thinking that it wouldn't be easily mistaken for anything else. That's something else you want in a diplomatic ship."

"Maybe," Mara said. "Or maybe the Chiss just like lumpy ships. Does make me wonder what the docking bay's going to be like, though."

Luke winced. Back when he'd first presented the *Jade Sabre* to Mara, after she'd thanked him for it, she'd made it casually clear what would happen to anyone who so much as scratched the paint. This could be trouble.

Fortunately, it wasn't. The starboard-side docking bay they were escorted to—more of a half port, really, than a full-sized bay—was smooth-walled, without any decorative angles or corners intruding on the approach. It also had maneuvering room to spare, and Mara got the *Sabre*'s nose into position and locked into the clamps on her first try. "We're in," she announced. "Now what?"

"Looks like they're moving a transfer tunnel toward the portside hatch," Luke said, craning his neck to peer out the side of the canopy. "Let's go meet our host."

It took a few minutes for them to shut the ship down to standby and then make their way back to the hatchway. Someone was already waiting there, tapping politely and discreetly on the metal. "Here we go," Luke murmured, and touched the release.

The hatchway slid up to reveal a young Chiss female dressed in an exotically cut jumpsuit composed of shades of yellow. "Welcome to the Diplomatic Vessel *Chaf Envoy*," she said. Her Basic was far better than the fighter pilot's had been, with only a trace of an exotic accent flavoring the words. "I am Chaf'ees'aklaio, aide to Aristocra Chaf'orm'bintrano. I would be honored if you would call me by my core name, Feesa."

"Thank you," Luke said. "I'm Luke Skywalker—call me Luke. This is Mara Jade Skywalker—Mara—my wife and fellow Jedi."

"Luke; Mara." Feesa repeated the names, bowing low from her waist. "We are honored by your presence. Please; come this way."

She turned and headed down the tunnel. "You speak our language very well," Luke commented as he and Mara fell into step behind her. "Is it common among your people?"

"Not at all," Feesa said. "It was introduced many years ago by the Visitors, but only a few have felt the desire to learn it."

"The Visitors?" Mara asked. "You mean the people aboard Outbound Flight?"

"No; the Visitors," Feesa said. "The ones who came before."

"*Before* Outbound Flight?" Mara asked, frowning. "Who would have come out here before that?"

"I do not know their names." Feesa half turned to regard Mara over her shoulder. "But it is not my place to speak of such things," she added. "You must not ask me anything more."

"Our apologies," Luke said, sending a warning thought at Mara and sensing in return a flicker of frustration at his tacit suspension of her investigation. Probing for information was one of Mara's specialties.

Ahead, the tunnel came to an end at a wide hatchway opening up into a large room beyond. Feesa stepped through into the room and moved to the side of the hatchway, making room for the other two to enter. Luke stepped through—

His only warning was a flicker in the Force, a brief and unfocused sense of danger. But it was enough. Reflexively, he threw himself forward into a low dive as something whipped through the space he'd just vacated.

Feesa gasped something as Luke hit the deck and rolled onto his back, kicking off the flooring with his heels. The momentum of his kick pushed him backward away from the point of danger, simultaneously shoving him back up off the cold metal. Half a second later he was back on his feet, poised in combat stance with his lightsaber blazing ready in front of him.

His first concern was Mara. To his relief, he saw she was still in the tunnel, just inside the protection of the hatchway, her lightsaber ignited and ready. For a moment their eyes met, exchanging assurances that each was unhurt. Feesa, he noted peripherally, was sprawled on the deck; apparently Mara had used the Force to shove her down where she'd hopefully be out of danger. Mentally warning Mara to stay where she was, he shifted his attention to search for the source of the attack.

It wasn't hard to find. A thick, heavy-looking cable anchored to the high ceiling was swinging ponderously alongside the wall, apparently having come loose just as Luke was stepping through the hatchway. Grimacing with a mixture of relief and annoyance, he closed down his lightsaber. "It's all right," he called to Mara, measuring the swing of the cable with his eyes. Another five seconds and it would cut back across the hatchway, but until then it would be safe to cross. "Come on through."

Mara came through, all right, but in typical Mara fashion. She waited four of the five seconds, then suddenly leapt out and up, spinning 180 degrees around in midair. As the cable swung past, she slashed upward with her lightsaber.

He'd expected her to cut the end completely off as a mark of her displeasure at what had just happened. But the blue blade merely slashed past the flying cable without any apparent effect at all.

She landed back on the deck, the cable clattering noisily along the wall as it swung past her. "You all right?" she asked Luke, closing down her lightsaber and returning it to her belt.

"I'm fine," Luke assured her. "I was feeling like a little exercise anyway."

A movement to his right caught his eye, and he turned to see a pair of Chiss males enter the room through a high archway, both considerably older than Feesa, both wearing elaborate outfits that were almost certainly robes of state. The shorter Chiss, his blue-black hair liberally sprinkled with white, wore a long, flowing robe in subdued shades of yellow with gray trim. The taller Chiss's outfit was shorter, more like a long tunic than an actual robe, and was predominantly black, though with small swatches of dusky red at various places on the sleeves and upper shoulders. "Greetings to you, Jedi of—" the black-clad Chiss began.

He broke off abruptly, his eyes narrowing, as the last echo of his words bounced briefly between the high walls. "What is this?" he demanded.

"There was an accident, noble sir," Feesa said, jumping quickly to her feet. "The cable broke and nearly struck Master Skywalker."

"I see," the Chiss said, the threatening tone fading from his voice. "My apologies, Master Skywalker. Are you injured?"

"No," Luke assured him as he and Mara crossed to meet the newcomers. "Aristocra Chaf'orm'bintrano, I presume?"

The Chiss shook his head. "I am General Prard'ras'kleoni of the Chiss Defense Fleet," he said stiffly. "Military commander of this expedition."

He half turned to the Chiss in yellow. *"This,"* he said, "is Aristocra Chaf'orm'bintrano."

Luke shifted his attention to the other Chiss. Alien ages were always hard to judge, but there was something about Chaf'orm'bintrano that marked him as being much older than the general. A presence, perhaps, or something in his face or stance. "My apologies, Aristocra Chaf'orm'bintrano," he said.

"Hardly necessary," the other said easily. "No one would expect you to know one Chiss from another. I trust you had an uneventful journey?"

"Quite uneventful, thank you," Luke said. Chaf'orm'bintrano's accent was somewhat thicker than Feesa's, but his ease in speaking indicated he knew the language better even than she did.

"Aside from this last bit," Mara interjected, nodding toward the cable still swinging along the wall. "You speak our language well, Aristocra Chaf'orm'bintrano. Did you also learn it from the Visitors?"

"From the Visitors, and others," the Chiss said. "Since the arrival of your people at Nirauan, it has by necessity become a small but growing field of study. All personnel aboard this mission are familiar with it, in fact, and I have instructed them to use it whenever possible as a courtesy to you."

"Thank you, Aristocra Chaf'orm'bintrano," Luke said, nodding his head. "That's an unexpected but welcome kindness."

"You're welcome," Chaf'orm'bintrano said. "Following

that same pattern of courtesy, I would also request that you address me by my core name, Formbi. I believe that will make our conversations easier."

"It will indeed," Luke assured him, feeling a definite relief at Formbi's thoughtfulness. He'd never been nearly as good with alien languages and pronunciations as Leia or even Han, and C-3PO was a long way away at the moment. "Again, I thank you."

"It's only a reasonable courtesy," Formbi continued, as if feeling he had to somehow justify the decision. "After all, full names are mainly reserved for formal occasions, for strangers, and for those who are our social inferiors. As representatives of the New Republic, all of you must surely be considered to be on a level with the very highest of the orders."

Luke glanced at Mara, caught the flicker that showed she'd spotted it, too. *All of you?* Shouldn't he have said *both of you*? "That's certainly one way to look at it," he agreed.

"Good," Formbi said. "You may likewise address General Prard'ras'kleoni as General Drask."

Luke looked at the general, caught the brief hardness about the other's mouth before he carefully smoothed it away. Apparently, Drask wasn't nearly as happy with upsetting the normal social order as Formbi was.

Or else he just didn't like humans.

"But come," Formbi added, gesturing back toward the archway he and Drask had entered by. "Let me show you the public areas of the vessel before Feesa takes you to your personal quarters."

He turned and led the way back across the room toward the archway. "Pretty big room for an entry area," Mara commented as they passed under the archway and into a curving hallway. Unlike the ship's outer hull, the interior surfaces were all smooth and even. "Our ships usually can't afford to waste that much space."

"Do you view courtesy and formality as a waste, then?" Drask growled. "Perhaps politeness is unnecessary, too, or positions or social levels—"

"General." Formbi spoke the title quietly, but there was something in his voice that instantly silenced the other. "Our guests don't do things as we do. Obviously, they don't understand."

He looked back at Mara. "This is a diplomatic vessel of the Fifth Ruling Family, and we often welcome high-positioned officials aboard. Each social and professional position requires its own proper expanse, decor, and pattern. In each of those situations the reception area can be automatically reconfigured and decorated before the guest's arrival."

He shrugged. "As it is, the room is barely large enough to properly welcome a brother or sister of one of the Nine Families. Fortunately, most of them travel but little, and then mainly in vessels of their own."

"I see," Mara said.

Formbi frowned at her, and Luke caught a sudden ripple of uncertainty. "Did you expect some ceremony of that sort?" he asked. "Admiral Parck told me that Jedi neither required nor wished such recognition. Was he incorrect?"

"No, not at all," Luke hastened to assure him. "Officials of our position don't require any formal rituals or treatment."

"Especially not on a mission like this one," Mara added. "If we're ever in a situation where ceremony is required, we'll inform you then, and instruct you in the proper patterns."

"As we of course will expect you to do for us if the situation is reversed," Luke said. "Until then, consider us to be merely fellow travelers come to see the remains of an ancient Republic ship."

Formbi nodded, the uncertainty smoothing away. "Then we shall do that," he declared. "Now that all have arrived—"

He broke off as a trilling group of tones cut through the air. "Incoming vessel," a gentle voice announced from somewhere above them. "*Paskla*-class; unknown configuration."

Drask muttered something under his breath. "Combat preparations," he called toward the ceiling as he took off at a run down the corridor.

"Come," Formbi said, gesturing them forward as Drask

disappeared from view around a curve. "We were going to the public areas anyway. We might as well begin with the command center."

He led them through a dozen twists and turns to a small balcony overlooking a room that was, as near as Luke could judge, buried nearly dead center in the core of the ship. It was about the same size as the reception area had been, but with a much lower ceiling. Unlike the reception room, it was crammed full of consoles, displays, wall monitors, and Chiss. Most of the aliens were dressed in the same black as General Drask, though their outfits were tighter fitting, less elaborate, and clearly more functional. Luke spotted Drask himself on a circular podium in the center of the room, conferring with a Chiss wearing an outfit similar to his but with green patches where the general's uniform showed red.

"This is the command center," Formbi said, as calm as if he was leading a tour through an interesting display of painted shellfish. "The officer wearing green patches is Captain Brast'alshi'barku, the line commander of this vessel— you may address him as Captain Talshib. And *that*," he added, pointing across to the largest of the wall displays, "is apparently our incoming vessel."

Luke focused on the image. The alien ship looked like a slightly squashed sphere, light-colored but with a close-order pattern of dark spots covering the hull that could have been viewports, vents, or even just decoration. There was no scale on the display that he could see, but if the ships now swarming around it were more of the fighters that had run escort for the *Jade Sabre*, then the intruder was decently sized.

"Doesn't look like a warship," Mara commented from beside him. "They usually have at least one low-silhouette, high-firepower plane available to present to an approaching enemy. That thing's going to be a perfect target no matter what direction it comes at you from."

"You forget the Death Star," Luke reminded her. "It was shaped more or less like that."

"And its design stunk, too," Mara retorted. "It just happened to be big enough and mean enough to get away with it."

"Mostly," Luke couldn't resist saying.

"Whatever." Mara gestured. "This thing, on the other hand, doesn't seem to be even half the size of a Dreadnaught."

Formbi turned to Feesa. "Feesa, please go and ask the ambassador to join us," he said. "He, too, may find this interesting."

"I obey," Feesa said, bobbing her head in a quick bow and then hurrying off.

"The ambassador?" Mara asked.

"Yes," Formbi said. "Did I understand you to say you knew of a vessel of this type?"

"No, just a battle station of a similar shape," Luke said.

"It was destroyed a long time ago," Mara added. "Now, about this ambassador?"

She was interrupted by another trilling tone, a different combination of notes than the one they'd heard earlier. "Signal alert," Formbi identified it. "They're trying to communicate."

One of the smaller displays to the side cleared to reveal a pair of alien faces with large violet eyes, flattened ears rising high on the skull, and a pair of small mouths set just above the jawline. The skin was light tan, with a hint of exotic gold marbling about the jaw and cheeks. "What are they?" Luke asked.

"It's not a species I've seen before," Formbi said, leaning forward a little as if trying to see the image better.

"I thought you were the dominant species out here," Mara said. "Don't you know all your neighbors?"

"We have a significant number of stars and star systems, yes," Formbi said. There was neither arrogance nor apology in his voice; he was simply stating a fact. "But the Nine Families have long discouraged our people from probing or prying into the territories of others. Certainly the Defense Fleet and all official personnel are required to stay within our own borders."

He shrugged. "Besides which, there are also many small groups in this region of space, remnants of pirate attack or refugees of mass destruction by other aggressors. Plus, of course, there are those same pirates and aggressors. Even if we wished to do so, it would be a great undertaking to try to know them all."

"There are a hundred different threats out there that would freeze your blood if you knew about them," Mara murmured.

Formbi frowned at her. "I beg your pardon?"

"I was just remembering something a Chiss once told me," Mara explained. "A warrior named Stent, back on Nirauan."

"Yes," Formbi said, his tone a little odd. Perhaps he didn't like being reminded that Parck had a lot of renegade Chiss working with him. "In actual fact, he may have underestimated the number. The galaxy outside Chiss territory is not a very safe place to be."

On the display, one of the aliens opened his mouths, and a flow of melodic sounds suddenly filled the room. Luke stretched out with the Force, wondering if he could get a sense of the words the way he'd once done with the Qom Qae and Qom Jha of Nirauan.

But those species' communication had had a Force component to it. This one did not, and his efforts were of no use.

"Ah," Formbi said. "At least they've been around the region long enough to pick up Minnisiat."

"What's that, a trade language?" Mara asked.

"Exactly," Formbi said, glancing at her with an approving look. "Minnisiat is the chief trade language among the various peoples of this area. Most Chiss know at least some of it, particularly those who live on border worlds like Crustai."

"What's he saying?" Luke asked.

Formbi pursed his lips. " 'Greetings to the noble and compassionate people of the Chiss Ascendancy,' " he said slowly. " 'I am Bearsh, first steward of the Geroon Remnant.' "

From the podium, General Drask was speaking now. It seemed to be the same language, though his voice was considerably less melodic than the Geroon's. " 'I am General

Prard'ras'kleoni of the Chiss Expansionary Defense Fleet,' "
Formbi translated. " 'What is your business in Chiss territory?' "

To Luke's ears, Drask's question hadn't seemed particularly angry or threatening. The Geroon, though, apparently
heard something different than he did. Bearsh's voice abruptly
took on what seemed to be an alarmed tone, a sense that
Formbi's translation merely confirmed. " 'We mean no af-
front. Please do not harm our vessel. We wish merely to
honor those who died to free our people.' "

Drask looked up from his podium, his eyes searching
briefly before locating Formbi on the observation balcony.
"Aristocra?" he called. "Are you familiar with the event he
refers to?"

"I have no knowledge of any such event," Formbi called
back. "Ask him to explain."

The general turned and began speaking again. "I thought
you didn't go out of your way to help people outside your
territory," Mara said.

"We don't," Formbi said. The Geroon spoke again, and
Formbi's glowing eyes narrowed as he listened. "I see," he
said. "Interesting. Listen: 'We have heard you have located
the bones of the Republic vessel known as Outbound Flight.
The people who traveled in it sacrificed their lives that we
might be freed from our enslavers.' "

"Wait a minute," Luke said, turning to Mara. "I thought
you said Thrawn destroyed Outbound Flight."

"That's what Parck told me," Mara confirmed. "Maybe he
was wrong."

"Or maybe this happened before Thrawn got to it?" Luke
suggested.

Drask was speaking again. "General Drask is asking who
their enslavers were," Formbi said, a thoughtful tone in his
voice. "I wonder . . ."

His voice trailed off. "You know something?" Mara
prompted.

"I have a thought," Formbi said. "Let's first see what the
Geroon says."

Bearsh answered, stepping back from the holocam and waving his hands in a complicated pattern. "What's that behind him?" Luke asked, frowning as he tried to see past the two alien faces that were now only partially filling the screen. The area behind them seemed to be a large open room, possibly even larger than the reception area he and Mara had come through earlier. The walls and ceiling were colored a white-textured blue, and he could just see the tops of some kind of open structures above the aliens' heads.

And then, as he watched, two small figures moved into view, climbing hand over hand on the nearest structure. "What in the—?"

"It's a playground," Mara breathed. "It's a *children's playground.*"

"You're right," Luke said. One of the small Geroons reached the top of the structure he was climbing, pulling a red headband from around his ears as he did so and waving it in triumph. "Looks like a version of Hilltop Emperor."

"Complete with flag and loud gloating," Mara agreed. "What in the world is a playground doing aboard a starship?"

"The Vagaari," Formbi murmured.

"What?" Luke asked, turning to him.

Formbi gestured to the display. "He has just confirmed my expectations," the Chiss said darkly. "He says it was the Vagaari who enslaved them."

"I take it that *is* a species you've seen before?" Mara asked.

"Not seen, but far too familiar with," Formbi said. "They were a great race of nomadic conquerors and slavers who once flew freely through this region of space, taking and destroying at will, particularly among the smaller species and worlds."

"Are they still around?" Luke asked.

"They and their deeds have not been seen for many years," Formbi said. "Not since the battle where the Outbound Flight was destroyed, in fact."

Luke and Mara exchanged startled looks. "They were at that battle?" Luke asked.

"And on whose side?" Mara added. "Outbound Flight's, or the Chiss's?"

"There was no 'Chiss' side of the battle, Jedi Skywalker," Formbi countered, his red eyes flashing at her. "There was only Syndic Mitth'raw'nuruodo and his one *very* small picket force. They did not represent the Chiss Defense Fleet, or the Nine Ruling Families, or any other group of the Chiss people."

"Yes, we understand that," Luke assured him hastily. "Mara was simply wondering how exactly the battle lines were drawn up."

Formbi shook his head. "I arrived after the battle was over, after all the destruction had already taken place." He rumbled deep in his throat. "Syndic Mitth'raw'nuruodo was not very informative on what exactly had taken place."

"So it's possible that the Jedi aboard Outbound Flight really *did* help them against the Vagaari?" Luke asked.

Formbi shrugged. "You know the Jedi," he said. "You must tell *me* whether that is possible."

Luke looked back at the display and the pleading Geroons. Faced with both a pirate gang and Thrawn's forces, threatened by both, what *would* the Jedi have done? "I'm sure they would have tried to help," he said slowly. "How much they could have done . . . I don't know."

"Though the Geroons clearly think they did something significant," Mara pointed out. "You suppose Outbound Flight and Thrawn could have combined forces long enough to stomp the Vagaari before Thrawn turned on them?"

Luke shrugged. "I suppose that's possible," he said. "Hard to believe he could have conned six Jedi Masters into wasting their strength against pirates when he knew all along he was going to attack them afterward."

"Unless they knew that, but decided to risk it anyway in order to save the Geroons," Mara suggested. "You Jedi Masters get all noble and self-sacrificing at the oddest moments."

"Thank you," Luke said dryly. "The question is—"

"Ah," Formbi said, turning. "Here he is now."

Luke turned to see Feesa coming toward them. Striding

along behind her was a medium-tall human male with silver hair and a close-cropped silver beard, his face lined and dark with the evidence of too many of his years spent under unforgiving suns. "Welcome, Ambassador," Formbi greeted him. "We seem to have more visitors."

"I see," the man said, looking past the group toward the command center's displays. His voice was deep and rich, full of intelligence and quiet confidence. Up close now, Luke could see that his eyes were an unusual shade of gray. "Interesting. Do we know them?"

"They call themselves the Geroons," Formbi said, turning back as someone called his name. "Excuse me, but I'm needed below. Come, Feesa."

"Introductions?" Mara murmured, her eyes on the newcomer.

"I'm sorry," Formbi said as he and Feesa paused at the top of the short stairway that linked the balcony to the main floor of the command center. "Ambassador, may I present Jedi Master Luke Skywalker and Jedi Knight Mara Jade Skywalker."

There was a flicker of something in the man's eyes, but his smile showed nothing but easy friendliness. "Pleased to meet you," he said. "I've heard many things about you both."

"And this," Formbi continued, "is the person Coruscant and the New Republic have sent as their representative.

"Ambassador Dean Jinzler."

CHAPTER 4

FORMBI HURRIED OFF DOWN THE STAIRWAY TO WHERE GENERAL Drask was waiting, Feesa following close behind.

Leaving the three humans gazing at each other.

Jinzler broke the silence first. "I see you've been talking to Talon Karrde," he said.

"What makes you say that?" Luke asked, his voice giving nothing away.

"Your expressions," Jinzler said. He smiled faintly. "Or, rather, your complete lack of them. You probably want to know what this is all about."

"Why don't you tell us?" Luke suggested. From the calmness in his voice it was clear he was willing to give the man the benefit of the doubt, at least for the moment.

Which was a full moment longer than Mara herself was interested in giving him. She threw a quick glance down at the command floor, wondering what Luke would say if she called Formbi back up here and denounced Jinzler on the spot.

But Formbi seemed to be having a quiet, three-way argument with Drask and Talshib on the podium. Interrupting them at this point might not be a smart thing to do.

"For starters, let me assure you I'm not here for any kind of financial gain," Jinzler said. "I'm not looking for power or influence or blackmail, either."

"Well, that cuts out all the interesting possibilities," Mara said tartly. "How about telling us what you *are* here for?"

"I can also promise you that I won't make any trouble," Jinzler continued. "I won't try to influence the Chiss or get in the way of whatever negotiations or other diplomatic plans you have."

"You're already making trouble, just by being here," Mara told him.

"You're also stalling," Luke said. "What do you want?"

Jinzler took a deep breath, let it out in a controlled huff. "I have to see Outbound Flight," he said quietly, his gaze drifting to the display and the image of the Geroon ship. "I have to . . ."

He closed his eyes briefly. "I'm sorry, but it's extremely personal."

"Very touching," Mara said. "Also very inadequate. Let's try it from a different direction. Why are you impersonating a New Republic official?"

Jinzler's throat tightened. "Because I'm a nobody," he said, a touch of bitterness edging into his voice. "And because the only way to get to Outbound Flight is aboard an official Chiss ship, at the invitation of the official Chiss government. You really think they'd let me aboard if they knew the truth?"

"I don't know," Luke said. "Why don't we try it?"

Jinzler shook his head. "I can't risk it," he said. "I have to see that ship, Master Skywalker. I have to . . ." He shook his head again.

"How did you expect to get away with it?" Luke asked. "Did you think we wouldn't notice you weren't a properly credentialed ambassador?"

"I thought you might not get the message in time and would miss Formbi's deadline," Jinzler said. "If you did make it—" He shrugged uncomfortably. "I hoped you'd understand."

"Understand what?" Mara retorted. "You won't even tell us what it is we're supposed to understand."

"I know." He smiled wanly. "Pretty foolish of me, I guess. But it was all I had."

Mara looked past him at Luke, a sour taste in her mouth. An accomplished actor, she knew, could pull off a performance this good. So could most of the good con men she'd known throughout her life.

But acting ability and deep sighs weren't nearly enough to fool a Jedi. Try as she might, she couldn't ignore the fact that her senses were picking up the same earnest emotional struggle in his mind as was coming out in his face and words.

The man was rash, not much of a long-range thinker, possibly even an out-and-out fool. But he was also completely sincere.

But then, she'd been sincere, too, the whole time she'd served Palpatine as the Emperor's Hand. She'd done everything he'd ordered her to, including assassinations of corrupt officials and Rebels alike, with all the sincerity anyone could ever have asked for.

No, sincerity alone didn't count for much. In fact, when you came right down to it, it didn't count for anything at all.

"Mara?" Luke invited.

"No," she said firmly. "Unless he's willing to tell us—right now—exactly why he wants aboard, I say he gets tossed off."

She lifted her eyebrows at Jinzler. "Well?"

The lines around Jinzler's eyes deepened, and his shoulders seemed to sag a little. "I can't," he said softly. "It's just—"

He broke off, his gaze flicking over Mara's shoulder. "Aristocra Formbi," he said, the indecision and pain abruptly gone from his voice, though not from his sense. "What's the situation with our guests?"

Mara turned to see Formbi climbing back up the steps toward them, an odd tightness in his face and tread. "They're coming with us," he said.

"What, all of them?" Luke asked.

"Apparently, that is exactly what you are seeing," Formbi said soberly. "The Geroon Remnant, all that remain of their people, packed into that single vessel."

"What happened?" Jinzler asked.

Formbi shrugged. "Apparently, their release from slavery by those aboard Outbound Flight came too late," he said.

"The Vagaari had already caused too much damage to their world for it to continue to support life."

"Like the Caamasi," Luke murmured. "Or the Noghri."

"I'm not familiar with those peoples," Formbi said. "At any rate, in the end, after plagues and starvation, they had no choice but to leave. Even now they search for a new world where they may live again in peace."

"That's terrible," Jinzler murmured. "Can you help them?"

"Perhaps," Formbi said. "A delegation will come aboard presently to examine some of our star charts. Perhaps we can find an uninhabited world outside Chiss territory where they can settle."

"I take it General Drask isn't too pleased with that?" Jinzler asked.

"He's not pleased at all," Formbi agreed with a wry smile. "Though to be honest, he's not pleased to have all you humans aboard, either. But in the end, my counsel prevailed."

"What about their request to visit Outbound Flight?" Luke asked.

"We'll allow their vessel to accompany us to the edge of the cluster where the remains are located," Formbi said. "At that point, I may need to have another discussion with General Drask. Still, I'm sure at least a small delegation of their people will be continuing on with us."

"What exactly do they want there?" Jinzler asked.

Formbi sighed. "To pay their respects to those who saved them," he said. "To say their final farewells."

It was all Mara could do to keep from jerking backward. The sudden flood of emotion that erupted from Jinzler's mind was like a stun burst from a blaster rifle.

She looked at him sharply. But aside from a twitching muscle in his cheek, his face showed nothing of the sudden anguish and heartache that had been triggered by Formbi's comment.

To pay their respects. To say their final farewells . . .

"At any rate, with all now assembled, we may finally proceed," Formbi continued. "Feesa will show you to your personal quarters, Master Skywalker."

"Thank you," Luke said. He looked at Mara, a question in his eyes.

Again, there was a sour taste in Mara's mouth. But there'd been something in Jinzler's silent burst of emotion that had touched a part of her she hadn't even known was there.

Or perhaps she had. Perhaps it was her own past as the Emperor's Hand, and her own reluctance to talk about it, that his presence had brought to mind.

She took a deep breath, caught the expectation in Luke and the quiet dread in Jinzler as she did so. Both of them knew exactly what she was about to say.

Both of them were wrong. "I thank you, as well, Aristocra Formbi," she said. "We'll look forward to spending more time with you."

She had the minor satisfaction of catching the surprise from both men at her comment. "You're quite welcome," Formbi said, oblivious to what was going on beneath the surface. "We shall meet again in a few hours. There will be a reception dinner; Feesa will meet you at your quarters shortly beforehand to escort you there. I will then introduce you to the rest of the vessel's officers and diplomatic staff."

"Thank you, Aristocra," Luke said. "We'll look forward to both the dinner and the meetings."

"Yes," Mara agreed, looking pointedly at Jinzler. "And I'm sure we'll have a chance there to talk more fully, Ambassador."

Because she *would* find out about this man, she promised herself as Feesa led them back down the curving corridor. She would find out about him, and she would find out the reason he was here.

And she would do so before they reached Outbound Flight. Guaranteed.

THE QUARTERS FEESA TOOK THEM TO WERE SMALL BUT WELL laid out, with a compact conversation area as well as the usual sleeping room and refresher station. "Not bad," Luke commented as he looked around. "A lot roomier than some shipboard berths I've been put up in."

"Yes," Mara said, watching the door slide shut behind her, her thoughts still on Jinzler and his disturbing emotional reaction.

"You're not even looking at it," Luke said, stepping through an archway into the bedroom and flopping backward onto the bed. "Let me guess. Jinzler?"

"Since when does a Jedi Master have to guess?" Mara asked dryly, trying to shake away the questions long enough for at least a perfunctory glance around the room. Overall, the decor was simple, as one would expect of shipboard accommodations. But at the same time it had the small touches of elegance that showed someone had put thought and care into it. The Chiss, apparently, took their host responsibilities seriously.

"Even Jedi Masters sometimes have trouble sorting through a plate of prunchti noodles," Luke countered, just as dryly. "That's about what you're looking like right now."

"What an appetizing image," Mara said. "And with dinner—" She looked at the chrono on the wall. "—still almost three hours away. Maybe there's a cantina aboard where I could get a snack."

"You want to talk about it?" Luke asked.

She shrugged. "I don't think he's a con man," she said. "Too emotionally connected to the whole thing. I can't see him acting as an agent for someone else, either, for the same reason. I suppose—"

"I meant you," Luke interrupted her gently. "Your reaction."

Mara grimaced. One of the minuses of having a Jedi husband was that you were never completely alone. "I don't know," she confessed. "There was just something in Formbi's comment about paying respects that got to me somehow."

"Any idea why?"

"Not really." She looked around the room, a small shiver running through her. "Or maybe it has to do with this place. Going back to Nirauan; and now the Chiss—"

"And Thrawn?"

"Maybe Thrawn," she agreed. "Though I don't know why that should bother me so much."

Luke didn't reply, but she could sense his invitation. Crossing the room, she lay down on the bed beside him. He slipped his arm around beneath her shoulders, and for a minute they just lay snuggled together, their minds and emotions wrapping around each other in much the same way. "Maybe it's the Force, then," Luke suggested. "Maybe there's something you need to work through, something you've been putting off or suppressing, and the time has come for you to deal with it. That's happened to me once or twice."

"I suppose," Mara said. "I just wish the Force would pick a time when things are quieter if it's going to push me into something."

She sensed his smile. "Me, too," he said. "If you ever figure out how to schedule things that neatly, let me know."

"You'll be the first," she promised, reaching up to pat the hand around her shoulder.

He caught her hand and held it. "Until then," he said quietly, stroking her hand with his fingertips, "just remember that I'm here for you. For whatever you need from me."

She squeezed his hand. "I know," she said, feeling his warmth and strength and commitment flowing into her, flooding into the dark areas that Jinzler's emotions had opened in her.

One of the plusses of having a Jedi husband, she thought contentedly, was that you were never completely alone.

They lay there together for a few minutes. Then, with a sigh, Mara forced her mind back to business. "So," she said. "What do you think of the rest of this setup?"

"Well, it's definitely not as cheering as we might like," he said. "Did you notice the way Formbi looked when he came up after that talk with General Drask and Captain Talshib?"

Mara thought back. She'd been concentrating mainly on Jinzler at the time, and all she could remember about Formbi was his general expression. "He looked tired," she said.

"It was more than that," Luke said. "It was as if he'd just fought a battle, and wasn't sure whether he'd won or lost."

"Mm," Mara said, slightly annoyed at herself. Usually she was better at catching details like that. "You think Drask and Talshib aren't happy about having all these aliens aboard a Chiss ship and are giving Formbi a hard time about it?"

"They're certainly not happy about *some*thing," Luke said. "Though it sounds to me like an Aristocra is higher in rank than a general."

"That's never stopped anyone else from complaining," Mara pointed out. "And I've seen a higher-ranking person give in just to shut the complainer up."

"So have I," Luke said. "We'll want to keep an eye on things and see how Drask does as we go along."

"Uh-huh," Mara murmured. "Tell me, do you think Drask might be annoyed enough about us to actually do something about it?"

"Such as?"

"Such as that accident with the cable in the reception room," Mara said. "The timing there was almost too good to be coincidence."

For a few seconds Luke didn't answer. Mara listened to the silence, watching the kaleidoscope of thought and emotion go through his mind as he examined the possibilities. "I don't know," he said at last. "It probably wouldn't have killed me even if it had hit me dead-on. But it could easily have put me out of action for a time while I went into a healing trance."

"Which would have left me more or less on my own," Mara said. "Alternatively, it might have given Drask an excuse to kick us off the mission completely."

"He would have had a tough job selling it," Luke pointed out. "It's pretty clear Formbi wants us along."

"Maybe, but at least it would have given him an added lever," Mara said.

Abruptly, she came to a decision. "I'll be back," she said, making sure her lightsaber was securely fastened to her belt as she headed for the door.

"Where are you going?" Luke called after her, propping himself up on an elbow.

"Back to the reception room," Mara said. "I want a closer look at that cable."

"You want me to come with you?" Luke asked, starting to stand up.

"Better not," Mara said, shaking her head. "One Jedi poking around is idle curiosity; two of them is an official investigation. There's no point in adding fuel to Drask's fire."

"I suppose." Reluctantly, Luke sat back down on the bed. "Whistle if you need any help."

"Of course," Mara said, giving him an innocent look. "Don't I always?"

She managed to get out of the room before he could come up with a suitably sarcastic reply.

THE CORRIDORS BACK TO THE RECEPTION ROOM WERE FAIRLY quiet. Mara saw perhaps a dozen black-uniformed Chiss on her way, and most of them pretty much ignored her. A few seemed interested or intrigued by her alien appearance, but even that small handful said nothing as they passed by. Either the culture was just naturally polite, or else Formbi had given strict instructions as to how his guests were to be treated.

It was interesting, though, how much more of their emotional states she was able to pick up this time around. Back on Nirauan, during her first brush with groups of Chiss, she'd barely even been able to sense their presence. Experience and practice apparently paid off in this area.

Of course, back then she hadn't been a true Jedi, either. Maybe that was part of the difference.

Not surprisingly, the reception room was deserted when she reached it. Somewhat more surprising was the fact that the loose cable that had nearly hit Luke had already been reattached.

She stood just inside the archway for a moment, eyeing the cable. It was nestled into a cable groove between the ceiling and the bulkhead, a good six meters off the deck. That wasn't an impossible jump for a Jedi, but a simple jump wouldn't accomplish very much. She needed to be able to sit there for a minute or two in order to examine the end where it had either broken or been cut. And as far as she knew, even Jedi couldn't hover in midair.

But there might be another approach. Formbi had said that the reception area could be automatically reconfigured and decorated for arriving guests . . .

It took a minute for her to find the control panel, set into the bulkhead just inside the archway and hidden behind a plate colored the same neutral gray as the rest of the paneling. The controls consisted of a dozen buttons, each labeled with an alien mark. Experimentally, she pushed one of them.

Smoothly, and in complete silence, the room began to change. A dozen wall sections of various sizes and shapes began to swing outward, exposing intricate symbols or painted patterns on their other sides, then settled back against the bulkheads with the patterns now showing. Parts of the ceiling likewise swung free to hang like flags or else began to lower as rectangular or circular columns to various heights, leaving the room with a sort of stylized stalactite look.

The deck itself underwent the most dramatic changes. Instead of large panels flipping or rotating or otherwise changing, tiny lights that had hitherto been invisible came to life, forming intricate spirals and patterns of color. As she watched, the patterns altered, giving a sense of water flowing from the hatchway over to the arch.

A minute later, it was finished. Mara looked around at the entirely new room that had appeared, impressed in spite of herself, wondering which level of Chiss official could command this particular brand of welcome.

She tried two more buttons in turn. Each time, she noted, the room went back to neutral before changing into its new configuration.

Unfortunately, none of the changes did anything with the cable she wanted to examine. Through it all, that particular edge of ceiling stayed where it was, with the cable remaining firmly out of reach.

Which meant she was going to have to be clever.

She went back to the first button she'd tried, studying the

positions of the swinging wall panels and lowering ceiling columns and counting off the seconds to herself. It would just be possible, she decided. And in her philosophy, anything that was possible might as well be tried.

She put the room back into neutral and prepared herself for action. *One Jedi poking around is idle curiosity,* she'd told Luke. She wondered if Formbi would really take it that way if he caught her.

Taking a deep breath, she touched the button and ran.

She caught the lowermost of the panels before it had swung more than a few degrees open, leaping up and grabbing its top edge with her fingertips. Her first fear, that it would break off under her weight and dump her ignominiously onto the deck, didn't happen. She didn't give it the chance to change its mind, either, but quickly pulled herself partway up and then shoved off it, lunging toward the next panel a meter to her right. She caught the top of this one about a quarter of the way open, again pulled herself up, and again shoved off for the next in the climbing pattern she'd worked out. By the time her last stepping-stone panel was about to swing closed, she was where she needed to be. Pushing off one final time, she leapt across a meter and a half of empty space and wrapped her arms around the side of the nearest of the lowered ceiling columns.

For a moment she just hung there, catching her breath and stretching out to the Force to draw renewed strength into her muscles. The column's texture was rough enough for a good grip and, like the wall panels, seemed perfectly capable of handling her weight. Getting a grip on the lower part of the column with her knees, she started up.

The going wasn't particularly easy, but the thought of some Chiss wandering in and catching her hanging up here like an oversized mynock added motivation to the climb. Halfway up, she reached another column and switched to a back-and-feet chimney-style ascent. Reaching the top, she grabbed on to one of the flaglike ceiling sections that was now hanging straight down. Using it as a pivot point, she swung over to a column hanging down in the corner.

And with that, she finally had a close-up view of the rogue cable.

She squinted at it, wishing she'd thought to bring a light. The room itself was well lit, but the end where the cable had been reattached to its connector was inconveniently lying in shadow from the ceiling column she was hanging on to.

Still, a Jedi was never entirely without resources. Looking awkwardly over her shoulder toward her waist, she reached out through the Force and unhooked her lightsaber from her belt. Levitating it carefully, she maneuvered it over to the corner, turning the handle over so that the blade would be pointing safely downward. Then, eyeing the stud, she ignited it.

The *snap-hiss* somehow sounded louder than usual in the corner of a quiet room. The lightsaber didn't put out all that much light, but it was enough.

The cable had not, in fact, been cut, which had been her first suspicion. On the other hand, the connection appeared to be a double screw-type linkage, which was almost impossible for vibration or tension to work loose.

So how *had* it come apart?

Moving the lightsaber as close to the connection as she could without risking damage, she peered at it. On the side of the cable, just above the connector, was a slight indentation. Lifting her gaze to the ceiling itself, she spotted a small round opening above and to the right of the groove.

Adjusting her grip on the column, she freed one hand and gingerly extended a finger into the opening. Nothing. She moved the finger around in a circle inside the opening, searching for the machinery or electronic connectors or heat radiator vanes that should naturally be behind any opening on a ship.

Or rather, the equipment that should be behind any opening that was part of a ship's actual design. The lack of anything up there strongly implied that this particular hole had been put in as an afterthought.

She was still working through the possibilities when a flicker of sensation touched her mind.

Instantly, she closed down the lightsaber, shutting off its

gentle hum. In the sudden silence, she could hear footsteps coming her way. Several sets, by the sound, but in too close a step to be Chiss on a casual stroll around the ship. This group was definitely military.

And here she was, trapped in a compromising position six meters in midair.

She looked around her, biting back an old curse from her days with the Empire. The column she was hanging on to was the only cover anywhere within reach. Problem was, she was hanging on the wrong side of it, in full view of the room below. She would have to work her way around to the wall side if she was going to have any chance of concealment; and from the speed those footsteps were approaching, she wasn't likely to have enough time.

Reaching out her free hand, she grabbed her lightsaber and reestablished a firm two-armed, two-kneed grip on the column. Then, moving as quickly as she could, she started maneuvering herself around toward the far side.

She was almost halfway around when the intruders marched in beneath the archway. She froze in place, shifting her gaze downward to look.

As she did so, her heart seemed to turn to stone.

Those weren't Chiss soldiers, sent by General Drask to hunt her down. They weren't even Chiss soldiers on routine patrol, searching for suspicious activities.

There were five figures below her, standing just inside the reception room in a loose box formation. The one in the center was a human male, young looking, wearing a gray Imperial uniform modified with rings of red and black trim on the collar and cuffs.

The other four were Imperial stormtroopers.

CHAPTER 5

MARA STARED DOWN AT THE STORMTROOPERS, A SUDDEN FLOOD of memories whipping around her like stones and debris in a hurricane-strength wind. She'd worked with stormtroopers many times through the years she served Palpatine as his Emperor's Hand. She'd ordered them to do her bidding; occasionally, she'd led small groups of them on special missions.

She'd stood by and watched as they killed.

It was impossible. It had to be. The elite cadre of stormtroopers was all but extinct, wiped out in the long war against the Empire. Most of the cloning tanks used to create them so many years ago were gone, too, tracked down and destroyed so that no one else would ever again unleash such a terrible wave of death and destruction upon the galaxy.

And yet, there they were. It wasn't an illusion, or a fraud, or a twisting of her own memories. They stood like stormtroopers, they held their BlasTech E-11 blaster rifles like stormtroopers, they wore stormtrooper armor.

The stormtroopers were back.

The young Imperial was looking around the room, his hand resting on the belted DH-17 blaster pistol riding his hip. One of the stormtroopers murmured something, and he looked up. "Ah," he called. His voice sounded young, too. "There you are, Jedi Skywalker. Are you all right?"

With a supreme effort, Mara found her voice. "Sure," she called back. "No problem. Why?"

He seemed a bit taken aback. "We heard the sound of a lightsaber being activated," he said. "With a Jedi, that usually means there's trouble."

"Trouble for whom?" Mara asked pointedly.

"Just trouble in general." The Imperial seemed better on balance now. "Do you need any help getting down from there?"

"Who said I wanted to come down?" Mara countered.

He snorted under his breath, and Mara caught a hint of annoyance. "Fine," he said. "Have it your way. I just thought you might be interested in talking, that's all."

"About . . . ?"

"About what you're doing up there, for starters," the young man said. "Maybe we could discuss this whole crazy mission, too."

She frowned, stretching out with the Force. It was hard to read a stranger, especially at this distance. But as near as she could tell he seemed sincere.

Though she'd concluded the same thing about Jinzler, and had already decided how much simple sincerity was worth.

Still, if these Imperials were out to kill her, the simplest time to try it had already passed. And if she and they were on the same side, comparing cards might not be a bad idea. "Fine," she said. "I was mostly done anyway."

"You need any help?"

"No, thanks," Mara said, setting her teeth as it occurred to her that there was perhaps one more tactical advantage he was waiting for before ordering his stormtroopers to open fire. Time for a small calculated risk. "On second thought, you can hold my lightsaber for me. Here—catch."

She tossed it toward him. The young man stepped forward and deftly caught it.

There was no shout of triumph as he held her only defensive weapon in his hand. More importantly, none of the stormtroopers raised his BlasTech and started shooting.

She started breathing again. So they really *didn't* mean any mischief. At least, not yet. "Okay," she called. "Stand clear."

She shifted her gaze to the control panel in the corridor behind them and stretched out with the Force, activating one of the buttons.

Once again, the room began to reconfigure. Mara swung herself over to one of the other columns as hers retracted toward the ceiling, then pushed off and down to grab hold of a swinging wall panel. A brief pause to catch her balance, and she jumped down to the next one in line. Three panels later, she landed on the deck.

"Thanks," she said, stretching out her hand to the Imperial, her senses alert for a last-second betrayal.

But he merely handed over her lightsaber, most of his attention on the room itself. "Impressive," he commented as the room hit neutral and then began shifting into the mode Mara had keyed it for. "Instant redecoration, whenever the mood strikes you."

"It's a little more functional than that," Mara said. Up close, he looked even younger than he had from the ceiling, no older than his midtwenties. *Like a kid playing soldier,* the irreverent thought struck her. "Didn't Formbi explain it to you? Or didn't you get one of these rooms when you came in?"

"We haven't talked to Formbi much," the young man said. "Or any of the other Chiss. We've been trying to keep a low profile since we came aboard." He smiled tightly. "I don't think General Drask is exactly thrilled by our presence here."

"General Drask doesn't seem very easy to thrill," Mara said. Stepping past the group to the control panel, she keyed the room back to its original neutral mode. "So," she said, turning back to face them. "You going to tell me who you are? Or do I have to guess?"

"Oh, I'm sorry." He stiffened to full attention. "I'm Commander Chak Fel, warrior of the Hand. You may remember meeting my father a couple of years ago."

"Very well," Mara said, smiling tightly at the memory. "I'm sure General Baron Fel remembers *me*, as well."

"With the greatest respect and admiration," Fel assured her. "He asked me to send you his greetings, and to tell you he still has hopes that you'll bring your talents to the Empire of the Hand someday."

"Thanks, but I've had my fill of Imperial service," Mara

told him. "*Any* Imperial service. So you knew I was going to be here?"

"I hoped you would be," Fel said. "Admiral Parck told me you and Master Skywalker had been invited, though he wasn't sure you'd be willing or able to come."

"He didn't let you know we'd contacted him a few days ago?"

"No," Fel said. "Of course, we were already on our way. Maybe he didn't think it was worth recalling us at that point."

"Which brings us to the rest of your party," Mara said, looking at the silent stormtroopers.

"Oh, yes." Fel waved a hand to encompass his escort. "This is Unit Aurek-Seven of the Imperial Five-Oh-First Stormtrooper Legion."

Mara felt her stomach tightening. The Imperial 501st: Vader's personal stormtrooper unit during the Rebellion. Dubbed "Vader's Fist," its very arrival in a star system had often caused Rebel forces and corrupt Imperial officials alike to run for cover. Nonhumans of every sort, even innocent bystanders, quickly learned to tremble at the sight of those white armored face masks. The Emperor's bias against aliens had impressed itself indelibly onto the combat psychology of all his stormtrooper legions, but even more so on the soldiers of the 501st.

And so, of course, that was the specific unit Parck had revived for his Empire of the Hand. That said a lot right there as to how the admiral was running things. "I guess the old saying is right," she said stiffly. "The one about old units never really dying."

Fel shrugged noncommittally. "So what exactly were you doing up there?"

Mara glanced around. Still no Chiss in sight, but that wouldn't last forever. "Not here," she told Fel. "Follow me."

Turning her back on them, she headed down the corridor. A moment later, without complaint or question, they had formed up behind her.

The Force connection between her and Luke wasn't nearly as clear and precise as most people in the New Republic thought, as if it were a mental comlink conversation. He became aware of her approach as she neared their quarters, and she could tell he was also aware that she was bringing company.

But it wasn't until he opened the door for her that he realized just what kind of company it was.

As usual, he recovered quickly. "Hello," he said calmly, nodding in greeting. "I'm Luke Skywalker."

"Commander Chak Fel," Fel said, nodding in return. "This is my escort guard, Unit Aurek-Seven of the Five Hundred and First."

Mara caught Luke's flicker of recognition at the name and the unit designation. But he merely nodded again. "Honored, Commander," he said. "Won't you come in?"

"Just the commander," Mara said before Fel could reply. "There's no room for everybody, and I'd just as soon not have Drask's people see stormtroopers hanging around outside our quarters."

"Good point," Fel agreed, giving the stormtroopers a hand signal. "Return to the ship."

"Acknowledged," one of them said in that flat, mechanically filtered voice that was one of the marks of a stormtrooper. Turning in perfect unison, they marched away.

"Now," Mara said, waving Fel toward the conversation area as the door slid shut behind him. "Let's start with you, Commander. What are you doing here?"

"I thought I'd explained that," Fel said, lowering himself into one of the chairs. "Admiral Parck wasn't sure you'd be coming, so he sent me to act as his representative."

"And Formbi went along with it?" Mara asked, sitting down beside Luke across from the young Imperial.

Fel shrugged. "Actually, Formbi didn't seem to have a problem. As I said, it was mostly General Drask who objected."

"He doesn't seem too happy with our presence, either," Luke told him.

"Or Ambassador Jinzler's," Mara added, watching Fel closely.

But there was no bump of reaction at the mention of Jinzler's name. "Yes, I've noticed," Fel said. "Frankly, I don't think Drask likes anyone. Certainly not aliens. Possibly not even Formbi."

"So why did Parck send you and a bunch of stormtroopers instead of coming himself?" Mara asked. "The way Formbi talks about it, you'd think Outbound Flight was the diplomatic high point of the year. Or does Parck just like irritating Chiss generals?"

"Not a hobby *I'd* like," Fel said. There was a flicker of something— "Actually, I really don't know why we're here."

Liar. Mara didn't have to look at Luke to know he'd caught it, too. "All right," Luke said, not giving any hint that they'd caught Fel's prevarication. "Let's try this, then. Why didn't Parck mention you when he talked to us?"

Fel shook his head. "I don't know that, either. I more or less assumed he had."

That one, at least, did seem to be the truth. "But then—" Mara began.

"Just a moment," Fel said, cutting her off with a lifted finger. "I've answered a whole batch of questions. It's your turn now. What were you doing climbing around the ceiling of the entry chamber that way?"

Mara had already decided there was no point in playing coy with this one. If Fel was involved in the cable incident, he already knew what had happened. If not, there was no reason for him not to know. "There was a small accident when we first arrived," she said. "A heavy cable attached to the ceiling came loose and nearly knocked my husband across the room."

Fel's eyes shifted to Luke, gave him a quick once-over. "No, it missed me," Luke assured him. "But as Mara said, it was close."

"I wanted to see if the cable might have been deliberately cut," Mara continued. "It had already been put back up, so that's where I had to go to look at it."

"What did you find?" Fel asked.

"No evidence that it had been cut, but it also shouldn't have come loose by itself," Mara said. "Still, I did find indentations on the end like you might get if it had been held in a spring clip for a while."

"Um," Fel murmured thoughtfully. "As if someone had had it already disconnected and held in a clip, so that they could release it at just the right time. Unless they swapped out the entire cable?"

Mara shook her head. "I marked the original with my lightsaber before we left the area," she told him. "Just a nick in the insulation, but visible enough if you know where to look. No, it was the same cable."

"So you suspect it was a deliberate attack framed to look like an accident," Fel said. "Just as well—" He broke off.

"Just as well what?" Mara demanded.

Fel reddened. "I'm sorry," he said. "I wasn't supposed to tell you. Admiral Parck sent us along because he thought you might be in danger on this trip." He smiled self-consciously. "We're sort of your escort."

Mara looked at Luke, saw her same surprise mirrored there. Unlike hers, though, his surprise had a touch of amusement to it. "Very kind of Admiral Parck," Mara said tartly. "You can tell him thanks on your way out."

"Now, Jedi Skywalker—"

"Don't *Jedi Skywalker* me," Mara retorted. "We don't want a bunch of stormtroopers clattering along behind us everywhere we go. Drask is already glowering more than I like. So climb aboard whatever shuttle you came in on and get out."

Fel looked pained. "I'm afraid it's not as easy as that," he said. "Yes, we're here to protect you—"

"Which we don't need."

"No, I agree completely," Fel said. "The idea of us protecting Jedi . . . but at the same time, I'm under Imperial orders, not yours."

"Besides, Formbi's already given them permission to come along," Luke pointed out.

"So what?" Mara demanded.

Luke shrugged. "You and I were wondering if Formbi was using this mission as a pretext for opening full diplomatic relations with the New Republic," he reminded her. "Maybe he's looking to do the same thing with the Empire of the Hand."

"What makes you think Parck even *wants* diplomatic relations with the Chiss?" Mara countered.

"We do," Fel said quietly. "Very much."

Mara glared at him. *There are a hundred different threats out there that would freeze your blood if you knew about them* . . . "All right, fine," she said between clenched teeth. "This isn't my ship. You want to hang around, fine. Just don't get in our way."

"Understood," Fel said. "Do you want me to start any inquiries as to who aboard might have wanted Master Skywalker injured?"

"Absolutely not," Mara said. "We'll handle that. You just stay in the background and keep quiet."

Fel smiled slightly. "As you wish," he said, getting to his feet. "If you'll excuse me, then, I'll return to our transport and prepare for dinner."

"We'll see you there," Luke said.

"Good talking with you." Fel crossed to the door, opened it, and left.

"Great," Mara growled. "Just what we needed. Our own private entourage."

"Oh, I don't know," Luke said soothingly. "It's no worse than a group of Noghri following us around."

"Of course it's worse," Mara retorted. "Noghri at least know how to be invisible. You ever see a stormtrooper who wasn't as obvious as a Wookiee at a formal dinner?"

"Well, they're here, and we might as well get used to it," Luke said. "Now, what about this cable?"

"It was deliberately dropped," Mara said, reluctantly changing gears. She wasn't really finished ranting about Fel yet, but she was practical enough to realize there were higher-priority matters that needed to be dealt with. "There was also a hole bored in the ceiling where the spring clip would have come through to hold the cable."

"So it could have been handled by remote control?"

"Easily," Mara said. "Which means Drask himself might have been the one to trigger it."

"Or Feesa," Luke pointed out. "She was in the best position to handle the timing."

"I thought she was Formbi's assistant, though," Mara pointed out. "Formbi's the one who wants us aboard."

"Does he?" Luke asked. "Or is he under orders from above that he himself doesn't necessarily agree with?"

"Point," Mara conceded, frowning as she thought back to their encounters with the Aristocra. "I don't know, though. He seemed genuinely pleased to have us here."

"Yes, but there's something else going on below the surface," Luke said. "Some extra tension he's trying to hide. Of course, that could be nothing more than the fact he's having to deal with so many aliens."

"Possibly with the future of the whole Chiss diplomatic structure hanging on how well he does?"

"That could be part of it," Luke agreed. "So if we leave Formbi off the list, who's left? Drask?"

"Who's left is basically everyone except the Geroons," Mara said. "And only because they weren't here at the time. It could have been Drask, Jinzler, or Fel and his group." She snorted. "The Five-Oh-First. Can you imagine Parck reviving *that* one? I guess old units die hard."

Luke shrugged, a little too casually. "Old units aren't the only thing," he murmured.

"What was that?" Mara asked suspiciously.

"I was just noticing how easily you slipped into the role of Imperial commander a few minutes ago," Luke said. "You led them here, you ordered the stormtroopers away, and you basically told Fel what you wanted him to do."

"So?" Mara said with a shrug of her own. "Since when have I been shy about telling *anyone* what I wanted them to do?"

"I know," Luke said. "I'm just pointing out how comfortably you took back that role, that's all. I'm not saying anything else."

"You'd better not be," Mara said darkly. But whether he

said it or not, she could sense there was something else behind his words. Something not entirely comfortable with the way she'd behaved.

Her first impulse was to have it out right now, to insist that he bring his thoughts on the subject out into the open where she would have the chance to knock them down one by one.

But something held her back. Perhaps she sensed it wasn't the proper time or place for that kind of discussion.

Or perhaps she wasn't so sure she *could* knock them all down.

He was right in a way. She *had* found it disturbingly easy to slip back into that role. It had been refreshing to deal with soldiers who took orders without question, instead of a mixed group of humans and Bothans and Devaronians and Mon Cals, all of whom had their own prejudices and perspectives and who sometimes heard or obeyed orders in entirely different ways.

I've had my fill of Imperial service, she'd told Fel. But had she? Really?

"Anyway, we should probably go back to the *Jade Sabre* and see if we've got anything that'll pass as formal wear," Luke went on. Apparently, he didn't want to have it out yet, either. "Dinner's going to be served soon, and we'll want to be ready when Feesa comes to get us."

CHAPTER 6

AFTER THE SIZE OF THE RECEPTION ROOM, LUKE HAD EXPECTED the *Chaf Envoy*'s main dining salon to be equally grand and expansive. To his surprise, it was in fact built more along the lines of a standard ship's wardroom, though decorated with the same sort of elegant touches he'd already noted in their quarters. Apparently, once the high-level dignitaries had been ushered aboard in proper style, the pomp and ceremony diminished considerably.

Perhaps the dignitaries' wardrobes were supposed to make up for it. Formbi and Drask were dressed even more elaborately than they had been at the *Jade Sabre*'s landing, though each maintained the same color scheme he'd been wearing then. Fel had switched to a dress uniform that bordered on the regal, with much of the tunic's upper left covered with rows of colored bits of metal that apparently denoted specific campaigns or victories. Jinzler had done equally well, with a layered robe-tunic that would have fit right in with a diplomatic reception on Coruscant. Mara wasn't too far behind him, with her flowing wraparound gown and embroidered bolero jacket.

It made Luke feel decidedly out of place in his plain dark jumpsuit and sleeveless, knee-length duster. Next trip, he made a mental note, he was going to have to make sure to bring a couple of fancier outfits along.

Still, he was far from being the worst-dressed guest at the party. The two Geroons on the far side of the wide circular table looked positively shabby in comparison with the Chiss staffers seated on either side of them. Both aliens wore simple but heavy-looking brown robes of some kind of thick material over long tan tunics. One of them, the Geroon who had spoken to Formbi from the refugee ship, also had what appeared to be a complete dead animal thrown over his shoulders, its long-snouted head and clawed forepaws hanging down across his chest nearly to his waist, while most of the torso and hind legs hung down behind his back. An elaborate blue-and-gold collar glittered around the animal's neck, about the only real decoration anywhere in the Geroon's outfit.

"I trust the food is pleasing?" Feesa asked from her seat at Luke's left.

"It's excellent, thank you," he assured her. In actual fact, it was a little too spice-heavy for his taste, and the combination fork-knife he'd been given to use left an oddly metallic aftertaste after each bite. But it was so clearly an attempt to create a New Republic–style banquet that he certainly wasn't going to quibble over minor details. More than once, he wondered if Parck had supplied the recipes.

"Interesting trophy Steward Bearsh is wearing," Jinzler commented from Feesa's other side. "That dead animal thing?"

"The wolvkil, yes," Feesa said, nodding. "I heard Steward Bearsh say they were a feral variant of a predator creature the Geroons once domesticated as pets. The one he wears is a mark of honor that has been in his family for four generations."

"Pets, huh?" Jinzler shook his head. "Frankly, I don't think I'd even like to meet it in the woods, let alone have it curled up by my bed."

"I doubt that will happen soon," Feesa said, a note of sadness in her voice. "All remaining wolvkils died with the Geroon world."

"I see," Jinzler murmured, and again Luke caught a flicker of emotion from him. For all his surface calm, he was clearly a man who felt things deeply. "A terrible tragedy, that. Was Aristocra Formbi able to help them find a new world?"

"Our knowledge of the regions outside our borders is very

limited," Feesa said. "I don't believe anything suitable was found."

"I hope the Aristocra isn't giving up this quickly," Jinzler said, a note of challenge in his voice. "They couldn't have had more than a couple of hours to study your star charts."

"Perhaps more study will be scheduled," Feesa said diplomatically. "Aristocra Chaf'orm'bintrano has not told me his plans."

Across the table Bearsh stirred and looked over at Luke, linking his fingers and dipping both hands and head in a sort of unified bow. Luke nodded in reply; and as he did, the Geroon picked up his fluted drink glass and got up from his seat. Circling the table, he came up behind Luke. "Good evening," he said, the words coming out from both his mouths. "Am I correct in the belief that you are Jedi Master Luke Skywalker?"

Luke blinked in surprise. Back in the command center, he'd only heard the Geroon speak in the Chiss trade language. "Yes, I am," he managed. "Please forgive my surprise. I didn't realize you spoke Basic."

The Geroon opened his mouths slightly, showing a double row of small teeth in each. A smile? "Should we not know at least a portion of the language of our liberators?" he countered. "It was we who were surprised to learn that the Chiss aboard this vessel could understand it."

"Yes, they do," Luke agreed, feeling suddenly like a hopeless bumpkin who'd just been dropped off the bantha cart at the edge of town. He understood probably a dozen languages, but all were anchored solidly to the cultures that dominated the Core Worlds and Inner Rim. It had never even occurred to him to try to add an Outer Rim trade language to his repertoire.

Which now meant that everyone else out here was having to go out of their way to accommodate his shortcomings.

But then, to be fair, this was hardly a situation he would normally have expected to find himself in. At least not without C-3PO or some other protocol droid along to assist with language duties.

"It is their way of honoring those of Outbound Flight, no doubt," Bearsh said, a note of reverence in his voice. "If I may intrude, I overheard you and Feesa speaking of our search for a world for our people."

"Yes," Luke confirmed. "I hope you will succeed."

"As do I and all the Geroon Remnant," Bearsh said, a note of sadness replacing the reverence. "That is indeed why I came across to see you. I hoped you might be willing to help."

"In what way?"

Bearsh waved his hand, nearly spilling his drink in the process. "I am told your New Republic has great resources and vast territories within its borders. Perhaps when you are finished with your meal you would be kind enough to search your records to see if any of your worlds near this region of space might be available for our use." He ducked his head. "We would of course pay for any world you might find to offer us. Our resources are small, but all Geroons stand ready to serve with their hands and minds and bodies until any such debt is repaid."

"If we find a suitable world, I'm sure something can be worked out," Luke assured him. "Actually, I'm finished now if you'd like to accompany me to my ship."

The Geroon started back. "You would take me aboard your vessel?" he breathed.

"Would that be a problem?" Luke asked cautiously, wondering if he'd made some terrible mistake in etiquette. Were the Geroons afraid of strangers and strange ships? And yet, they were *here*, aboard a Chiss ship. "Because if it would make you uncomfortable—"

"Ah, no," Bearsh said, dropping suddenly onto one knee and bowing his head low to the deck. This time some of his drink *did* slosh up over the rim and dribble down over his fingers. "It is too much. There is too much honor for one Geroon. I cannot accept."

"Maybe I should just give you the data cards, then," Luke suggested. "Though you might not be able to read them," he added as that thought belatedly struck him. "I'd have to bring a datapad along, too."

"You would be willing to allow us to honor you?" Bearsh asked eagerly. "You would come aboard our humble vessel?"

"Certainly," Luke said, touching his mouth with his napkin and standing up. "Shall we go?"

"The honor is great," Bearsh said, bowing repeatedly as he stepped back. "The honor is great."

"You're welcome," Luke said, feeling decidedly awkward. The sooner he got himself and this groveling Geroon out of here, the better.

He turned to Mara, who was practically radiating her amusement at his fumbling. "I'll see you back at our quarters," he told her, sending her a silent warning with his eyes that she ignored completely. "If you need me, I'll be in the Geroons' shuttle."

"Understood," Mara said blandly. At least her voice was polite enough. "I'll see you later. Have fun."

"Thanks," Luke growled, turning back to the still-bobbing Geroon. And Leia made this diplomatic stuff look so easy. "Lead the way, Steward Bearsh."

THE GEROON SHUTTLE, AS IT TURNED OUT, WAS DOCKED ON THE starboard side of the *Chaf Envoy* about twenty meters aft of the *Jade Sabre*. Luke ducked into the *Sabre* as they passed and grabbed a set of astrogation data cards and a datapad, then followed Bearsh back to their ship.

Twenty-two years before, back at the Mos Eisley spaceport, he could remember gazing at the *Millennium Falcon* and wondering how a ship that looked like that could even be permitted to fly the Imperial space lanes. Now his first reaction to the Geroon shuttle was that such thoughts had done the *Falcon* a disservice. Not only *should* this thing not be flying, he couldn't see how it even *could* be flying.

The entire interior was a patchwork of repaired, reworked, or readapted equipment, patched pipes and conduits, and power cables that would have had a New Republic safety inspector scrambling for emergency cutoff switches. Two of the bunkrooms and a storage compartment had been sealed off with vacuum-leak warnings on the doors, and half the displays on the control deck seemed to have been permanently shut down. Overlaying it all was a faint odor that seemed to be a mixture of lubricating compound, battery solution, maneuvering fuel, and hydraulic fluid. It was, Luke thought more than once, astonishing that the thing had managed to make it here from the main Geroon ship.

Or perhaps the *Chaf Envoy* had a really good set of tractor beams.

There were three other Geroons in the ship when he and Bearsh arrived, and it was quickly evident that the steward's adulation in the dining salon had actually been greatly restrained. The other Geroons clustered around him practically from the moment he ducked through the rusty hatchway, blathering excitedly and repeating over and over again how much of an honor it was to have him aboard, until he was about as embarrassed as he'd ever been in his life.

Several times he tried gently to explain that he wasn't really someone who deserved such adulation. But all it did was inspire fresh salvos of praise even more insistent and pathetic than what had gone before.

Eventually, he gave up. Whatever those aboard Outbound Flight had done for these people, it was so deeply ingrained that even after fifty years there was no holding it back. All he could do was endure it, try not to let it go to his head, and hope they would eventually run out of adjectives.

"All right," he said when they had finally quieted down enough to sit around a small table together. "I've pulled all the information I have on Outer Rim systems. Just bear in mind that a lot of these systems aren't members of the New Republic, and a lot more give only token allegiance. But if we can help you, we will. Now, what sort of world exactly are you looking for?"

"One with air like this," Bearsh said, waving a hand around him. "Less full and flavorful than the Chiss air."

Probably meant a lower oxygen content, Luke decided. "Okay," he said, keying that parameter into the datapad. "I presume you need water, too. What about climate and terrain?"

"We need places for the children to play," one of the other Geroons put in eagerly. "Many places, for many children to play."

"Peace, young one," Bearsh soothed, his mouths opening in another toothy Geroon smile. "On an entire world, there will be plenty of places for the children."

He turned back to Luke. "You must excuse Estosh," he said quietly. "He has never known life anywhere but within our vessel."

"I understand," Luke said. "I can tell your people put great store in your children, too."

"How do you know that?" Bearsh asked, his face puckering oddly. Then it cleared. "Ah—of course. The great and renowned powers of the Jedi."

"Actually, there was nothing special needed on this one," Luke said. "We saw your earlier conversation with the Chiss. Any people who would put a playground right in their command center must certainly care a lot for their children."

"Ah," Bearsh said. "Yes. Our vessel was originally built for scientific surveys. That space was designed to contain the center for instrument responses." His face puckered again. "It was the only place large enough for a proper play and exercise area. All the rest of the vessel is composed of small rooms for the singles and families. We had no need for the instruments, so we took them out and gave the space to the children."

He straightened his head and shoulders, his eyes unfocusing as if gazing into the future. "But one day," he said firmly. "One day we will have a *real* place for the children. And then you will see, Jedi Master Skywalker, what the Geroon people can become."

"I'll look forward to it," Luke promised. "Now, about terrain?"

Bearsh seemed to come back from his dreams. "We will live in whatever grounds you find for us," he said. "Mountains or lakes, woodlands or plains—it does not matter."

"All right," Luke said. They certainly weren't a picky lot. "What about temperature ranges?"

Again, Bearsh waved his hand. "The temperature in this vessel is somewhat warm for us," he said. "But we will adapt and adjust to whatever—"

He broke off as the deck beneath them gave a sudden gentle jolt. "What was that?" Estosh asked fearfully, looking quickly around.

A second later they had their answer as a distant thunderclap echoed faintly through the open hatchway. "An explosion," Luke told him, jumping to his feet and sprinting toward the entry tunnel, stretching out to the Force as he pulled out his comlink. The opposite side of the ship, he estimated from the sudden surge of consternation in that direction, somewhere in the aft quarter. "Mara?"

"We've got an explosion and fire on the aft port side," her voice came back. "I'm heading back to see if I can help."

"I'll join you," Luke said, clearing the end of the entry tunnel and heading for the nearest cross-ship corridor. "Any idea what's back there?"

"Fel's transport, for one thing," Mara told him. "No idea what else, but from the way Drask took off I'd guess something serious. Vital equipment, or possibly fuel storage."

Luke winced. "Right. See you there."

The air began to smell of smoke before he was halfway down the main portside corridor. He kept going; and then, suddenly, he was there, braking to a halt behind a dozen Chiss with handheld extinguishers running into a half-open door through which smoke was pouring. He spotted Mara off to one side with Fel and eased his way past a Chiss in military dress uniform shouting orders in a sharp, staccato language. "Situation?" he called to Mara.

"The fire's right by a nexus of maneuvering jets and their fuel supply," she told him grimly. She'd stripped off her fancy jacket and gown, and was dressed now only in the gray combat leotard and softboots she'd been wearing underneath the formal wear. "The stormtroopers are already inside with extinguishers, trying to keep it away from the tanks."

Luke looked over at Fel. The young Imperial was wearing a stormtrooper's headset comlink, an intense expression on his face as he stared through the open door. "Don't they have automatic extinguisher systems?" he asked.

"They used to," Mara said. "Apparently, a malfunction in the system was what caused the explosion in the first place."

"That's useful," Luke said, blinking back tears as the acrid smoke stung his eyes. Some of the Chiss who had gone into the fire zone were starting to come out now, most of them staggering slightly as they trailed plumes of smoke. "How come the stormtroopers are in there?"

"They were the first ones on the scene with self-contained breathing equipment," Fel said before Mara could answer. "Speaking of breathing, how are Jedi in oxygen-poor atmospheres?"

"We can handle a few minutes," Luke said. "Less, if there's a lot of physical or mental exertion involved. What do you need?"

"Some delicate lightsaber work." Fel pointed to the doorway through which the smoke was pouring. "They've got the fuel tanks isolated for the moment, but the fire's got too much of a head start and it's pushing in on them. They think they've located the extinguisher system—"

"They *think*?"

"That's why the work needs to be delicate," Fel said. "Otherwise, they'd just blast the lines open and be done with it. What we need is for you to lightly scratch the conduits, just enough to let out a few drops so we can see exactly what kind of liquid's inside. The last thing we want is to dump more fuel or something else flammable."

"No kidding," Mara said. "Assuming they're right, then what?"

"Then you cut them all the way open," Fel said. "It looks like the explosion only warped the area around the main spray valves, so if you can open the lines behind them we should be able to flood the compartment and put it out in short order."

Luke looked over at the dress-uniformed Chiss, now huddled with a pair of crewers strapping on air tanks and breather masks. Protocol, he knew, probably dictated that they clear this with one of the ship's officers before going in.

But the officer looked too busy to listen to passengers. And if the fire was already getting close to the fuel tanks . . . "All right," he said, coming to a decision. "How do I find the conduit?"

"How do *we* find it?" Mara corrected, her lightsaber already in hand.

"Mara—"

"Don't even think it," she warned. "Besides, I'm better with delicate work than you are."

Unfortunately, she was right. With an effort, Luke forced back his instinctive reaction to shield her from danger wherever possible. "Fine," he said. "How do *we* find the conduit?"

"They'll guide you in," Fel told him. "Watch for a bright light."

"Right." Unhooking his lightsaber from his belt, Luke took a deep breath and stretched out to the Force. He lifted his eyebrows at Mara, got her confirming nod, and ducked through the doorway.

The smoke was considerably thicker inside the room than Luke had expected, swirling madly around as the compartment's venting system tried its best to clear it away. Ahead, through another half-open door, he could see the blaze of the fire, the crackling of flames punctuated by the hiss from fire extinguishers. Squinting against the smoke, he slipped through the second doorway, dodging around staggering crewers and trying to stay clear of the flames as he looked around for the stormtroopers.

There was no sign of them. But there *was* another doorway angling off to the right where the fire was burning even more intensely. Even as he sent a questioning thought toward Mara, a dim light suddenly shone out from the room, the narrow beam fighting its way through the smoke.

Mara had seen it, too. Luke caught her wordless signal, sent back an equally wordless confirmation, and started picking his way through gaps in the flames. He managed it with only a few minor burns, and a minute later eased into the room.

The four stormtroopers were standing in the far corner, arranged in a combat semicircle with their backs to an extensive array of fuel tanks, sending short bursts of spray from their extinguishers at any tendril of flame that threaded its way too close. The one shining his light through the doorway looked over as the two Jedi came in and flipped the light upward, centering the beam on one of a set of five conduits snaking their way across the ceiling. Luke nodded acknowledgment and looked for a way through the flames.

Unfortunately, there wasn't one.

He peered into the smoke, listening to his heartbeat counting out the seconds. Even Jedi breath control had its limits, and he and Mara were getting dangerously close to them. He could use the Force to lift his lightsaber to the conduit, of course, but he wasn't at all sure he would have enough control at that range for the delicate scratch Fel wanted. The only other option he could see would be to lift Mara there directly and let her do the job.

It would be risky. That much activity would put a severe strain on his system in his current oxygen-deprived state, quickly running him to the limit of his breath control and leaving him at the mercy of the smoke still filling the room. If the smoke also contained toxic gases, he could be in serious trouble.

He would have to chance it. Turning to Mara, he replaced his lightsaber on his belt and gestured toward the conduit. He could sense her own doubts, but she knew better than to waste time arguing. She nodded her readiness, and he stretched out to the Force to lift her gently off the deck. Keeping her as high over the flames as he could without banging her head against the various pieces of equipment jutting down from the ceiling, he moved her into position. She had her lightsaber ignited before he eased her to a stop, giving the conduit a quick and almost casual-looking slash with the tip of the blade.

For a long moment nothing happened. Then, through the

haze of smoke, Luke saw a few drops of liquid collect on the underside of the conduit. They coalesced into a single large drop and fell onto the deck below.

With a sizzle audible even over the crackle of the flames, the particular tongue of flame directly below flickered and went out.

Mara didn't wait for further instructions. Her lightsaber slashed again, slicing the conduit lengthwise; and suddenly the room was filled with a noisy spray of liquid, splattering against the ceiling and walls and showering down onto the fire.

It was almost too late. Luke's vision was starting to waver now as his body ran out of air, and it was all he could do to keep from dropping Mara onto the dying flames and fire-heated deck below her.

Clenching his teeth, he hung on. *A few more seconds,* he told himself sternly. A few more seconds and the fire would be out, or near enough. Then he could set Mara down and they could both start breathing again.

Unless between the lingering smoke and the extinguisher spray the room contained nothing but those toxic gases he'd wondered about earlier. In that case, he would just have to hope that the fire would be mostly gone before he blacked out, or at least that the stormtroopers would notice and pull him out of anything before he burned to death. A few more seconds . . .

He jerked as something suddenly came down over his head. He blinked; but even as his eyes registered the vision-enhancing eyepieces in front of them, his skin registered something far more important: the feel of clean, cool air being blown at his face.

He reached a hand up to his head, the fingertips bumping against something hot and hard. But the reaction had been pure reflex anyway, because he'd already figured out what was happening. One of the stormtroopers, recognizing his desperate need for air, had come to his side and put his own helmet over Luke's head.

He took a deep, careful breath. The air smelled as good as

it felt. He took another breath, and another, filling his lungs and replenishing the oxygen in his bloodstream. His thoughts flicked to Mara, but before he could ask he sensed that she, too, was being given the same care by a stormtrooper standing on the hot but no longer burning deck beneath her. He eased his Force-hold on her, lowering her down into the Imperial's waiting arms.

There were a pair of hands on his shoulders now, half guiding, half pushing him back the way he'd come. A moment later they reached the doorway and stepped through. "I'm all right," he called, taking one final breath and pushing the helmet away. Its owner caught it on its way up, and Luke got just a glimpse of an intense, dark-skinned face before the other slid the helmet back down over his own head again. He glanced back over his shoulder to make sure Mara was all right—

And froze, feeling his mouth drop open in astonishment. Like him, Mara had taken a few breaths of clean air and was in the process of returning the borrowed stormtrooper helmet to its owner.

Only the head sticking up out of the white armor wasn't human. It was green with touches of orange, dominated by large eyes and a narrow highlighting of glistening black scales that curved over the top and sides of the head almost to the nose. He caught sight of Luke staring at him and his mouth gaped open in what had to be a grin.

Luke could only stare back. The 501st Stormtrooper Legion—Vader's Fist—the absolute epitome of Emperor Palpatine's hatred of nonhumans and his determination to bring them under human domination.

And one of its own members was an alien . . .

UNDER THE CIRCUMSTANCES, LUKE HAD TO PRIVATELY ADMIT, General Drask was surprisingly polite about the whole thing. "We appreciate the assistance," he said, standing like a small, immovable pillar in the smoke-stained corridor as a small river of Chiss moved past and around him on cleanup duty. His voice was under careful control, but there was no mistaking the smoldering fire in his glowing red eyes. "But in the future, you will not take action aboard this vessel without specific authorization from myself, Aristocra Chaf'orm'bintrano, Captain Brast'alshi'barku, or another command-rank officer. Is that understood?"

"Clearly," Fel said before either Luke or Mara could say anything. "I apologize for overstepping our bounds."

Drask nodded shortly and brushed past them, heading aft toward the damaged area. "Come on," Fel said to Luke, lip twitching in an ironic half smile. "Our work here appears to be done."

They headed forward. "Certainly a gracious bunch, aren't they," Mara commented sourly as more Chiss hurried past them going in the other direction.

"You have to look at it from his point of view," Fel reminded her. "First of all, we're supposed to be honored diplomatic guests, not volunteer firefighters."

"That's *Formbi's* point of view, not Drask's," Mara countered. "At least the *honored* part is."

"Doesn't matter how he personally feels," Fel said. "He has his orders, and when a Chiss accepts orders he carries them out, period. Still, that said"—he smiled suddenly—"I suspect he's chewing hull fasteners right now. He doesn't like anything about the Empire of the Hand or humans in general, and it has to gall him no end for us to have saved his ship for him."

"Which brings up a more serious question," Luke said. "Namely, what exactly happened back there? Accident, or sabotage?"

"I'm sure they'll be looking into that," Fel said. "But if it was sabotage, it was a pretty poor job of it. Even if those tanks had ruptured, it would only have put one relatively minor sector of the ship out of action. It certainly wouldn't have killed everyone aboard or anything so dramatic."

"Unless that's all the damage the saboteur needed," Mara suggested. "Maybe all he wanted to do was scuttle the mission, or delay it while another ship was brought out for us to use."

"Fine, but why would anyone want to delay the mission?" Fel asked reasonably. "Everyone aboard seems pretty eager to get on with it."

"*Seems* being the operative word," Mara pointed out. "Someone could easily be faking."

"Really," Fel said, frowning. "I thought you Jedi could pick up on things like that."

"Not as well as we'd sometimes like," Luke said. "We can pick up on strong emotion, but not necessarily subtle lies. Especially if the liar is good at it."

"Or maybe our saboteur *does* want to get to Outbound Flight, but doesn't want all the rest of us getting there with him," Mara said thoughtfully. "If he could manage alternate transport for himself while we were left hanging, that again might be all he needs."

"But what would getting to Outbound Flight first gain him?" Luke asked. "Besides, the Chiss have already been there, haven't they?"

"Actually, all they did was a long-range fly-by," Fel said. "They got enough readings to figure out what they'd found, then hightailed it out of there and forwarded the data to the Nine Ruling Families with a request for instructions. The Families held a quick debate, declared the area off limits, and put Formbi in charge of getting in touch with all of us."

"Then let's try backing up a step," Luke suggested. "What is it about Outbound Flight that anyone might particularly want?"

Mara shrugged. "It's Old Republic technology," she pointed out. "Fifty-plus years out of date. That makes it pretty much of historical value only."

"Only to the three of us here," Fel said. "A lot of the cultures in this part of space are pretty primitive, technologically. Any one of them could learn a lot from a set of Dreadnaughts in even marginal condition. I daresay even the Chiss military would learn something if they had the time to take everything apart and study it."

"Or maybe the Geroons figure they can trade what's left

for a new home." Luke shook his head. "I wish we had more information."

"We do," Fel said, sounding puzzled. "Or rather, *I* do."

Luke looked at him in surprise. "You do?"

"Sure," Fel said. "Before we left, Admiral Parck went looking in Thrawn's records for anything he might have on Outbound Flight. Turns out he had a complete copy of the project's official operational manual."

"The whole thing?" Luke asked, frowning.

"The whole thing," Fel confirmed. "Four data cards covering personnel lists, inventory manifests, technical readouts and maintenance guides, flight operations checklists and procedures, schematics—everything. You want to take a look?"

"I thought you'd never ask," Mara said dryly. "Let's go."

The Imperial transport was docked in a mirror image of the half port and reception room that the *Jade Sabre* was using on the opposite side of the ship. The stormtroopers were already inside in the ready room, stripping off their armor to check for damage from their battle against the fire and talking quietly together about the incident.

"You know, I don't think I've ever seen a stormtrooper without his armor before," Luke commented as Fel led the way through the ready room and into a narrow corridor. "Not a conscious one, anyway."

"They *do* come out on occasion," Fel said with a grin. "Though never in public, of course."

"Fine, but why stormtroopers?" Mara asked. "Why didn't you just design and create your own elite force if that's what you wanted?"

Fel shrugged. "Mainly because the psychological advantage was already in place," he said. "Thrawn had brought several stormtrooper legions out here, and used them very effectively against a whole series of troublemakers. Once potential enemies came to respect and fear men in stormtrooper armor, it paid to keep using it."

"Even if not all those inside the armor are men anymore?" Luke asked.

Fel smiled. "Yes—Su-mil. Also goes by the warrior name Grappler."

"Your stormtroopers have names?" Mara asked. "I thought they were just assigned operating numbers."

"Even some of Palpatine's stormtroopers had names," Fel told her. "We all have names here. In case you're interested, Aurek-Seven consists of Grappler, Watchman, Shadow, and Cloud."

"Colorful," Mara commented. "I hope you don't expect us to keep track of them in public." .

"Especially since they don't seem to have gotten around to imprinting their names on their helmets," Luke added.

"And they never will," Fel said. "We don't put that kind of identification on stormtrooper armor. That way, no one can tell whether the stormtroopers he's facing are the absolute best the Empire of the Hand has to offer or a set of freshly trained recruits facing their first genuine action. It keeps our enemies from playing the odds against us."

"Were Su-mil's people one of those enemies?" Mara asked.

"Not at all," Fel assured her. "Su-mil is an Eickarie, one of the latest peoples to join the Empire of the Hand. They were a fragmented tribal people whom we helped liberate from the domination of a very organized warlord with a relative handful of disciplined troops."

"Helped how?" Mara asked. "Threw him out, then moved in yourselves?"

"Hardly," Fel said. "The Eickaries were actually very good fighters. They'd just gotten used to fighting among themselves over the years, and the Warlord took advantage of that to keep them working at cross-purposes. All we did was help organize and arm them. They did all the rest."

"And once they were free they simply decided to join up with you?" Luke asked.

"We're not Palpatine's Empire, either, Master Skywalker," Fel said. "We're more like a confederation than a true empire, in fact, with allies instead of conquered peoples. We keep the name, again, mainly for the historical aspects."

"And the psychological value, of course," Mara murmured.

"Of course," Fel agreed. "If you've gotten used to the notion of the Empire of the Hand being unbeatable, you're likely to give up that much sooner when a Star Destroyer appears over your planet or a squad of stormtroopers blows a hole through your defensive perimeter. Frankly, our philosophy is that the best battles are those where the enemy gives up before any shots have to be fired at all."

"You still don't strike me as a stormtrooper officer type," Luke commented. "What does your father think of your career choice?"

Fel shrugged. "Actually, I'm in the fleet end of the Imperial military," he said. "My usual command is a fleet-arm of clawcraft." He grinned again. "And my father is very proud of me."

They emerged from the corridor onto a deserted command deck. "No one on duty?" Luke asked, looking around.

"Is there anyone on duty in your ship?" Fel countered reasonably as he crossed to what appeared to be the main sensor station and waved his guests to a pair of chairs at nearby consoles. "Actually, we don't have a separate flight crew. This kind of transport is designed for a stormtrooper unit to be able to fly by itself, at least on routine operations. Takes some of the strain off our pilot cadre."

"Does that mean you're low on trained personnel?" Mara asked as she and Luke sat down.

"Everyone's always low on skilled pilots," Fel said, sitting down and swiveling his chair toward a rack of data cards. "I doubt the New Republic's any different. But at the moment we're doing all right. There are at least two alien groups within the Empire that have shown very good aptitude for general flight operations . . ."

He trailed off, and Luke caught a sudden dark flicker in Fel. "What is it?" he asked.

Slowly, Fel swiveled back to face them. "Well," he said, his voice studiously conversational. "I think I know now what that fire was all about. Whoever it was figured the Imperial Five-Oh-First would go charging back to help, nobly oblivious to our own safety."

"What are you talking about?" Mara demanded.

Fel gestured to the rack of data cards. "The Outbound Flight operational manual," he said. "It's gone."

CHAPTER 7

MARA LOOKED AT LUKE, TO FIND HIM LOOKING BACK AT HER. "Really," she said, looking over at Fel. "That's handy."

"Isn't it, though," Fel said. His voice was still quiet, but his face suddenly seemed older and harder. More mature, somehow, than Mara's first impression of him as a kid playing soldier. "Yes, that's certainly one way of putting it."

"I take it you don't have another copy?" Luke asked.

"This *was* the copy," Fel said. "The original records are back on Nirauan."

"Of course," Luke said. "What I meant—"

"I know what you meant." Fel passed a hand across his face; and when he had lowered it, some of the hardness had faded. "Sorry. I'm just . . . I messed up. I hate when I mess up."

"Welcome to the club," Mara said, an odd feeling flickering through her. In all her time with the Empire, she wondered, had she *ever* heard an Imperial officer actually admit to having made a mistake? "Let's skip the finger pointing and see if we can figure out who's got it. You have any idea how many people are aboard?"

"Not that many," Fel said, sounding a little more on balance. "I think this size ship runs a crew of only thirty to thirty-five. There seems to be an honor guard running around, too—call it two squads of six warriors each. Typical ambassador's staff runs to twenty, plus Formbi, so that's sixty-eight Chiss, max."

"Plus five Geroons, you and four stormtroopers, Jinzler,

and us," Luke said. "Unless there's someone else we don't know about."

"Right," Fel said.

"Wait a second," Mara said, frowning in concentration as she searched her memory. "You said Formbi had a staff of twenty?"

"I said that was typical for an ambassador," Fel corrected. "I haven't actually run the numbers myself."

"And I presume most of them would be from Formbi's family," she said. "That means they'd all be wearing yellow, right?"

"That's the Chaf family color, yes," Fel confirmed. "Why?"

"Because I didn't see more than four yellow outfits at dinner tonight," Mara said. "Formbi, Feesa, and two others. Everyone else was wearing black."

"She's right," Luke agreed. "Which family wears black?"

"None of them," Fel said, frowning. "That's the Chiss Defense Fleet. Black's a combination of all colors, since the military draws from all the families."

"What about his honor guard?" Mara asked. "Would they be from his family?"

Fel shook his head. "All honor guards wear military black. Huh. I wonder what he's done with the rest of his entourage."

"Maybe he had to leave them behind," Luke suggested. "With a mission of this sort the Nine Families might not have wanted any one family too heavily represented."

"I suppose that would make sense," Fel agreed slowly. "There's always been a tricky balance of power among the families."

"We can do a head count in the morning," Mara said. "Let's go on. How many of these assorted people might have known you had those files?"

Fel grimaced. "That's not going to narrow it nearly as much as you think. I was talking about it to Ambassador Jinzler this evening in the reception corridor before we were seated for dinner."

"You told *Jinzler* about it?" Mara bit out.

"Yes," Fel said, frowning at her vehemence. "I wanted to

know if he'd brought any records of his own I could compare against ours. Why, shouldn't I have done that?"

Mara waved a hand in disgust. Of course Fel had no way of knowing the man was a fraud. "Skip it," she said. "Did he?"

"What, have any records?" Fel shook his head. "No. He said everything useful the New Republic might once have had had been lost or destroyed."

"Probably true," Luke murmured. "Could anyone have been able to overhear this discussion?"

Fel exhaled noisily. "Could *every*one have been able to overhear it, you mean," he said. "The whole dinner crowd was milling around the corridor being sociable."

"Yes, but the whole dinner crowd wasn't paying attention," Mara countered. "Tell us who was."

Fel frowned into space, searching his memory. "For starters, of course, there were several Chiss," he said slowly. "I remember Feesa passing by at one point—I think she'd just brought you two in. Then there was—"

"Wait a minute," Luke said, straightening in his chair a little. "We were there by then?"

"Yes, but you were all the way across the corridor," Fel said. "Talking with Formbi, I think."

"That's not the point," Luke said, looking at Mara. "What do you think?"

"Worth a try," she agreed. "Just hold those thoughts a minute, Fel. We'll be right back to you."

Taking a deep breath, she closed her eyes and stretched out to the Force. The memory-enhancement technique the Emperor had taught her only worked on short-term memories, but the reception corridor ought to be recent enough to be accessible. She let the pictures flow backward through her mind's eye: the fire, the dinner, the flow of conversation before dinner . . .

There it was: Formbi stepping forward to greet them as Feesa brought them into the gathering. She and Luke speaking with him, assuring him their quarters were quite satisfactory and that, no, they didn't know very much about Outbound Flight but were looking forward to the voyage.

And in the background, Fel and Jinzler across the corridor by one wall, deep in conversation.

She froze the image, studying it. Then, slowly, she let it run forward again, watching everything and everyone around them.

All too soon, she had her answer. With a sigh, she slipped out of the trance and looked over at Luke.

He was already finished with his own memory enhancement. "What do you think?" he asked.

"He's right," she said in disgust. "It'd be simpler to figure out who *didn't* know. I spotted at least two Geroons close enough to listen in, plus a couple of the Chiss crewers and two command-rank officers."

"Including General Drask," Luke agreed. "About the only likely suspects who couldn't have known were Formbi and us."

"And, of course, Feesa works for Formbi," Mara reminded him. "She could have clued him in at any time."

Luke lifted a hand, let it fall into his lap. "Which leaves you and me. Dead end."

"Not necessarily," Mara said as a sudden thought struck her. "Okay, so they got the data cards. But they'd also need a datapad to read them with. That leaves only Jinzler."

"*And* the Geroons," Luke said. "I was talking to them when the explosion went off, and I left my datapad behind in their shuttle."

"Sorry, but that's a dead end, too," Fel spoke up, pointing to another rack above the console. "Whoever took the data cards also helped himself to a datapad." He brightened suddenly. "Which means it's *not* Jinzler or the Geroons," he said. "Like you said, they wouldn't need to take one."

"Unless they deliberately took it to throw us off the trail," Luke pointed out gently.

Fel's face dropped. "Oh. Right." He muttered something under his breath. "Sorry. This sort of thing is a little outside my area of expertise."

"Ours, too," Luke assured him. "Don't worry, we'll figure it out. If necessary, we can always ask Formbi to search the ship."

"What do you mean, if necessary?" Fel asked, frowning. "Don't we want him to do that anyway?"

Luke shrugged. "There are any number of places aboard a ship like this where you can hide something as small as four data cards," he pointed out. "Or the thief could easily have copied them into a different system—a droid, even—and then gotten rid of the originals."

"The Chiss don't have droids," Fel said. "But I see your point."

"On the other hand," Luke went on, "if we *don't* make a fuss, the thief won't know whether or not we've even missed them. That might give us a whole different set of advantages."

"Maybe," Fel said, not sounding entirely convinced.

"Trust me," Luke assured him. "Knowledge of any sort is power, as Talon Karrde always says."

"As Grand Admiral Thrawn usually proved," Fel rejoined.

"Don't remind us," Luke said ruefully. "Do you know if this ship carries any hypercapable transports or shuttles?"

"I believe this class usually carries one," Fel said, forehead wrinkling in concentration. "The commander's glider, it's called, though on a diplomatic ship like this it would probably be assigned to Formbi instead of Captain Talshib. Why?"

"You might still be right about someone trying to delay us and get a head start," Luke explained. "Especially now that he's got an operational manual in hand. If so, he'd need a way to get there once he'd disabled the ship. With your transport, ours, and Formbi's, that means he's got at least three to choose from."

"Plus the Geroons' shuttle and whatever Jinzler used," Mara put in.

"You can forget the Geroons' shuttle," Luke said, shaking his head. "I wouldn't trust it to fly to the far side of the *Chaf Envoy*."

"That bad, is it?" Mara asked.

"It makes my old T-sixteen look good by comparison," Luke said wryly. "Anyway, I don't think it has a hyperdrive."

"Okay, so that leaves Jinzler's ship," Mara concluded. "Fel, do you know what he's got?"

"Actually, I don't think he has a ship," Fel said. "I didn't see him arrive—he got here before we did—but I believe Formbi mentioned he'd gotten a ride from someone."

"He got a *ride*?" Luke asked incredulously. "Out *here*?"

Fel shrugged. "All I know is what Formbi said. Maybe he contacted Nirauan and Admiral Parck arranged something."

"Maybe," Mara said. Personally, she didn't believe that for a minute, but there was no point arguing about it. "So what's our next move?"

"*Our* next move is to go back to our quarters," Luke said firmly. "I don't know about you, but I've got a few small burns that need to be attended to."

"Oh, I'm sorry," Fel said, getting up quickly from his chair and starting toward one of the medpacs fastened to the wall beside the emergency oxygen tanks. "I didn't even think about—"

"No, no, that's all right," Luke hastened to assure him. "We don't need medical help. We'll be able to fix ourselves up just fine overnight with a Jedi healing trance."

"Oh." Fel stopped short, and Mara could sense his embarrassment. "I'm sorry. I guess I don't know as much about Jedi as I thought I did."

"Have you ever even met one before?" Mara asked.

"Well, no," Fel admitted. "But I have read up on them. I mean, on you. I mean—"

"We know what you mean," Luke said, smiling slightly. "Don't worry about it." He stood up. "Mara?"

"We'll see you tomorrow, Commander," Mara said, getting to her feet.

"All right," Fel said. "I'll see you out."

"Don't bother," Luke said. "We can find the way. You'd better go see to your men."

"Maybe discuss some new security arrangements," Mara added.

Fel made a face. "Point taken. Good night."

The stormtroopers had vanished from the ready room as Luke and Mara passed through, their armor hung neatly on the racks lining the walls. "That last comment was a little unfair, you know," Luke commented as they walked down the corridor toward their quarters. "I'm sure he *did* have some security set up."

"That's why I said they needed a *new* set of arrangements," Mara countered. "The old ones obviously weren't good enough."

"Mm," Luke said. "Maybe. Maybe not."

Mara looked sideways at him. "You have a thought?"

He shrugged, glancing casually behind them. "I don't know if it occurred to you, but we only have Fel's word that there were any data cards here in the first place."

"Or that he really did talk to Jinzler about them before dinner," Mara agreed. "He could just be venting waste gases here, trying to get us to look suspiciously at everyone except him. You think we ought to pay a little visit to Jinzler before we lock down for the night?"

Luke shook his head. "Not worth it. We definitely need to talk with him sometime before we get to Outbound Flight, but I don't want to do it with these burns distracting us. Besides, even if Fel did talk to him about Outbound Flight, it doesn't prove anything. By Fel's own admission he was trying to see what Jinzler knew about the mission. If Jinzler didn't have anything, but said he wanted to see Fel's records—"

"Records Fel didn't have," Mara murmured.

"Right—records he didn't have," Luke said, "then Fel would still have to fake a robbery. It'd be easier to fake it to us than wait until Jinzler came by."

"Except that we might catch him at it," Mara pointed out.

"You're forgetting the sequence of the conversation," Luke reminded her. "It wasn't until we told him we couldn't always catch people in lies that he even mentioned he had the data cards."

Mara played back the memory. Blasted if he wasn't right. "You're really making me look bad tonight," she growled. "I thought *I* was the one who was supposed to have had the investigative training."

"It's all the time I've spent hanging around Corran Horn," Luke said dryly. "Some of it rubs off on a person. Besides, you've got other things on your mind."

Mara felt her muscles stiffen. "What do you mean?" she asked cautiously.

He shrugged, too casually. "I was hoping you'd tell *me*," he said. "All I know is that there's something still churning around behind those beautiful green eyes of yours."

Mara snorted under her breath. "So it's flattery now, is it? That's a sure sign you've run out of logical arguments and persuasive skill."

"Or else it's a sign of my sincerity and commitment to your continued happiness as my wife and companion," Luke countered.

"Ooh—I like that," Mara said approvingly. "Commitment to my continued happiness. Make sure you use that one again sometime."

"I'll make a note," Luke promised. His smile faded into seriousness. "You know that I'm always ready to listen."

She caught his hand, squeezed it. "I know," she assured him. "And it's no big deal—really it isn't. I just have to do some thinking on my own before I can talk about it, that's all."

"Okay," Luke said, and she could feel his concern fading a little. But only a little. "Oh, and there's one more factor here we shouldn't forget. Fel's stormtrooper squad isn't exactly homogeneous."

Mara frowned. "Are you talking about that alien, Su-mil?"

"Yes," Luke said. "We don't know anything about him or his people, after all. It's possible he's running with his own agenda."

"Possible, but unlikely," Mara said, shaking her head. "The Five-Oh-First wasn't exactly your run-of-the-star-lane storm-trooper unit. They were an elite among elites, and I can't imagine Parck reviving it without holding to those standards."

"I didn't say it was likely," Luke reminded her mildly. "I would hope that Fel hadn't just thrown chance cubes when he picked his people for this mission. I just thought it was something we should keep in mind."

THEY DID MAKE ONE SHORT SIDE TRIP ON THE WAY BACK, STOPping by the *Jade Sabre* to make sure she was properly locked down against intruders. After that admittedly snide comment to Fel, Mara knew she would never live it down if her own ship got broken into. Back in their quarters, they were preparing for bed when Formbi's official announcement came over the shipwide speaker system that the fire damage had been repaired and that the mission would continue without interruption. He made no mention of the assistance the Chiss had received in battling the blaze; nor was there any comment as to the cause of the explosion that had started the fire in the first place.

Later, lying beside Luke in the darkness, Mara stared at the ceiling and wondered what exactly *was* going on inside her.

It had come on so quickly, this quiet feeling of guilt that had suddenly taken hold of her like a hand gently gripping her throat. Suddenly, all the things she'd done through the years she was Palpatine's agent were coming back to haunt her. The heavy-handed investigations; the casual brushing aside of even the limited rights that had existed under the Empire; the summary judgments.

The summary killings.

But she'd put all that behind her. Hadn't she? She'd never truly been on the dark side, after all—Luke himself had pointed that out to her three years ago. She'd served Palpatine and the Empire as best and as honestly as she'd known how, based on the admittedly slanted information he'd given her. Certainly the fact that she was now a Jedi seemed to support the view that her actions were redeemable.

So what was it that was bringing all this back? Fel and his stormtroopers, the most visible image of Imperial rule and excesses? The mission itself and its constant reminder that the destruction of Outbound Flight had been one of Palpatine's early atrocities?

Or was it something else entirely, something more subtle? After all, Palpatine had paid for his deeds with his life. So had Darth Vader and Tarkin and all the other Grand Moffs. Even Thrawn, whom she now realized had probably been nobler than all the rest of them put together, was gone. Only she, Mara Jade, the Emperor's Hand, had survived.

Why?

She rolled uncomfortably over onto her side, transferring her stare from the darkness of the ceiling to the darkness on the far side of the room. *Survivor's guilt,* she remembered hearing someone call it once. Was that what Fel and Outbound Flight had sparked in her? If true, it was pretty stupid, particularly at this late date.

Unless it was what Luke had suggested earlier. That there were still things about the Empire that she was reluctant to let go of.

She took a deep breath, let it out quietly. Luke was still awake, too, she knew, watching her emotions swirl around, ready to join her in her struggle whenever she was ready to invite him in.

She reached over and found his hand. "We're supposed to be doing Jedi healing trances, right?" she murmured.

He took the hint. "Right," he murmured back. "I love you."

"I love you, too," she said. "Good night."

"Good night."

She closed her eyes, settling herself more comfortably against the pillow and stretching out to the Force. After all, Luke had accepted her, dark past and all. If he could do it, she certainly ought to be able to.

MARA'S BREATHING SLOWED, HER MIND AND EMOTIONS QUIETING as she slipped into the healing trance. Luke watched her lovingly as she went silent, then gently disengaged his hand from hers and rolled over to face the opposite wall. It had been a long and busy day, and he had his own burns to deal with. He'd best get to it.

But the calmness and concentration necessary for the healing trance refused to come. Something was going on aboard this ship, something wrapped in a dark and murky purpose. Someone aboard—maybe more than one someone—was going to Outbound Flight for some other reason besides respect or penance.

He shifted his shoulders uncomfortably beneath the weight of the blankets. But then, to be perfectly honest, didn't he have an ulterior reason of his own for being here?

Of course he did. Outbound Flight was a relic from the last, turbulent days of the Old Republic, its existence and records offering the chance to fill in some of the gaps in the New Republic's history of that period. But even more importantly, it might offer a detailed look into the ways and organization of that last generation of the full Jedi Order. There might be information aboard that would fill in the gaps in his own knowledge and understanding, showing him what he was doing right.

And, more importantly, what he was doing wrong.

He grimaced in the darkness. Luke Skywalker, Jedi Master. *The* Jedi Master, as far as most of the New Republic was concerned. Founder, teacher, and leader of the resurgent Jedi Order.

How in the worlds had he wound up in this position, anyway? How was it that he had been loaded with the responsibility for rebuilding something that had taken past generations centuries or more to create?

Because he had been all that there was, that was how. *When gone am I,* Yoda had said in those final moments, *the last of the Jedi will you be. Pass on what you have learned.*

He'd done his best to live up to Yoda's command. But sometimes—too many times—his best hadn't been enough.

Yoda's training had helped, but not enough. The Holocron had helped, but not enough. Advice and correction from Leia and Mara had helped, but not enough.

Was there something that had survived aboard Outbound Flight that might also help? He didn't know. To be honest, he was almost afraid to find out.

He was going to search for it just the same, because he had to. He and Mara had both felt the gentle but unmistakable leading of the Force in accepting Formbi's invitation, and he knew too well that ignoring that nudge would bring bitter regret somewhere down the line. For good or evil, they were going to Outbound Flight.

And who could tell? Maybe there was even something aboard that would finally lay to rest his questions about Jedi marriage. Dissenting opinions from other Jedi Masters, perhaps, or even an indication that the whole Order had been wrong in the prohibition.

But he wouldn't know until they arrived. And he might as well arrive healthy. Taking a deep breath, letting the doubts and concerns slide away from him, he stretched out to the Force.

ALL THE NOISE AND BUSTLE IN THE CORRIDORS OUTSIDE HAD died down by the time Dean Jinzler put aside his datapad and started getting ready for bed. It had been a long, strange day, full of odd people and odd events, and he was tired with the kind of weariness that had haunted him for so much of his adult life.

And yet, at the same time, there was a fresh excitement underlying the fatigue. An excitement, and a darkly simmering dread.

Outbound Flight. After half a century, he was finally going to see the huge, mysterious project that had taken Lorana away from the Republic. He would stand where she had stood, see what she had seen. Perhaps, if he was very lucky, he would even be able to catch an echo of the idea or goal that had captured her own imagination, and to which she had dedicated her life.

And he would see where that all-too-short life had ended.

He gazed at his reflection in the refresher station mirror as he cleaned his face and teeth. Behind the lines and wrinkles, he could still see a hint of the much younger face that had sneered at Lorana and resented her for so many years, the face that had sent her off without even a proper farewell. The eyes gazing back at him—had her eyes been that same shade of gray? He couldn't remember. But whatever the color, he knew her eyes hadn't been cold and hard like his, but warm and alive and compassionate. Even toward him, who hadn't deserved any compassion at all. The hard set to his mouth hadn't been there, of course, way back then.

Or maybe it had. He'd carried this edge of quiet bitterness with him for a long time.

Rather like that young woman he'd met earlier, the stray thought occurred to him: that Mara Jade Skywalker. There was an air of old and bittersweet memory about her, too. For all the evidence of recent smoothing he could see in her face, it was clear that some of those memories would take a long time to fade.

Some memories, of course, never faded completely, no matter how much one might wish them to. He was living proof of that.

He finished in the refresher and stepped back into the bedchamber. And yet, for all the traces of old hardness and cynicism he could see in her face, he also knew that it had been Mara who had made the final decision not to expose him to Formbi.

That made him nervous all by itself. Compassion was something he'd long ago learned to dislike, and compassion from Jedi was even more ominous. Jedi, if you believed the old stories and New Republic propaganda, were supposed to be able to read people's characters and attitudes with a single glance. Could they also read minds and thoughts and intentions? If so, what exactly had Mara read in him?

He snorted. Nonsense. How in the name of Outer Rim bug-eaters could she possibly read his feelings when he himself couldn't even sort them out?

He didn't have an answer. Maybe she would, if he asked her.

Or maybe she would just decide that her mercy and second chances would be better spent on someone else, and turn him in to Formbi after all.

No. The chance cube had been thrown, and all he could do now was to sit back and see it through to the end. And as for the Jedi, his best bet would be to simply keep his distance from both of them.

Turning off the light, he settled himself down into the bed. And tried to push back the memories long enough to sleep.

CHAPTER 8

THE NEXT TWO DAYS WENT BY QUIETLY. LUKE SPENT MUCH OF the time with the Geroons, poring over New Republic planetary listings and trying hard to be patient with their continual and wearying mixture of hero worship and eagerness to please. Between world searches he tried to draw out some details of their encounter with Outbound Flight, but their stories seemed so confused and half mythic that he soon gave up the effort. Clearly, none of these particular Geroons had been there, and those who had hadn't done a very good job of reporting the event.

He didn't see Mara much during that time except at meals and in the evenings after they had settled in for the night. But a comparison of notes showed she was doing far better at the task of information gathering than he was. With Feesa as her guide, she had begun a methodical study of the *Chaf Envoy* and its crew.

Her first task had been to confirm some numbers. It turned out Fel had been right about the crew complement: besides General Drask there were four officers, thirty other crew members, and twelve line soldiers, making a total of forty-seven wearing the black Defense Fleet uniforms. Formbi's staff, in contrast, consisted only of Feesa and two other members of the Chaf family.

She never did get a proper explanation as to why Formbi was traveling so light, though Feesa did mention that under normal circumstances the entire ship's crew would have been Chaf, with no Defense Fleet personnel present at all. Eventually, she and Luke concluded that he had been right about the Nine Families' reluctance to have a single family get too much of the credit for the Outbound Flight expedition. The credit, or anything else that might come out of it.

The Chiss, for the most part, seemed fairly neutral to Mara's presence and the various questions she put to them during her tour. Drask continued to be gruffly polite when she ran into him, though there was no way of knowing how much of the courtesy was because of Mara's own status and how much was the fact that Formbi's aide was standing right there, ready to report any slippage in proper behavior toward the Aristocra's guests.

Formbi was even busier than the general, spending most of his time consulting in private with his other two staffers, Drask, or Talshib and the other ship's officers. Mara saw him a few times, but only at a distance, and usually in deep conversation with someone else. After that first formal evening meal together, he also began eating elsewhere, leaving his host duties mainly to Feesa and Talshib's officers.

As near as she could tell, Fel and his stormtroopers also kept largely to themselves and mostly out of sight of everyone else. On the handful of occasions outside of mealtimes when she ran into Fel, he was cordial enough, though she reported sensing a certain preoccupation beneath the surface. Neither of them mentioned the stolen data cards.

And though she readily admitted she couldn't prove it, she also had the distinct impression that Dean Jinzler was avoiding her.

If so, Luke mused, and particularly under the current circumstances, it was probably not the smartest move he could have made. Though Mara didn't actually say so, it wasn't hard for him to read between the lines and see that by the middle of the second day she had set herself the task of deliberately seeking Jinzler out wherever and whenever she could.

Even with that, though, the man was mostly successful in not letting himself be found. That irritated Mara all the more, and at one point Luke had to endure a prickly late-night hour in their quarters when he suggested to her that she might want to ease back a bit.

Finally, thankfully, late in the evening of the second day, Formbi summoned his passengers to the command center observation deck.

But not, as it turned out, for the reason everybody thought.

"I WELCOME YOU TO BRASK OTO COMMAND STATION," FORMBI announced, gesturing to the double-pyramid-shaped mass of glistening white metal floating in the center of the main viewing display. "It is here where you must all pause and consider."

There was a multiple buzz from the Geroons, like a cluster of honeydarters hovering over a promising flower bush. "Pause and consider what?" Bearsh asked. "Are we not arrived at Outbound Flight?"

"We are not," Formbi said. "As I said, you are here to consider."

"But we were told we had arrived," Bearsh persisted, sounding as upset as Luke had ever heard him. Small wonder, really, given the extent to which the Geroons had dressed for the occasion. Not only were they wearing elaborate robes covered with tooled metal filaments that looked to be twice as heavy as their usual garb, but all of them had also come to the meeting outfitted with their own shoulder-slung wolvkil body. Added to the already uncomfortable heat of the Chiss ship, they must have been sweltering under their loads.

"We have arrived at the point where the difficult part of the journey begins," Formbi told him patiently. "All must hear of the dangers we will face, then make a final decision whether you wish to proceed."

"But—"

"Patience, Steward Bearsh," Jinzler soothed the Geroon. Even here, Luke noted, Jinzler was standing as far away from the two Jedi as he could without being obvious about it. "Let's hear what he has to say, shall we?"

"Thank you, Ambassador," Formbi said, inclining his head

toward Jinzler. He gestured behind him, and the double-pyramid station vanished from the display.

Luke inhaled sharply as a murmur of similar astonishment rippled through the assembled dignitaries. Centered on the display was a stunningly beautiful globular cluster, hundreds of stars tightly packed into a compact sphere.

"The Redoubt," Formbi identified it. "Within this group of stars lies the last refuge of the Chiss people should our forces ever be overwhelmed in battle. It is impregnable, impossible for even a determined enemy to quickly or easily penetrate, with war vessels and firepoints scattered throughout. There are also other surprises that nature itself has created for the unwary."

"Starting with some really tricky navigation," Fel commented. "Those stars are awfully close together."

"Correct," Formbi said. "And that is where the principal danger lies, to us as well as any potential enemy."

He gestured again at the display. "As you say, the stars lie close together, and the routes between them have not been entirely mapped out. We will need to travel slowly, making many stops along the way for navigational readings. The journey will take approximately four days."

"I thought your ships had already located the planetoid where Outbound Flight crashed," Fel reminded him. "Can't we just follow their course?"

"We indeed will use their data as our starting point," Formbi confirmed. "But inside the Redoubt, nothing is ever constant or stable. There is a great deal of radiation to which we will be subjected each time we halt for readings. There are also many planetoids and large cometary bodies that travel on unpredictable paths, driven by the constantly changing battle of gravitational forces. These, too, pose a significant hazard."

"We waste time," Bearsh spoke up. The annoyance had passed, and his voice was calm again. "Those of Outbound Flight gave their lives for us. Shall the Geroons shy away from danger as we seek to honor their memory?"

"Agreed," Fel said firmly. "We're going in."

"As am I," Jinzler added.

"We're in, too," Luke said, making it unanimous.

"Thank you," Formbi said, inclining his head toward them. "Thank you all."

Luke felt a strange shiver run up his back. Formbi's thanks, of course, had been addressed to all of them. But at the same time, he had the oddest feeling that the words had somehow been specifically directed at him and Mara.

Formbi turned to the Geroons. "And now, Steward Bearsh, you and your companions must say farewell to those aboard your vessel. They cannot accompany us farther, but must wait here for our return."

"I understand," Bearsh said. "If you will prepare a signal frequency, I will speak with them."

Formbi nodded and gestured again. For a few seconds the Redoubt cluster remained centered on the display. Then the image cleared away to reveal a Geroon standing in front of the children's playground they had seen earlier. "You may speak," Formbi said.

Bearsh drew himself up to his full height and began speaking in an alien language whose singsong tones ran mostly to two-part harmony. The kind of language, Luke decided, that a species with twin mouths might logically be expected to create.

Formbi had drifted off to one side and was gazing down into the command center. Trying to be unobtrusive, Luke drifted over to join him.

"Master Skywalker," Formbi greeted him softly. "I'm pleased you will be accompanying us the rest of the way."

"That's why we came," Luke reminded him. "I was wondering exactly how tricky the navigation is going to be for this trip."

Formbi smiled, his glowing eyes glittering in the relative dimness of the observation deck. "It won't be simple, but it certainly won't be impossible, either," he said. "Why do you ask?"

"There are some Jedi techniques that can help with hyperspace navigation," Luke told him. "Especially with something as complicated and crowded as this Redoubt cluster. We can sometimes find easier or safer routes than a nav computer can come up with."

"An interesting thought," Formbi said. "I wish we could have borrowed some of you Jedi when we first set out to study the cluster. Many lives would undoubtedly have been saved."

Luke frowned. "Are you saying you only just started building this haven?"

"I make a small joke," Formbi admitted. "No, we began studying the cluster more than two hundred years ago, before we even knew of your existence." He turned back to gaze at the Geroons on the display. "Though I will also say that it has only been in the past fifty years that the work has been set at the current pace of urgency," he conceded. "Fortunately, it now nears completion."

"I see," Luke said. Fifty years ago: just about the time Outbound Flight made its appearance in this area. Was the Old Republic the "determined enemy" that had worried the Chiss so much that they'd started in earnest to build a place to hide? Or could they have foreseen the rise of Palpatine and the Empire? Thrawn might have, certainly, if the other leaders had been willing to listen to him.

It would probably have worked, too. Even a man as arrogant as Grand Moff Tarkin might have hesitated before taking his Death Star into a maze like that. "I see now why your people don't need to bother with preemptive strikes," he commented. "With a refuge like this, you can afford to let any enemy take the first shot."

Formbi swiveled sharply to face him. "That has nothing to do with the Redoubt," he said stiffly. "It is completely and purely a matter of honor and morality. The Chiss are *never* to be the aggressor people. We cannot and will not make war against any until and unless we have been attacked. That has been our law for a thousand years, Master Skywalker, and we will not bend from it."

"I understand," Luke said hastily, taken aback by the vehemence of Formbi's response. No wonder Thrawn and his aggressive military philosophy had rubbed these people backward. "I didn't mean to imply anything else. Please forgive me for not making myself clear."

"Yes, of course," Formbi said, the fire in his eyes fading somewhat as he pulled himself back under control. "And forgive me in turn for my outburst. The subject . . . let's simply say that it's been a matter of strenuous discussion in recent days among the Nine Ruling Families."

Luke lifted an eyebrow. "Oh?"

"Yes," Formbi said in a tone that said, *Drop the subject*. "At any rate, I thank you for your offer of assistance, but your Jedi powers of navigation should not be needed."

Luke bowed. "As you wish, Aristocra. If you choose to reconsider, we stand ready to assist." Turning, he headed back toward where Mara was standing, wondering yet again how Leia could make this diplomacy stuff look so simple.

The Geroons, he noted, seemed to be near the end of their conversation. The alien on the display was humming something that sounded like a cross between a military fanfare and a Huttese opera excerpt, and Bearsh had just started his equally musical reply.

"What was that all about?" Mara asked as Luke came up beside her.

"I was offering Formbi our help in navigating the Redoubt," Luke said, frowning. There was a new tension in his wife's face that hadn't been there when he'd left a minute ago. "He says they can do it themselves. What's wrong?"

"I don't know," Mara said, her eyes narrowed as she swept her gaze slowly around the room. "Something just hit me . . ."

"Something bad?" Luke suggested, stretching out to the Force as he tried to read the pattern of her thoughts. "Something dangerous?"

"Something not right," she said. "Something very much not right. Not dangerous, I don't think, at least not in and of itself. Just . . . not right."

Across the observation deck, the two-toned music stopped. "Thank you, Aristocra Formbi," Bearsh said, switching back to his stilted Basic. After the Geroon language, the words sounded startlingly drab. "My people express regret that they cannot all pay homage to the heroes of Outbound Flight, but we understand your concerns."

His mouths made quick chopping motions. "At any rate, our vessel would most certainly not survive the voyage. And if the Geroon people perish, what use then would be Outbound Flight's sacrifice?"

"What use, indeed," Formbi agreed. Turning toward the command floor, he lifted his voice. "We are ready, Captain Talshib," he called. "Take us to Outbound Flight."

FEESA HAD CALLED THIS PLACE THE FORWARD OBSERVATION lounge during their inspection tour of the *Chaf Envoy*, Jinzler remembered as he sipped the drink he'd brought with him and gazed out the curved viewport stretching across the entire end of the room in front of him. It had had a spectacular view of the Chiss starscape at the time, as well as a large collection of comfortable-looking chairs and couches, and he'd made a mental note to come back later after things had quieted down.

Now, of course, half a standard hour into their trip to Outbound Flight, the view wasn't nearly so interesting. Hyperspace, after all, looked pretty much the same anywhere you went.

But the couch was still comfortable, he had his drink and his solitude, and they were on their way to Outbound Flight. At the moment, that was all he asked out of life.

He lifted his glass to the mottled patterns of hyperspace streaming by. *To Lorana*, he gave a silent toast.

Behind him, the lounge door slid open. "Hello?" a voice called tentatively.

Jinzler sighed. So much for the solitude part. "Hello," he called back. "This is Dean—Ambassador Jinzler," he corrected himself.

"Oh," the other said tentatively, and as Jinzler turned he could see a shadowy figure move into the darkness. "I am Estosh. Do I intrude?"

One of the Geroons. The youngest, in fact, if Jinzler was

remembering the introductions correctly. "No, of course not," he assured the alien. "Come in."

"Thank you," Estosh said, groping his way through the maze of furniture to Jinzler's couch. "What do you do here?"

"Nothing, really," Jinzler said. "I was just watching the light-years fly past, and thinking about Outbound Flight."

"They were a great people," Estosh said softly, sitting gingerly down beside Jinzler. "Which of course makes you yourself a great person," he hastened to add.

Jinzler grimaced in the dark. "Perhaps," he said.

"You are great," Estosh insisted. "Even if you do not feel it."

"Thank you," Jinzler said. "Tell me, what do you know about what happened?"

"I was not yet alive at that time, so I know only what I have been told," Estosh said. "I know that long before your people arrived the Vagaari came to our worlds, conquering and destroying and taking everything of value to themselves. They used us as laborers and craftspeople and slaves. They sent us into unsafe mines and dangerous mountains, and forced us to walk before them on warfields that we might die instead of them." He gave a shiver that shook the whole couch. "They wore us down until we were almost nothing."

"And then Outbound Flight came?"

Estosh sighed deeply, a sound like a whistle in a deep cave. "You cannot imagine it, Ambassador Jinzler," he said. "Suddenly they were there before us, weapons blazing from all directions, shattering our oppressors' vessels and destroying them."

Ahead, the churning hyperspace sky faded abruptly into starlines, and the starlines collapsed into a brilliant mass of stars. "Must be one of the navigation stops Aristocra Formbi mentioned," Jinzler commented, gazing out at the view. "Impressive, isn't it?"

"Indeed," Estosh said. "It is a shame the Chiss have no worlds here they would be willing to give us. To live here among such beauty—"

"Quiet," Jinzler cut him off, listening hard as a quiet warning bell went off in the back of his mind. Something was wrong . . .

Abruptly, it clicked. "The engines," he said, scrambling to his feet. "You feel that? They're sputtering."

"Yes," Estosh breathed. "Yes, I do. What does it mean?"

"It means something's wrong with them," Jinzler said. "Or with the control lines. Or," he added grimly, "with the people in the command center."

MARA HAD JUST PULLED OFF HER BOOTS IN PREPARATION FOR bed when the deck seemed to shiver beneath her feet.

She paused, stretching out to the Force, all her senses alert. "Luke?"

"Yes," he murmured, frowning in concentration. "Feels like something funny's going on with the engines."

"They've picked up a wobble," Mara said, flipping her legs up over the edge of the bed and rolling across to Luke's side, the side that had the comm panel. Stretching out, she jabbed the button. "Command center, this is Jedi Skywalker," she called. "What's going on?"

"There is nothing to be worried about, Jedi Skywalker," a Chiss voice answered. "There is a problem with the control lines to the aft end of the vessel."

"What kind of problem?"

"It is not your concern," the voice said tartly. "It is a small problem only, and we will deal with it. Stay in your quarters."

There was a click as the connection was cut from the other end. "I can hear the soothing tones of General Drask's voice in that order," Luke said, grabbing his shirt and starting to put it back on. "Sounds like he's been talking to his people about us."

"We going to check it out anyway?" Mara asked, rolling back to where she'd left her boots.

"Actually, I was thinking we might try a different approach," Luke said, finishing with his shirt and reaching for his lightsaber. "We've already seen one noisy diversion aboard this ship, and there's a lot of the same smell to this one."

"I agree," Mara said, picking up her own lightsaber. "He said the problem is aft. We go forward?"

"Right," Luke said. "You've been studying the ship. What's up there someone might be interested in?"

"All sorts of good stuff," she told him. "Forward navigational sensors, meteor defense systems, shield generators, some crew quarters, and bulk storage."

"Including food?"

"Right," Mara said. "Best of all, not very far back from the bow is the commander's glider."

"The hyperdrive-capable boat Fel told us about?"

"That's the one," Mara said. "Pick your target."

"Well, you can't expect him to make it easy on us," Luke said philosophically. "Here's the plan. You head for the bow along the main starboard corridor, watching for anyone or anything suspicious. I'll backtrack past the Geroon shuttle, see if there's any unusual activity in that area, then cross over to port side and check out the Imperials' transport. If everything looks okay, I'll head forward along the port-side corridor and meet you at the bow."

"Sounds good," Mara said. "See you there. And watch yourself."

"You, too."

The starboard corridor was largely deserted as Mara made her way forward, her senses alert for trouble. Most of the on-duty crewers were apparently aft, dealing with the engine trouble, while the rest were either snugged comfortably in their beds or engaged in other late-evening relaxations. The fact that the whole crew had obviously not been turned out implied that Drask did indeed consider the problem to be a minor one. Just the sort of low-key, not-quite-crisis-level event their mysterious data card thief might use for his next bit of sleight of hand.

She just wished she knew which of the possible targets he was after this time. Still, with a little luck, maybe she'd get a chance to ask him.

She was nearly to the bow when the corridor lights abruptly went out.

She froze in her tracks, pressing her back against the side wall in a pocket of shadow thrown by a misaimed emergency light. Wisps of sensation seemed to swirl around her as she stretched out with the Force, marking the presence of thoughts and emotions somewhere ahead. Someone was definitely moving around nearby. Maybe two someones.

Maybe even three.

She scowled to herself, peering into the darkness as she fought to push the hazy impressions into something solid. Between the Chiss and Geroons, the presence of so many unfamiliar minds surrounding her was severely limiting her ability to focus. There, ahead and to the right? Was that one of the beings she was sensing?

And then, from a side corridor in that direction, came a barely audible *clink*, as if someone had brushed the bulkhead with something hard. Holding her lightsaber ready, she slipped toward the archway leading into the corridor, keeping to the shadows as much as she could.

There was another faint *clink* as she reached the archway, this one much closer. She pressed her back to the wall and lifted her lightsaber high, thumb ready on the activator.

For a second she held the pose. Then, in a sudden smooth surge of motion, she swung around, igniting her lightsaber as she rotated, and planted herself in combat stance squarely in the center of the archway—

To find herself facing an Imperial stormtrooper as he simultaneously swung out from behind a coolant pump into the same stance, his BlasTech E-11 pointed squarely back at her.

Mara's first impulse, from somewhere deep in the dark corners of her mind, was to lower her weapon and order him to lower his. Her second impulse, from a more recent frame of reference, was to slash the blue lightsaber blade forward and cut him in half. Her final impulse, as her brain finally caught up with the conflicting reflexes, was to simply do nothing.

Fortunately, perhaps, the stormtrooper himself seemed to have no such confusion of loyalties or responses. Even as

Mara fought back the urge to kill, he snapped the muzzle of his weapon upward away from her. "Jedi Skywalker," he said. "My apologies."

"No problem," Mara said, fighting the words out through a momentarily stiff throat as she closed down her lightsaber. That unexpected surge of past patterns had been incredibly disconcerting. "What are you doing here?"

"Commander Fel heard of the problem with the ship's engines and ordered me to secure the bow from potential danger," he said. "You?"

"Same thing," Mara said, peering down the darkened corridor over his shoulder. "You find anything?"

"The area around the glider appears secure," he said. "My intention was to continue forward and check the shield generators."

"Fine," Mara said. "We'll go together."

"Acknowledged," he said. Without asking, he stepped past her and moved into point position, ahead and slightly to Mara's left. In silence, they continued forward.

They had gone perhaps ten more meters when Mara caught a glimpse of something ahead. "Hold," she murmured, running through the Jedi sight-enhancement techniques as they stopped. It hadn't been a movement she'd seen, exactly, but something else.

The stormtrooper, with his helmet's own vision enhancements, got it first. "We're looking through the archway into the shield generator room," he murmured back. "That was a reflection from the generator shell."

"Right," Mara agreed, trying to overlay the view ahead onto her mental schematic of this part of the ship. A reflection off the semispherical cap of the shield generator meant someone was inside the room, moving port and possibly aft.

Unfortunately, there were three other exits from the compartment in that direction: one heading aft toward the shield monitor room behind it, one heading forward toward a small cluster of crew quarters, and the third all the way across the chamber to a mirror-image archway into the portside corridor. Three possible ways out, with only her and one storm-trooper available to cover them all.

Except that Luke should be on his way toward that far portside exit. *Luke?* She sent out the mental call.

Coming, the reply came, accompanied by a glimpse of the portside corridor. It was apparently as dark over there as it was on this side of the ship, but he seemed to be making good progress and she had the sense that he was nearby.

At any rate, they couldn't afford to wait any longer. "All right," she murmured to the stormtrooper. "You keep going straight ahead. Make sure he doesn't double back and get out through the starboard archway up there. If it looks like you can do it without risking him getting behind you, go ahead and sweep him portside. I'll head back to that last cross cor-ridor and try to cut him off before he can get out through the monitor room."

"Acknowledged," the stormtrooper said. Lifting his Blas-Tech, he moved cautiously forward.

Mara didn't wait to see how he fared, but turned and moved as quickly and silently as possible back to the cross-corridor. Unlike the main passageway, this one had several jogs in it as it wended its way around and between rooms of various sizes and shapes. That meant more cover for her, of course; unfortunately, it also meant she wouldn't get a glimpse of the exit she was trying to block until she was practically on top of it. Setting her teeth, stretching out to the Force, she headed in.

She'd gone maybe five steps when the whole thing fell completely apart.

From somewhere ahead came a sharp shout and the sud-den scuffle of running feet. Breathing a curse, Mara ducked ahead around the next jog in the corridor, coming into view of the generator room exit just in time to see the reflected blue flash of a Chiss charric heat weapon. Someplace in the distance, over the ruckus, she heard the distinctive *snap-hiss* of Luke's lightsaber. Sprinting to the doorway, she ducked through—

There was just the briefest flicker of warning, and she

barely got her lightsaber ignited in time to block another charric blast that would have burned her upper right shoulder if it had gotten through. "Hold it!" she snapped, ducking back into the relative protection of the doorway as another pair of charric bolts shot past her face.

"Halt!" a harsh Chiss voice countered. "Identify!"

"Who do you think?" Mara shot back. "How many people have you got aboard with lightsabers?"

For a moment there was no reply. But at least the shooting had stopped. "Very well, Jedi Skywalker," the Chiss said in a somewhat more polite tone. "Come forward."

Warily, Mara stepped into the room. Over by the starboard shield generator to her right were two armed Chiss dressed in leisure clothing, apparently having come straight from the crew quarters a couple of corridors away. Behind them was the stormtrooper she'd sent in, his BlasTech held in ready position across his chest. Possibly the reason they'd stopped shooting at her, the cynical thought crossed her mind.

She turned her head to her left. At the far end of the generator room, Luke was coming toward the party from the portside archway, his lightsaber blade looking brighter than usual in the gloom.

And in the long gap between Luke and the Chiss, standing straight and tall and yet looking strangely vulnerable and forlorn, was Dean Jinzler.

CHAPTER 9

"THERE'S REALLY NOTHING TO TELL," JINZLER PROTESTED AS Mara led him to one of the lounge's couches and gave him a not-entirely-gentle push down onto it. "I was sitting right here, watching the stars, when the lights went out."

"Were you alone?" Luke asked, stretching out with the Force. The man clearly knew he was in trouble, yet was amazingly calm for all that. It was the sort of calm Luke had seen before, sometimes in a person who no longer had anything to lose.

Unfortunately, he'd also seen it in people with hidden tricks up their sleeves, or in people who fully believed they could lie their way out of anything. So far, he still couldn't tell which category Jinzler fit into.

"By then I was," Jinzler said. "A little earlier I'd been talking with one of the Geroons—Estosh, the young one—but he left when the engines started acting up. He said he was worried there was going to be another fire. I stayed here until the lights went out, as I said, at which point I decided something serious must be happening and started back toward my quarters."

In the ceiling above them, the lights abruptly came back on. That part, at least, was apparently fixed. "Why did you go through the Chiss quarters?" Luke asked. "Why didn't you use one of the outer corridors? They're better lit."

"Yes, I know." Jinzler shrugged. "I didn't really think about it, I suppose. At any rate, I heard someone moving around in the darkness and went to investigate."

"Like a complete idiot," Mara pointed out, standing behind him. "Suppose he'd taken a shot at you?"

Jinzler's lips compressed briefly. "I guess I didn't think about that, either."

Mara glowered a look over his head at Luke. Luke shrugged microscopically: he couldn't detect any lie either.

Which, unfortunately, wasn't conclusive proof one way or the other. "All right, so you heard someone," he said. "What did you see?"

Jinzler shook his head. "Nothing, I'm afraid. Whoever it was must have heard me coming, because there was no one in the generator room when I got there. I was looking around, trying to see if I could spot anything out of place, when all of you burst in on me."

Luke looked back at the lounge door, where the stormtrooper and the two Chiss were silently observing the interrogation. The Chiss, he noted, had made a point of standing as far away from the armored Imperial as they could without abandoning the doorway entirely. "Thank you all for your assistance," he told them. "Jedi Skywalker and I will handle it from here. You may return to your other duties."

"He was found in a restricted area," one of the Chiss said stiffly. "He must answer to General Drask."

"He's an ambassador from the New Republic government," Luke countered. "There are certain rights and privileges associated with that title. Furthermore, I don't remember General Drask or Aristocra Formbi saying anything about any part of the ship being restricted."

"What about him?" the other Chiss demanded, jabbing a contemptuous finger toward the stormtrooper. "*He* cannot claim ambassador's privileges."

"He was with me," Mara said. "Or were you planning to deny ambassador's privileges to me, as well?"

The Chiss looked at each other, and Luke held his breath. Technically, neither he nor Mara had any official standing here, apart from being Formbi's guests. He still didn't know what had gone wrong with the *Chaf Envoy*'s lights and engines, but he suspected Drask would be perfectly justified in declaring a state of emergency and confining all non-Chiss to their quarters.

In which case, Mara's attempt to pull rank might be looked upon very suspiciously, reflecting not only on them but on Formbi as well. In the subtle pull-war going on between the two Chiss leaders, that might have long-reaching consequences.

But for now, at least, the crewers didn't seem inclined to make a challenge out of it. "We will wait in the corridor," the first Chiss said. "When you are finished here, we will escort you back to the public areas of the vessel."

He looked at the stormtrooper. "The faceless soldier is invited to return to his proper place right now," he added.

The stormtrooper stirred, as if choosing from among the various possible responses. "Go ahead," Mara said before he could pick one. "Please thank Commander Fel for your assistance."

"Acknowledged." Swiveling in a crisp military about-face, the stormtrooper disappeared out the door. The two Chiss gave short bows and followed.

Quietly, Luke let out the breath he'd been holding. One of the best things about stormtroopers, he reflected, was their willingness to instantly and unquestioningly obey orders. It was, of course, also one of the worst things about them. "All right, Jinzler," he said, pulling a chair up in front of the older man and sitting down facing him. "We've been very patient with you up to now. But game time is over. We want to know who you are and what you're doing here."

"I know you've been patient," Jinzler said, nodding. "And I very much appreciate it. I know you've both stuck your necks out for me—"

"Stalling time is over, too," Mara interrupted, coming around from behind the couch to face him, remaining on her feet as she leveled the full weight of her stare down at him. "Let's hear it."

Jinzler sighed, some of the stiffness going out of his shoulders as he dropped his gaze to the deck. "My name's Dean

Jinzler, just as I told you," he said. "I work sort of on the edges of Talon Karrde's intelligence organization—"

"We know all that," Mara cut him off again. "What are you doing here?"

"A gentleman came to me a little over eight weeks ago," Jinzler said. "A rather old gentleman, flying a spacecraft of a type I'd never seen before."

"What was his name?" Luke asked.

Jinzler hesitated. "He said he didn't want me spreading it around . . . but I suppose you two would be all right. He said his name was Car'das."

Luke looked at Mara, feeling a ripple of shock from her that echoed his own surprise. *That* was a name he remembered quite well.

"Car'das?" Mara demanded. "*Jorj* Car'das?"

"That's the one," Jinzler said, nodding. "He said he'd once been an associate of Karrde's. Do you know him?"

"Never met the man," Mara said, her voice carefully neutral. "Though not from lack of trying. How do *you* know him?"

"I don't, really," Jinzler said. "I'd never seen him before that day. He came to me and suggested—strongly—that I put in for a transfer to the sector relay post at Comra. He said there would likely be a message coming through soon that would be of great personal interest to me."

"And you just went?" Luke asked. "Not even knowing who he was?"

"I know it sounds crazy," Jinzler admitted. "But frankly, I had nowhere else to be just then. Besides, there was something about him . . ." He trailed off.

"Okay, so you transferred to Comra," Mara said. "I take it this message he mentioned was the transmission addressed to Luke that you filched?"

Jinzler winced. "Yes," he admitted. "It showed up about, oh, I guess it was a little over a week ago now. I—" He looked up at Mara, his lip twitching in a slightly shamefaced smile. "—I filched it, grabbed one of our courier ships, and headed for the rendezvous point Formbi had specified."

"Only the ship didn't make it," Luke commented.

Jinzler blinked. "How did you know that?"

"We're Jedi," Luke reminded the other pointedly. "What happened?"

"The hyperdrive gave out in the Flacharia system," Jinzler said. "It would have taken me more than a week to repair it by myself, and I didn't have enough money to hire out the job. Fortunately, at that point Car'das showed up again and offered me a lift."

"Really," Mara said. "What an intriguing coincidence."

Jinzler lifted a hand, palm upward. "Maybe he was following me to make sure I got here okay. I never saw him on my sensors, but with a courier that doesn't mean a whole lot. He did say—" He broke off.

"He did say what?" Luke prompted.

"It didn't make any sense to me," Jinzler said. "All he said was that he was trying to fulfill a promise he'd been neglecting for a very long time."

"Did he say what that promise was?" Mara asked. "Or to whom it had been made?"

"Neither," Jinzler said. "Actually, the way he said it, I had the odd impression he wasn't talking to me so much as he was talking to himself."

"Okay," Luke said. "Go on."

"That's all there is, really," Jinzler said. "We came into the outer Crustai system and Car'das sent a message in. Formbi came out in the *Chaf Envoy*'s glider and picked me up."

"What did he think of Car'das?" Mara asked. "Or had Car'das left by then?"

"Actually, the two of them had a long talk together while I was transferring across to the glider," Jinzler said. "I didn't understand the language, but it sounded a lot like the one the Geroons were speaking when they first arrived. They finished their conversation, I introduced myself as Ambassador Jinzler from Coruscant, and Formbi brought me back to the ship. And that was that."

Luke nodded. Straightforward enough, and they could presumably confirm some of the details with Formbi. Assuming Formbi was willing to talk about it, of course. "Okay, that's the *how*," he said. "Now let's hear the *why*."

"There was a Jedi aboard Outbound Flight," Jinzler said. "Well, actually there were several Jedi aboard. This particular one was named Lorana Jinzler."

He seemed to brace himself. "She was my sister."

He stopped. Luke frowned at Mara, caught her own suspicious puzzlement. "And?" he prompted.

"What do you mean, *and*?" Jinzler asked.

"So your sister died with Outbound Flight, and you wanted to go pay your respects to her memory," Luke said. "So what was so dark and personal that you couldn't tell us earlier?"

Jinzler lowered his eyes, his hands wrapping tightly together in his lap. "We didn't part on . . . very good terms," he said at last. "I'd rather not say any more if you don't mind."

Luke felt his lip twist. More evasion, which seemed to be an integral part of this man.

But at the same time there was the sense of truth to his pattern of thought and emotion. He glanced a question at Mara, caught her reluctant agreement. "All right," he said. "We'll let that part sit for now. *But*."

He let the word hang in the air a moment like a threatening sandstorm in the distance. "We may need to hear more before we're done here," he continued. "If and when that time comes, you *will* tell us everything. Clear?"

Jinzler straightened up. "Clear," he agreed. "And thank you."

"Don't thank us yet," Luke warned, nodding toward the door. "The Chiss are waiting. Go back to your quarters."

"And the next time you think you hear something suspicious, use one of the corridor comm panels to call it in," Mara added. "If you'd done that, we might have caught him."

"I understand," Jinzler said. "I'll see you in the morning."

He crossed the lounge and disappeared into the corridor. "Well?" Luke asked as the door slid shut behind him. "What do you think?"

"For starters, I'm getting tired of this piecemeal approach,"

Mara growled, stalking over to the viewport and leaning against it as she stared out at the stars. "I'd like nothing better than to sit him down and drag the whole story out of him. With hydrogrips, if necessary."

"You really think that's the best way to approach it?" Luke asked, crossing to the viewport to stand beside her.

"No, of course not," she said with a sigh. "I just wish we could, that's all."

"At least we've got a few new puzzle pieces to work with," Luke pointed out. "Let's start with Jorj Car'das. You think this is the same man Karrde asked you and Lando to try to track down ten years ago?"

"Who else could it be?" Mara countered. "Contacting someone working for Karrde's organization and flying a ship that wasn't a New Republic design? No, it's got to be him."

"What makes you think his ship wasn't a New Republic design?"

"Jinzler has a certificate in hyperdrive tech," Mara reminded him. "If *he* didn't recognize the ship, it had to be something pretty exotic."

"Mm," Luke said. "I don't suppose you ever got Karrde to open up about who Car'das actually was."

"Karrde, no," Mara said. "But I *was* able to coax a bit out of Shada a couple of years ago. Apparently sometime in or around the Clone Wars era Car'das started up a smuggling operation, building it up into something that rivaled even the Hutts' organizations. A few years after that, he suddenly and mysteriously disappeared, and one of his lieutenants took over for him."

"Karrde?"

"Right," Mara said. "No one apparently heard anything of or from Car'das until you found that beckon call on Dagobah after Thrawn's return and Karrde sent Lando and me out hunting for him. When the Caamas Document crisis hit three years ago and the New Republic started to tear itself apart over what to do about the Bothans, Karrde and Shada took the *Wild Karrde* and went out hunting for him themselves."

"Did they find him?"

"Shada was rather evasive on that point, but it seems clear that they did," Mara said. "Reading between the lines, I'd also guess Car'das had something to do with the dramatic collapse of that Return-of-Thrawn hysteria that happened while we were out on Nirauan. She also mentioned a huge data card library that she said rivaled the official New Republic archives on Coruscant."

"Karrde's former mentor," Luke murmured thoughtfully. "And Karrde with his deep and abiding interest in gathering information. It fits, I suppose."

"What fits?" Mara asked. "The bit about Car'das knowing something was in the works and pointing Jinzler to exactly the right place at the right time to intercept an incoming message?"

"Guessing the right place, at least, wouldn't have taken anything special," Luke pointed out. "Comra's the logical spot to pick up a transmission coming from Nirauan or Chiss space. If Car'das knew or guessed Formbi would be contacting us, that's where the message would come through."

"That assumes he knew the message was on its way," Mara pointed out.

"Right," Luke agreed. "And that part *would* have taken something special. Though even there you'll notice he seemed to be a bit off on his timing. Jinzler was at the station a good seven weeks before the message came through."

"Maybe Formbi had to argue with the Nine Families longer than he expected before he got permission to contact us," Mara suggested. "You can't dock Car'das points for someone else's bureaucracy."

"I suppose not," Luke conceded. "There's also the question of how he could have found out about Jinzler and his sister."

"Yes—Jinzler's sister," Mara growled. "I presume you've noticed that up until a couple of days ago there would have been a perfect way to check out that part of his story."

Luke nodded. "Fel's Outbound Flight operational manual and its personnel lists."

"Except that it was stolen," Mara said. "And now all of a

sudden he comes up with a sister. Convenient timing, wouldn't you say?"

"I might," Luke had to admit. "But that's not proof that he took the manual."

"We're not exactly rolling in proof on any part of this," Mara pointed out. "Still, if Jinzler didn't take the cards, who did? And why?"

"I don't know," Luke said, half turning to look back toward the lounge exit. "Right now, I'm more intrigued by the question of what someone was doing lurking in the dark up here. Unless you think Jinzler made that part up to try to deflect suspicion from himself."

"Oddly enough, I don't," Mara said slowly. "He strikes me as being too smart to trot out such a lame story without dressing it up a bit."

Luke frowned. "Dressing it up how?"

"Suppose he wanted to do some mischief in the shield generator room," Mara said. "Say, someplace over at the starboard end. The first thing a real professional would do when he got inside would be to go to the *portside* end and open one of the storage cabinets there. Not too obviously, but enough to see if you were looking for it. Then, if he gets caught, he still spins his story about chasing down an intruder, but adds that he got a glimpse of someone over by the portside cabinets before he took off."

"The investigators go to look, and they find the open cabinet," Luke said, nodding his understanding.

"Right," Mara said. "Not only does it make his story play better, but it also automatically shifts attention away from his real target."

Luke nodded. "Simple, but effective."

"All the best tricks are," Mara agreed. "It's basically the same thing we assumed our saboteur was doing right from the start: drawing attention to the engines, then going and hitting something in the bow."

"Right," Luke said. "Assuming the engine thing *was* a diversion."

"Also true," Mara admitted. "It could just as well be that

that was a genuine accident, and that Jinzler or someone else simply took advantage of it to do some late-night skulking."

Luke shook his head. "This is starting to make my head hurt," he said. "If Jinzler set the fire to steal Fel's Outbound Flight data, shouldn't that have been the end of it? What would he have needed to do up here?"

"Who knows?" Mara said. "He may be on some special mission, either for Car'das or someone else, and had to steal the operational manual first so that we couldn't crack his story."

"And since most of what we know comes solely from him, we wouldn't even be able to guess from that what he's really up to."

"Actually, *everything* we know about him comes solely from him," Mara corrected. "Karrde told us about Dean Jinzler's background, but we only have our gray-eyed friend's word for it that he really *is* Dean Jinzler."

Luke hissed between his teeth. That one hadn't even occurred to him. "Which means what I said about us having a few more puzzle pieces is meaningless, isn't it?"

"They could be pieces to an entirely imaginary puzzle," Mara agreed. "And it gets worse. It could even be we have *two* different sets of late-night skulkers, each with different agendas, working either parallel or at cross-purposes to each other. Don't forget, we had not only Jinzler up here but at least two Chiss crewers and one of Fel's stormtroopers, as well."

"And if Jinzler's telling the truth, one of the Geroons," Luke reminded her. "All we're missing is Formbi and Drask to round out the suspect list."

"Right," Mara said. "On the other hand, Jinzler's the only one who got caught where he wasn't supposed to be. How does that story about just happening to head through the Chiss quarters strike you?"

"It's actually not as far-fetched as it sounds," Luke said. "If there *was* a Jedi in his family, he could easily be Force-sensitive enough to be nudged to the right place at the right time without knowing how or why he'd done it. Not many people know enough about Jedi family patterns to spin that sort of subtlety into a lie, either."

"Car'das might have known," Mara said. "And whatever he senses or doesn't sense, Jinzler still needed Car'das's advice to get himself transferred to Comra in time." She waved a hand. "Yes, I know that's not the same thing."

"Still, we do keep coming back to Car'das, don't we?" Luke murmured. "I wonder what he and Formbi might have had to talk about."

"No idea," Mara said. "As far as I know, Karrde himself never did any work out in the Unknown Regions. If Car'das made it out this far, it was before he and Karrde met."

"Or after Car'das disappeared," Luke pointed out. "We don't know anything about him during that period, either."

"Maybe we should go ask Formbi," Mara suggested.

"Sure, why not?" Luke said. "We need to warn him to check the shield generators, anyway."

Mara shook her head. "I don't think the generators were the target," she said. "I think it was something else."

"Any idea what?"

"Not really," Mara conceded. "But if I had to vote, I'd vote for someone putting a tap on the sensor lines. Remember when we were called into the command center earlier this evening and Formbi was listing all the dangers we would be facing inside the cluster?"

"Yes," Luke said, wondering where she was going with this.

"Among the various natural hazards to life and happiness, he also mentioned something called firepoints," she went on. "I've been meaning to ask him what exactly those are, but I think I may have figured it out." She pointed out the viewport. "You see that asteroid over there? The one with all the dark spots?"

Luke peered out into the brilliant starscape. A spotted asteroid . . . "Yes," he said as he picked it out of the shadows.

"Ten to one it's either a missile cluster or a fighter nest," Mara said. "Those dark spots are almost certainly the ends of launching tubes."

"A firepoint," Luke murmured, studying the asteroid. There were a *lot* of dark spots on it, too. "Aptly named."

"Very aptly named," Mara agreed. "An unfriendly ship that stops here for a nav check is going to be in for a world of hurt."

She looked at Luke, her expression grim in the reflected starlight. "Anyone who might be thinking about taking on the Chiss would have a definite interest in locating as many of those defenses as possible."

Luke felt his stomach tighten. "Fel?"

"Or the Geroons might have an interested client with an unused planet to swap them," Mara said. "Jinzler could be fronting for someone, too."

"Car'das?"

She shrugged. "Could be. We do know that Car'das likes collecting information. This would certainly come under that heading."

"Point," Luke said, taking one last look around at the stars. *The last refuge of the Chiss people,* Formbi had called it. Who out there would be interested in learning its secrets? "I think we've pushed this set of puzzle pieces around as much as we can. Let's go see if we can pick up another piece or two."

Mara pushed away from the viewport. "Formbi?"

Luke nodded. "Formbi."

THEY FOUND THE ARISTOCRA IN A SERVICE CORRIDOR MIDWAY between the control center and the main engines, watching in silence as a pair of Chiss crewers dug into an open conduit access panel with long, tonglike probes. A third crewer stood expectantly by with a sealed metal container. "Ah, our noble Jedi," Formbi said as they maneuvered past the workers in the cramped space and came to his side. "I understand you've been busy this evening."

"I see you have, too, Aristocra," Luke pointed out. "Have you found the problem?"

Formbi nodded. "Line creepers, as we suspected."

"Line creepers?"

"Long, slender creatures that chew their way into power

and control systems and live on the electrical power generated within," Formbi explained. "They're a vermin we've worked very hard to destroy or contain."

"Sounds like conduit worms," Mara commented. "That's a type of vermin *we've* tried hard to destroy."

"With no more success than we've had, I suspect," Formbi said.

"True," Luke said. "What was this particular batch working on? The engine control lines?"

"Yes," Formbi said. "That's what caused the flutter you apparently felt earlier. We're clearing them out now."

"What about the lights in the forward part of the ship?" Mara asked. "Did they get in there, too?"

"No," Formbi said. "It appears someone merely shut them down."

"Accidentally?" Mara asked.

Formbi's glowing eyes seemed to blaze a bit brighter as he looked at her. "What do you think?" he countered.

"We think the *Chaf Envoy* has some serious problems," Luke said. "We're not sure everyone aboard wants this mission to succeed."

He stretched out to the Force, hoping for a telling reaction. But Formbi merely shook his head. "You're wrong, Master Skywalker," he said quietly. "Everyone aboard very much wishes the mission to succeed."

"Maybe so," Mara said. "But it may not be the same mission as the one you have scheduled."

"I presume you've heard of the incident in the bow a few minutes ago?" Luke asked.

"I have," Formbi said. "Captain Talshib is already searching for damage or theft in that part of the vessel."

"Good," Mara said. "What did you and Jorj Car'das talk about?"

Luke had been trying, without success, to spark a reaction from the elderly Chiss. Mara's attempt was just as futile. "Jorj Car'das?" Formbi asked, lifting his eyebrows politely, his composure not even flickering.

"The human who brought Ambassador Jinzler to Crustai," Mara said. "The ambassador said you two spoke at length."

Formbi smiled faintly. "And you suspect something sinister about it?" He shook his head. "Not at all. He introduced the ambassador to me and listed his credentials and honors. I greeted him in turn, and welcomed him on behalf of the Chiss Ascendancy."

"And you did all this in that trade language, Minnisiat?"

"At the time I doubt he was aware I could speak your New Republic Basic," Formbi said.

"And you'd never met Car'das before?" Mara persisted.

"How could I possibly know anyone from the New Republic?" Formbi asked patiently. "I've never been farther than a few light-years outside Chiss space. Ah."

He pointed over Luke's shoulder. Luke turned to see one of the workers pull a long, segmented worm from the conduit with his tongs. The third Chiss had his container open, and the first eased the worm carefully into the opening. "A line creeper," Formbi identified it as the third crewer sealed the container again. "A young one, too, from its size. If left undisturbed long enough, they can grow to be as long as an adult Chiss and thick enough to nearly fill a conduit that size."

"I can see why you don't want them around," Luke said. "Any idea how it got in there?"

"Not yet," the Aristocra said. "We'll begin a thorough search of the vessel in the morning." His eyes bored into Luke's. "Of our vessel, and all others associated with it."

"Of course," Luke said, sensing Mara's sudden wariness. "May I ask exactly what this search will entail?"

"For you, it will most likely be noninvasive," Formbi assured them. "Line creepers exhale a distinctive mixture of gases that is quite easy to detect. If none of those gases is detected in your vessel's compartments, that will be the end of the procedure."

"And if you *do* detect any?" Mara asked.

"Then we will of course need to examine those areas more thoroughly," Formbi said. "But you should have nothing to

be concerned about. If you haven't opened your vessel elsewhere in this region of space, it's highly unlikely you could
have picked up any vermin. But we must check nevertheless."

"We understand," Luke said. "Actually, if one of these
things *is* aboard the *Sabre*, we'd be just as glad for you to get
rid of it. Is there anything we can do to help?"

"Thank you, but no," Formbi said. "We'll alert you before
entering your vessel, of course."

"We thank you in turn," Luke said, sensing the dismissal
in his tone. "We'll see you in the morning, then."

"One other thing," Formbi said as they turned to go. "I'm
informed that both you and Jedi Skywalker activated your
lightsabers during your search this evening."

"Yes, we did," Mara said. "We were hunting a possible
saboteur, if you recall. Not to mention defending ourselves
against a Chiss warrior with a twitchy trigger finger."

"Yes—that," Formbi said, sounding embarrassed. "An unfortunate occurrence. The warriors have been spoken to, and
it will not happen again."

Something seemed to flicker through the Aristocra's eyes
too fast for Luke to catch. "But in return, I must ask you not
to activate your weapons again as long as you are aboard a
vessel of the Chiss Ascendancy."

Luke frowned. "Not at all?"

"Not at all," Formbi said flatly.

"What if we're in danger?" Mara demanded. "Or if you or
one of *your* people is in danger?"

"Then of course you may do whatever you deem necessary," Formbi said. "But General Drask has insisted that the
casual waving of alien weapons aboard the *Chaf Envoy* will
no longer be tolerated."

"Casual?" Mara echoed disbelievingly. "Aristocra—"

"We understand," Luke hurriedly cut her off. "We'll do our
best to comply with the general's order."

"Thank you," Formbi said, dipping his head slightly.
"Until the morning, then."

The corridors were deserted as they made their way back.

Just the same, Luke waited until they were in the privacy of their quarters before breaking the silence. It made for better security, and also gave his quietly seething wife time to cool down. "What do you think?" he asked when the door was solidly sealed behind them.

"My low opinion of General Drask just dropped a few points," she said darkly. "Of all the stupid, childish—"

"Take it easy," Luke soothed, sitting down on the bed and pulling off his boots. "And don't blame Drask, at least not directly. I don't think he was the one who gave the order."

Mara frowned. "Then who did? Formbi?"

Luke nodded. "That's the feeling I was getting."

"Interesting," Mara murmured thoughtfully. "And the reason?"

"No idea," Luke said. "But don't forget how annoyed Drask was when we helped the Five-Oh-First put out the fire. Formbi may be playing politics again, trying to give Drask fewer things to complain about."

"Terrific," Mara muttered as she started again to get ready for bed. "It's so nice to spend time with an honorable people like the Chiss."

"It could be worse," Luke pointed out. "We could be doing this with Bothans. What did you think about his story?"

"The one about Car'das?" Mara snorted under her breath. "He's lying through his teeth on that one, too. There's no reason to let Car'das rattle off Jinzler's list of alleged credentials in an exotic trade language when he understands Basic. He could have switched languages anywhere along the way, just as soon as it was his turn to speak."

"I was thinking that, too," Luke said. "The obvious conclusion is that they didn't want Jinzler to know what they were talking about."

"Exactly," Mara said. "You'll also notice Formbi never actually answered my question as to whether he knew Car'das from somewhere else. *And* don't forget that they held their little rendezvous in the outer Crustai system where Drask and the rest of the Chiss couldn't eavesdrop."

She shook her head. "They're planning something, Luke,"

she said darkly. "Something devious. Possibly devious *and* nasty."

"I know," Luke said, pulling her down onto the bed beside him and wrapping his arm around her. "Do you want to leave?"

"Of course not," she said. "I still want to see Outbound Flight, assuming that part of the story isn't a lie, too. Besides, if there's some trap being spun here—whether for us, Fel, or Drask—we're really the only ones available to stop it."

She shifted position to nestle herself more comfortably against his side. "Unless, of course, you want to leave that to the Geroons?" she added.

Luke smiled at the thought. "No, I think we'd better handle it," he agreed. "Pleasant dreams, Mara."

His last mental image, as he drifted off to sleep, was a darkly amusing one of Bearsh and Estosh and the other Geroons shaking in terror as they stood huddled in one of the ship's corridors, trying desperately to hold blasters steady.

FEL LOOKED UP FROM HIS DESK AS GRAPPLER SAT DOWN ACROSS from him. "Yes?"

"It is in place," the other said, his large eyes reflecting the light from Fel's desk lamp. "Tapped into the navigational repeater lines."

Fel laid aside the datapad he'd been reading. "That was quick," he commented. "Any chance of the Chiss spotting it?"

The orange highlights of Grappler's green skin faded to yellow, the Eickarie equivalent of a head shake. "Not by any casual search," he said. "It is in a conduit behind a cabinet, not directly behind an access panel."

Fel nodded. "Nicely done," he said. "What about our Jedi? Do they suspect anything?"

"Of course they suspect," Grappler said, the highlights becoming orange again. "But they know nothing." His mouth opened in a sardonic grin. "Jedi Skywalker asked me to thank you for my assistance to her."

"Don't underestimate them," Fel warned. "I've heard stories about these two, both from my father and from Admiral Parck. They're sharp, they're quick, and they're very, very deadly."

"I would have it no other way," Grappler assured his commander, stiffening his shoulders proudly. "I look forward to learning their full measure in combat."

Fel took a deep breath. So the game had begun. Time to sit back and let it play. "You'll get your chance," he promised Grappler softly. "I guarantee it."

CHAPTER 10

THE VERMIN SEARCH BEGAN EARLY THE NEXT MORNING, WITH four pairs of Chiss armed with atmosphere sniffers starting at the bow and stern and checking every room, storage compartment, conduit, access panel, and supply package aboard the *Chaf Envoy*. They reached the *Jade Sabre* about midday, and Mara watched in polite but stolid silence as they made their methodical way through her ship.

Fortunately, Formbi's prediction proved to be correct. No line creepers were found, and within half a standard hour the search team had departed down the transfer tunnel, leaving nothing behind but a faintly metallic aroma from their equipment.

Fel's Imperial transport was searched with equal speed and efficiency. The Geroon shuttle, in contrast, took nearly three times as long to be cleared. Most of that was due to the fact that so much of the vessel had been repaired, rebuilt, or replaced that there were virtually none of the sealed equipment modules that most ships carried and that would normally not have to be checked. The search would have taken even longer if the bunkrooms and storage compartment Luke had noticed on his first visit hadn't been open to space behind their vacuum-sealed doors. The Chiss confirmed the doors' pressure readings, assured Luke that line creepers couldn't survive in vacuum, and moved on.

The whole procedure took most of the day. In the end, they found nothing.

"So we apparently have two options," Luke commented to Mara as they sat together in the forward lounge watching the hyperspace sky roll past. "Either a single group of line creepers got in and ignored everything else while they worked their way nearly to the center of the ship, or else someone brought them in and deliberately let them loose in that spot."

"Guess which option *I'd* pick," Mara invited.

"I know which one you'd pick," Luke said dryly. "What bothers me is that our saboteur seems to have had only that one group. What if he hadn't accomplished whatever he'd intended the first time around and had needed to create another diversion?"

"Maybe he had a few spares and spaced them before the search started," Mara suggested.

"Which means what?" Luke asked. "That he lost his nerve and dumped the evidence even though he wasn't finished with it?"

"More likely that he *did* accomplish what he set out to do last night," Mara said. "And that one *really* bothers me."

"Why?"

"Because I can't figure out what that was. Drask's been over every piece of equipment in the forward third of the ship and hasn't found anything. So what did the diversion gain anyone?"

Luke stroked thoughtfully at his cheek. "Maybe Drask is looking in the wrong place," he suggested. "Maybe we're looking at a two-stage diversion: line creepers in the control lines and doused lights in the bow, while the actual work went on somewhere else."

"Fine," Mara said. "But where? And what? Don't forget, the Chiss checked every cubic centimeter of the ship today."

"Looking for line creepers."

"Looking at everything," Mara corrected. "I watched them go through the *Sabre*, Luke. Even when they were sampling the air they were looking around. If there'd been any spare weapons or explosives or anything else out of place in there, they'd have spotted it. And I'll bet that goes double for the Imperials and Geroons."

"Probably triple for the Imperials," Luke conceded. Outside, the mottling vanished into starlines and collapsed into stars. Yet another navigational stop, apparently. Idly, he wondered what sort of firepoints the Chiss had waiting at this one. "So what's our next move?"

"Unfortunately, that's probably up to him," Mara said, not sounding at all happy about it. "The initiative always lies with the attacker. About all we can do is be ready—"

She broke off as a raucous trilling tone suddenly sliced like a vibroblade through the lounge. "Alert T-Seven!" a Chiss voice snapped over the speakers. "Arc twelve-two. Repeat: Alert T-Seven; arc twelve-two."

The nearest comm panel was at the far end of the next couch over. Luke got there first. "This is Master Skywalker," he said. "What's going on?"

"This does not concern you—"

"This is Aristocra Formbi, Master Skywalker," Formbi's voice cut into the circuit. "Please come to the Geroon vessel as quickly as possible."

"On our way," Luke promised. "What's happened."

There was a hint of a sigh from the speaker. "One of the Geroons has been shot."

THERE WERE A DOZEN CHISS SWARMING ABOUT THE CORRIDOR outside the Geroon shuttle when Luke and Mara arrived. Two of them, Feesa and someone in Defense Fleet black, were kneeling beside the writhing and moaning figure of a Geroon, working on him with one of the ship's medpacs. Formbi, looking grim, was standing off to the side where he'd be out of the way. "What happened?" Luke asked as they were passed through the outer circle of Chiss.

"He was shot with a charric as he left his vessel," Formbi told them. "Upper back, left side. We're searching for the weapon now."

Luke stepped around Feesa and looked down, his heart sinking inside him as he got a look at the victim's face. It was Estosh, the youngest of the Geroons, his features twisted in pain at the charred and blackened skin across his left shoulder.

"You are a Jedi," Formbi went on. "I'm told Jedi have healing powers."

"Some of us do," Luke said, kneeling beside Estosh and studying the injured area. Behind him, he could feel Mara's sympathetic pain as she gazed down at the wound. She'd been shot with a Chiss charric once herself and knew exactly how it felt. "Unfortunately, neither of us has any special skills in that area."

"Is there nothing you can do?" Feesa asked.

Luke pursed his lips, trying to think. With himself or another Jedi, a healing trance would be the obvious answer. He might even be willing to risk it with Fel or one of the human stormtroopers, if the victim had been one of them.

But with an alien, especially one with unknown physiology and a mental and emotional structure he was unfamiliar with, it would be far too dangerous unless there was no other choice. "Can you tell me how bad it is?" he asked Feesa. "Is it life threatening, or only very painful?"

"It is certainly painful," Feesa said stiffly. "I do not know the rest. What does it matter?"

"It matters a great deal," Luke told her, looking around the corridor. The rest of the Geroons, he noted with surprise, were nowhere to be seen. "Where are Bearsh and the others?"

"Inside their vessel," Formbi said. "They say they are afraid for their lives."

Luke grimaced. But he supposed he couldn't really blame them. "Someone go tell them to get out here," he said. "Tell them there's nothing to be afraid of."

"They will not come," one of the Chiss said contemptuously. "They fear now that the whole of the Chiss Ascendancy stands against them." He made a clicking sound in the back of his throat. "They are an easily terrified species."

"They can be terrified on their own time," Luke told him shortly. "Right now, I need someone to tell me how bad this is."

"I'll go," Mara volunteered, crossing toward the entryway

room. "If they don't trust the Chiss, maybe they'll trust a human."

Whatever it was she said to them, it obviously worked. Two minutes later Bearsh and the others emerged hesitantly from the transfer tunnel, looking around like children in a festival frighthouse. "Come here, Bearsh," Luke said, beckoning. "I need to know how bad this injury is."

"It is terrible," Bearsh moaned as he sidled nervously past the Chiss to Estosh's side. "How could someone do this to him?"

"We hope to learn that soon," Formbi said. "In the meantime, Master Skywalker needs to know if his injuries are life threatening."

Bearsh knelt down gingerly, his fingers probing the edges of the burned skin. Estosh tensed, but said nothing. "No," Bearsh said after a moment. "But he is in great pain."

"I know," Luke said reluctantly. "But I'm afraid there's nothing I can do for that. Jedi healing powers can be dangerous to use. I can't risk it if he'll most likely heal by himself."

"Of course not," Bearsh said, his voice sounding bitter. "He is only a Geroon, after all."

"I meant it would be dangerous for him," Luke said, trying hard not to be irritated. None of this was *his* fault, after all. "About all I can do is help you get him inside."

"That would be most kind," Bearsh murmured, his flash of bitterness subsiding. "Thank you."

"No problem." Luke stretched out to the Force, reaching for a mental grip on Estosh—

"That won't be necessary," Formbi said suddenly before he could begin lifting. "A medical litter is on its way. My people will take him inside."

Bearsh stood up. "We would prefer the human's help," he said stiffly. "We would prefer the Chiss not enter our spacecraft again."

"You don't have a choice," Formbi said flatly. "The *Chaf Envoy* is a vessel of the Fifth Family of the Chiss Ascendancy. As travelers within that vessel, you come under Chiss law and custom. If we choose to enter your vessel, we will do so."

For a long moment the two aliens stood facing each other in silence, Bearsh looking ridiculously small and fragile in front of the tall, regal Chiss. Then, with a sigh, Bearsh's shoulders seemed to sag. "Of course," he murmured, turning away. "As you wish."

Luke stirred, starting to take a step forward. Formbi was being completely unreasonable—

No.

He stopped in midthought and midstep as Mara's urgent warning flowed into his mind. He looked back around at her, caught the similarly warning look in her eyes.

His intended protest died away unsaid. It *was* Formbi's ship, after all. If the Aristocra wanted to make that point obvious to everyone present, it wasn't Luke's place to argue with him.

From down the corridor came two Chiss guiding a floating medical cart between them. Luke looked at Mara again, caught the fractional tilt of her head, and stepped away from the injured Geroon to give them room. A minute later, they had Estosh on the litter and were moving him inside. The rest of the Geroons walked beside them in stony silence.

"That's all, then," Formbi said, turning his glowing eyes on Luke and Mara as the party disappeared down the transfer tunnel. "Thank you for your assistance."

With a supreme effort, Luke merely nodded. "You're welcome," he said. "I don't suppose Estosh saw who shot him?"

Formbi shook his head. "He told Feesa the shooter fired as he entered the corridor. He wasn't even certain where the shot came from. We're searching for the weapon now."

"I see," Luke said. "Please let us know if you find it."

"Of course," Formbi said. "Good night."

"They won't find anything," he muttered to Mara as they threaded their way through the milling Chiss and headed toward their quarters. "Ten to one it's back in its rack or holster or wherever it was taken from."

"You think that's what our friend last night was looking for?" Mara asked. "A weapon?"

"Maybe, only he didn't take it then," Luke said. "If he had, the search parties today would have noticed it was missing. No, all he wanted yesterday was to find where a weapon was conveniently located so that he could grab it tonight, shoot the first Geroon who came out of their shuttle, then put it back before it could be missed."

"But why shoot a Geroon, of all people?"

"I don't know," Luke said in disgust. "Maybe someone wants to drive a wedge between them and the Chiss. Or maybe just between them and Formbi. Someone who doesn't want to see them get a world of their own."

"Or maybe someone looking to stir up trouble between Formbi and us," Mara pointed out. "You were within half a heartbeat of arguing with him in front of his own people. You think he could have let you get away with that?"

"He was being petty," Luke said with a sigh. "But you're right. His ship; his rules. Anyway, good guests don't argue with their hosts."

"So be a good guest," Mara said, taking his arm soothingly as they walked. "And while we do that, we can also see about watching his back."

He gave her a sideways look. "You think Formbi's in danger?"

"Someone's trying to scatter chaos around this ship," she reminded him. "A major political assassination, or even just an attempt, would pretty well end the whole thing, don't you think?"

Luke shook his head. "I wish I knew what was on Outbound Flight that's so important."

"Me, too," Mara said. "I guess we'll find out soon enough."

THE SEARCHERS FOUND THE CHARRIC HALF AN HOUR LATER IN a ventilation intake a few meters down the corridor from where Estosh had been shot. Further investigation showed it had been stolen from an arms locker in the stern of the ship near the main engines, a locker whose fasteners had been carefully gimmicked for quick opening. Luke's guess, Mara had to admit, had been right on the nose.

There was, of course, no indication as to who had actually taken the weapon or fired the shot.

For the next two days Mara did some quiet poking around on her own, examining the scene of the attack, learning everything she could about charrics and their operation, and holding casual conversations with everyone who would talk to her.

The interviews were, unfortunately, less than illuminating. Most of the crewers had stopped being neutral toward her and her questions and gave halfhearted answers or none at all. The non-Chiss passengers were friendlier but even less helpful. Most had been alone at the time of the shooting, with no way of corroborating their stories. Only the stormtroopers claimed to have been together in Fel's ship, and even there careful questioning established that they weren't in sight of each other during much of the critical period.

She also spoke twice with Estosh, trying to draw out a more complete description of the incident. But he, too, was of little help. He'd been facing away from the shooter, his thoughts on other matters, and the shock and pain of the injury itself seemed to have thrown an extra layer of haze over his memories. About the only positive thing that came out of those discussions was the fact that he was definitely on the path to recovery.

It was frustrating to hit so many blind alleys. And yet, paradoxically, she found the process itself strangely exhilarating. In many ways this kind of investigation was exactly what she'd been trained for, back when Palpatine had been preparing her to be his silent agent. Certainly it had been one of the most stimulating aspects of her service to him.

Only now it was even better. Here, there was none of the brooding air of hopelessness that had seemed to be the normal state of affairs under Palpatine's Empire, a hopelessness that had hung like a black cloud over every job and every mission. No one aboard *Chaf Envoy* cringed as she approached, hating and fearing her, or else welcomed her with the false courtesy of someone hoping to twist her authority to his own private ends.

True, most of the Chiss crewers still seemed to heartily dislike the Imperials. But it was a contemptuous dislike, born of a sense of superiority of culture and purpose, not the terrified, hopeless hatred those under the Empire's heel had displayed toward their masters. Fel, in response, walked about with his head held high, not with the arrogance of a Grand Moff or Imperial general, but with a sense of pride about who he was and what he and the Empire of the Hand had accomplished. It was the same kind of pride that she'd often seen in Han or Leia, or in the pilots of Rogue Squadron, or even in Luke himself.

And as she observed and analyzed it all, she couldn't help but compare it to the very different flavor of life she'd left behind in the New Republic. To the squabbling in the Senate that mirrored the hundreds of tensions and clashes between neighboring star systems, or to the factions and power centers maneuvering for position and supremacy on Coruscant that constantly siphoned off energy and resources that could be far better spent in other ways.

Palpatine had been hateful, vicious, and destructive, especially toward the hundreds of alien species under his domination. But she had to admit that, at least on a purely practical level, the efficiency and order of his Empire had been a vast improvement over the bloated bureaucracy and bribe-driven operation of the Old Republic that had preceded it.

What would that Empire have been like, she couldn't help wondering, if people like Parck and Fel had been in command instead of Palpatine? What could that efficiency and order have accomplished, for that matter, in the hands of someone like Thrawn, himself a nonhuman?

And more than once, late at night as she lay in bed beside Luke, she found herself wondering what it would have been like to serve an empire like that.

What it would *be* like to serve an empire like that.

It was the late part of ship's night after one of those speculative moments that the room's comm panel buzzed them abruptly awake. Twitching away from her, Luke rolled over to key it on. "Yes?" he called.

"This is Aristocra Formbi," the voice noted. "You and Jedi Skywalker may wish to wake and get yourselves dressed."

"What's wrong?" Mara called.

"Nothing's wrong," Formbi said. "We've arrived."

"There," Formbi said, pointing at the main command center display. "There, just to the right of center. Do you see it?"

"Yes," Luke said, peering at the image. There was a ship there, all right, its once shiny hull blackened and crackled with multiple laser and missile impacts. It lay poised just over the crest of a steep hill on the planetoid's surface, as if it had been somehow frozen in the act of toppling over the edge.

And as the *Chaf Envoy* continued its inward spiral, he saw how it was the ship managed to stay suspended in midair. From points near the bow and the stern slender tubes could be seen extending from the underside of the hull, stretching downward at a shallow angle and connecting with another vessel mostly buried in the rubble at the foot of the hill. Midway along each of the tubes, he noticed, another pair of curved tubes veered off, stretching down and inward and coming together as they disappeared into the rocky hillside.

"Is that your Outbound Flight?" Formbi asked quietly.

Luke nodded. The ship was a Dreadnaught, all right: six hundred meters long, armed with an awesome array of turbo-lasers and other weapons, capable of carrying and supporting nearly twenty thousand crewers and passengers.

Or it had been once. Not anymore. Gazing at the battered hull, he felt a stirring of distant pain for those who had been aboard when this had happened. "I think so," he told Formbi. "It fits the description, anyway."

"Engines look mostly intact," Mara commented. Her voice was calm, almost clinical, but Luke could feel the pain and turmoil behind the words. "The turbolaser blisters and shield bays were pretty well pounded, but the rest doesn't seem too bad. With some work, it might actually be able to fly again."

"The vessel on the surface appears capable of sustaining life," Formbi agreed. "The sensors indicate it has air and heat, and is using low levels of power. The other vessel, the one half visible at the foot of the hill, exhibits none of those characteristics."

"No surprise there," Luke murmured. "You can see a dozen places where the connecting tubes between it and the upper ship have been blasted open."

"What about the rest of it?" Jinzler asked. "I understood Outbound Flight was composed of six Dreadnaughts."

"The rest must be underground," Fel said. "What's left of them, anyway."

"Underground?" Bearsh echoed, sounding awed. "This vessel can even travel underground?"

"No, of course not," Formbi said. "Perhaps it would be more accurate to say the rest of it is beneath the—" He hissed thoughtfully. "I don't know the right word. The loose, fine stone in the valley between the hills."

"The scree?" Luke suggested. "Moraine?"

"Scree, I think," Formbi said slowly. "At any rate, our instruments indicate the loose stone is very deep in that place and that there is definitely metal beneath it."

"Do you have any idea what shape it's in?" Jinzler asked. "The parts that are underground, I mean."

"Our instruments cannot say," Formbi said. "We will have to wait until we are aboard to determine that."

"Assuming the connecting tubes under the rock are in better shape than those others," Luke pointed out. "If they are, we may be able to follow them around the circle. If not, we'll have to dig."

"Assuming enough of the circle of ships is there to make it worth the effort," Fel said.

"How did it get here in the first place, though?" Mara asked. "That's what *I* want to know."

"That remains a mystery," Formbi conceded. "Obviously, Thrawn must have had it towed here for future examination. Yet there is no evidence he or anyone else ever returned for any such study."

"I was actually thinking more about the mechanics of the operation," Mara said. "You said he was commanding a small picket force at the time. Did every junior Chiss officer know how to get in and out of the Redoubt cluster?"

"Absolutely not," Formbi said. "He would have had to search deep into high-ranking information archives to have gained such information."

"That certainly sounds like Thrawn," Fel commented. "Information was his passion."

"Yes," Mara said grimly. "And killing was his business."

A quiet shiver ran up Luke's back. According to Admiral Parck, there had been fifty thousand people aboard those six Dreadnaughts when Outbound Flight was destroyed.

Would the bodies still be aboard, lying where they'd fallen? Certainly he'd seen dead bodies before, but most of those had been the remains of Rebel and Imperial soldiers killed in battle. Here most of the deaths would have been civilians, possibly including children.

With an effort, he shook away the thought. Whatever was there, he would simply have to deal with it. "So what's the plan?" he asked.

"The planetoid is too small to hold significant atmosphere," Formbi said, nodding toward the display. "We will therefore land the *Chaf Envoy* on top of the hill beside the upper vessel and run a transfer tunnel to the portside docking port near the aft end. Then all those who will be going aboard will do so."

He gazed at the display, where the Dreadnaught was growing steadily larger as the Chiss ship closed the gap. "Once we're aboard, there will be a short ceremony in which I will recount the Chiss part in the vessel's destruction and express the depth of our regret," he went on. "I will then ask for forgiveness on behalf of the Nine Ruling Families and the Chiss Ascendancy, and formally return the vessel's remains to Ambassador Jinzler, representing the New Republic, and Master Skywalker and Jedi Jade Skywalker, representing the Jedi Order."

"And us?" Bearsh asked anxiously. "Will there be a place in the ceremony for the Geroon people to express our gratitude?"

"Whether or not you are permitted to speak will be a decision for Ambassador Jinzler," Formbi said gravely.

"Of course you may," Jinzler assured the Geroon, smiling encouragingly at him. "As will you, Commander Fel," he added, nodding to Fel. "Though I'm still not certain what exactly your interest is in Outbound Flight."

"Remembrances come in all sizes and shapes," Fel said obliquely. "As do acts of repentance and atonement for past failures. Regardless, we'll be honored to participate in the ceremony."

"Then I suggest all return to your quarters or vessels and prepare," Formbi said. "In one hour, we shall begin."

LANDING THE *CHAF ENVOY* BESIDE THE EXPOSED DREADNAUGHT was a straightforward enough operation, though there had been some concern that the loose rock wouldn't adequately support its weight, especially given the possibility that a structurally damaged vessel might be buried beneath it. Fortunately, everything seemed solid enough. Setting up the connecting tunnel was handled with equal efficiency.

At that point, they ran into an unexpected problem. The docking bay hatchway Drask had selected, which had looked completely functional, turned out to be warped just enough to be impossible to open, and the Chiss ended up having to use cutting torches to carve out an access.

It was a slow process. Even the relatively thin hatchway of an Old Republic warship was incredibly tough, and the need to maintain a margin of safety in the enclosed area limited how much power the Chiss could run to their torches. More than once as he watched them work, Luke considered going to Formbi and offering to do the job with his lightsaber instead. It would be easier and cleaner and a *lot* faster.

But each time he suppressed the impulse. The Aristocra's midnight discussion about the casual waving of alien weapons was still fresh in his mind, and he'd already learned enough about Chiss pride to know that Formbi and the others would probably rather do it their way than accept his help. Particularly when that help wasn't really necessary.

And so the company waited as the crewers finished the job. Once they'd broken through the hatchway there was another short delay as the ship's medic tested the atmosphere, confirming that none of the microorganisms, trace gases, or suspended particulates present would be dangerous to Chiss or human. With only a few days' worth of data on Geroon biochemistry he was less certain as to whether there would be any adverse effects on them, and there was some talk of rigging protective suits for the four who would be coming aboard.

But Bearsh declined the offer. The proper ritual clothing would be impossible to wear inside such suits, he stated, and assured Formbi that he and his people were willing to take whatever risks were necessary.

With all the delays, it was actually closer to three hours before the party was finally ready to go.

A strange-looking party they were, too, Luke reflected as they lined up on the Chiss side of the transfer tunnel. Drask and Formbi were dressed in the same stately outfits they'd worn at the first night's reception dinner, while Feesa and a black-uniformed Chiss warrior carrying an elaborate banner on a pole wore much simpler and more functional clothing. Fel was back in his dress uniform, and Luke would swear that the four stormtroopers had put extra effort into making sure their armor was gleaming. Jinzler had discarded his earlier layered robe-tunic in favor of something simpler and less constrictive, and Luke found himself wondering if the older man was expecting dirt and close quarters aboard the Dreadnaught or whether he was just tiring of his ambassadorial play-acting.

Each of the four Geroons who would be attending wore one of the blue-and-gold-collared wolvkil bodies over the shoulders of his thick brown robe, making an odd contrast to Estosh and the bandages he was wearing on *his* shoulder. The young Geroon had argued at length with Bearsh in their melodic language about going along, and was clearly still not happy that he was merely there to see the others off. He stood off to one side, nursing his shoulder and looking even more lost and pathetic than usual.

Luke was back in his dark jumpsuit and duster, but Mara had passed up her formal gown in favor of a jumpsuit similar to Luke's that she could move more freely in if necessary. Still, her natural poise and elegance made him feel as if she were far better dressed than he was. "Next trip," Luke murmured to her as the Chiss standard-bearer led the way into the tunnel, "remind me to pack a couple of formal outfits."

"I've always said you and Han are the scruffiest heroes I've ever met," she murmured back.

He looked sideways at her. The comment was typical Mara—that sarcastic manner that had proved so useful in distracting and irritating opponents in the past.

But this time he could tell that the words were pure reflex. There was something going on behind her eyes, some strange concentration.

Shifting his eyes back forward, Luke stretched out to the Force. If something was bothering Mara, he'd better get up to speed, too.

They emerged from the tunnel into an entryway and storage area that was probably half again the size of even the extravagant equivalents aboard the *Chaf Envoy*. A few boxes were still stacked along the bulkheads, their markings somewhat faded with age, but most of the room was empty. Everything seemed to be coated with a thin layer of dust. "Amazingly clean," Jinzler commented, looking around as the group gathered in the center of the room. His voice echoed strangely from the bare metal walls. "Shouldn't there be more dust?"

"Must be some housekeeping droids still functioning," Fel said. "Or at least there were. Repair droids, too—see where they've patched the cracks in the hull?"

"These machines can still function after all these years?" Bearsh asked in wonderment. "With no one to supervise or repair them?"

"Everything aboard Outbound Flight was well automated," Fel said. "It was all internal rather than being linked to a lot of other ships. Otherwise they would have needed probably sixteen thousand people on each Dreadnaught just to crew it."

"So few?" Bearsh asked, looking around. "Our own vessel is less than half this size, yet it carries more than sixty thousand Geroons."

"Sure, but this wasn't just a colony ship with everyone packed tightly inside," Fel pointed out. "The Dreadnaughts were warships, the biggest the Old Republic had before the Clone Wars, with weaponry and equipment—"

Formbi cleared his throat. Fel took the hint and subsided.

"On behalf of the Nine Ruling Families of the Chiss Ascendancy, I welcome you all to this solemn and sorrowful occasion," the Aristocra began, his voice deep and resonant. "We stand today on the deck of an ancient vessel that lies here as a symbol of human courage and Chiss failing . . ."

Luke let his eyes drift around the group as Formbi continued his speech. Off to the side, he noticed, Bearsh was murmuring into a bulky comlink in the melodic Geroon language. Probably giving Estosh a running commentary on the ceremony, he decided, and found himself wondering why the young Geroon had been left aboard the *Chaf Envoy* in the first place. Surely this short a trip wouldn't have strained his injuries *that* much. About the only thing he could come up with was the fact that the positioning of Estosh's injuries precluded his wearing one of the ceremonial wolvkils.

Personally, Luke considered that a rather ridiculous reason to leave him behind. But he'd been with the New Republic long enough to know that not every aspect of an alien culture had to make sense to him. It was enough that such rules and customs were important to the people who lived under them, and that as such they were worthy of his respect if not necessarily his approval.

And then, without warning, something touched Luke's mind. The last sensation he would ever have expected.

He twisted his head to look at Mara. One glance at her

widened eyes was all he needed to show she'd caught it, too. "Luke—?" she whispered tightly.

"What is it?" Formbi demanded, cutting off his speech in midsentence. "What's happened?"

Luke took a deep breath. "It's Outbound Flight," he said, stretching out harder to the Force. No mistake. They were there: minds—*human* minds, not Chiss—somewhere deep beneath them. A lot of them. "We're not alone, Aristocra Formbi. There are survivors aboard."

CHAPTER 11

SOMEONE GASPED, A SHARP INTAKE OF AIR, JUST AS QUICKLY cut off. "What did you say?" Bearsh demanded, his comlink sagging forgotten in his grip. "You say . . . *survivors*?"

"Unless the Chiss are running a vacation transport service," Mara said, stretching out harder to the Force as she tried to sort out the twisting tapestry of sensations. "There are humans down there, at least a hundred of them. Probably more."

"But that's impossible," Jinzler said, his voice hoarse. "This ship died fifty years ago. It *died*."

Mara frowned, drawing some of her concentration away from the distant minds to focus on Jinzler. His lined face was tight, his sense swirling like storm clouds in a crosswind, every mental barrier stripped away in a strange combination of hope and dread and guilt.

And in that moment she knew that he hadn't been lying, at least not about his sister having been aboard.

Or was she possibly still aboard? Was that the thought that was sending this emotional groundquake through him? "Maybe the ship died, Ambassador," she told him. "But not everyone aboard died with it."

"Well," Fel said, his voice studiously matter-of-fact. "This complicates things."

"It does indeed," Formbi said, his glowing eyes narrowed in concentration. "It complicates things tremendously."

Mara caught Luke's eye. "What do you think?" she asked. "Shall we leave them here to discuss the diplomatic ramifications while you and I just go find these people?"

The gambit worked. "No," Formbi insisted, snapping out of whatever deep thoughts he'd been working on. "You cannot go alone."

"Absolutely not," Drask agreed, gesturing to the standard-bearer. "You—return to the *Chaf Envoy* and instruct Captain Brast'alshi'barku to issue a *drace-two* alert. He is to prepare three squads—"

"Wait a minute," Luke interrupted. "You can't bring a contingent of soldiers in here."

"This vessel is still the property of the Chiss Ascendancy," Drask said, glaring warningly at him. "We will do whatever we please."

"I'm not disputing that," Luke said. "I'm simply concerned about what the passengers may do if they see a group of armed Chiss coming down the corridors toward them."

"He raises a fair point," Formbi said reluctantly. "They may remember that it was a picket unit of the Chiss Defense Fleet that destroyed their vessel."

"And so they will be afraid until we can speak with them and assure them of our intentions," Drask said impatiently. "I do not think a few minutes of fear is too much to ask of them."

"I wasn't worried about how they would feel," Luke said. "I was thinking about what they might *do* if they saw a corridor full of armed Chiss. Bearing in mind what happened the *last* time they saw a group like that."

"Syndic Mitth'raw'nuruodo did not send warriors aboard," Drask said. "There is no record in any testimony of his doing so."

"But they would have seen *someone* with blue skin and red eyes," Mara pointed out. "Either Thrawn himself or some other envoy. Unless you're suggesting he would have attacked without even offering them the chance to surrender?"

Drask glared at her. "No," he growled. "Not even Mitth'raw'nuruodo would have done that."

"Right," Mara said. "So they'll have known who the enemy was. *And* they've had fifty years to prepare for attack."

"And as Commander Fel pointed out, Dreadnaughts were designed as warships," Luke added.

There was a moment of silence from the others as the implications of that finally sank in. "What do you suggest?" Formbi asked.

"What Mara just said," Luke told him. "She and I go find them. Alone."

"No," Bearsh pleaded. "You must not leave us apart. We wished to pay tribute to the memories of these brave people. How much more should we not pay tribute to the people themselves?"

"We can bring you down afterward," Mara told him. "Once we've explained the situation—"

"No," Bearsh repeated, starting to become agitated. "You must not leave us apart."

"Your plan is unacceptable to us, as well," Drask put in. "I accept your reasoning as to why we should not bring a full boarding party. But Aristocra Chaf'orm'bintrano and I must at least be present at your first contact with these survivors. And the Aristocra must have a guard."

"He'll have the Five-Oh-First, General," Fel reminded him. "They can handle anything these people can throw at us."

"Your assurances are welcome but insufficient," Drask said stiffly. "We will bring a half squad of three Chiss warriors. No fewer."

He looked a challenge at Luke. "Do you argue that, Jedi?"

"No," Luke said, giving up. "Three warriors should be all right. I take it you're coming, too, Ambassador?"

"Absolutely," Jinzler said firmly. His tension had faded a bit into the background of his mind, but it was definitely still there. "My si—my superiors on Coruscant would insist on it."

"Then it's unanimous," Fel commented. "Good. Now all we're doing is wasting time."

"After fifty years, I do not think a few more minutes will make any difference," Drask said acidly. He turned back to the standard-bearer, who had stopped when the discussion began and was standing awaiting orders. "Return to the *Chaf Envoy* and signal *drace-two* alert," the general said. "Then order the Number Two Honor Squad to report to this chamber. They must be standing ready in the event we require immediate assistance." His blazing eyes dared anyone to argue with him.

No one did. "Very well, then," Formbi said. "Let us all return to the *Chaf Envoy* and obtain such equipment as each person wishes to carry on this journey through the past." He glanced down at his elaborate robes. "And perhaps a change of clothing would be in order, as well," he added. "We will reassemble here in thirty standard minutes and begin our search."

THE FIRST STRETCH OF THE TRIP WENT SMOOTHLY ENOUGH. THE place felt like an extended tomb, with the bare metal decks and bulkheads dully reflecting the dim glow of the permlight emergency panels set into the ceilings and the brighter light from the party's own glow rods. But at least the passageways were open and relatively uncluttered by debris. Various rooms opened off the main corridor, some of them large enough for the glow rod beams to fade into the darkness, and the distant walls and ceilings of those larger rooms echoed their footsteps eerily as they stepped briefly inside for a look. Most of the rooms were loaded with silent equipment or dusty storage boxes. Occasionally they came across a sleeping area with rows of empty bunks and personal items scattered on the deck around them.

Mara walked up front with Luke, trying to read beyond the reach of her glow rod beam and wondering a little how this particular marching order had been set up. She and Luke were the most reasonable ones to take point, of course, and she had no particular problem with Formbi, Drask, and Jinzler following directly behind them.

But then came Fel, Feesa, and one of the stormtroopers, with the Geroons behind them. At the very back, walking silently despite their armor, came the other three stormtroopers.

The more she thought about it, the more the arrangement bothered her. Her own training would have put Fel and all four stormtroopers at the back, where they could act as a rear guard in case of trouble from that direction. If Fel still insisted on detaching one of his men, that spare stormtrooper ought to be closer to the front, probably directly behind her and Luke, where his firepower would be available without him having to worry about shooting around Jinzler and both of the senior Chiss.

Twice in that first stretch she thought about halting the party and calling for a rearrangement. But both times something stopped her, and eventually she gave up on the idea. Fel's military training was certainly more recent than hers, and it was possible the Empire of the Hand's tacticians had come up with a more efficient military doctrine than she'd been taught.

After the first fifty meters, travel abruptly became more difficult. Shattered slabs of insulation material, buckled bulkheads, and twisted support beams seemed to be everywhere, littering the corridors and sometimes blocking doorways and the smaller side corridors completely.

"What happened here?" Feesa murmured as Luke carefully pushed aside a set of dangling power cables covered with splintered armor sheaths.

"We've reached the part of the ship where the main turbolasers were located," Fel told her. "You remember Mara pointing out that the weapons blisters had been severely damaged? They would have been Thrawn's primary target."

"He did a thorough job, too, I see," Formbi said. "Why haven't the maintenance machines fixed this?"

"None of the droids they had aboard would have been big enough to handle damage this extensive," Fel said. "The survivors must have decided it wasn't worth the trouble to clear it away themselves."

"Or were unable to work in safety," Drask added. "With so

many stars in such close proximity to each other, the radiation levels are higher inside the Redoubt cluster than most humans are accustomed to."

"Are we therefore in danger?" Bearsh asked nervously.

"We won't be here long enough for that," Luke assured him. "The outer hull is thick enough to stop most of the radiation. You'd have to live here months or years before you started having problems."

"Which probably explains why they decided to live in one of the lower Dreadnaughts," Mara put in. "Whatever the hull doesn't block, all that rock out there should be able to handle."

"Or else the other Dreadnaughts aren't damaged this badly," Fel said.

Luke shrugged. "We'll find out."

"Is that where we're going?" Jinzler asked. "To the lower ships?"

"That seems to be where the survivors are," Luke said. "Before we try to find the way down, though, I'd like to see if we can work our way up a few levels to the command deck. If it's in decent shape, there may be records left that'll tell us exactly what happened."

Bearsh made a subdued whistling sound in the back of his throats. "And what truly is the chance of that?" he asked darkly. "We see here how thoroughly this Thrawn was committed to its destruction."

"Thrawn never destroyed more than was absolutely necessary," Fel said. "There would have been no reason to wreck the command deck if taking out the shield generators and turbolasers was all he needed."

Jinzler turned his head. "What in the worlds are you talking about?" he demanded. "All he *needed*? What did he *need* to destroy Outbound Flight for in the first place?"

"He had his reasons," Fel insisted.

"He had reasons for killing civilians?" Jinzler shot back. "Men, women, and children who never did him any harm? What, he just needed some target practice that day and they conveniently happened along? And *you*." He turned his glare on Formbi and Drask. "You Chiss. What did *you* do to stop him?"

"That's enough, Ambassador," Mara put in, flashing a warning at him with her eyes. Formbi had already said the Chiss were carrying their own load of guilt over this thing. There was no need to hammer it into the ground. "The past is over and done with."

"Is it?" Jinzler asked her pointedly. "Is it really?"

"Yes," Luke put in firmly. "And bringing up anyone's failures—*anyone's*—isn't going to accomplish anything. Let's concentrate on finding these people and seeing what we can do for them, all right?"

"Of course," Jinzler muttered. "I'm sorry. I'm just—"

"Something's coming," the stormtrooper beside Fel cut in, swinging his BlasTech toward a half-crushed equipment crawl space branching off the corridor to their right.

The other three stormtroopers were at his side in an instant, spreading themselves into a defensive semicircle between the crawlspace and the rest of the party, their weapons leveled at the opening. "Steady," Fel warned. "If there's going to be shooting, we don't want to be the ones to start it."

Soft but steady footsteps could be heard now. Mara drew her lightsaber but didn't ignite it, stretching out to the Force. There didn't seem to be any presence that direction that she could detect. "Probably a droid," she said.

"What kind of walking droid could fit through that opening?" Fel objected.

A few seconds later he got his answer as a low-slung, badly dented box about half a meter long and a few centimeters high rolled into view on battered treads. "A walking droid with a bad limp?" Luke suggested as one of the treads gave a soft *thunk* that sounded exactly like a footstep. "What is that, a floor cleaner?"

"Probably does floors and small-object retrieval," Fel said, stepping back as the droid rolled past his feet toward a pile of shattered plastic insulation, leaving faint tread marks in the dust as it went. "Part of the main cleaning system, I'd guess."

"I see," Luke said, looking over at Mara.

She nodded back. Given the layer of dust on everything, it seemed unlikely that their group had shown up just as the cleaner was starting its monthly or yearly run. It was far more likely that the droid had been equipped with a holocam and comlink and sent to check out the intruders.

Either as an observer, or as a decoy.

She shifted her attention away from the droid, searching the corridor ahead. There was too much debris to see very far, but it looked like the passageway widened a short way ahead. A perfect place for an ambush. She caught Luke's eye and nodded toward it; he nodded back and slipped past her into the corridor.

"It is truly amazing," Bearsh said, shaking his head in wonderment as they watched the cleaner droid extend a pair of slender arms and begin sorting through pieces of the insulation. "So that is a droid. And it runs all by itself?"

One of the stormtroopers looked over at Luke as he disappeared behind a section of hanging ceiling material, the armored chest lifting slightly as he took a breath to speak. Mara shook her head in warning; his helmet dipped slightly in acknowledgment and he remained silent. "This one's probably connected to a central housekeeping computer," Jinzler told the Geroon. "Small units like this don't have the logic capacity to run completely on their own."

"I see," Bearsh said. "But there *are* those that do, correct?"

"All sorts," Jinzler confirmed. "Everything from protocol droids to astromech droids to medical droids."

"And battle droids and droidekas?" one of the other Geroons asked. "Did they also run independently?"

"Some of the later versions could," Jinzler said. "But again, most of them were run off a central computer system."

"A terrifying weapon," Bearsh murmured.

"Not really," Fel said. "The whole droid army concept is pretty well outmoded these days, at least in the Empire of the Hand. How about in the New Republic, Ambassador?"

"A few systems still use droidekas," Jinzler said. "Mostly smaller colonies on undeveloped worlds in Wild Space where people need perimeter guards at night to protect against native predators."

Bearsh shivered. "Such awesome power in your hands. Yet you make no use of it?"

"We're not in the conquering business anymore, Steward," Jinzler reminded him.

"Besides, power's only one part of the equation for good soldiers," Fel said. "The problem with battle droids was that they were really pretty stupid . . ."

Mara felt the urgent touch of her husband's mind. Leaving Fel to his lecture, she slipped quietly down the corridor.

Luke was standing just inside the wide area she'd spotted earlier. "What've we got?" she murmured.

He pointed at a stack of flat gray boxes along the left-hand bulkhead. "Looks a little too neat for random debris," he murmured back. "Booby trap?"

Mara ran through the Jedi sensory-enhancement techniques and took a slow, careful breath. The subtle background smells of the ship suddenly jumped into full focus: dust, plastic, metal, rust, a general odor of age. She took another breath, sorting through them all.

And this time she caught the faint but unmistakable tang of explosives.

"If it's not, it's a terrific imitation of one," she confirmed, letting the odors fade into the background again. "Remote-triggered, you think?"

"You're the demolitions expert in the family," he reminded her. "They can't have it on timer, though, and I can't see anyone wasting a droid to come in and set them off."

"Me, neither," Mara agreed. "I presume we're not stupid enough to just rush the stack?"

"I don't even think we're stupid enough to get anywhere near it," Luke said. "Let's back up a bit and see if we can find another route."

"I don't know," Mara said doubtfully, looking around at the devastation. "There's enough damage here in the central corridor. The other, smaller passageways are likely to be even worse."

"Only until we get through the weapon and shield sections," Luke said. "The rest of the ship may be in better shape. Actually, this is one of *four* central corridors through this part of the ship. They run parallel to each other on opposite sides of the centerline, collapsing down to two main corridors as you get closer to the bow."

"Really," Mara said, frowning. "Since when do you know so much about Dreadnaughts?"

"Since Han and I had a running battle with a bunch of Imperials aboard the *Katana*," Luke told her dryly. "You learn a lot about a ship's architecture when you're dodging blaster bolts. Come on, let's go tell the others."

Fel had finished his lecture by the time they rejoined the group. "There you are," Drask said, his eyes flashing. "Where did you go?"

"Just scouting ahead," Luke assured him. "Looks like we're going to have to cross to one of the other corridors."

Drask's eyes narrowed. "Why?"

Luke looked over at the housekeeper droid, still picking through the rubble. "There's a booby trap in there," he said. "I'd just as soon not have to take the time to disarm it. There's another cross-corridor we can use about ten meters ahead that'll get us back to this one."

"There is a *trap*?" Bearsh gasped. "But why would anyone wish to hurt us? We have come to honor them."

"Yes, but they don't know that," Luke said. "All we can do is try to avoid trouble until we can explain it to them."

"Until then, we must make certain such a meeting does in fact take place," Drask said grimly, pulling out a comlink.

"Wait a minute," Fel said. "What are you doing?"

"Summoning an escort," Drask said. "This is no longer a matter for diplomats."

"We *have* an escort," Fel countered. "Trust me: the Five-Oh-First can handle things."

"That is not sufficient," Drask insisted. "Even if they are

as good as you claim, they cannot adequately protect us all. We require a stronger force."

"That might not be a good idea, General," Luke warned. "If the inhabitants are monitoring our progress, a show of that much force might be taken as a threat."

"He's right," Formbi said, not sounding particularly happy about it. "Leave the warriors in reserve for now, General Drask. We'll retreat and use the route Master Skywalker suggests."

"I disagree completely," Drask growled. But he put the comlink away without further argument. "Very well, Master Skywalker. Lead the way."

THE SIDE CORRIDORS LUKE HAD CHOSEN WEREN'T ANY EASIER to navigate than the main corridor had been. There was less actual debris lying around underfoot, but the state of the bulkheads and ceiling more than made up for it. Many of the bulkheads had buckled, twisting wall plates out at crazy angles into the corridor, many of them broken and sharp-edged. Something in here must have exploded during the battle, Mara decided as the group eased gingerly past the rubble.

It took them more than an hour to pick their way through that first 150 meters. They saw two more droids in that time, both of them housekeeping types, both of them eliciting words of amazement from the Geroons. It was clear, at least to Mara, that someone was indeed watching their progress.

But there were no other booby traps, at least none that they were able to detect. Certainly nothing went off in the confining spaces. Perhaps, as Luke had hoped, whoever was monitoring the droids had gotten the message that their visitors had no ill intentions toward them.

Or else they were simply preparing a more memorable reception farther in.

As expected, once they were past the main turbolaser batteries the damage began to drop off considerably. Fifty meters after that, it became no worse than a sort of dusty clutter.

"What is this place?" Bearsh asked as they passed through a large room lined with consoles and monitor displays.

"This is the fleet tactical room," Fel said. "In a battle, this is where this ship would coordinate combat with the rest of its companion ships."

"The Vagaari must have had rooms like this aboard their vessels," one of the other Geroons said. "Larger even than this, perhaps. They had huge fleets."

"Yes," Bearsh agreed, a shiver running through him. "They darkened the sky when they passed through the air of our world."

"This appears to be in a workable state," Drask commented, stepping over to one of the consoles for a closer look. "Would this be a place Mitth'raw'nuruodo might have deliberately spared?"

"It's possible," Fel said. "The six Dreadnaughts were presumably coordinated directly from the primary command ship, without any need for this room to even be crewed."

"Unless this *is* the command ship," Jinzler reminded him.

"And of course, we don't know whether any of these consoles actually works," Mara added, frowning as she stretched out to the Force. There seemed to be a flicker of a presence lurking somewhere ahead of them. But the sensation came and went, as if the person was appearing and then disappearing. Someone only half conscious, perhaps?

"Might be worth trying to start them up," Luke suggested, throwing a glance at Mara. So he'd caught the tentative contact, too. "What do you think, Commander?"

Fel's forehead furrowed briefly, then cleared as he caught on. "Sure, why not?" he agreed with false enthusiasm. "In fact, it might be easier to find records back here than it would on the command deck. That console you're looking at, General—let's see if we can get it started."

Drask stepped back and gestured toward the board. "Go ahead."

"Right," Fel said, pulling out the chair and sitting down. "Let's see now . . ." Tentatively, he keyed a few switches. The console beeped twice, and a few of its indicators came reluctantly to life. "Okay. Let's try this . . ."

Luke, Mara noted, was already gone. She waited until the entire group was watching Fel, then slipped out after him.

He was waiting for her just outside the tactical room. "You felt her, too?" he asked quietly.

Her? Mara's mind flashed back to Jinzler's story about his sister. "I felt something, but it kept coming and going," she said. "You think it's a woman?"

"A girl, actually," he said. "Too young to be Lorana. Sorry."

"Well, it *was* a long shot," Mara conceded, trying not to feel too disappointed. "Let's see if we can find her before we're missed."

"Too late," a voice murmured darkly from behind her.

She glanced at Luke, caught his grimace. "Hello, General," she said as she turned around.

Drask was standing alone in the corridor, his posture stiff. "You must think we are fools," he bit out. "You and Commander Fel both. Do you really think the Chiss can be so easily deceived in the same way twice?"

"Forgive us," Luke said, bowing to him. "We were merely concerned for your safety."

"I do not need my safety guarded," Drask countered. "I do not know how you humans do such things, but Chiss leaders do not merely sit behind the young warriors and watch them fight."

"I understand," Luke said. "Perhaps I misspoke. I meant we were concerned for the Aristocra's safety."

"Better," Drask rumbled. "But be advised: this is still a Chiss vessel, and you will not again move ahead of me."

"Understood," Luke said. "Again, our apologies."

"Very well." Drask glanced back over his shoulder. "Then let us continue before the others notice our absence."

They had gone perhaps ten meters when the wisp of sensation again touched Mara's mind. Luke had been right: it was definitely female. "She's just ahead," she warned Luke, peering at the equipment and occasional piles of debris as she tried to pin down the girl's location. Five meters ahead, the corridor opened into a large room with its door frozen partially open, and she could see more of the same type of consoles as they'd found in the tactical room.

"She must be in the sensor room," Luke said, pointing toward the frozen door. "You want to hang back while General Drask and I check it out?"

Mara bit back a retort. Obviously, Luke was being diplomatic. "Sounds good," she said. Stepping to the side, she planted her back against the corridor wall. Luke and Drask continued forward, the general's hand resting on the charric belted at his waist. They stepped to the sensor room door and Luke ducked down and started to ease his way beneath it—

"Are you Jedi?" a soft voice asked from behind Mara.

Mara spun around, old combat reflexes flaring as her hand automatically went to her lightsaber. The girl standing quietly in the corridor was no older than ten, plainly but neatly dressed, her dark auburn hair glistening in the light. She was looking at Mara with bright, unblinking blue eyes.

Standing in the corridor *behind* Mara. How in blazes had she managed *that*?

Mara found her voice. "Yes, we are," she told the girl. "We're here to help you."

"Oh," the girl said. For a moment she seemed to study Mara, an uncertain look on her face. Then she shifted her gaze to Drask and Luke, eyeing her in turn as they stood together by the sensor room door. "And a Blue One," she went on. "Are you here to hurt us?"

"No one will hurt you," Drask assured her. "As the Jedi said, we are here to help."

"Oh," the girl said, her voice completely matter-of-fact. "Well, you can tell him that." She gestured to an alcove just behind her. "He's waiting for you."

"We'll look forward to seeing him," Luke said, wondering who she was talking about. The survivors' leader, perhaps? "What's your name?"

"I'm Evlyn," she said. "Will you follow me, please?"

"We must first alert the others of our group," Drask added, pulling out his comlink.

"They'll be all right," Evlyn assured him as she stepped into the alcove. "They'll be brought through right behind us."

She touched a control. The wall blocking the far end of the alcove slid smoothly up into the ceiling, revealing a short corridor with another door at the far end. "Come on," she invited, stepping inside and heading for the door in the opposite wall.

Mara frowned. Aside from the door at the far end and another one midway along the left-hand wall, the corridor was completely bare. A security transit, perhaps, with hidden sensors that would allow whoever was beyond to get a close look at prospective visitors?

Possibly. It could also be another booby trap.

Still, unless the rest of the survivors were prepared to sacrifice the girl, it ought to be safe enough. Provided, of course, she and the others got inside with the girl before she disappeared through the far door.

Again, Luke's thoughts were mirroring hers. "Mara, you and the general had better stay here," he said as he stepped into the corridor behind Evlyn, taking long strides as he tried to catch up without looking too obvious about it. "He can call back and alert the rest of the party."

"No," Drask insisted, brushing past Luke in turn and striding into the corridor ahead of him. "You do *not* go ahead alone."

Evlyn had reached the far end and was reaching for a small control panel set into the wall beside the door. Mara hesitated, stretching out to the Force, trying to reach back to Formbi's group behind them. There was no fear or sudden surprise back there that she could detect.

Abruptly, she made up her mind. If this whole thing was legitimate, it wouldn't hurt to be separated from the others for a few minutes, especially with Fel and the 501st there to guard them. If it was a trap, two Jedi always had a better chance than one. "We can call them on the way," she decided, stepping in behind Drask.

She was just in time. Even as she ducked beneath the door,

it slid down behind her. "Hurry," Evlyn said, beckoning them forward. Mara took a long step to catch up to Luke—

She caught the warning flicker an instant before it happened. But it was too late. Even as she and Luke grabbed for their lightsabers, two doors abruptly slammed down from the ceiling, one in front of Drask, the other behind Mara, cutting the corridor into thirds and trapping them in the center section.

With a lurch, the floor dropped out from under them.

CHAPTER 12

"JEDI!" DRASK BELLOWED, MAKING THE WORD A CURSE. "DO something!"

But for that first terrifying second there was nothing either of them could do. Luke fought for balance, feeling Mara's chagrin mixing with his own. The room kept falling, far faster than the planetoid's own weak gravity could possibly have pulled it. Too late, now, he realized they'd been decoyed into a disguised turbolift car.

Then, so unexpectedly and abruptly that he nearly fell over, the car braked to a halt.

"Good day, Jedi." The disembodied voice came from the control panel beside the side door. "Good day, Blue One."

"We are called *Chiss*," Drask corrected the voice tartly.

"Ah," the voice said. "Good day, then, Chiss. I'm Jorad Pressor, Guardian of the People."

"Interesting way you have of greeting peaceful visitors," Mara commented. "You at least going to come out where we can talk face to face?"

"Whom I deal with is my decision, not yours," Pressor said. "For the moment, that's not going to be you."

"For a very *short* moment," Mara countered. "Or do you really expect this box to hold us for long?"

"Long enough," Pressor assured her. "Let me explain. The reason you've stopped moving is that your turbolift car is currently sitting at a gravity eddy point being balanced by two equal and opposite focused repulsor beams. If either of them is cut off, you'll be instantly shot through the tube to smash into either the Dreadnaught you just left or the Dreadnaught you were intending to travel to. Either way, it will be very messy."

"For your vessel as well as for us," Drask warned. "Such an impact may do serious damage to your structural integrity."

"I don't think so," Pressor said. "Of course, none of you would ever know for certain."

"True," Luke conceded. "I presume there's more?"

"I know about Jedi lightsabers," Pressor said. "I know you could normally cut your way out of the car with ease. In this case, however, I'd strongly advise against trying it. The power and control cables for both repulsor beams are wrapped in random patterns around the car. Cut any of the wires, upsetting the balance of forces, and it will be the last thing you ever do."

Luke looked at Mara. "You've spent a lot of time thinking this out," he said. "Have you had a lot of Jedi visitors in the past fifty years?"

"We haven't had any visitors at all," Pressor said, his voice suddenly cold and bitter. "But I've always known that someday the Republic would send someone to hunt us down. It seemed only prudent to take precautions."

Luke shook his head. "You've got it all wrong," he said, putting all the persuasion he could into his voice. "We're not here for revenge or retribution or whatever. We're—"

"Don't bother trying to communicate with the rest of your people, either," Pressor interrupted him. "All comlink frequencies are being jammed. Make yourselves comfortable, and cultivate that renowned Jedi patience."

There was a click, and the voice was gone.

"Interesting," Drask commented, turning to face Luke. "Aristocra Chaf'orm'bintrano has often stated that the Jedi are honored and admired by all. Apparently, he was mistaken."

"Very much mistaken," Luke agreed, looking slowly around the car. Up close, the walls appeared to be solid metal, with no signs of tampering. If their captors were monitoring them, the holocams and voice pickups had to either be hidden in the control board or else buried in the line where the walls and ceiling met, where numerous age cracks had opened up in the metal. "There are any number of people who don't like Jedi," he continued, lifting his eyebrows at Mara. She nodded to the control panel, then put her hands together in a right angle.

So she'd come to the same conclusion he had. Nodding back, Luke slipped off his emergency-kit backpack and popped it open.

Mara picked up the explanation: "Of course, most of them are criminals or warmongers." She had her own backpack off now, her fingers sorting through the contents. "Jedi are supposed to keep the peace, so of course those groups hate us."

"Corrupt politicians don't like us much, either," Luke added, digging beneath the ration bars and water tubes and pulling out his liquid-cable dispenser. Mara was already ready with her contribution: her medpac's tube of synthflesh wound healer. "I wonder which category Pressor falls into."

"Maybe none of them," Mara said. Stepping to a corner of the room, she began laying a thin bead of the synthflesh into the line between ceiling and wall. "Maybe he just doesn't think talking to us would get him anywhere."

"Maybe," Luke said, coming up beside his wife and playing out an equally thin line of liquid cable on top of the synthflesh before it could solidify. "Not here in Chiss space, anyway."

"If they even know where they are," Mara said. "Maybe once we've persuaded them we're here to help we can all sit down together and hear the whole story."

An uncomfortable silence descended on the car. Mara reached the corner and continued on along the next wall, Luke right beside her. Liquid cable, which solidified instantly on contact with the air, was designed specifically not to be sticky so that it wouldn't hang up on anything as it was being extruded. The synthflesh, on the other hand, was designed just as specifically to stick solidly to wounds, protecting them from the air and further injury. Together, they made a perfect barrier against the age cracks and anything that might be hidden behind them.

Once they finished with the walls, it would be a simple matter to block the view from the control panel with one of their all-temperature cloaks. If Pressor didn't interfere, they should be finished in a few minutes.

Pressor didn't, and they were. "There," Luke said at last, stepping back to admire their handiwork. "That should at least keep them from watching us."

"A useful start," Drask said, his tone neutral. Clearly, he wasn't all that impressed. "Yet we are still inside. What now?"

"Now," Luke said, smiling tightly at Mara, "you'll get to see how Jedi do things."

FROM SOMEWHERE AHEAD CAME A DISTANT *CLUNK*. "WHAT WAS that?" Feesa asked, looking up.

"Machinery," Grappler said, lifting his BlasTech and taking a step toward the passageway Luke and Mara had disappeared down a few minutes earlier. "Possibly a door sealing."

"The Skywalkers!" Jinzler said sharply, looking around. "They're gone!"

"It's all right, Ambassador," Formbi said calmly. "They went with General Drask to scout ahead." He peered in that direction. "It's time we joined them."

Fel suppressed a grimace. He'd assumed the two Jedi would be back before they were missed, or at least before it was time to move on. This was going to play havoc with his marching order. "Stormtroopers, form up," he ordered. "Two and two, front and rear."

"I'd prefer they hold rearguard position, Commander," Formbi said. "You"—he gestured to the three Chiss warriors—"come with me."

Without waiting for comment or argument, he strode off down the corridor, one of the Chiss warriors taking point two steps ahead of him as the other two moved into position on either side of him.

Fel hissed between his teeth as Jinzler, Feesa, and the

Geroons moved off behind the procession. He hated being stuck all the way in the back this way. "Rearguard formation," he ordered the stormtroopers.

He was striding along behind Bearsh when a young, auburn-haired girl stepped out of concealment in front of the lead warrior, bringing the whole group to an abrupt halt. "Hello," she said calmly, as if visitors dropped by Outbound Flight every day. "Are you here to see the Guardian?"

Formbi glanced at Jinzler, then back to the girl. "We're here to see the survivors of Outbound Flight, and to help them," he said. "Is the Guardian the one we need to see?"

"Yes," the girl confirmed. "Come; I'll take you to him."

She turned and headed down the corridor toward the forward sensor room. "Who are all of you?" she asked over her shoulder.

"I am Aristocra Chaf'orm'bintrano of the Fifth Ruling Family of the Chiss Ascendancy," Formbi identified himself. "This is my aide, Chaf'ees'aklaio. This"—he gestured to Jinzler—"is Ambassador Dean Jinzler of the New Republic. Our expedition also includes representatives of the Geroon Remnant and the Empire of the Hand."

"So many people here to see us," the girl commented, turning into an alcove to her left.

"Yes," Formbi said. "May I ask your name?"

"I'm Evlyn," she said. "This way, please." She touched a control on the wall, and a door slid open in front of her. Gesturing the others to follow, she stepped inside.

Fel stepped close beside Cloud as Formbi and the others filed through the doorway. "Are you picking up Drask or the Jedi anywhere?" he murmured.

"I have no sensor contact," the stormtrooper murmured back. "But there's a lot of metal and electronic equipment in here. It may be shielding them."

"Maybe," Fel said, pulling out his comlink as he and the stormtroopers reached the doorway. The opening led into a short corridor, he saw, with another door at the far end and a third door midway down the wall on the right. Formbi, the Chiss warriors, and two of the Geroons were right behind the girl, while Jinzler, Feesa, Bearsh, and the fourth Geroon had fallen a couple of paces behind the leaders as they looked around the empty corridor. "Cloud, Grappler: go catch up to Formbi," he ordered quietly. At the far end of the corridor, Evlyn touched a control, and the door slid up in front of her. "We'll stay back here and—"

He never finished the sentence. Evlyn stepped through the door; but instead of staying open, the panel slammed violently down right in Formbi's face. Even as Fel drew his blaster, another door dropped out of a groove in the ceiling in front of Cloud, cutting the Imperials off from the rest of the party. He spun around in time to see the door they'd come though slam down in turn, isolating them from the rest of the ship.

An instant later, the floor seemed to drop out from under him as their newly created prison began to fall.

It braked to a stop before he had time for more than a single curse. "Good day," a voice said from a speaker in the control panel. "My name is Guardian Pressor. You're in a turbolift car that is being held in suspension between two opposing repulsor beams. Do you understand this?"

"Perfectly," Fel said, trying to keep his voice calm. "I'm Commander Chak Fel of the Empire of the Hand. Interesting trap you've got here."

"Merely making use of limited resources," Pressor said. "The six turbolift cars running through this pylon were designed to operate independently, but could also be connected together for large cargoes."

"Ah," Fel said. "I take it this pylon you mentioned is the connecting tube between these particular two Dreadnaughts?"

"The wiring that feeds power to the repulsor beams also wraps randomly around the outside of the car," Pressor said, ignoring the question. "I'd therefore advise against trying to shoot or cut your way out."

"Understood," Fel said. Clearly, Pressor wasn't interested in a long conversation. "What is it you want from us?"

"From you, nothing," Pressor said. "I'll speak with you again when I've come to a decision concerning your group."

"Very well," Fel said, looking casually around the car. There would be at least one hidden monitor in here, he knew. "Would it help to tell you we come in peace, and in the hope of helping you and your people?"

"Not really, no," Pressor said.

The speaker clicked off. "Anyone?" Fel invited sourly.

"They're jamming our comlinks," Shadow offered. "I can't raise any of the others."

"Big surprise there," Fel said. "What about monitors?"

"One," Grappler said, pointing his BlasTech toward the control panel. "I mark the monitor system feed in there."

"Concur," Watchman agreed.

Fel nodded. "All right, then," he said, digging into his emergency pack. "The others are off by themselves, out of our reach and protection. That is unacceptable."

His fingers located the insulator blanket and emergency food paste he'd been looking for. So Pressor was proud that he could make use of limited resources? Fine. As far as Fel was concerned, the Empire of the Hand had *invented* that particular operational philosophy. "So let's make ourselves a little privacy," he continued, crossing toward the hidden monitor, "and then see what exactly we can do about this."

". . . SO I'D ADVISE AGAINST TRYING TO SHOOT YOUR WAY OUT," Pressor said, wiping the sweat from his forehead in the hot room as he once again ran through the warning message he'd prepared. "Is that understood?"

"Clearly," the Blue One—Chiss—who had identified himself as Aristocra something-or-other said calmly. He'd ended up in the Number Four Turbolift Car, along with three more Chiss and two of the other, unknown aliens. "We'll await your decision," the Aristocra continued. "I would simply say that we've come here to help you, not to harm you."

"I understand," Pressor said. "I'll speak with you soon."

He cut off the speaker, scowling blackly at the fuzzy image that was the best the turbolift monitors could handle anymore. Of course they weren't here to harm anyone. Just like those strange soldiers with their white armor and hidden faces weren't here to harm anyone, or the Jedi weren't here to harm anyone.

Jedi.

For a long minute Pressor stared at the image of the two Jedi on the Number Two display. It was hard to tell on the ancient and failing equipment, but they looked young, probably younger than he himself was.

But of course, age didn't mean anything. According to Director Uliar, the Jedi culture and methods were centuries old, passed down from one generation to the next with all the passion and rigidity of a system kept alive through sheer inertia. If these two were following in that same tradition, they would be exactly like the Jedi who had set out with Outbound Flight all those years ago.

He shifted uncomfortably in his seat. Of course, he'd only been four when Outbound Flight died, and admittedly nowhere near the center of the action. But still, he remembered those Jedi.

Or at least, he remembered one of them.

The control room door slid open, letting in a blast of even hotter air, and Evlyn stepped inside. "Do we have all of them?" she asked.

"Every one," Pressor assured her, gazing back at his niece's bright blue eyes. They might look innocent—Evlyn herself might look innocent—but Pressor wasn't fooled. There was something odd about the girl, something he'd been aware of since she was three years old. Something the others would eventually notice, too.

"Good," Evlyn said, taking another step toward Pressor to allow the door to slide shut behind her. "It's a lot cooler in here."

"A little cooler, anyway," Pressor said. "The repulsorlift generators are running pretty hot."

"That's not good, is it?" Evlyn asked, peering over his shoulder at the monitors.

"Not if one of them gets hot enough to fail, no," he conceded, swiveling back around in his creaky chair. "At least it would be a fast way to die."

He glanced over the bank of monitors, frowning. One of the displays was suddenly showing nothing except black, the one in the Number Six Car. Muttering a curse at the antiquated equipment, he reached for the controls.

"That's not going to help," Evlyn said. "The man in the gray uniform put a piece of cloth over the monitor. I saw him do it as I was coming in."

Pressor glared over his shoulder at her. "And you didn't say anything?"

"What could you have done about it if I had?"

Disgustedly, he turned back around. She was right, of course, but that wasn't the point. "Next time you see something important, tell me," he growled. The low conversation coming from the Number Six speaker had vanished along with the video image, he noted, disappearing into a faint hum. Cranking up the volume did nothing but increase the intensity of the hum. "Did they do something to the voice pickup, too?" he asked Evlyn.

"I didn't see anything," she said, sounding puzzled. "That sounds a lot like the hum from the repulsor generators, though."

"Of course it does," Pressor growled as the explanation hit him. The cloth they were using to block the camera was heavy enough to pick up the vibration from the wall and amplify it over the voice pickup, deafening him as well as blinding him with a single move. So much for keeping tabs on the armored soldiers and their officer.

And from the looks of things, the two Jedi were trying to shut him down, too. "Blast them all, anyway."

"You could," Evlyn reminded him.

Pressor grimaced. Yes, he could blast them, all right. He could blast all of them. A flick of a switch, and they would be slammed down the turbolift pylon hard enough to turn them into jelly. "We'll let them be for now," he told the girl. "Anyway, whether we can see them or not, they're still trapped."

He shifted his attention to the Number Five Car's monitor. The man the Aristocra had identified as Ambassador Jinzler was in there, plus a young-looking Chiss and two of the aliens with the twin mouths, one of whom was currently pounding on the control panel as if trying to break it open.

Talking with them would be a risk, he knew, especially if this New Republic they'd mentioned was anything like the Republic Outbound Flight had left all those years ago. But he had to talk to *someone*. And of all those in the boarding party, at least none of this particular group was carrying any weapons.

"Go ahead and release Number Five," he told Evlyn. "Actually, give me a couple of minutes to talk to them and then release it. You remember how to deactivate the trap and put the car back on normal?"

"Sure," she said, reaching into a pocket and pulling out the command stick he'd given her. "Seven-three-three-six."

"Right," he said. "Bring them back up here and take them to the pilot ready room. I'll be waiting for them there."

"Okay," she said, taking a step backward. The door behind her slid open, letting in another blast of hot air, and she was gone.

Pressor reached for the comm control, checking over the readings one last time. *Ambassador Jinzler*—he repeated the name in his mind, making sure he had it right. *Jinzler. Jinzler.*

His fingers froze a centimeter from the comm switch. *Jinzler?*

He sucked in a lungful of hot air, staring at the man on the display. Ambassador Jinzler, here aboard his ship. Jedi Lorana was how he'd known her, but her full name had been Jedi Lorana Jinzler.

With an effort, he forced his fingers to travel that last centimeter. "Hello, Ambassador Jinzler."

WITHOUT WARNING, TWO HUGE PANELS SLAMMED DOWN IN front of and behind them, the resonating *thud* as they hit the floor cutting across Feesa's sudden scream of fright. "It's all right," Jinzler said reflexively, reaching out an arm to catch her around her shoulders as she half fell, half lunged against his side. She jerked at his touch, but didn't pull away. "It's all right," he repeated as soothingly as he could.

It wasn't soothing enough, evidently. Her body was trembling as she pressed against him, her glowing eyes narrowed. Jinzler tightened his grip around her shoulders, looking helplessly at Bearsh and the other Geroon who'd wound up trapped in here with them.

But neither alien was in any shape to give him any assistance. Bearsh's companion had pulled his heavy wolvkil drapery half over his head, gripping it by its blue-and-gold collar, as if instinctively preparing to throw off the extra weight and make a run for it, or else just as irrationally hoping that he could hide underneath it. Bearsh himself was half crouched beside the door, his twin mouths repeating the same agitated tones over and over as he clutched the other Geroon's arm with one hand and pounded uselessly on the small control board beside the door with the other.

Jinzler looked around, searching for some clue as to what he should do. But with the exception of the door and the control panel Bearsh was still pounding on, the room was completely devoid of decoration or instrumentation. The control panel itself didn't offer much, either. There were only five options for stops, marked D-4-1, D-4-2, D-5-1, D-5-2, and SC, plus the usual emergency buttons and a droid socket that would do them no good without a droid. Jinzler himself was unarmed, though what he would have done with a blaster even if he'd had one he couldn't guess. He did have a comlink connected to the *Chaf Envoy*, but whoever had sprung this trap would surely have thought to jam their communications.

Still, it was worth a try. Slowly, carefully, he dug into the proper pocket of his survival pack.

There was a loud *click* from the control panel. Bearsh jumped back, twitching as if he'd been stung. "Hello, Ambassador Jinzler," a man's voice said. "My name is Pressor, Guardian of this colony."

"Hello, Guardian," Jinzler said, trying to keep his voice calm. "This has been something of a surprise."

"I'm sure it has," Pressor said. "And I apologize for that. But I'm sure you understand that we have to take precautions."

"Of course," Jinzler said, though he didn't, entirely. "May I ask what's happened to the rest of my party?"

"They're perfectly safe," Pressor assured him. "At least for now. What ultimately happens to all of you, of course, is still undecided. I'd like to bring you out for a discussion, if I may."

An unpleasant thrill tingled across Jinzler's skin. *Ambassador Jinzler.* He'd started this whole charade purely to get himself aboard Formbi's expedition. Quite unintentionally, he'd apparently sold these people on that story, as well.

And unless he was misreading the tone of Pressor's voice, he was about to be dropped into negotiations regarding the fate of everyone aboard the expedition.

For a long second panic bubbled in his throat. He wasn't a diplomat, trained in mediation or negotiation. He was only an electronics tech. Mostly a failed one, too, like he'd been a failure at everything else he'd tried. Luke and Mara should be handling any talks with Guardian Pressor. Them, or Aristocra Formbi—after all, this territory belonged to the Chiss, not the New Republic. Even Commander Fel probably had more experience with foreign cultures than he did.

But he was the one Pressor had chosen. Arguing the point would probably be a bad idea, and admitting his deception would be even worse. Whether he liked it or not, it was up to him. "Certainly," he told the disembodied voice. "Just tell me what you want me to do."

"When the door opens you will step outside," Pressor said. "The girl who met you earlier will take you to a nearby room. I'll be waiting for you there."

"I understand," Jinzler said, glancing down at the top of Feesa's head. "What about those in here with me?"

"They'll have to wait there until we're finished."

Feesa gave a soft whimper. "Please," she whispered. "Please. No."

"You cannot leave us here alone," Bearsh agreed softly. "Please, Ambassador Jinzler."

Jinzler grimaced. This could get very awkward. "I understand your concerns, Guardian," he said. "But my companions . . . they're not exactly what you'd call heroic."

"We have no need of heroes here, Ambassador," Pressor said, his voice dark. "We don't need them, and we don't like them."

"Of course," Jinzler said hastily. "My point is that it's going to be a severe hardship for them to stay here alone. Besides which," he added as inspiration finally struck, "First Steward Bearsh and the other Geroons came a long way to pay you honor for saving them from slavery to the Vagaari all those years ago. I know they would very much like to be present at our discussions."

There was no answer. Jinzler remained motionless, holding on to Feesa and mentally crossing his fingers. "Very well," Pressor said at last. "They may all accompany you, provided they remain silent. I trust you are willing to guarantee their behavior?"

"I am," Jinzler said firmly. "No one wants to hurt any of you. We're only here to help."

Pressor snorted. "Of course you are."

WITH ONE FINAL DELICATE SLICE OF HER LIGHTSABER, MARA cut away the twenty-centimeter-square section of the turbolift car wall she'd been working on, leaving everything behind it untouched. The piece of metal fell inward, stopping abruptly in midair as Luke caught it in a Force grip. "Okay," he said, easing it to the floor as warm air flowed in through the opening. "Let's see what we've got."

"Mostly a lot of wires," Mara said, switching off her lightsaber and stepping closer to the wall.

Luke moved to her side. She was right: in just the small section she'd opened up there were no fewer than eight wires of different colors crisscrossing their way across the gap. "Guardian Pressor wasn't kidding about the power cables being wrapped around the car," he commented.

"He sure wasn't," Mara agreed, pushing experimentally on one of them. It gave about a centimeter and then stopped. "Wrapped pretty tightly, too. We're not going to be able to push them far enough out of the way to squeeze between them."

"What good would that do anyway?" Drask asked. "Even if we left the car, we would still be suspended in midair."

"Sure, but as long as we stayed out of the repulsor beams, we'd be all right," Luke told him. "All we'd have to deal with along the edges would be standard ship's gravity, and there should be access ladders built into the sides of the tube we can use to get down."

"Except that the wires prevent us from reaching them," Drask said tartly. "Have you any other ideas?"

"We're not finished with this one yet," Mara countered, just as tartly. "What do you think, Luke? Should mine be on the other side?"

"Yes," Luke agreed. "Back to back always seems to work best."

"Right."

Crossing to the opposite side of the car, Mara ignited her lightsaber again. With the delicacy of a surgical droid, she began to cut a second opening. "And this will accomplish what?" Drask asked.

"If we do it right, it'll get us out of here," Luke told him.

"And if we don't," Mara added helpfully, "at least it'll kill us quickly."

Drask didn't reply.

WATCHMAN RAN HIS INDUCTION METER TO THE LOWER EDGE OF the rear wall and straightened up. "Well?" Fel asked.

"The topside repulsor cable comes around the corner right about here," the stormtrooper reported, marking the spot with a daub of synthflesh from his medpac. "It's in slightly worse shape than the power line to the underside generator—the field leakage is definitely stronger."

"Right." Fel shifted his attention to Grappler as he ran his own sensor over the edges of the door. "Anything there?"

"Yes, but not promising," the other said. "If Watchman is right about the differential in leakage levels, it appears the opposing sets of power cables were dropped into a cross-connection pattern right after the door closed behind us."

"So if we try to force it open, we break one of the circuits?" Fel suggested.

"Actually, we'd eventually break both of them," Watchman said dryly. "At least in theory. In actual practice, we'd probably be slammed into something solid one direction or the other before the second circuit popped."

"Let's try to avoid that," Fel said, trying not to sound sarcastic. His stormtroopers' apparently casual attitude, he knew, was just that: apparent. Beneath the surface they were all working as hard as he was to sort through the facts and options. "Anyone have a less lethal suggestion to offer?"

There was a moment of silence. Then Cloud cleared his throat. "I'm not as tech-trained as Watchman and Grappler," he said. "But if we drain some of the power to one of the repulsors, wouldn't the strength of the beam diminish?"

Fel rubbed his cheek thoughtfully. That was an interesting direction to go. "Watchman?"

"I don't think so," the stormtrooper said slowly. "Not with the power cables themselves."

"But we may be able to do something with the control lines," Grappler suggested. "If we can adjust them enough to lower their output, we may be able to lower the car to ground level."

"Right," Watchman concurred. "Of course, we'll only be able to get to the control cables if they're also wrapped around the car. You think they were careless enough to do that?"

"I don't know," Fel said. "Let's find out."

THE PLACE EVLYN LED THEM TO REMINDED JINZLER OF THE meal room back at the Comra relay post: a drab, viewportless place enclosed in undecorated metal, furnished only with a long, plain table and a handful of equally plain chairs.

Seated in the chair at the far end of the table was a dark-haired man in his midfifties with a lined, brooding face, dressed in the same simple fashion as the girl.

"Good day," Jinzler said with a nod, trying to remember how diplomats usually talked on the holodramas he'd liked to watch in the days when such entertainments could still interest him. "Do I have the honor of addressing Guardian Pressor?"

"You do," Pressor acknowledged. His eyes flicked to Feesa and the Geroons, lingered a moment on the wolvkils slung over the aliens' shoulders, then came back to Jinzler. "Sit down."

"Thank you," Jinzler said, choosing a seat midway down the table. Feesa took the chair beside him; Bearsh, perhaps sensing the lack of welcome, sat himself and his compatriot at the far end of the table, as far from Pressor as possible.

"Let's make this simple, Ambassador," Pressor said as the group settled in. "First of all, I don't trust you. Any of you. You arrive suddenly and without warning, invading my ship without even attempting to communicate with us first."

"I understand your feelings and your concerns," Jinzler said. "But the fact is, we didn't know anyone was here until we were already aboard. Even then, if it hadn't been for the Jedi, we probably wouldn't have known about you until we stumbled over Evlyn here."

"Yes," Pressor murmured. "Well, we'll let that pass for the moment. Right now, I'd like to hear why I should permit any of you to come farther into our world."

Jinzler smiled faintly. This was starting to sound and feel almost familiar. Maybe Pressor had learned his diplomatic technique from the holodramas, too. "Don't you mean, why should you permit any of us to live?" he suggested. "Because that really *is* the question, isn't it?"

At least Pressor had the grace to blush. "I suppose so," he admitted gruffly. "What can you offer that's worth risking the betrayal of my people?"

At the far end of the table Bearsh stirred in his seat. Jinzler threw him a sharp look, and he subsided without speaking. "I don't know exactly what happened to you," he said, turning

back to Pressor. "It's obvious you've all suffered tremendously. But I'm here—*we're* here—in the hope of bringing
that suffering to an end."

"And then what?" Pressor demanded. "A glorious return
to the Republic? Most of us volunteered for this voyage
specifically to *escape* the very thing you're offering."

"We're not the Republic you left," Jinzler said. "We're the
New Republic."

"And, what, you no longer have squabbles among factions
and members?" Pressor countered. "The bureaucracy no
longer exists? The leaders are wise and benevolent and
just?"

Jinzler hesitated. What exactly was he supposed to say?
"Of course we still have a bureaucracy," he said carefully.
"It's impossible to operate a government without something
of that sort. And there are certainly still squabbles and factions. But we've already tried the other option: rule by a single, monolithic Empire. Most of us prefer the alternative."

"An Empire?" Pressor asked, frowning. "When was this?"

"The wheels were already in motion when Outbound
Flight left Coruscant," Jinzler said, wondering how much he
should say. His goal was to convince Pressor that the New
Republic offered hope to these people, not to give the full
history of one of the politicians' more spectacular failures.
"At first, Palpatine only seemed to want peace—"

"Palpatine?" Pressor cut him off. "Supreme *Chancellor*
Palpatine?"

"That's the one," Jinzler confirmed. "As I was saying, at
first he only seemed to want to bring the Republic together.
It was only afterward, in hindsight, that we were able to see
how he was drawing more and more power to himself."

"Interesting," Pressor said. "But that's the past. This is the
present. And I'm still waiting to hear a good reason why we
should trust you."

Jinzler took a deep breath. "Because you're all alone out
here," he said. "You're in foreign territory, surrounded by the
hazards and lethal radiation of a tightly packed globular
cluster, sitting in a ruined and useless ship."

"This ship is hardly useless," Pressor said stiffly. "With all the work my father and the droids put into it, this particular Dreadnaught is pretty much ready to fly."

"Then why haven't you loaded everyone aboard and left?" Jinzler countered. "I'll tell you why. You haven't left because you have no idea how to get out." He locked gazes with the other man. "The bottom line is this, Guardian. If you don't trust us—if you kill us, or even if you just send us away, you and your descendants will be here forever."

Pressor's lip twitched. "I can think of worse fates."

"And if it were just you, I wouldn't have any problem with that decision." Jinzler turned to look at Evlyn, standing silently just inside the door. "But it isn't just you, is it?"

Pressor muttered something under his breath. "Well, one thing hasn't changed between the Old and New Republics," he said. "The politicians and diplomats still know how to fight dirty."

He waved a hand as Jinzler opened his mouth. "Never mind. I guess that's how the game has always been played."

"I'm not trying to push you into anything," Jinzler said quietly. "We're not in any rush, and you don't have to make any decisions right now. But ultimately, you have to be aware that your decision is going to affect more than just your own life."

Pressor didn't reply. Jinzler listened to the silence, trying to think of something else to say. "While you're thinking," he said as he finally found something, "we'd very much like to meet the rest of your people and see your ship. It's a testimony to your ingenuity and perseverance that you were all able to survive for so long, particularly after suffering so much devastation."

For another long minute Pressor gazed at him with narrowed eyes, as if trying to decide whether the request was genuine or simply one more diplomats' word game. Then, abruptly, he nodded. "All right," he said, pushing back his chair and getting to his feet. "You want to see our home? Fine; let's go see it."

"What about the others?" Jinzler asked, standing up as well. "The Skywalkers and Aristocra Formbi and the rest?"

"They'll keep for now," Pressor said, circling the table toward the door. "If we decide we're going to deal with you, I'll release them."

"It would be a nice gesture to at least release Aristocra Formbi," Jinzler said, pressing the point cautiously. "You're in Chiss space, and he's a high-ranking member of the Chiss government. You'll certainly need their help before this is over."

Pressor's lips compressed briefly. "I suppose," he said reluctantly. "All right. The Aristocra and his group can join us. But the Jedi will stay where they are." He considered. "So will those armored soldiers, I think. I don't much like the looks of them."

Jinzler bowed his head. "Thank you, Guardian," he said. To be perfectly honest, he didn't much like the looks of the stormtroopers, either. Fel could talk all he liked about how his Empire of the Hand wasn't the despotic tyranny Palpatine had created. Maybe he was even telling the truth. But Jinzler had lived under an empire once, and he'd long ago learned that words cost nothing to produce.

Pressor reached the door. Then, abruptly, he turned back around. "One other thing," he said, his voice pitched just a bit too casually. "Your name: Jinzler. Any relation to the Jedi Knight Lorana Jinzler?"

Jinzler felt a hard lump form around his heart. "Yes," he said, forcing his voice to be as casual as Pressor's. "She was my sister."

Pressor nodded. "Ah."

He turned around again. "This way."

CHAPTER 13

"WHAT WAS THAT?" DRASK ASKED ABRUPTLY. "DID YOU HEAR something?"

Across the car, Mara closed down her lightsaber. Luke stretched out with the Force, straining to hear. There was the sound of a door closing . . . one of the repulsorlift generators seemed to change pitch subtly . . .

"One of the turbolift cars is moving," Mara said, her head cocked to listen. "Down, I think."

"Which one?" Drask demanded. "Can you tell which one?"

Luke frowned with concentration. The sense of those in the car . . . but between the Geroons and Chiss, there was too much alienness all around for him to get a good reading. "I don't know," he said. "Mara?"

"I think Jinzler's aboard," she said, shaking her head slowly. "I can't get anything else."

Drask muttered something under his breath. "We must get out of here," he said. "Aristocra Chaf'orm'bintrano may be in grave danger."

"We're working as fast as we can," Luke pointed out, trying to suppress the sudden misgivings circling his stomach. If Jinzler was on the move, did that mean Guardian Pressor had decided he was the one the colonists should be talking to? Had that been Jinzler's plan the whole time, in fact—to be the one to make first contact with them?

He shook the thought away. No—that was ridiculous. How could Jinzler have possibly known there was anyone left aboard?

Still, even if there was no malice in the man, there was also no diplomatic training. "Mara?" he murmured.

"Working as fast as I can," she reminded him, scratching the tip of her lightsaber blade gently across the metal.

Luke grimaced, but he knew as well as she did that this couldn't be rushed. If she cut too far through the metal and nicked one of the repulsor power lines, none of them would be helping Formbi or Jinzler or anyone else. He fingered his own lightsaber hilt, cultivating his Jedi patience.

And then, all at once, the square of metal popped out of the wall. Caught slightly by surprise, Luke let it fall nearly to the floor before he was able to nab it in a Force grip and lower it more gently the rest of the way. "Okay," Mara said, closing down her lightsaber and stepping aside. "Your turn."

"Right." Stepping to the spot Mara had just vacated, he ignited his lightsaber. Stretching out to the Force, he eased the tip of the blade between the crisscrossing of wires behind the wall.

"Careful," Drask warned, taking a half step toward him. "If you touch the wrong wire—"

"Don't worry," Mara said, waving him back. "He knows what he's doing."

Luke pursed his lips. He knew what he was doing, certainly, at least in theory. Whether he could actually pull it off was another question entirely.

Just above the lightsaber blade a bright red wire stretched horizontally across the opening. Preparing his mind, he twitched the blade toward it.

Not close enough to actually touch it, of course. But close enough to activate the short-range prescience that gave the Jedi what appeared to be superfast reflexes.

And for that single brief instant, he could feel a sudden pressure against the soles of his feet.

"Red wire powers the upper repulsor," he announced, closing down the lightsaber and stepping back.

"Right," Mara said, going to the opening and marking the indicated wire with a bit of the dark brown coating from one of her ration bars. "One to go."

Luke nodded and turned around toward the first opening she'd made in the wall. Choosing a blue wire this time, he ignited his lightsaber and again twitched the tip of the blade toward it.

Nothing.

He tried again with a green wire, then a red wire, then another blue wire, with similarly negative results. Then, finally, he waved the blade toward a black-striped white wire and felt a brief sensation of the floor dropping out from under his feet. "There," he told Mara, backing away. "Black-striped white."

"Got it," she confirmed, marking it as she had the red wire on the other side. "Okay. We ready?"

"Ready as we'll ever be," Luke agreed, getting into position again facing the black-striped white wire. Mara stepped behind him, pressing her back to his as she faced the other side and the red wire he'd identified.

"Just a moment," Drask said, sounding more than a little alarmed. "What exactly do you plan here?"

"It should be clear enough, General," Mara said. "We're going to cut the power lines."

"But—" Drask broke off. "You really can do this?"

Luke could feel Mara's red-gold hair shift against the back of his neck as she turned to face the Chiss. "Trust us," she said.

Her hair resettled itself as she turned back to her target, and with a *snap-hiss* she ignited her lightsaber.

And with a sensation Luke still found astonishing, he felt her mind flow into, around, and through his.

For that exquisitely stretched-out moment in time they were truly a single mind, a single spirit poured into two separate bodies. They thought as one; they felt as one; they moved as one.

And their lightsabers struck as one, each of the two glowing blades slashing through its targeted power cable in perfect synchronization.

There was a slight jerk, more imagined than truly felt; and with a decided feeling of anticlimax, the turbolift car began to sink downward. Luke took a deep breath . . .

As suddenly as it had begun, the melding ended. The sensation of oneness faded away, leaving only the warmth of the memory behind. "There," Mara said. To Luke's ears, her voice sounded a little strained as she, too, worked to regain mental and emotional balance after their moment of unity. "See? No problem."

"What do you mean, no problem?" Drask bit out. "We are *falling.*"

"Don't worry," Mara said. "Now that we're traveling at a normal speed, there are built-in safeties to catch us at the other end. The problem was that Pressor's repulsors would have slammed us down too fast for them to trigger."

"That was a dangerous chance to take," Drask growled.

"You want out of here or not?" Mara countered.

The Chiss hissed between his teeth. "You Jedi have the arrogance of untested power," he told her bluntly. "One day, you will take one too many chances, and it will destroy you."

There was a gentle jolt from above, as if the car had momentarily shivered. "What was that?" Luke asked, glancing at the ceiling.

"We have changed direction," Drask said, cocking his head oddly to the side. "We are now traveling more vertically than before."

"How do you know?" Luke asked. Standing in the car's artificial gravity, he couldn't feel anything different.

"I simply know," the Chiss said. "I cannot explain. It simply *is.*"

"All right, fine." The last thing Luke wanted right now was something else to argue about. "But in that case, where are we going?"

"Perhaps Guardian Pressor enjoys layering his traps," Drask said, his hand on his charric. "This may lead to a special place reserved for anyone who defeats the first layer."

"I don't know," Mara said, looking around. "Seems a little like overkill. Luke, do you remember what this setup looked like from the outside? There were a pair of curved tubes leading off the main one, right?"

"Right," Luke confirmed, pulling up the image from his

memory. "They looked like they were heading toward each other when they disappeared into the hill."

"One coming off each side of the tube," Mara added. "Like they were branch routes you could take from either of the two Dreadnaughts."

"Branch routes heading to the central supply core," Luke said, nodding as the explanation suddenly hit him. "Of course: the SC button on the control panel."

"Right," Mara agreed. "That must be where we're going."

The words were barely out of her mouth when the car abruptly jerked again, and the floor seemed to drop gently out from under them. Reflexively, Luke tensed, then relaxed as he realized what had happened. Now that the car was out of the main tube and Pressor's trap, it had been grabbed by the branch tube's normal repulsor beam and was being pulled sedately downward toward the storage core. "We are turning over," Drask said, again doing that head-cocking thing.

"Must be lining up with the storage core's gravity direction," Luke said.

"Is that good?"

"Definitely," Luke assured him. "Shipboard gravity is usually tied in with the rest of the environmental system. If the gravity is working, chances are the core's got air and heat, too."

A few seconds later the car settled to a stop, and the door slid open to reveal a large, musty-smelling cavern.

Luke stepped out of the car, lightsaber ready in his hand. The room stretching out in front of him was only dimly lit, with perhaps a third of the permlight emergency panels still operating. The nearest true bulkhead was ten meters away toward the forward end of the core, with another bulkhead twenty meters in the other direction toward the rear. The space right in front of the turbolift was reasonably open, but the rest of the room had been partitioned by a grid of floor-to-ceiling meshwork panels dividing the floor space into three-meter-by-three-meter sections. A few of the sections had been partially or completely emptied, but most still held stacks of crates.

"Haven't made much of a dent, have they?" Luke commented as the others stepped out to join him.

"This facility was supposed to supply fifty thousand people for up to several years," Mara reminded him. "I'm surprised they got even this far into it."

"This may have been used up during the first part of the voyage, when all were still alive," Drask said, moving the beam from his glow rod down the labels of one of the stacks. "Surely not many of the original crew could have survived."

"How *any*one survived is still beyond me," Luke said, shifting his glow rod to point at the aft bulkhead. Just visible at the edge of the beam were two doorways: one human sized, the other obviously built for cargo. "Let's head aft and see what else is back—"

He broke off as the comlink at his waist emitted an odd chirping noise. He pulled it from his belt, peripherally aware that Mara and Drask were doing the same with theirs, and clicked it on.

A burst of static crackled at him, and he quickly shut it off again. "That's strange," he said, frowning at it. "It sounded like something was coming through just then."

"Same here," Mara said, turning her comlink over in her hand. "Yours, too, General?"

"Yes," Drask said, sounding thoughtful. "It was as if—" He stopped.

"As if?" Mara prompted.

"As if someone had used a—I do not know the proper word in your language," the Chiss said. "It is a signal that stretches across all parts of the communications range in an attempt to penetrate jamming."

"Some kind of full-spectrum burst," Mara said, nodding. "We use that technique ourselves sometimes. Usually between vehicles or ships, though—I've never seen it used on anything as small as a comlink."

"Do Chiss comlinks have that capability?" Luke asked Drask.

The other hesitated. "Certain of them do," he said. "Those I equipped our party with do not."

"Let's put it a different way," Mara said. "Are there any of these more sophisticated comlinks aboard the *Chaf Envoy*?"

Drask looked away. "There are," he conceded.

Mara looked back at Luke. "Terrific," she said. "So someone's able to communicate with the ship. Only that someone isn't us."

"Maybe it was just the survivors talking among themselves," Luke suggested, hunting for a less ominous explanation. "Maybe Pressor needed to send a signal to one of the other Dreadnaughts."

Mara shook her head. "Intership comms ought to be hard-wired."

"Unless some of the lines are out."

"Maybe," she said. Clearly, she didn't believe that for a second.

Unfortunately, despite what she still sometimes called his farmboy naïveté, neither did Luke.

Someone aboard Outbound Flight was communicating through Pressor's jamming. The question was, who?

And what were they saying?

He looked at Mara, but she just shrugged. "Nothing we can do about it right now," she said. "Come on, let's see what's back this way."

"IN HINDSIGHT, I SUPPOSE WE SHOULDN'T HAVE BEEN SUR-prised to find you here," Ambassador Jinzler commented as Pressor led the group back toward the Number Five Turbolift Car. "Even in the most adverse of conditions, humans always seem to find a way to survive."

"Yes," Pressor said, keeping his voice neutral as he waved the others ahead of him into the car. The two Geroons, he noticed, hesitated before stepping through the doorway. Jinzler himself didn't even break stride. The man was either very trusting, very overconfident, or very stupid. "Though the fact we lived through all of that certainly wasn't for lack of trying on *somebody's* part," he added.

"Indeed," Jinzler murmured as he and the female Chiss stepped to one of the rear corners of the car. "Exactly how this all happened is one of the things we hope to find out."

"Perhaps you'll have that chance," Pressor said, pulling out his command stick and plugging it into the droid socket on the control board. "Unfortunately, most of the records were ruined in the attack." He touched a button, and the barrier between Cars Four and Five slid open.

The three black-clad Chiss in the car reacted like dolls on twitch-strings, spinning around as one of the walls of their prison vanished, their hands darting to their holstered weapons. The two Geroons, in contrast, lifted their arms and surged forward toward their compatriots as if they'd been separated for years instead of just a few minutes. The older Chiss, the one dressed in yellow and gray, merely turned casually toward Pressor and nodded. "Good day," he said, his Basic oddly accented but quite understandable. "I am Aristocra Chaf'orm'bintrano of the Fifth Ruling Family, representing the Chiss Ascendancy. You may address me as Aristocra Formbi. Do I have the honor of addressing Guardian Pressor?"

"You do," Pressor said, returning the nod. The least he could do was show himself to be as cultured and polite as his visitors. "I welcome you to Outbound Flight, Aristocra Formbi, and apologize for the necessity of greeting you as I did."

"No apology required," the Aristocra assured him. Those glowing red eyes flicked to the female Chiss still hovering close to Jinzler, as if checking to see that she was all right. "Your caution is completely understandable."

"Guardian Pressor is going to take us to see his people," Jinzler spoke up. "After that, I presume we'll be discussing the possibility of their return to the New Republic."

The Aristocra frowned. "The possibility?"

"That's correct," Pressor said. "I'm not at all sure we'll choose to go back to the Republic. Or to go anywhere at all, for that matter." He made an adjustment on the command stick.

"You didn't tell him where they are?" Formbi asked, his eyes on Jinzler.

Pressor paused, his finger poised against the activation button. "What do you mean, where we are?" he asked.

"I'm afraid our conversation didn't get that far," Jinzler admitted.

Pressor looked at Formbi, feeling a knot forming in his stomach. "Why don't you tell me now?" he invited.

Formbi's mouth twitched. "You're deep within a high-security defensive position of the Chiss Ascendancy," he said. "Traveling here is forbidden without special authorization. Now that we know about you, I'm afraid you can't be permitted to stay."

The knot in Pressor's stomach tightened. "I see," he said, putting his voice back into neutral mode. "And if we refuse to leave?"

"I would hope you wouldn't," Formbi said, matching Pressor's tone. "We will, of course, give you any assistance you might require in moving your people wherever you wish to go. It's little enough compensation for what you've suffered."

"I see," Pressor said again. "Well, you can present your case before Director Uliar and the Managing Council. They'll be the ones who'll make the final decision."

Jinzler cocked his head. "Who is Director Uliar?"

"He's the head of the colony," Pressor told him, pressing the activation button on his command stick. Behind him the door to the alcove slid shut and the double car began to descend.

"I see," Formbi said. "I'm sorry—I'd assumed *you* were the leader."

"I'm the Guardian," Pressor said. "My Peacekeepers and I keep order within the colony. Director Uliar and the Managing Council make all the policy decisions."

"Sounds rather like a corporation," Jinzler commented.

"And why not?" Pressor retorted. "Corporations work a lot better than the political mess we left behind."

"Yes, of course," Jinzler said hastily.

"How many of you are there?" Formbi asked.

Pressor turned his face away from them. "I think I should let Director Uliar handle any further questions."

The car fell silent except for the distant creaks and rumblings of the turbolift equipment, and the melodic murmuring of the four Geroons as they huddled together in a back corner. Probably still assuring each other that they were all right, Pressor decided, eyeing the dead animals wrapped across their shoulders with a mixture of distaste and fascination.

With a raucous squeak and a vibrating thump, the double car came to a stop, snapping Pressor out of his thoughts. "This way," he said, touching the door release on the command stick. "We'll go find Director Uliar." He stepped outside—

And came to an abrupt halt. At the back of the turbolift lobby, as he'd prearranged, three of his Peacekeepers were standing ready, their faces displaying expressions ranging from wary to hostile to simply nervous.

Standing in a silent group beside them were Director Uliar and the two Survivor members of the Managing Council. Beside Uliar, her auburn hair glinting in the corridor's light, was Instructor Rosemari Tabory. Pressor's sister, and Evlyn's mother.

And *that* part Pressor had most certainly *not* prearranged.

"Director Uliar," he said in greeting as he crossed the lobby toward the group, trying to keep his voice steady. "Councilor Tarkosa; Councilor Keely," he added, nodding to each of the other two old men in turn. "What brings you here?"

"Don't act the innocent, Guardian," Uliar advised, the age wrinkles around his eyes deepening as he gazed at the group emerging from the turbolift car. "It doesn't suit you. So these are our visitors, are they?"

"These are some of them," Pressor said, flicking a quick look at his sister. Rosemari's expression was stiff, with a hint of paleness to her skin. "This is hardly the place for a historic diplomatic meeting, you know." He looked significantly at the two councilors. "Or the correct attendance for one, either."

"The entire council will be summoned in due course," Uliar said. "But I think those of us who actually lived through the Devastation have first rights to face our destroyers."

"This is a major event, with a major decision attached to it," Pressor insisted, keeping his voice low. "Probably the most significant thing that's happened since we arrived here. The Charter specifically requires that the entire Managing Council, Survivor *and* Colonist members, be present."

"And they will be," Uliar promised. He twitched a smile. "Until then, I daresay Instructor Tabory can act as observer for the Colonists."

"But—"

"Which ones are the Jedi?" Keely cut in, his nervous eyes darting back and forth across the group that had now paused a little uncertainly by the turbolift door. "Guardian? Which ones are the Jedi?"

"None of those here," Pressor told him. "The Jedi are still being held in one of the turbolift cars."

"No one here is a Jedi, you say?" Uliar said. "Not even—? Why look, Instructor Tabory; there's your daughter. Imagine that."

Pressor felt his stomach tighten as he glanced behind him. Evlyn was just emerging from the car behind the last of the Geroons, the calmness in her face in sharp contrast to the tension in her mother's. "She was assisting me," he said, looking back at Uliar.

"Was she really," Uliar said, as if it were a surprise to him. "You took your niece up to Four, exposing her to all the extra radiation up there? Not to mention putting her at risk from potentially dangerous intruders? What an extraordinary thing to do."

"She likes spending time with her uncle Jorad," Rosemari put in, her voice firm for all the concern in her face. "She always has."

"Indeed," Uliar said as Evlyn slipped past Jinzler and

Formbi and came to stand beside her mother. "Hello there, Evlyn. How are you?"

"I'm fine, Director Uliar," Evlyn said with a seriousness that looked strangely out of place on someone so young. But the quick hug she gave her mother was pure ten-year-old. "You don't have to worry about me. Uncle Jorad did everything just right. I wasn't in any danger."

"I'm sure you weren't," Uliar said, eyeing Pressor again. "Just as you weren't in any danger two years ago, hmm? Back when Javriel went crazy and tried to take the entire nursery hostage? You were helpful to your uncle then, too, if I remember correctly."

"You do," Pressor confirmed, feeling sweat starting to gather beneath his collar. So Uliar had noticed Evlyn's abilities, too. He should have known the old Survivor would catch on. And of all the possible times for him to decide to make an issue of it—

He felt his throat tighten. Or had Uliar in fact deliberately chosen this moment? A moment when there were outsiders—including Jedi—aboard his ship for the first time in fifty years? Outsiders who, not knowing the realities aboard Outbound Flight, might be willing and able to confirm his suspicions about Evlyn?

"Indeed," Uliar said. "You have a strange way of returning your niece's affection, Guardian."

"I needed her help today," Pressor said. "The same help I needed from her back then: to act as decoy. It wasn't a job any of my Peacekeepers could handle."

"But your own niece?" Uliar persisted. "Why not pick someone else?"

He smiled crookedly, the giveaway sign that he was about to close the jaws of his verbal trap. "Or," he said smoothly, "does she have special qualifications or talents that make her suited for such tasks?"

"My daughter has many special talents, Director," Rosemari put in, her arm wrapped protectively around her daughter's shoulders. "For one thing, she doesn't panic under pressure. She's quick and smart, and she knows Four as well as anyone else in the colony. Certainly now that most of the work is done and almost no one goes up there anymore."

"Did she also join the Peacekeepers while I wasn't looking?" Uliar countered, throwing a quick glare in her direction. His trap had been set for Pressor, and he clearly didn't appreciate Rosemari jumping in and blunting its teeth. "As long as we're quoting from the Charter, Guardian, I believe it explicitly states that you and your Peacekeepers are the ones who are supposed to stand between the colony and potential dangers."

"He just said he needed someone to decoy them," Rosemari said, her voice starting to match the director's own annoyance level. She gestured to the three Peacekeepers standing uncomfortably at the edge of the debate. "You think they would have just walked into a disguised turbolift behind Trilli or Oliet or Ronson?"

She shifted her finger to point squarely at Uliar's chest. "Or should he have asked someone else? One of your granddaughters, maybe?"

"A decoy shouldn't have been necessary," Uliar insisted. "Guardian Pressor has assured us over and over that between the various traps and the droid surveillance, Four is perfectly secure."

"Oh, so now you want to set off explosives and wreck it completely?" Rosemari asked scornfully. "After all the time and effort my father and the others poured into putting it back together?"

She drew herself up to her full 1.58-meter height. "Or don't you mean it when you say you want to take us out of here someday?" she demanded. "Are you so comfortable in your private little kingdom that you want to keep us all here?"

"Silence, woman," Tarkosa rumbled, his eyes glinting ominously beneath his bushy eyebrows. "You have no idea what you're talking about."

"Yes, be silent," Uliar seconded gruffly. "I didn't bring you here to listen to you make excuses for your brother."

"Then you apparently don't know her very well," Pressor

told him, a small part of him starting to enjoy this. "Meanwhile, our guests are waiting."

Uliar's lips pressed briefly together as his eyes flicked over Pressor's shoulder. "Very well," he said reluctantly. "Introduce us."

"Certainly," Pressor said, half turning and waving the others forward. Uliar hadn't given up, he knew. All he'd done was abandon this particular probe, at this particular time.

But he would be back. He would definitely be back.

Walking at the head of the group, Jinzler stepped to Pressor's side and stopped expectantly. "May I present the representative of the New Republic," Pressor said, watching Uliar's expression closely. "Ambassador Dean Jinzler."

The director was good, all right. There was barely a twitch from the corners of his eyes as the name registered. "Ambassador," he said smoothly. "I'm Chas Uliar, current director of the Outbound Flight Colony. These are Councilors Tarkosa and Keely, two of the original Survivors of the Devastation."

"Honored, Director," Jinzler said, bowing from the waist like a diplomat from some old holodrama. "We're pleased to find you alive."

"Yes," Uliar said, a little too dryly. "I'm sure you are."

"This is Aristocra Formbi of the Chiss Ascendancy," Pressor went on, "and First Steward Bearsh of the Geroon Remnant, along with their assistants."

"Such a varied group," Uliar commented as he exchanged nods with Formbi and Bearsh. "I understand you brought two Jedi along with you, as well."

"Yes," Jinzler said. "Guardian Pressor informs us they're still being held, along with the others."

"Others?" Uliar asked, looking questioningly at Pressor.

"Five others, in a separate car," Pressor confirmed. "Representatives of a government calling itself the Empire of the Hand."

"Empire of the Hand," Uliar repeated, as if to himself. "Interesting. I presume, Ambassador, that you'll wish both groups released at once to join you?"

Pressor held his breath. A simple, obvious suggestion; but

he'd long ago learned not to trust simplicity when it came to dealing with Uliar. Was the director's question in fact an attempt to find out who was really in charge of this expedition?

Jinzler hesitated, perhaps also sensing a trap. "I'm sure they're fine where they are, Director," he said carefully. "We'll want them released eventually, of course, but we can certainly begin our discussions without them."

"Good," Uliar murmured. Apparently, Jinzler had passed the test. "Well, then. The Managing Council chamber is located a short distance back this way. If you'll follow me? . . ."

"Thank you," Jinzler said, bowing again.

Uliar turned and headed aft down the corridor, the two councilors falling into step beside him, Jinzler and Formbi following a couple of paces behind them. Pressor caught the eyes of his three Peacekeepers and nodded toward Uliar; nodding back, Ronson and Oliet moved into flanking positions beside the three Survivors. The black-clad Chiss were already walking in a military-precise, lockstep line behind Formbi, with the Geroons following somewhat more tentatively and not at all in step with the rest of the group or even each other. "We're certainly starting off with a bang," Pressor muttered to Rosemari as the procession marched away. "You'd better take Evlyn and—"

He broke off as he glanced down at his sister's side. Evlyn was nowhere to be seen. "*Blast* her," he snarled under his breath, looking around. There she was, of course, halfway down the corridor, walking between Aristocra Formbi and the three black-clad Chiss striding along behind him. "How does she *do* that?"

"I don't know," Rosemari murmured grimly. "But if she doesn't quit it, Uliar won't need any help figuring out what she is."

"No kidding," Pressor said, a tightness settling into his stomach. "You'd better catch up and go with her."

"What, to a council meeting?" Rosemari countered. "I'm not authorized to be in there."

"Sure you are," Pressor told her. "You're representing the Colonists in these negotiations, remember? Uliar said so."

"And that was as much of a fraud as asking why you keep using Evlyn for these stunts," Rosemari shot back. "Speaking of which—"

"Save it," Pressor cut her off. "Look, if you *don't* go, Evlyn's going to crash the party by herself. What do you think Uliar will say when he finally notices her and doesn't remember seeing her coming in?"

"You're right," Rosemari conceded reluctantly. "But you'd better be there, too."

"I fully intend—"

Pressor broke off as the comlink at his belt gave an odd twitter. Frowning, he reached down and pulled it free.

"That's weird," Trilli murmured, stepping to his side, his own comlink in hand. "Your comlink just say something, Chief?"

"I thought it did," Pressor said, tapping the switch. On the normal channel was only the static of his jamming, while on the special twist-frequency command line there was silence. "Strange."

"Want to know what's stranger?" Trilli pointed down the corridor at the departing crowd. "I saw Jinzler and Formbi go for their comlinks, too."

Pressor frowned, an uncomfortable feeling creeping across his back. With the jamming still in place, there shouldn't have been *any* communications getting through. Not to *anyone's* comlinks. "Get back upstairs and double-check the jamming," he ordered Trilli. "Our guests may have a trick or two we don't know about."

"Right."

Trilli started to go; stopped again as Pressor caught his arm. "And while you're there," the Guardian added quietly, "put a lock on the controls for the forward trap cars' repulsors. Make sure no one but us can turn them on or off."

"Sure," Trilli said, sounding puzzled. "You afraid someone's going to accidentally bump into them or something?"

Pressor gazed at Uliar's receding back. Uliar, who had lived through the destruction of Outbound Flight and still carried the scars from that event. Uliar, who knew where the Jedi and Imperials were currently being held.

Uliar, who was leading the way toward a meeting room far from the turbolifts and the turbolift controls, where Pressor and the others wouldn't be in a position to notice if someone slipped up to Four and started playing with control switches.

"Yeah," Pressor said softly to Trilli. "Or something."

WITH A DISCONCERTING THUMP, THE TURBOLIFT CAR BEGAN moving. "Steady," Fel warned, putting a hand on the vibrating wall for balance and watching closely as Watchman and Grappler adjusted the power splitters they'd cobbled together. "Take it real easy. We're not in any particular hurry."

"We're keeping it slow," Watchman assured him. "It's running real smooth."

"Good," Fel said, not entirely sure he believed it. The car's vibration seemed to be increasing, and a low-pitched rumble had started in from somewhere.

On the other hand, if the trick failed, they would probably be dead before it even registered. Comforting.

"You still want us to head for the storage core?" Grappler asked.

"If you can manage it, yes," Fel said. That other car they'd heard, the one with Jinzler and possibly Formbi aboard, seemed to have gone straight down to the next Dreadnaught in the ring. It didn't seem like it would be a good idea to just burst in full-bore behind them, especially if Pressor had other surprises prepared for unwanted company. Far better if they could bypass that ship entirely and find a way to come up on it from below.

Out of the corner of his eye, he saw Cloud's head twitch. "Commander?" the stormtrooper asked. "Did you get that?"

"Get what?" Fel asked, straining his ears against the rumbling.

"My comlink just chirped," Cloud said.

"Mine, too," Shadow confirmed. "Sounded like someone sending a message burst."

Fel frowned. He hadn't heard any such noise from his own

comlink; but then, the pervasive rumbling could easily have masked it. The stormtroopers, with their comlinks built into their helmets, would be less affected by outside noises. "Could you get any kind of fix on it?" he asked. "Either direction or distance?"

"Negative," Cloud said. "My gear wasn't rigged for that."

"Well, rig it now," Fel ordered, looking around. Suddenly, the car seemed a little smaller and a lot more vulnerable. "And let's risk a little more speed," he added. "If Pressor's talking to his friends, I want us out of here as soon as possible."

"And if it wasn't Pressor?" Shadow asked.

Fel looked up at the ceiling. "Then I want us out of here even faster."

CHAPTER 14

THE DOORWAY OPENED INTO ANOTHER STORAGE ROOM, IDENTI-cal to the one they'd come in through except that in this one there was no turbolift access door. It also didn't appear that any of the supply crates piled behind their meshwork panels had ever been touched.

Neither had the crates in the next room back. Or in the room behind that. "It's one thing to talk about ten years' worth of supplies for something this big," Luke commented as they walked past the stacked crates toward the next door leading aft. "It's something else to actually *see* them."

"And this is just one level," Mara murmured, an odd sensation creeping through her as she gazed at the rows of stacked cartons. All those people—nearly fifty thousand of them—all gone. Destroyed in a matter of seconds or minutes or hours.

Murdered on the orders of the man she'd once proudly served.

"Hey?"

She shook off the mood. Luke was looking at her, concern in his face. "You all right?" he asked.

"Sure," she assured him. "I'm fine."

Like she could actually fool him. "More ghosts from the past?" he asked quietly.

She looked over at Drask, off examining a stack of crates a few meters away. "It's strange," she told her husband softly. "I thought I'd been through this already. That I'd put it all behind me. But back on the *Chaf Envoy*, I actually started feeling . . . I don't know. It's hard to explain."

"You started feeling comfortable?" Luke suggested.

Mara tried out the word in her mind. "Yes, I suppose that's it," she agreed. "Fel and this new Five-Oh-First Legion seemed so different from what Palpatine had created that it felt like something I could actually enjoy being a part of."

Luke's forehead creased. "You're not seriously thinking of taking Parck up on his offer of a job with the Empire of the Hand, are you?"

"Of course not." Mara hesitated. "Well, no, that's not entirely accurate," she confessed. "I mean, I certainly wouldn't go anywhere without you. But at the same time . . ." She shook her head.

"I know," he said. "The New Republic hasn't exactly been a shining example of how to run a galaxy lately, has it?"

Mara snorted. "The understatement of the month," she said. "All those stupid little brush wars and conflicts—I thought they'd all die down after we finally found that intact copy of the Caamas Document. But half of them are still simmering, and the Senate hasn't done a thing to stop them."

"That's not entirely true," Luke said. "But you do have a point. Things were a lot quieter under the Empire, weren't they?"

"At least until your Rebellion got going," Mara countered. "Then it got noisy again."

"We tried," Luke said, smiling back. The smile faded, and he shrugged fractionally. "You can't play the what-ifs, Mara. Palpatine may have suppressed all those regional conflicts, but he also suppressed freedom and justice, especially for nonhumans. If someone else had been in charge . . . but we'll never know."

"I understand all that," Mara said. "But that's not really the point. The point is that I was just starting to feel kindly, even nostalgic, toward the Empire."

She gestured at the dusty stacks of crates around her. "And then I come face to face with something like this: supplies carefully laid in for people he knew he was going to have murdered." She let her hand drop to her side. "There was just something about the cold-bloodedness of it that was a sudden kick in the teeth, that's all."

"I know," Luke said, taking her hand and squeezing it gently. "You never really saw the results of Palpatine's policies, did you?"

"No, not usually," Mara said with a sigh. "Not the big ones, anyway. Alderaan and that sort. Mostly I dealt with individuals or small groups, and half of them were Imperial officials suspected of embezzlement or treason. I never saw anything on Outbound Flight's scale."

"It makes sense that he shielded you from as much of that as possible," Luke pointed out. "You might have started having doubts, and he couldn't risk that."

"Jedi?" Drask called.

Mara turned around. The general had moved to another stack of crates near the aft set of doors and was shining his glow rod on one about halfway to the ceiling. "Come."

"What is it?" Luke asked as he and Mara crossed to the other.

"These two stacks," Drask said, indicating them with his glow rod. "They have been moved here from somewhere else."

Mara frowned at Luke, getting a similarly puzzled look in exchange. "What do you mean?" Luke asked. "How do you know?"

"In the previous storerooms these stacks all followed a specific pattern," Drask said. "Foodstuffs of several particular types, clothing, replacement components, various other types of supplies, emergency equipment, and so on. They were all placed in specific positions, with the proportions of each type always the same."

Luke looked at Mara. "Is this making any sense to you?" he asked.

"Actually, yes," she said. "If you proportion out each room according to the rate of expected supply usage, you can more or less empty one area at a time and don't have to keep going back and forth among half a dozen storerooms for what you want. That would also make it quicker and easier to apportion things if you decided to plant a colony somewhere."

"Ah," Luke said, nodding. "I get it. You give your colonists a Dreadnaught and, say, two levels' worth of supplies. No sorting needed: you just take aboard everything from those two levels."

"Right," Mara said. "And you say these stacks are out of order?"

"Yes." Drask gestured. "This group consists of electrical and fluid maintenance supplies. It should instead be food-stuffs."

"I'll take your word for it," Luke said, looking around. "Well, it doesn't look like they came from anywhere in here."

"Unless someone rearranged the whole room," Mara pointed out.

"No," Drask said. "The other stacks are properly placed."

"Maybe the next room back, then," Luke suggested. "Let's take a look." He led the way back to the smaller of the two aft doors and touched the release.

Nothing happened.

"That's funny," he said, frowning as he touched the release again. Again, the door didn't budge.

"Let's try the big door," Mara suggested, moving over to the cargo hatchway and tapping the release for that one.

It didn't move, either. "Now that," Luke said thoughtfully, "is very peculiar. All the other doors have worked just fine."

"Perhaps there is something in there the survivors do not wish us to see," Drask suggested, his voice ominous. "You have lightsabers. Cut it open."

"Let's not be too hasty," Luke said, running a hand along the smaller door. "Maybe we can do it the easy way. Mara?"

Mara pulled her lightsaber from her belt and stepped to the doorway. "Ready."

"Okay." Luke took a deep breath, and Mara could sense him stretching out to the Force. A moment later, with a creak of metal that had been sitting too long in one spot, the door began to slide up into the ceiling.

Mara was ready. The gap was barely waist-high when she ducked under the rising panel, igniting her lightsaber as she leapt into the room.

But there was nothing there except another storeroom, empty except for the usual stacks of boxes, exactly like all the previous four storerooms they'd looked at.

She frowned, lowering the lightsaber blade a little. No; not exactly. Back toward the center of the room, half a dozen sections of the mesh had been cleared out.

And inside them . . .

"Mara?"

"All clear," she called, closing down her lightsaber and looking around. Lying against the near wall was a piece of slightly twisted girder. Stretching out to the Force, she lifted it and set it upright beneath the door Luke was still holding up. "See if that'll hold it," she said.

Carefully, Luke lowered the door onto the girder. The metal creaked but held. "Odd thing to have lying around," he commented, frowning at the girder as he ducked under the door and into the storeroom. "I haven't seen anything like that in any of the other rooms."

"You haven't seen anything like this, either," Mara said as Drask came in behind Luke. "Take a look."

"Furniture storage?" Drask asked, frowning past Luke's shoulder.

"It's a little more interesting than that," Mara said as the three of them crossed over to the cleared sections. The contents were little more than a jumbled mess of broken furniture and tangled furnishings. But to her the signs were obvious. "You can see three cots in that first one—they've been a little broken up, but there are definitely three of them. Looks like there were four in the next. Probably four in that back one there, too."

"That round thing was probably part of a small table," Luke said, pointing. "I don't see any chairs, though."

"Perhaps they had only stools," Drask suggested. "Those short pieces, perhaps."

"Right," Mara agreed. "There are probably a lot of other pieces tangled in with those blankets and draperies, too. And of course, those boxy things have got to be portable 'fresher stations."

"But this makes no sense," Drask objected. "What you are describing are living quarters. Yet the vessels above are adequately intact. Why would anyone have chosen to live here instead?"

"Maybe all the Dreadnaughts were too badly damaged right after the battle," Luke suggested. "It may have taken a while for the droids to make them livable again."

Mara shook her head. "You're both missing the point. What did we have to do to get in here?"

"We had to lift—" Luke broke off. "Are you saying this was a *prison*?"

"What else?" Mara asked. "Small cubicles with minimal furnishings and not much privacy, stuck away from everywhere else in the place, all of it behind a door that doesn't open. What else could it be?"

"Interesting," Drask commented. "It would seem that your Outbound Flight experiment was a failure from the start. For there to have been a need for a prison so quickly implies the passengers were not well chosen."

"Or that something drastic happened to them," Mara said. "Some kind of space madness or something."

"Any chance it could have been a medical quarantine instead?" Luke suggested.

"Unlikely," Drask said. "There are not enough beds here for a large disease outbreak. A smaller problem would surely have been better dealt with in the vessels' own facilities."

"He's right," Mara agreed. "Besides, I don't see any sign of medical equipment in here." She gestured into the area. "And you see what else *isn't* here?"

Luke frowned. "No."

"I see," Drask said grimly. "There are no bodies."

"Or even the remains of bodies," Mara confirmed. "Which either means someone got in through that door sometime in the past fifty years and disposed of the dead—"

"—Or else they got out on their own," Luke finished for her.

"That's what I'm thinking," Mara agreed soberly. "I'm

also wondering if the timing of the breakout might have had an effect on the battle."

"Or perhaps it is connected with the unexplained appearance of this vessel in Chiss space," Drask pointed out. "That mystery has still not been solved."

"No, it hasn't," Mara said. "Luke, do you have any idea what sort of justice system was in place during that era? Specifically, what sort of people might the Jedi on Outbound Flight have locked up this way?"

"I don't know," Luke said, shaking his head. "But I can't see why anyone but the most violent or psychotic sorts would be buried this far away from the rest of the expedition. There would certainly have been a brig on each of the Dreadnaughts for dealing with standard lawbreakers."

A whisper of sensation touched Mara's mind. "Someone's coming," she said, unhooking her lightsaber from her belt.

"Who?" Drask asked, drawing his charric. "Guardian Pressor and his forces?"

Mara focused her mind, trying to isolate and identify the approaching minds. They definitely seemed familiar, but they were still too far away to identify.

Luke got there first. "It's all right," he said, returning his own lightsaber to his belt. "It's Fel and the stormtroopers."

"Is Aristocra Chaf'orm'bintrano with them?" Drask asked.

"No," Mara said. "Neither are Feesa or the Geroons. It's just the five Imperials."

"They pledged to protect him," Drask said ominously. "Why are they not with him?"

"I don't know," Luke said, heading for the propped-open door. "Let's go ask them."

They met up with the Imperials two rooms back toward the turbolifts. "Well, well," Fel commented as the two groups crossed the room toward each other. "I certainly wasn't expecting to find *you* three here. Not that I'm displeased, of course. What did you think of our host's little trap?"

"Where is Aristocra Chaf'orm'bintrano?" Drask cut in before either Luke or Mara could answer. "Why are you not protecting him?"

Fel seemed taken aback. "Relax, General," he said. "He's hardly alone up there. Your three warriors are with him, remember?"

"Besides, if Pressor wanted any of us dead, he could have done it long before now," Mara added.

"She's right," Fel agreed. "I'm sure the Aristocra's fine."

"Your calmness is very reassuring," Drask bit out. "Do you even know where he is?"

"Not exactly," Fel said. "But from the sounds their turbolift car made as it headed down, we're pretty sure they're on D-Five, the next Dreadnaught around the circle from where we came in."

"Then why did you not follow them after you made your own escape?" Drask asked.

"Because I thought it might make more tactical sense to come in from a direction they weren't expecting," Fel said, starting to sound a little annoyed himself. "There are three other turbolift tubes we can use to get up to D-Five: one straight aft along this deck, the other two fore and aft around that direction." He gestured to his right.

"Wait a minute," Mara said. "If the Dreadnaughts are in a ring, shouldn't the turbolift connections be on a lower deck instead of this one?"

Fel shook his head. "It has to do with the way the gravity directions were set up," he explained. "All the Dreadnaughts are oriented with their bellies pointing inward toward the supply core, while the supply core runs its own gravity toward its own center, sort of like a cylindrical planet, with the lower decks 'down' from the upper ones. That means that from any of the Dreadnaughts, 'down' is always toward the core, while from the core 'up' is always toward the nearest Dreadnaught."

"Strange approach," Mara commented.

Fel shrugged. "My guess is that they probably figured doing it any other way would mean attaching the connecting pylons in different places on each of the Dreadnaughts. This way, all the ships could be modified in exactly the same way, with two turbolift pylons connecting to the starboard belly, fore and aft, and the other two to the portside belly, fore and aft. It certainly doesn't matter to the crew; all the gravity changes are handled automatically as you travel from one place to another, with the turbolift cars rotating so that you're matched with your destination by the time you get there."

"So Formbi and the others are where, exactly?" Luke asked.

"Dreadnaught-Five," Fel said. "D-Five for short. The one we came into from the *Chaf Envoy* was D-Four."

"So that wasn't the primary command ship?"

Fel shook his head. "I assumed it would be, too, but the labels on the turbolift controls clearly showed we came in on either D-Four or D-Five. Given the ships' orientations, the one on the surface is definitely D-Four."

"I presume you are getting this information from the Outbound Flight data cards you have in your possession?" Drask asked.

"The data cards that *used* to be in my possession, yes," Fel corrected. "Fortunately, we'd studied the layout before they were stolen."

"They were *stolen*?" Drask asked, his eyes narrowing. "When?"

"While we were helping put out that fire just after we left Crustai," Fel said. "Whoever set it apparently did so as a diversion to get aboard our transport."

Drask looked at Luke and Mara, then back at Fel. "Why was I not informed?"

Mara sensed Fel's hesitation, and wondered if he would have either the honesty or the audacity to tell Drask that he hadn't been told because he was one of the suspects. She rather hoped he would; Drask's reaction would probably be very interesting.

To her mild disappointment, Fel went with the diplomatic answer instead. "It didn't seem likely the thief could be found regardless," he explained. "I thought we might have an advantage if the culprit didn't know we'd noticed the loss."

"What advantage did you expect to have?"

"I don't know, exactly," Fel conceded. "I just thought there might be one."

"You just *thought* there might be one." In a being of lesser inherent dignity, Mara reflected, Drask's words and tone might have sounded small-minded or even childish. But from a command officer of the Chiss, it came across as bitingly and righteously angry. A neat trick, that. "In the future, Commander Fel, you will not *think* when aboard a vessel of the Chiss Ascendancy. You will instead bring any and all concerns of this sort to the commanding officer at once. *He* will decide what thinking is to be done. Is that understood?"

"Completely, General," Fel said, his voice under careful control.

"Good," Drask said, not sounding particularly mollified. "Now. You will lead us to these alternative turbolifts so that we may rejoin Aristocra Chaf'orm'bintrano."

"Just a moment," Luke said. "Would the command ship have been designated D-One?"

"Right," Fel said.

"So with six Dreadnaughts, D-Four would be all the way on the far side of the circle from it?" Luke persisted.

"Right again," Fel said, his forehead wrinkling.

"Is this important at this precise moment?" Drask put in impatiently.

"It might be, yes," Luke told him. "Because, logically, D-One is where they should have been flying Outbound Flight from. So why is that ship the one that ended up farthest underground when they crash-landed?"

"Interesting question," Fel agreed thoughtfully. "They must have been having some serious control problems there at the end."

"Maybe," Luke said. "Or maybe they had unwanted help on the command deck."

"Indeed," Drask said, the impatience in his voice temporarily subdued by a touch of interest. "The criminals, perhaps?"

"Criminals?" Fel asked, blinking.

"There seems to be a makeshift prison back there," Luke said, gesturing aft. "No human or alien remains, though."

"Hmm," Fel said. "And considering the shape the Dread-naughts would have been in after the battle, they might well have been in the best position to get to the command deck and make trouble."

"Or we could have it completely backward," Mara warned. "Maybe the *prisoners* were the ones in command, and some-one else managed to get Outbound Flight flipped over this way trying to stop them."

"Interesting speculation," Drask said. The moment of in-terest had passed, and he was getting impatient again. "But this is all ancient history."

"Perhaps," Luke said. "But then, ancient history is why we're here, isn't it?"

"We must rejoin Aristocra Chaf'orm'bintrano," Drask in-sisted.

"We will," Luke promised. "But first, I want to go have a look at D-One. Anyone going with me?"

Mara looked around the group. From Fel's expression she could tell that he wanted to go, and she could sense definite interest from the four stormtroopers, as well.

But Drask's agitation was practically bouncing off the stacks of crates, and once again Fel's sense of diplomacy won out. "Thanks, but we'll wait for the second tour," he said, turning to Drask. "Whenever you're ready, General, we'll escort you to D-Five."

For a moment Drask's eyes bored into Luke's face, as if es-timating his chances of either talking him or ordering him out of going on what he clearly considered a time-wasting side trip. Apparently, he decided it wasn't worth trying. "Thank you, Commander," he said, turning back to face Fel. "You said there were three other turbolifts available?"

"Yes," Fel said. "Actually, the best approach would proba-bly be to go a little farther around the core and escort Luke and Mara to the turbolift they'll need to get to D-One. We can use the same one to get to D-Six, from which we can then travel to D-Five."

"It sounds as if that will be a longer trip than going di-rectly to D-Five," Drask pointed out.

"It will be, a little," Fel conceded. "But it's occurred to me that if Pressor's people are hiding any surprises we ought to know about, they'll most likely be on either D-One, D-Two, or D-Six."

"Why?"

"Because they're the three farthest underground, which means they have the best radiation shielding," Fel explained. "Luke and Mara will already be checking out D-One; if we at least take a look at D-Six on our way to D-Five, we'll have two of the three covered."

Drask hesitated, then nodded. "Very well," he said. "Provided you do not propose to search the entire Dreadnaught with only the six of us."

"We'll just take a quick look," Fel promised. "If they're using the other Dreadnaughts for anything at all, it should be obvious pretty quickly."

"Very well," Drask said again. "Lead on."

Fel nodded. "Stormtroopers: escort formation. This way, General."

CHAPTER 15

"THIS IS THE MAIN SCHOOL AREA," ULIAR SAID, POINTING across the corridor toward a room with a small plaque beside the door identifying it as AA-7 FIRE CONTROL ROOM. A neatly printed sign had been fastened to the wall above the plaque that read PRELIMINARY TIERS. "All the lower tiers are in the complex of rooms back there," he went on. "There's also a university of sorts two decks above us, up where the main scientific and technical sections of the ship were."

"Interesting," Jinzler said, looking at the door and wondering if he dared ask to go in and take a look. "What courses do you teach?"

"Everything we can, of course," Uliar said, half turning to look at Evlyn and her mother, walking silently behind Formbi. "This is actually Instructor Tabory's field of expertise. Instructor, would you care to elaborate?"

"Many of the records were lost in the Devastation, of course," Rosemari said. "Either destroyed or buried in the wreckage of D-One where we couldn't get to them."

She waved at the schoolroom door. "But the Survivors had fair amounts of skills and knowledge among them, so as soon as they could they set up a school to teach the children what they would need to know. In the lower tiers we teach history, science, reading, galactic languages, political science, and a few others—the usual curriculum of a Republic school back home. At the university level—though of course it's not a *real* university—we teach mechanics and electronics, higher mathematics, basic astrogation and starship operation, plus the sorts of things we'll need when we finally get out of here and settle down on a real world again."

"Ah," Jinzler said. "And you were trained as an instructor?"

She shrugged. "That's what I do now, but my actual training is in meteorology and music. I'm not very good at the latter, though." She smiled down at the girl beside her. "Evlyn's much better than I am. And of course, there are a *lot* of advanced maintenance classes."

"That being particularly important to our survival," Councilor Tarkosa added gruffly, glaring briefly at Rosemari. Apparently, her comment about leaving Outbound Flight wasn't sitting well with him. "Even with many of the old droids still functional, this ship still chews up a huge number of worker-hours in repairs and maintenance. And the droids need constant maintenance of their own."

Jinzler nodded. "What about basic life necessities?" he asked. "Food, water, and energy?"

"Fortunately, we have all of that in abundance," Uliar said. "The central storage core suffered only minor damage in the Devastation, and we were able to bring the D-Five and D-Six fusion generators back online before the emergency power supplies were exhausted."

"You speak as if you were there," Formbi suggested.

Uliar favored him with a somewhat brittle smile. "Yes, I was," he said. "I was twenty-two, in fact, when your people viciously attacked and destroyed us."

It took every bit of Jinzler's strength to keep his face from reacting. With all of Uliar's politeness and hospitality, and the almost homey atmosphere of the place as the inhabitants had fixed it up, he'd nearly forgotten what had actually happened here. Hearing Uliar's straightforward reminder had hit him harder than he would have expected. "Yes," Formbi murmured. "Though it was not the will of either the Nine Ruling Families or of the Chiss people that that happen."

"Well, it was the will of *some*one with blue skin and red eyes," Uliar said bluntly. "And I'm constrained to point out that even after all that, knowing that it had happened, you waited until now to come see what had become of us."

He peered closely at Formbi. "Or *is* this your first time here? Have you actually been watching us all along, just for your own amusement?"

"Not at all," Formbi said, his voice even. "We didn't even know this vessel had survived until a few handfuls of days ago. Even then, we had no reason to assume anyone had survived."

"Then why *did* you come?" Uliar countered. "Was it the ship itself you wanted? Secrets from the Republic you hoped to plunder?"

He turned his unblinking stare on Jinzler. "Or was it you and this so-called New Republic of yours? Were *you* the ones who wanted it?"

Jinzler shook his head. "We came solely from a desire to see the place where so many of our people had died," he said, trying to match Formbi's calm diplomatic tone.

"And to honor those who gave their lives defending our people," Bearsh spoke up from the rear.

"That's correct," Jinzler said. "No one here wants to take anything away from you."

Uliar smiled coldly. "No. Of course not."

The smile vanished. "At the very least I'm sure you didn't expect to find anyone aboard who still remembered," he said. "You see, *Ambassador* Jinzler, I recognize your name. I knew that other Jinzler, too, the one who deserted us at our time of greatest need. Who was she, a relative? Sister? Cousin?"

"She was my sister," Jinzler said, staring at him in disbelief. Lorana, desert these people in the middle of trouble? No—that had to be a mistake.

"Your sister," Uliar repeated, the darkness in his voice deepening. "Deeply beloved, of course, which is why you've come all this way to honor her memory." He crossed his arms across his chest defiantly. "Well, we *don't* honor her memory here, Ambassador. Are you still so eager to help us?"

Jinzler took a careful breath. "She wasn't beloved," he

said, fighting to control the trembling of emotion flowing into his voice. "At least, not by me."

Uliar lifted his eyebrows with polite skepticism. "No?"

"No." Jinzler looked the other man straight in the eye. "As a matter of fact, I hated her."

The statement seemed to throw Uliar completely off his stride. He blinked, then frowned; opened his mouth, then closed it again. "Of course you did," he said at last, clearly just to have something to say. He eyed Jinzler another moment, then turned resolutely back to Formbi. "The fact remains that it was your people who attacked us," he said, apparently trying to get back on course with his earlier tirade. "What do you and these Nine Ruling Families of yours intend to do about that?"

Formbi opened his mouth— "I'd like to see the school," Jinzler put in, suddenly tired of hearing Uliar talk. "As long as we're here anyway."

Again, Uliar seemed to falter. He looked at Jinzler, hesitated, then nodded. "Certainly," he said. "Instructor Tabory, perhaps you'd be kind enough to show the ambassador around?"

"Uh . . . sure," Rosemari said, her face puckering uncertainly. Jinzler's comment about his sister had apparently thrown her for a loop, too. "This way, Ambassador."

She turned and headed toward the door at a quick walk, her daughter beside her. Jinzler followed, fighting his way through the images and memories swirling around him . . .

"This is the second-tier classroom."

Jinzler blinked the images away, to find himself standing in a low-ceilinged room equipped with perhaps a dozen small desks arranged in a circle. In the center of the circle was a holoprojector showing a tree with three animals of various species standing beneath it. The children at the desks, four- and five-year-olds by the look of them, were busily scribbling away on their datapads while a young woman wandered around the outside of the circle silently inspecting their work.

"I see," Jinzler said, trying to generate some genuine interest in the proceedings. "Art class?"

"Art, plus elementary zoology and botany," she told him. "We combine disciplines and lessons as much as possible. The third-tier classroom is through here."

She led the way through an archway into another room with larger desks and no students or teachers. "Run out of thirders?" Jinzler asked.

"They must be on a field trip," she said, crossing over to a larger desk in the corner and peering down at a datapad lying there. "Yes; they're down in the nursery today learning about the proper care and feeding of babies."

"Sounds like fun," Jinzler commented. "And the art of proper changing, too, no doubt. You said *down*? I thought we were on the lowest deck."

"The nursery's on Six, the next Dreadnaught down," Pressor's voice said. Jinzler turned, vaguely surprised to see the Guardian walking behind him. Preoccupied with his memories, he hadn't even noticed the other follow them inside. "There's less solar radiation down there, so that's where all the pregnant women and those with children under three are housed."

"And their families, too, of course," Rosemari added. "We'd all move down there except that it suffered so much more damage in the battle that there's less usable space for people to live in. And besides, Director Uliar doesn't want us living too close to—"

"Rosemari," Pressor cut her off sharply.

Rosemari flushed. "Sorry."

"Sorry for what?" Jinzler asked.

"So, did you really want to see the school?" Pressor asked. "Or was that just an excuse to get away from Uliar and his ranting?"

Jinzler hesitated, studying Pressor's face. The man's eyes were hard, his expression set in pale stone. It would not, he decided suddenly, be a good idea to lie to this man. "Mostly the latter," he conceded. "He seems so . . . angry."

"Wouldn't you be?" Pressor countered. "The universe turned upside down, with everything you'd planned to do with your life suddenly cut off at the knees?"

"I suppose," Jinzler said. "Are he and the other two the last of the original survivors?"

"No, there are ten left," Pressor said. "But the other seven are old and weak and keep pretty much to themselves."

"Most of the fifty-seven Survivors were either injured in the attack or suffered badly in the months after Outbound Flight arrived here," Rosemari said. "It affected both their health and their life spans, which is why there are only ten left."

"We're talking about the adults, of course," Pressor added. "There were also several children like me who were alive during the Devastation but were too young to know what exactly was going on. We certainly didn't have any plans for our lives yet." His eyes bored into Jinzler. "Though of course, plans or otherwise, *our* lives were pretty well destroyed, too."

"Tell it to Aristocra Formbi," Jinzler advised, holding his gaze evenly. "*He's* the one accepting guilt for all this, not me."

To his mild surprise, Pressor actually smiled. "You're right," he said without apology. "I'm sure Uliar will remember to bring that up."

"Did you really hate your sister?" Evlyn asked.

Jinzler looked down at the girl. She was gazing up at him, her eyes steady, her face expressionless. "Yes," he said. "Does that frighten you?"

"Why should it frighten me?" she asked.

"Maybe you're wondering if I hate all Jedi," Jinzler suggested. "Maybe you're wondering if I hate *you*."

"No," Pressor bit out before Evlyn could answer. "Whatever you're thinking, stop it right now. There's absolutely nothing special about her."

Jinzler frowned. An unexpectedly harsh reaction, far more vehement than the comment deserved. "I just meant—"

"No," Pressor said, his voice softer and under better control now but just as firm. "You're imagining things. Leave it alone."

Jinzler looked at Evlyn; and in his mind's eye he saw her calmly leading them into the turbolift trap. Unafraid of armed alien strangers, as if she somehow knew they wouldn't shoot her the minute her back was turned.

And then stepping casually through the doorway with exquisitely precise timing as the trap was triggered.

He looked at Rosemari. "*Am* I imagining things?" he asked.

Rosemari sent a hooded look at her brother. "Jorad worries about things," she said obliquely.

"There's nothing to worry about," Jinzler assured her. "If she has Jedi abilities—"

"I said to let it alone," Pressor warned harshly. "She's not going to have that kind of life. I won't let her. Neither will Rosemari. You hear me?"

Jinzler swallowed. The Guardian, he suddenly noticed, had his hand wrapped around the grip of his blaster, and the knuckles were white. "I hear you," he said quietly. "But you're making a mistake."

"You just keep your mouth shut," Pressor said. His voice was still tight, but his gun hand seemed to have relaxed a bit. "You hear me?"

Jinzler sighed to himself. "Yes. I won't mention it again."

"Why did you hate your sister?" Evlyn asked.

Jinzler looked at her again, feeling a tightness in his chest like a logjam starting to break up. For more than half a century he'd kept these thoughts and feelings locked away in the dark privacy of his own mind, never speaking of them to family or friends or confidants. The closest he'd ever come to even hinting at them before today had been his admission to Luke and Mara that he and Lorana hadn't parted on good terms.

Perhaps he'd kept all of it in too long.

"She was my older sister," he said. "Third of four children, if you care. I was the youngest. We lived on Coruscant, pretty much in the shadow of the Jedi Temple. My parents worked there, in fact, as maintenance engineers on the electrical equipment."

His gaze drifted away from his audience to one of the empty desks, where a spare datapad was lying. "My parents adored Jedi," he said, the words coming out with difficulty. "Adored them, honored them—practically worshiped them, in fact."

"Did the Jedi return the affection?" Pressor asked.

Jinzler snorted. "What makes you think the grand exalted guardians of the Republic even noticed a couple of lowly workers scurrying around beneath their feet?" He shook his head. "Of course not. They had better things to do with their time.

"But that didn't matter to my parents. They still loved the Jedi, and they thought the greatest thing in the universe would be if they could have a Jedi child of their own. As soon as each of their children was old enough, they hustled us over there and had them run us through the tests."

"Was your sister the only one who made it?" Rosemari asked.

Jinzler nodded. "Right at ten months," he said, his throat aching. "It was the happiest day of my parents' life."

"How old were you when that happened?" Evlyn asked.

"I wasn't even born yet," Jinzler said. "Parents weren't allowed to even see their children once they'd been taken into the Temple, and my parents lost their jobs. Still, they would hang around outside and finagle a glimpse of her every once in a while as she passed by. I was four when I first saw her."

"The same age I was when I first met her," Pressor murmured.

Jinzler blinked. "You remember her?"

"Of course," Pressor said, sounding surprised that he would even have to ask. "Jedi Lorana, we called her. What, I look too young to you?"

"No, of course not," Jinzler said. "It's just that so much has happened since then that it seems like . . . you know. So what did you think of her?"

Pressor shrugged, too casually. "She seemed nice enough," he said, his voice guarded. "At least, for a Jedi. I didn't know any of them very well, of course."

"Yes, I suppose she could have become a nice person by then," Jinzler said, and immediately regretted it. "No, that's not fair," he amended. "She was probably just as nice when she was six. I just . . . I suppose I wasn't in a position to notice."

"Let me guess," Pressor said. "You'd already failed your own test."

"Very good," Jinzler said sourly. "My parents never said anything about it, but I knew without asking that they were disappointed. Anyway, when I was four they brought me to the Temple. The Jedi were coming out for some kind of public holiday. We waited and waited."

He took a deep breath. "And then, finally, there she was."

He closed his eyes, a whole flood of hated memories sweeping back through him. The rustling of Lorana's robes as she walked by them, a tall Jedi striding along watchfully beside her; the sudden tight grip of his mother's hands on his shoulders as she bent down and whispered Lorana's name in his ear.

"They were proud of her," he went on in a low voice. "So very proud of her."

"I take it you weren't impressed?" Pressor asked.

Jinzler shrugged. "She was six. I was four. How impressed should I have been?"

"What happened?" Rosemari asked. "Did she talk to you?"

"No," Jinzler told her. "The Jedi who was with her spotted us, and leaned over to say something. She looked in our direction, hesitated a second, and then the two of them turned and headed off. She never even got within ten meters of us."

"That must have been disappointing," Rosemari murmured.

"You'd think so, wouldn't you?" Jinzler said, hearing the bitterness in his voice. "But not with *my* parents. Even as she disappeared into the crowd of Jedi I could feel them practically swimming in love and respect and adoration. None of it, of course, directed at me."

"But they loved you, too, didn't they?" Evlyn asked, her voice low and earnest. "I mean . . . they must have loved you, too."

Even after all these years, Jinzler's throat ached at the memories. "I don't know," he told her quietly. "I'm sure they—I think they tried. But the whole time I was growing up it was clear that Lorana was the real center of their universe. She wasn't even there, but she was still their center. They talked about her all the time, held her up as an example of what people could make of their lives, practically made a shrine to her in a corner of the conversation room. I can't even count the number of times a scolding included the words *not something your sister Lorana would ever do* somewhere in the middle of it."

"Setting a standard none of the rest of you could ever live up to," Rosemari said.

"Not a chance in the galaxy," Jinzler agreed tiredly. "I tried, you know. I went into my father's own field—electronics—and pushed myself until I'd gone farther than he'd ever made it. Farther than he'd ever hoped to go. Droid repair and pattern design, starship electronics maintenance, comm equipment architecture and repair—"

"And politics?" Evlyn murmured.

Jinzler looked down at her, startled. She was gazing at him with a disturbingly knowing look.

Abruptly, he got it. *Ambassador* Jinzler. In the rush of ache and memory and old bitterness he'd completely forgotten the role he was playing here. "I tried as hard as I could to make myself into someone they could love as much as her," he said, wrenching himself out of his meanderings and back to the point. "And of course, they said they were proud of me and of what I'd done. But I could see in their eyes that I still didn't measure up. Not to Lorana's standards."

"Did you ever see her again?" Rosemari asked. "Lorana, I mean."

"I saw her a couple more times at the Temple," Jinzler told her. "Always at a distance, of course. Then we met just before Outbound Flight left the Republic." He looked away. "I don't want to talk about that."

For a long moment no one spoke. Jinzler stared at the empty classroom, watching the memories still parading themselves in front of his eyes, wondering why exactly he'd just bared his soul to a trio of total strangers that way. He must be getting old.

It was Pressor who eventually broke the silence. "We should get back to the others," he said, his voice sounding odd. "Uliar's suspicious enough of us as it is. We don't want him to think we're planning some conspiracy against him."

Jinzler took a deep breath, willing the ghosts of the past to go away. The ghosts, as usual, ignored him. "Yes," he said. "Of course."

THEY RETRACED THEIR STEPS THROUGH THE CLASSROOMS, Rosemari leading the way with Evlyn beside her. Not held quite so closely to her side, Pressor noted as he fell in behind Jinzler like a good Peacekeeper should. Apparently, his sister didn't feel quite as nervous about their visitor as she had a few minutes ago.

As for Pressor himself, he didn't know what to think anymore. He'd been fully prepared to hate Jinzler and the others, or at the very least to be extremely distrustful of them, their words, and their motives.

But now, all that nice convenient caution had been thrown for a twist. True, Jinzler's story just now could have been a complete lie, a performance carefully calculated to lull suspicions and evoke sympathy. But Pressor didn't think so. He'd always been good at reading people, and something about Jinzler's revelation had struck him as genuine.

Still, that didn't necessarily mean anything as far as the rest of the group was concerned. He'd caught the subtle hint in Evlyn's question about politics; clearly, Jinzler was no ambassador, or at least nobody who'd been officially sanctioned in that post. Either he was part of some complicated plot, which was seeming less and less likely, or else he'd wormed his way into this expedition under false pretenses. Either way, the logical conclusion was that the chief Chiss, Formbi, was the one in actual charge here, and so far Pressor hadn't been able to read him at all. Hopefully, Uliar was making some progress on that front. The outer school door slid open, and Rosemari stepped out into the corridor—

And nearly collided with Trilli as he shot past at a fast jog.

"Sorry," the Peacekeeper muttered, managing to avoid running them down. He caught sight of Pressor and came to an abrupt halt. "Jorad, I need to talk to you," he said.

Pressor glanced at Jinzler. Letting the pseudo-ambassador wander around alone would not be a good idea, he knew. But the look in Trilli's eyes was one that demanded immediate attention, and in private. "Rosemari, will you escort the ambassador to the meeting chamber?" he asked his sister. "I'll be along in a minute."

"Certainly," Rosemari said. "This way, Ambassador." Walking side by side, she, Evlyn, and Jinzler headed down the corridor.

"What is it?" Pressor asked when he judged the group far enough out of earshot.

"I went to lock down the turbolift controls like you said," Trilli said, his voice tight. "The other two trap cars—Two and Six—aren't midtube anymore."

Pressor felt his stomach tighten. "You mean they—? No, that's impossible. We'd have heard the crash."

"I'd sure think so," Trilli agreed. "But if the cars aren't there, and they didn't smash themselves to a group pulp, it means the Jedi and Imperials somehow ungimmicked them and got out."

Pressor hissed softly between his teeth. This was not good. This was *very* not good. "All right," he said slowly. "They didn't come down here—there are enough people wandering around that we'd surely have heard about it if they had. That means they either went back up to Four, or else they're down in the storage core. Could you tell where the cars ended up?"

Trilli shook his head. "We messed up all the positioning sensors when we rewired the cars way back when. We'd have to physically go in there and see."

"Yeah," Pressor said. "Okay, go scare up a couple of maintenance droids and send them into the shaft, one in each direction. Then get hold of Bels and Amberson and have them lock down all access from Four. If they went up, they're probably planning to come back with reinforcements."

"And if they went down?"

Pressor grimaced. From the supply core, the intruders would have access to both the main colony here on Five as well as the nursery on Six. And, of course—

"You think they know about Quarantine?" Trilli asked, echoing Pressor's own thought.

"I don't know how they could," Pressor said. "But they're Jedi. Who knows what they know?"

"Well, we sure as vacuum can't let them get back there," Trilli warned darkly. "If they find those people—worse, if they spring them . . ." He shook his head.

"Right," Pressor said grimly. "Who's on Quarantine duty?"

"Perry and Quinze," Trilli said. "You want me to send reinforcements?"

Pressor snorted. "Like who?"

"Yeah," Trilli said with a sigh. "We don't exactly have an army here, do we?"

"Hardly," Pressor agreed, frowning back over Trilli's shoulder. In the distance, in the direction of the forward turbolift lobby, some of the lights seemed to have gone off. Odd. "About all we can do is warn them. Better alert the maintenance crews to be on the lookout, too. Wired comms only on those; I want the comlink jamming kept in place for now."

"Right," Trilli said. "This could get ugly, Jorad."

Pressor looked the other way down the corridor, where glimpses of his sister and niece and Jinzler could still be seen through colonists going about their business. "Yes," he said. "I know."

CHAPTER 16

THE LAST TEN METERS OF THE TURBOLIFT PYLON LEADING to the command Dreadnaught were crushed and twisted, as if that part of the pylon had been hit with a powerful impact. The final two meters of that, in addition, were blocked by what seemed to be the remains of a car that had been caught in the wrong place at the wrong time. Even with lightsabers, it was a delicate task to cut enough of it away to get through.

"Finally," Mara said as she sliced through one last section of car wall to reveal the tube doors, as mangled and distorted as the tube itself. "Maybe we should have gone aft and tried the pylon back there."

"I doubt it would have been any faster," Luke said, stepping forward and carefully sniffing the air drifting in through the slightly open door. It smelled dank and stale, but otherwise livable. The door markings were upside down, he noted, which meant that the turbolift car hadn't made the usual rotation as it arrived, and D-1's gravity wasn't functioning. If the gravity was off, the rest of the environmental system probably was, too, with the air he was smelling just the leakage from the rest of the Outbound Flight complex. They would have to make sure they didn't get oxygen-starved. "Don't forget all the debris we had to wade through when we first came in up on D-Four," he reminded her as he stepped back and gestured in invitation toward the doors. "Thrawn probably made even more of a mess of the turbolaser and shield sections on this one."

"I suppose." With deft flicks of her lightsaber, Mara carved an opening through the door. "Shall we?"

It wasn't as bad as Luke had expected, at least as far as basic travel difficulties were concerned. It was strange to walk along the ceiling with the deck above them, and of course the planetoid's own gravity was far weaker than what they were used to, but that in itself didn't present any particular problems. The bulkheads and floors were horrendously crumpled and twisted, but there was relatively little actual debris lying around to contend with. Occasionally they had to use their lightsabers to clear away a support strut that was blocking a doorway, and twice they had to use the Force to move a wayward console that had broken away from its connections and was lying, dust-covered, across their path. But most of the obstacles were easily dealt with, and a handful of the permlights had survived to supplement the illumination from their glow rods.

The debris itself wasn't the tough part. The tough part was the bodies.

Not really bodies, of course, at least not the sort Luke had seen in the aftermath of the many battles he'd been through in his lifetime. After five decades, there was little left but piles of bones and scraps of clothing to show where someone had fallen. Sometimes he could see evidence of how death had come: severely broken skulls from flying equipment, or pulverized bone showing where a hit from a laser or missile blast had turned part of the inner hull into deadly shrapnel.

Most of the time, though, the remains showed no indication of what had happened. Those crewers, most likely, had either died of suffocation or from the impact when the Dreadnaught had slammed into the gravel pile where Outbound Flight now lay.

"You can see where the hull's been repaired," Mara commented as they picked their way forward toward the command deck. "See the weld marks?"

Luke looked where she was pointing her glow rod. The marks were very professional, precisely following the jagged hull cracks. "Repair droids?"

"Definitely," Mara agreed. "The attack must have smashed the hull in enough places to bypass the blast doors and emergency compartmentalization system, which then suffocated any of the crew and passengers still alive. But it didn't put all the droids out of commission, and they automatically began emergency repairs. By the time anyone else got here, enough of the ship was airtight again for them to fly it."

The damage seemed to increase as they moved forward. So did the number of bones. "The crew must have been trying to escape up here as Thrawn took out the turbolaser and shield blisters," Mara said as Luke sliced open yet another frozen blast door. "There normally wouldn't have been this many people this far forward."

"Especially since most of the ones on duty would have been farther forward on the command deck," Luke agreed, eyeing her closely. "How are you doing?"

"I'm all right," she said. "Why? Shouldn't I be?"

"I just wondered," he said. "I mean, down here with more . . ."

"With more evidence of what Thrawn and Palpatine did to these people?"

Luke winced. "Something like that."

"Oddly enough, I'm all right," Mara said, her eyes drifting around the room. "I guess I must have already worked through all that up above." She gestured toward an upside-down arch ahead of them, a doorway partially blocked by a half-closed blast door. "Looks like we're getting near the end of the line."

"I think you're right." Slipping through the opening, Luke looked around. It was a large room, with a lot of scattered chairs and broken consoles that had once apparently been lined up in neat rows, all of it covered with the same thick layer of dust that existed everywhere down here. "Definitely the monitor anteroom," he identified it as Mara joined him. "That would put the bridge just ahead, through that other archway in the middle of the far wall."

"What's left of it, anyway," Mara said, looking around. "It may be my imagination, but it looks like there's less actual battle damage here."

"It does, doesn't it," Luke agreed, frowning. She was right:

aside from a few of the droid-repaired fissures, most of the destruction seemed to be impact damage. "Either it happened when Outbound Flight plowed into this rock pile, or else Thrawn did some ship ramming during the battle."

"Thrawn, or someone else," Mara said. "Don't forget that according to Bearsh, the Vagaari were also at that battle."

"True." Luke surveyed the wreckage, a strange feeling of emptiness flowing into him. "I'd hoped we'd be able to find some intact records down here. Something about the Jedi of that time, maybe some details about how they'd been organized. But I can't see how anything like that could have survived."

"Doesn't look promising, does it?" Mara said. "Still, as long as we're here, we might as well go the whole way. You said that was the door to the bridge?"

"Should be," Luke said, ducking under a section of collapsed deck and stepping over to the archway and the warped metal door blocking it. Igniting his lightsaber, he sliced it open.

It was indeed the bridge, very much as he remembered from his brief time aboard the *Katana* some thirteen years before. Except, of course, that this particular bridge was littered with bones and broken consoles and ankle-deep in powdery dust.

And it was only about half as long as the other one had been.

"Now, *that's* impressive," Mara said. "I don't think I've ever even heard of a ship being crushed this badly, let alone seen it. They must have been really scorching space when they hit."

"Yes," Luke murmured. "Question is, whose idea was it to hit this hard?"

"You still thinking about those prisoners in the storage core?"

"Off and on," Luke said, frowning toward the crushed bow. There was something glinting dully over there amid the shards of the shattered observation bubble, something that didn't seem to fit with the rest of the wreckage they'd seen.

"We know they escaped somehow," he continued, stepping carefully through the debris, wincing as something snapped beneath his boot. "We also know that there were eighteen Jedi aboard Outbound Flight, and yet Thrawn was still able to beat them. I keep wondering if there's some connection."

"It could be that Thrawn had a bigger fleet than anyone wants to admit," Mara suggested, leaning over one of the consoles for a closer look.

"Formbi said it was just his picket force," Luke reminded her.

"Formbi is also lugging around about two bantha-weights of corporate Chiss guilt over the whole incident," Mara countered, moving on to the next console. "Maybe there was more official Chiss involvement than he's letting on."

"Could be," Luke said, squatting down among the transparisteel shards. There it was. Gingerly, he reached into the debris and got a grip on it.

He froze. Not *it*; *them*. There were two objects buried in the rubble, both archaic in design and yet instantly recognizable as they lay among two distinct sets of broken bones.

Mara picked up instantly on his emotional reaction. "What is it?" she asked, abandoning her survey and coming to his side.

"Exhibit One," Luke said, lifting up a dented cylinder that could only be a lightsaber. "And," he added quietly, holding up a tarnished, dented hand weapon, "Exhibit Two."

Mara inhaled sharply. "Is that what I think it is?"

"I think so," Luke told her, standing up and turning the weapon over in his hand. "It's a few decades out of date, but the style is unmistakable.

"It's a Chiss charric."

FOR A MOMENT NEITHER OF THEM SPOKE. THEN, STILL WORD-lessly, Mara held out her hand. Luke placed the unknown weapon in it, and for another minute she studied it in silence. "Yes," she said at last. "You can see Chiss lettering on it. It's a charric, all right."

"So what's it doing here?" Luke asked. "Drask told us Thrawn never sent a landing party aboard."

"And how exactly would Drask know whether he did or didn't?" Mara pointed out. "He wasn't there. Was he?"

"Not that I've heard," Luke admitted, taking the charric back from her. An odd thought was starting to take shape around the edges of his mind . . .

"Not much we can tell from the skeleton, either," Mara commented, squatting down and gently touching one of the bones the charric had been lying beside. "Humanoid, but definitely not human. That covers a lot of species, unfortunately."

"Including the Chiss," Luke said. "Tell me, Mara. You spent a lot of time talking to the Chiss on the trip here. Did any of them ever say they'd actually *seen* any of the Vagaari? Or seen holos of a Vagaari, or even heard a description of one?"

Mara frowned, and he could sense her stretching to the Force as she searched her memory. "No," she said. "In fact, I remember Formbi specifically saying they hadn't been seen anywhere in the region since Outbound Flight. Though to be fair, I never actually asked anyone that particular question."

"Well, I *did* ask Bearsh once," Luke said. "None of his generation of Geroons ever saw a Vagaari, either."

"Which would make sense if they all disappeared fifty years ago," Mara pointed out. "Are you going anywhere special with this?"

"The Chiss were at Outbound Flight," Luke said. "According to Bearsh and Formbi, so were the Vagaari."

He lifted his eyebrows. "What if they were in fact the same people?"

Mara blinked. "Are you suggesting the Chiss *are* the Vagaari?"

"Why not?" Luke asked. "Or at least, some particular group of Chiss were. We both know how devious and creative Thrawn was. Would it have been that hard for him to invent a completely fictitious race for his own purposes?"

"Probably wouldn't have been more than a lazy afternoon's work for him," she conceded. "But why would he do that?"

"*That's* the real question, isn't it?" Luke conceded. "I don't know. I just find it oddly suspicious that when Outbound Flight disappeared, so did the Vagaari."

"Mm," Mara murmured, frowning off into infinity. "Maybe we should sit Formbi down in a quiet corner somewhere when we get back to the rest of the group. It's about time he was straight with us about what's going on."

"It's well past time," Luke said. "And we'll need to get him off alone. I don't think we'll want Drask listening in."

"That goes without saying." Mara gestured to the dusty weapons in his hands. "Either of those still work?"

"I don't know." Aiming at an empty spot across the room, Luke squeezed the charric's firing stud.

Nothing happened. "Dead as Honoghr," he said, sticking it into his belt. Pointing the lightsaber away from him, he touched the activator.

The weapon's *snap-hiss* sounded weak and rather asthmatic. But the green blade that blazed out appeared functional enough. "Whoever built this built it to last," he commented, closing it down and peering more closely at it. "I wonder if it was C'baoth's."

"C'baoth's?"

"He was apparently the senior Jedi Master on the expedition," Luke reminded her. "This is probably where he would have been during the attack. And look." He pointed to the activator. "See this? Looks like some kind of gem."

"You're right," Mara said, leaning toward him for a closer look. "An amethyst, I think."

"I'll take your word for it," Luke said, sliding the lightsaber into his belt beside the charric. "Come on, let's finish and get back upstairs. That talk with Formbi is starting to sound more and more interesting."

THE TURBOLIFT CREAKED AND MOANED AS IT ARRIVED AT Dreadnaught-6, but it settled into place with only a couple of small bumps. "They've definitely been using this car," Fel commented.

"As we had already concluded below," Drask said pointedly.

With an effort, Fel held his tongue. *Yes*, Drask had noticed that the core's stack of supplies near this particular turbolift tube had been systematically raided; and, *yes*, Fel had agreed then with the general's conclusion that this probably meant at least part of D-6 was in use. But it didn't mean extra evidence shouldn't be noted and commented upon.

With a little more creaking, the doors slid open. Grappler, at point, stepped out into the corridor, his helmet turning back and forth as he scanned the area. "Clear," he reported, moving aside to let the others emerge. "Which way, Commander?"

"The most direct path to D-Five, of course," Drask growled before Fel could answer. "That is, after all, our chief purpose in being down here."

With an effort, Fel controlled his temper. Drask had been nothing but a blue-skinned lump of impatience and disapproval since he'd left Luke and Mara and linked up with the Imperials. Maybe, he thought unkindly, that was why the two Jedi had been so eager to go down to D-1 and foist him off on the Imperials. "We'll get to D-Five, General," he said with all the patience he could scrape together. "But as long as we're here, it wouldn't hurt to do a little looking around."

Drask rumbled something deep in his throat. "You do not understand," he bit out.

Fel looked aft along the corridor, trying to ignore him. The game of diplomacy, he decided, was rapidly losing whatever faint charm it once might have possessed. As soon as he reasonably could, he would indeed get back to the others, turn Drask back over to Formbi, and be done with him.

In the distance, somewhere beyond this particular Dreadnaught's fleet tactical room, he could see a glow that seemed stronger than anything permlights could put out. "Looks like the local civilization is back that way," he said, pointing. "Stormtroopers?"

There was a short pause as the stormtroopers turned their sensors in that direction. "Infrared and gas-spectrum analysis readings indicate approximately thirty to forty humans," Grappler reported.

"Picking up voices, too," Cloud added. "The pitch would suggest mostly females and infants."

Fel frowned. *Infants?* "Let's take a look."

Drask rumbled again. "Commander Fel—"

"We're going to take a look, General," Fel said shortly, sending the Chiss's glare right back at him. "If you choose to argue with me every third or fourth step, it's going to take a lot longer."

"Very well, Commander," Drask said, his eyes blazing. "As you wish. You *are* in command of this unit, after all."

And don't you forget it. Again leaving the words unsaid, Fel gestured the 501st forward.

They headed down the corridor, Grappler in the lead, Cloud and Shadow behind him, Watchman bringing up the rear behind Fel and Drask. The general maintained a stony silence, and possibly because of that they hadn't gone more than a handful of steps before Fel began to hear the sounds of infant squeals and gurgles and female conversation. A few steps after that, and he was able to see the light he'd noticed spilling gently out into the corridor from a large room he tentatively identified as the forward sensor analysis complex. "Easy, everyone," he murmured as Grappler neared the archway leading into the room. "We don't want to scare them. Better let me go first."

Grappler nodded, and the three stormtroopers in the lead slowed their pace and moved apart. Fel passed through the middle of the formation; to his annoyance, Drask stayed right at his side. "General—"

"If you pause to argue, this will take longer," Drask countered. "Let us finish and go to D-Five."

Fel squeezed his hand into a fist. Having a stranger drop in on unsuspecting women and children would be bad enough; having two strangers, one of them a glowing-eyed alien, would be an order of magnitude worse.

But there was a set to Drask's jaw implying that further argument would be a waste of time. Sighing to himself, Fel stepped into the archway.

Even at first glance it was clear why Cloud had picked up only female and infant voices: by its furnishings and decor, the room was clearly a large and well-equipped nursery. Perhaps twenty women were visible in the nearer section, sitting on comfortable-looking couches and chairs, some of them clearly pregnant, the rest just as clearly monitoring the activities of a herd of infants, crawlers, and toddlers. There were also about a dozen older children in the seven-to-eight-year-old range, that group standing in a half circle around another woman as if listening to a story or a lesson. He had just enough time to see every eye turn to him, and to catch the startled or frightened expressions on several of the women—

The attack came as a stuttering burst of full-auto blaster-fire from somewhere farther aft, a screaming volley of red bolts sizzling and spattering across the stormtroopers' armor. Instinctively, Fel ducked down, grabbing for Drask's arm only to find that the general's combat reflexes were better honed than Fel's and had already put him flat on the deck. The stormtroopers' reactions were just as quick: Watchman shouted something Fel didn't catch, and suddenly a set of green blaster bolts was scorching the air in the other direction.

"Cease fire!" Fel shouted over the din. "Stormtroopers: cease fire!"

"No!" Drask barked. "Lay down protective fire and retreat to the fleet tactical room. Fel, come."

Before Fel could even form a protest, Drask had the two of them back on their feet, rapidly retreating behind the stormtroopers' moving defensive screen. They reached the fleet tactical room, and with a quick look inside Drask shoved Fel through the doorway and jumped in after him. A second later, with one final burst of covering fire, the four stormtroopers were inside as well.

"Report," Fel ordered, feeling like an idiot and hoping the effects of the exertion would adequately cover his embarrassment. Getting shot at was hardly a new experience for him, but usually he was in the cockpit of a clawcraft at those times, with a familiar collection of sensors, shields, and weapons at his fingertips. Being attacked in dress uniform had startled him more than he would have expected. "Injuries?"

"No armor damage," Watchman reported. "Those bolts were weaker than standard."

"Comes of using the same Tibanna gas reserves for fifty years, I guess," Fel said. "All right, I guess that's that. Let's see if we can get back to the turbolift without getting ourselves blasted."

"No," Drask said. "We go back."

Fel felt his jaw drop a couple of centimeters. "What are you talking about? We're here to help these people, not trade shots with them."

Drask eyed him curiously. "Interesting," he said. "You have more restraint than I would have expected from one trained under Syndic Mitth'raw'nuruodo's authority." He gestured down the corridor. "But in this particular situation, such restraint is inappropriate. Those warriors are protecting something. I wish to learn what it is."

Fel took a deep breath, his opinion of Drask's soldiering skills dropping a few notches. "They were protecting that nursery," he said, as if explaining it to a small child. "Women and children. Remember?"

"No," Drask said. "If that had been their purpose, they would have been positioned between the turbolift and that room."

"Maybe there aren't any good defensive positions this far forward."

"We passed at least three of them," Drask countered. "I am a ground soldier, Commander. Such things are my business."

"He's right, Commander," Watchman put in. "Actually, for that matter, the position they were firing from wasn't very secure. Best guess is that they were on their way forward from somewhere else when they ran into us."

Fel stepped to the doorway and hooked a cautious eye

around it. Beyond the open nursery door, he could see two figures jump-stopping toward them along the corridor. "In fact, I would suspect they are right now taking advantage of the lull to move to better positions closer to us," Drask said from behind him.

"They're coming, all right," Fel confirmed, his estimation of Drask reluctantly returning to its previous level. "Looks like just two of them."

"Then let us move quickly," Drask urged. "If we hesitate too long before launching a counterattack, the subsequent battle will take place near the nursery and risk injury to the women and children. That is unacceptable."

"I thought launching attacks in general was unacceptable to the Chiss," Fel muttered under his breath as he gestured the stormtroopers forward.

"They fired first," Drask reminded him coolly. "They are now fair game. Do we go?"

Fel clenched his teeth. "We go," he confirmed. "Watchman? Clear out those snipers. Try to do it without killing them."

"Copy, Commander," the stormtrooper said promptly. "Grappler, Shadow, Cloud: Overrun Pattern Three. Go."

Grappler touched his fingertips to his helmet in acknowledgment and swung halfway out into the corridor, dropping onto one knee and opening up with his BlasTech on full auto. The other two stormtroopers gave the pattern half a second to settle in, then ducked out into the corridor and charged out toward the waiting enemy, Shadow adding his own blaster-fire to the barrage.

Fel held his breath. Five seconds later came the distinctive sputtering sizzle of a stun blast, and the firing abruptly ceased.

"All clear," Grappler announced, getting to his feet and disappearing down the corridor toward his comrades.

Silently, Fel let out the breath he'd been holding. He'd worked with units of the 501st on several occasions, but never under actual combat conditions. This was going to be an educational experience. "Let's go, General."

The women and children, he noted as they passed the nursery, had retreated to the farthest part of the room and were standing huddled together, some of them visibly trembling. He considered pausing to try to reassure them, decided that anything he could say or do would only scare them more, and continued on without breaking stride.

The two gunners were sprawled on the floor as he and the others reached the spot. Shadow was kneeling beside them, checking for the heart palpitations that sometimes occurred with stun blasts, while Cloud stood guard with his BlasTech pointed aft down the corridor. "They'll be all right," Shadow reported as he stood up. "Shall I leave them their weapons?"

Fel looked down at the antique blasters lying beside the sleeping men. Disarming the enemy was standard procedure, of course. But he hadn't come here to fight these people, and there was a chance that what had just happened had been some kind of misunderstanding. "Just put them up there," he ordered, pointing to a makeshift ledge a meter and a half above the deck that was supporting some reworked cable connections. "We don't want some kid from the nursery finding them."

"Yes, sir."

He watched as the stormtrooper complied, fully expecting Drask to object to his decision. But the Chiss said nothing. "Cloud?"

"I'm not picking up anyone else nearby," the stormtrooper reported. "There's a lot of the same sort of structural damage back there that we ran into on D-Four, though, and that could be masking them."

"Not to mention providing them with lots of choices for an ambush position," Fel said.

"Yes, sir," Watchman agreed. "Shall we go clean it out?"

Fel very much wanted to say yes. Antique weapons or not, those blaster bolts could still do considerable damage to an unarmored body if they connected. Staying here while the 501st did all the dangerous work made a lot of tactical sense.

But he couldn't do that. Not with Drask standing there listening. "We'll go together," he told Watchman.

"Yes, sir," the other said. "Stormtroopers: escort formation. Move out."

THE COUNCIL MEETING CHAMBER WAS SIMPLER THAN JINZLER had expected it to be. There was a long rectangular table in the center ringed by a dozen padded wire-mesh chairs, with another eight or nine chairs lined up against each of the two side walls. In each corner of the room were a pair of pedestals with oddly shaped sculptures sitting on them, clearly handmade, while a few more pieces of local art hung on the walls.

Uliar was seated at the far end of the table, flanked on one side by Councilor Tarkosa and on the other by Councilor Keely. Facing them from the other end of the table, the end nearest the door, were Formbi, Feesa, and Bearsh, the latter hunched over in his seat like someone fighting a losing battle with disillusionment. The other three Geroons were seated together in the chairs along the left-hand wall, looking equally dejected, while the three Chiss warriors sat stiffly against the wall to the right. Each of the two latter groups had one of Pressor's Peacekeepers standing watch beside its row.

The conversation, or perhaps more accurately the confrontation, was already under way as the door wheezed open and Jinzler, Rosemari, and Evlyn stepped into the room. "Not good enough, Aristocra Formbi," Uliar was saying. "The actions of your people have cost us fifty years of exile and deprivation, not to mention the loss of nearly fifty thousand of our companions' lives. If you genuinely wish to atone for this atrocity, you'll need to do far more than that."

He looked up at Jinzler. "Ah—Ambassador," he greeted him gravely, gesturing to the chair beside Feesa. "Did you enjoy your tour?"

"Yes, thank you," Jinzler said, moving reluctantly forward. This looked like a discussion he really didn't want to get involved in, and for a moment he wondered if he should try to come up with another excuse to get out of it.

But the door had already slid shut behind him, and the

others were all looking at him with varying degrees of expectation. He was apparently in for the duration.

So, it appeared, were Rosemari and Evlyn. Out of the corner of his eye he saw one of the Geroons bound eagerly from his chair and smilingly usher the mother and daughter to chairs beside the Chiss warriors. Uliar's forehead wrinkled dangerously at that, but he apparently decided it wasn't worth making an issue of. "We were just discussing the extent of reparations the Chiss government will be providing in contrition for the Devastation," he said instead.

"And as I've already explained, I cannot make the sort of agreement you seek," Formbi said. "I have no instructions or mandate for the situation we find ourselves in here. I can offer a certain level of monetary compensation from my own family's resources, the amount of which I've already stated. But I can make no promise that will bind the other families."

"On the other hand, the Nine Ruling Families *had* agreed to turn Outbound Flight's remains over to the New Republic," Jinzler pointed out as he sat down beside Feesa. "It shouldn't be stretching that offer too much to include returning all the Colonists, as well."

"And what makes you think we want to return to that part of the galaxy?" Uliar asked. "What makes you think we want anything to do with you *or* your New Republic?"

"Then what *do* you want?" Jinzler asked.

"In a perfect world, we'd want the slow executions of everyone involved with what was done to us," Tarkosa bit out. "But Aristocra Formbi informs us that most of them are unfortunately already dead. So we'll settle for a ship."

Jinzler blinked. "A ship?"

"Not just any ship, of course," Uliar cautioned. "We want a ship at least as big as one of our Dreadnaughts—no, make that twice as big—equipped with the best and most modern equipment available."

"And weapons," Keely murmured, his eyes staring darkly at something in the table apparently only he could see. "Lots of weapons."

From Jinzler's belt came a soft chirp, the same odd sound

he'd heard back in the turbolift foyer just after they'd been brought down here. He glanced at Bearsh across the table, but if the Geroon's comlink had made any such noise he wasn't reacting to it.

"Yes," Uliar agreed. "Plenty of weapons and defenses."

"You already have most of that list," Formbi reminded him. "According to Guardian Pressor, the uppermost Dreadnaught has been made capable of flight."

"Capable of flight, yes," Tarkosa said. "Capable of what we need, no."

"What *do* you need, then?" Formbi asked. "What exactly do you want with this new ship?"

"To fulfill our mission, of course," Tarkosa said. "Fifty years ago, we were commissioned to travel through the Unknown Regions to the edge of the galaxy and beyond in a search for new life and new worlds."

He glared at Formbi from beneath his bushy eyebrows. "The Chiss denied us that opportunity. We will therefore make it for ourselves."

Jinzler threw a startled look at Formbi. The Aristocra's face was settled in diplomatic neutral, but Jinzler could see a hint of surprise in his glowing eyes. "That's a rather ambitious project, Director," he said carefully, turning back to Uliar. "Especially for a group as small as yours."

"And what if your people don't wish to go?" Formbi added.

"The people will come," Keely said, his eyes still focused on the table. "If we lead them, they will follow. All of them."

"Of course," Jinzler said, a shiver running up his back. Was the councilor going senile? Or had the long exile driven him completely insane? "We will, of course, need to consult with our governments," he said aloud, deciding the best approach right now would be to stall and hope he didn't improvise himself into a corner. "We'll need to discuss how to locate and deliver a ship that will suit your needs."

"Good," Uliar said, leaning back in his seat. "Go ahead. We'll wait."

"It's not quite that simple," Formbi put in. "First of all—"

"Of course, of course." Uliar lifted a hand in an imperious gesture toward the young man standing beside the Chiss. "Peacekeeper Oliet? You may turn off the jamming."

The Peacekeeper reached for the antique comlink in his belt; hesitated. "I'm sorry, Director, but I don't think I should do that without Guardian Pressor's permission."

Uliar's face darkened. "Then get it," he said, his voice rumbling ominously.

To Jinzler's left, the door again slid open, and with perfect timing Pressor stepped inside. "There you are," Uliar said, his tone making the words an accusation. "Release the jamming. Ambassador Jinzler needs to contact his government."

"It's not the jamming that's the problem," Formbi said before Pressor could reply. "The fact is that communication with the outside galaxy is impossible from inside the Redoubt. If Ambassador Jinzler and I are to consult our governments, we'll need to leave Outbound Flight."

Uliar's eyes narrowed. "Will you, now," he said, his voice almost silky smooth. "How very convenient. Perhaps you won't find it so necessary if I tell you that one of you will be required to remain while—"

He broke off as, with a squeak of boots on decking, the Peacekeeper who'd taken Pressor aside earlier appeared from the corridor and came to a halt at Pressor's side. He grabbed the Guardian's arm and began murmuring urgently to him. "Guardian?" Uliar demanded. "Guardian!"

"Your pardon, Director; Councilors," Pressor said, most of his attention on the man still whispering to him. "A small matter that needs to be dealt with. I'll be back in a moment."

He flashed a hand signal to the two Peacekeepers standing guard over the Chiss and Geroons. Then he and the messenger hurried from the room, the door wheezing shut behind them.

Jinzler looked across the room at the guard beside the Geroons. The young man's face was suddenly tight and nervous, and his hand was now resting on the butt of his blaster. Whatever was going on, it was apparently far more serious than Pressor was admitting.

And it seemed to Jinzler that there were only two places trouble could be coming from right now. The Jedi, or the Imperials.

Swallowing, he turned back to Uliar. "Well," he said, searching for something to say. "As long as we have a few minutes, Director, why don't we get some details. I'd like to hear exactly what kind of ship you're looking for."

CHAPTER 17

MARA WAS ON HER KNEES, STUDYING THE SCATTERED BONES and trying to visualize what the owner of the charric might have looked like, when she felt the faint and distant sensation.

She paused, closing her eyes as she stretched out to the Force. Bits and pieces flowed into focus—*fear, surprise, anger, violence*—then flowed away again into the general roiling fog. She worked harder at it, trying to pull back from the details to get a bigger picture.

The larger view refused to come, and a moment later the sensation itself faded into the darkness and dust and ancient bones. But that moment had been enough.

Somewhere nearby, someone had died. Violently.

She opened her eyes and looked at Luke. His eyes were still closed, his mouth tight as he, too, chased after the last wisps of the vision. She waited, fingering her lightsaber and fighting for patience, until he too had lost the contact. "How many?" she asked.

"Several," he said, climbing hastily to his feet. "No injuries, either, just deaths. Quick ones, too, as if the victims were ambushed."

"You think it's real, then?" Mara asked as they headed back across the bridge and into the monitor anteroom. "I mean, it couldn't have been something from the past, could it?"

"You mean like an echo of what happened to Outbound Flight fifty years ago?" Luke shook his head. "No. One of us might possibly pick up something like that, but not both of us at the same time. No, this was real, and it happened just now."

They had to do some climbing through the rubble at the bottom of the turbolift shaft in order to reach their car, but they'd made sure to leave adequate hand- and footholds, and within a few minutes they were once again inside. "Were you able to tell where it happened?" Mara asked as the car began moving sluggishly upward.

"No," Luke said. "Someplace above us, but it all went by too quickly to pin it down any better than that. You?"

Mara shook her head. "All I could tell was that the deaths didn't seem human, somehow."

"Really," Luke said, looking at her thoughtfully. "Interesting. I had something of that same feeling, but I couldn't decide whether that part was real or just the fact that there are so many Chiss and Geroons around."

"Or maybe it was a little of both," Mara said. "If someone decided to start shooting at Jinzler or the Five-Oh-First, they wouldn't be likely to let Formbi and Bearsh just walk away."

The car lumbered to a halt in the storage core. "Where exactly are we headed?" Mara asked as they hurried through the silent storage rooms.

"We'll try the turbolift Fel and the stormtroopers used to go to D-Six," Luke said over his shoulder. "We should be able to reach either D-Six or D-Five with that one."

"Yes, that part I'd already figured out," Mara said. "I was asking which of the two Dreadnaughts you think we should start with."

"I don't know," Luke said as they reached the turbolift lobby where they'd taken their leave of the Imperials. "Fel went to D-Six; Jinzler and Formbi are probably on D-Five. Pick one."

The turbolift door slid halfway open and stopped. "Let's make it D-Five," Mara decided as they squeezed inside. "Even with three Chiss warriors along, the civilians are likely to be harder pressed if things have gotten messy."

"Sounds good," Luke said. Using the Force to pull the doors at least partially closed, he tapped the key for D-5.

The car didn't move.

"Uh-oh," he said, trying the key again. Still nothing.

"Terrific," Mara growled, pulling out her comlink. A quick on–off showed that the jamming was still in place. "Well, so much for the easy approach," she said. "Looks like our choices are to climb the shaft or head aft and hope the turbolifts back there are still working."

"Or to continue around to the turbolift Pressor had us trapped in," Luke reminded her. "Actually, given that we've already cut some of the repulsor controls in that pylon, it might be the easier one to climb."

"Probably safer, too," Mara pointed out, pushing the doors open again.

"Right," Luke agreed as they squeezed back out into the turbolift lobby and took off at a run toward the next turbolift lobby over. "It would be a little tricky to play Hilltop Emperor if the repulsor beams came back on."

Mara stiffened. Suddenly, unbidden, a horrible revelation had come like a thundering of blaster bolts chewing their way into her stomach. The Geroon ship—Bearsh's farewell to the rest of his people as the *Chaf Envoy* prepared to head into the Redoubt—the vague and nameless puzzle that had bothered her so tantalizingly at the time—

And the image of a Geroon child triumphantly waving a red headband.

"What is it?" Luke asked, his own step faltering at the abrupt spike he felt in her. "Mara?"

"*Blast* it," she bit out, sprinting past him as she doubled her speed. "Come on—no time to waste. Blast them all."

"What—?"

But she had left Luke and his bewildered question behind her. So simple; so embarrassingly simple.

And yet Mara Jade Skywalker, former Emperor's Hand, had missed it completely. Musing on the Empire that had been, and her former place in it, she had missed it completely.

She was nearly to their target turbolift, and over her panting breath she could hear Luke's footsteps as he caught up to her. *Steady,* his thought came, flowing calmness over her as he tried to soothe some of her agitation.

But even Jedi calm couldn't help her now. People had already died because of her carelessness. Unless they hurried, others would suffer the same fate.

Maybe even all of them.

THE TURBOLIFT LOBBY WAS ALMOST COMPLETELY DARK WHEN Pressor and Trilli arrived. "This is crazy," Pressor declared, looking around in disbelief. Even some of the emergency permlights were out, which should have been well-nigh impossible. "What could have caused all this?"

"You got me," Trilli said. "The power's all right at the generators—that was the first thing the techs checked. It's just getting lost somewhere along the way."

"So, what, we've got a short in the wiring?"

"It'd take a lot more than just one," Trilli pointed out. "And that wouldn't explain the permlights, anyway."

"Yes," Pressor conceded. "Have we got a tech crew on the way?"

"One's already here," Trilli told him. "They're a deck up, checking out the turbolifts. Apparently, that's where the outages started."

Pressor scratched his cheek. "The turbolifts that the two Jedi and Imperials were able to get past?"

"I thought about that, too," Trilli said. "But the power was just fine earlier after they got out."

"Maybe it's some sort of delayed reaction," Pressor suggested. "Something they set up to cover their tracks."

"I don't know," Trilli said doubtfully. "Seems kind of a waste of effort. Especially for Jedi."

Across the lobby, the faint sound of a ventilator fan went silent. "There goes another one," Pressor said, peering in that direction. "You know what this reminds me of? That infestation of conduit worms we had a few years after the landing."

"That's impossible," Trilli insisted. "We exterminated them thirty years ago."

"Unless we've just imported a new batch," Pressor said, jerking his head back down the corridor.

Trilli muttered something under his breath. "Uliar's not going to be happy about this at all."

"No kidding." Pressor started to reach for his comlink, remembered the jamming in time and headed instead toward one of the wall-mounted comms. "We'd better get a couple more tech teams down here," he said. "If it's conduit worms, we want them gone, and fast."

"Right," Trilli said. "You want me to wait here while you go tell Uliar the good news?"

Pressor made a face. "Let's both wait," he said. "There's no point in starting rumors until we know for sure what we've got."

"Besides which, you don't want to spring this on Uliar alone?"

Pressor keyed the wall comm for the tech section. "Something like that."

THE CENTER PORTSIDE CORRIDOR ON D-6 WAS AS SNARLED with rusted debris as anything Fel had seen up on D-4. The center starboard corridor, in contrast, was almost perfectly clear.

"They've definitely been using this one," Watchman commented as the group made their cautious way aft. "Not very much traffic, but it's steady."

"How do you figure that?" Fel asked.

"From the pattern of dust on the deck," Drask told him. "There are places where occasional footsteps have lifted or moved it. No more than twenty people come this way each day. Possibly fewer."

"Possibly as few as ten," Watchman agreed. "The two guards we left stunned back there, running three shifts a day, plus a few more would pretty well cover it."

"Commander?" Grappler, in the lead, called back over his shoulder. "I'm picking up voices ahead."

"Extend formation," Watchman ordered. "Not too far— make sure to stay in sight."

"I see a light," Grappler announced. "Looks like it's coming from one of the crew bunkrooms."

"Watch for trouble," Fel warned. "They may have had time to get reinforcements in position."

Apparently, they hadn't. A minute later, the group had arrived.

At a prison.

Fel hadn't been particularly impressed by Luke's claim that there had been an old prison down in the supply core, and Drask's description of the setup hadn't done anything to modify that skepticism. But about this place he had no doubts at all. The door to the old crew quarters had had a pair of narrow slits cut into it, one at eye level for observation, the other just above the floor and wide enough to pass a tray of food through. Supplementing the door's original lock was a heavy add-on with the kind of twin access ports that implied two separate codes were necessary to open it.

"Hello?" a woman's voice called tentatively from behind the door. "Perry? Is that you?"

Fel stepped to the door and pressed his face to the upper slit. The bunkroom had been divided into at least three sections, two of which were currently closed off by light, hand-movable panels. The center section, the one visible from the observation slit, had been set up as a recreation area, with chairs, a couple of small tables, games, and toys. Seated in two of the chairs were a pair of women, one in her twenties, the other much older, watching as four children with ages ranging between six and ten years old played or talked. The younger woman was leaning toward the door, squinting to try to see Fel through the narrow slit.

Abruptly, she stiffened. "You're not Perry," she said, her voice quavering a little. "Who are you?"

"I'm Commander Chak Fel of the Empire of the Hand," Fel identified himself as the children all paused in their activities and turned to see what was going on. "Don't worry, we aren't going to hurt you."

"What do you want?" the older woman asked.

"We're here to help," Fel assured her, frowning as he

looked around. These certainly didn't look like hardened criminals who deserved to be kept behind a double-coded lock and supplied through a zoo-style feeding slot. In many ways the room reminded him of the nursery they'd passed down the corridor, in fact, or perhaps a special classroom of some sort. "Who are you people?"

"We're the remnant of the Republic mission called Outbound Flight," the older woman said.

"Yes, we know that part," Fel said. "I mean you and the children. What are you doing in there?"

"Why, we're the dangerous ones, of course," the younger woman said bitterly. "Didn't you know?" She waved a hand to encompass the children. "Or rather, they are. That's why they're in Quarantine. We're just here to take care of them, poor dears."

"The dangerous ones, huh?" Fel asked, eyeing the children. As far as he could tell, they looked like any other kids he'd ever known. "What exactly did they do?"

"They didn't *do* anything," the older woman said quietly. Apparently she'd been at this long enough for her bitterness to decay into resignation. "All they were was a little bit different from everyone else. That's all. Director Uliar's imagination and hatred did all the rest."

"And what exactly does his imagination and hatred tell him?" Fel asked. "What does he think they are?"

"Why, pure evil, of course," the younger woman said. "Or at least, that's what he's afraid they'll grow up to be."

Fel looked at the kids again. "Pure evil?" he asked.

"Yes," the older woman added, her forehead creasing as if it should be obvious. "You know.

"Jedi."

CHAPTER 18

FEL JUST STARED AT HER, HIS BRAIN REFUSING TO FORM WORDS. Pure evil? *Jedi?* "Who told you Jedi were evil?" he demanded. "Some of them may have their moments, but . . ."

He trailed off. Both women were looking at him as if he'd just told them that red was green. "Don't you know anything?" the younger woman said. "They destroyed us. They betrayed and destroyed us."

"Did you actually see this happen?" Fel persisted. "Or is it just something you heard from—?"

"Commander," Drask said.

Fel turned away from the observation slit. "What?" he snapped.

"For the moment, this is irrelevant," the general said quietly. "We can learn more about their history when the Aristocra and ambassador are once again safely under our protection."

Fel felt his jaw tighten in frustration. But the Chiss was right. "Understood," he said reluctantly. "So we just leave them here?"

"Would you prefer we take them with us?" Drask countered.

"No, of course not," Fel conceded reluctantly. "I just—of course not. Back to the turbolift?"

"Yes," Drask said, his eyes flashing with quiet anger toward the locked room. "We have seen what we came here to see."

Fel nodded. He hated to just leave these people here, prisoners of some insane half-remembered myth or personal vendetta. But Drask was right. It could be dealt with later. "All right, stormtroopers, form up. We're heading back to the forward turbolifts."

He started to turn, and, as he did, something about Grappler's stance caught his attention. "Grappler?" he asked.

Reluctantly, he thought, the Eickarie came back to attention. "Your pardon, Commander," he said, his voice sounding even more alien than usual. "I was . . . remembering."

"Remembering what?"

"My people." Grappler gestured fractionally toward the Quarantine door with his BlasTech. "The Warlord took away many such innocents who were of no genuine threat and put them in places like this. Most were never heard from again."

"I understand," Fel said, leveling his gaze at the white faceplate. "But the best thing we can do right now is find Formbi and Jinzler and make sure they know about this. Rule One is that diplomats always get first crack at this sort of problem."

"And if they are unable or unwilling to do anything?"

Fel looked back at the locked door. "Rule Two is that soldiers get second crack," he said darkly. "Move out."

OUTBOUND FLIGHT'S DESIGNERS HAD CLEARLY NEVER CONSIDered the possibility that anyone would ever wish to travel through the connecting turbolift pylons without an actual turbolift car or at least a maintenance repulsorlift pack. As a result, they had kept the tube interior smooth, without any of the access ladders Luke had assumed would be there. There were also no other built-in handholds, and all the wiring was buried behind protective metal panels.

Fortunately, Jedi had their own resources.

"How's it going?" Luke grunted as he hauled himself another arm's length up the thick power cable.

"*I'm* doing fine," Mara countered from above him. "Question is, how are *you* holding up?"

"I'm fine, too," Luke assured her, taking a moment to look up at the woman sitting on his shoulders. It would have looked utterly ridiculous, he knew, had there been anyone around to see them: a man hauling himself hand over hand up a set of power cables while a grown woman sat high atop his shoulders like a small child watching a Victory Day parade.

But silly looking or not, it was working, and faster even than Luke had anticipated. With the metal access panels long since frozen shut by age and rust, there was no way to reach the cables beneath them except via a lightsaber wielded by a steady hand. Any other approach they could have used would have required each of them to cut away a section of paneling, haul him- or herself up to that level via the newly exposed cables, and then pause to cut away the next section. This way, Mara was able to concentrate on the task of precision cutting while Luke could give his full attention to the climb itself.

Or at least he could do so as long as his arms held out. Stretching out to the Force, letting its strength flow into his muscles, he kept going. It was just as well, he reflected, that they hadn't had to get out of the rigged turbolift car this way. Drask would never have made it.

"Watch it," Mara warned. "We're hitting the edge of another eddy."

"Right," Luke said, making sure to get an extra-firm grip with each pull upward. With the storage core and each of the Dreadnaughts running its own gravity direction, the tube had been designed to align incoming cars with the proper "up" before they arrived at their various destinations. The gravity eddy fields required for such an operation weren't too difficult to get past—he and Mara had already forded two of them—but getting caught unprepared could be trouble.

"I wish these things weren't tied into the ships' environmental system," he muttered as he felt the eddy current tugging at his body, trying to turn him around. Mara had abandoned her lightsaber work for the moment in favor of steadying herself with a grip on Luke's collar. "Without gravity in the pylon, we could have just floated up to D-Five."

"It would have taken us half a day just to find all the redundancies and shut them down," Mara pointed out, waving her free hand cautiously above her. "Okay, there's the upper edge of the eddy."

Luke eased them past the interface and they continued on their way. "So when are you going to tell me what this is all about?" he asked.

Even over the humming of her lightsaber he heard Mara's sigh. "It was that scene on the *Chaf Envoy*'s observation deck," she said. "Just before we headed into the Redoubt, when Bearsh and the Geroons were saying good-bye to their ship."

"I remember," Luke said. "You said at the time something about that wasn't right."

"I just wish I'd caught it sooner," Mara said, an edge of self-recrimination in her voice. "I *should* have caught it earlier. Remember when the Geroon ship first arrived, and on the comm display behind Bearsh we saw some children playing Hilltop Emperor?"

"Yes," Luke said, replaying the scene in his mind. "It looked all right to me."

"Oh, it looked just fine," Mara bit out. "Problem is, a couple of days later, when the Geroons were saying their farewells, the same scene was going on in the background."

Luke frowned. "What do you mean, the same scene? More children playing on the structure?"

"I mean the *same* children playing on the structure," she said. "Doing the same things, in exactly the same way."

Luke tightened his grip on the cables. "The whole thing was a *recording*?"

"You got it," Mara said bitterly. "There are no children aboard that ship, Luke. Bearsh was lying through his teeth. *Both* sets of teeth."

"And I missed it completely," Luke said, feeling like a fool. "I wasn't even paying attention."

"Why should you have been?" Mara pointed out. "There wasn't any reason to suspect them of anything."

"I still should have been more alert," Luke said, refusing to be mollified. "Especially after everything that was going on aboard the *Chaf Envoy*. So what exactly does it mean?"

"It means the Geroons are frauds," Mara said. "It means that ship of theirs isn't a refugee ship at all. Aside from that, I have no idea."

"Bearsh said the ship was mostly composed of small rooms," Luke said, trying to think it through. "That kind of structure is something our sensors might be able to check out, so we can assume he was telling the truth about that. What sort of ship would be composed of mostly small rooms?"

"A prison ship, maybe?" Mara suggested. "Or maybe a cargo ship like Outbound Flight's storage core? That's basically a series of small rooms."

"I wish we knew what size rooms they are," Luke said. "You ever ask Drask if he took any sensor readings of their ship?"

"No, but you'd think he would have said something if it didn't check out," Mara said.

"Maybe he did, only not to us," Luke said, visualizing the Geroon ship in his mind. Big and spherical, with a regular pattern of dark spots covering the hull. Viewports, he'd tentatively identified them at the time. Or vents, or decoration—

He drew in a sharp breath. "Or ejection ports," he said aloud.

"What?"

"Ejection ports," he repeated. "Those dark spots on the hull are just like the ones we saw on that firepoint asteroid on our way into the Redoubt."

"Ejection ports for fighters," Mara bit out. "The thing's a *carrier*."

"And we left it sitting right next to the Brask Oto Command Station," Luke reminded her grimly.

"Terrific," Mara grunted. "So much for the Geroons being peace loving."

From behind Luke's head, barely audible over the sound of Mara's lightsaber, came a soft chirp. "Did you hear that?" he asked.

"Hear what?"

"Another of those comlink chirps," he told her. "The kind

Drask said sounded like someone communicating over the jamming. It came from your comlink."

"I missed it," she said, the tone of her lightsaber changing slightly as she sliced away more of the metal. "The Geroons, you think?"

"I don't think anyone else has lied to us as consistently as they have," Luke said grimly.

"Not even Formbi?"

"Not even Jinzler," he said. "And I'm getting a very bad feeling about this. How much farther?"

Her weight shifted slightly on his shoulders as she peered upward. "Fifteen minutes at this rate," she said. "Maybe more."

Luke set his teeth, stretching out to the Force for strength. "Let's make it less."

"NO." WITH A CONTEMPTUOUS FLICK OF HIS WRIST, TARKOSA sent Jinzler's datapad sliding back across the tabletop toward him. "Completely unacceptable, all of them."

"What's wrong with the Rendili *Battle Horn*-class?" Jinzler asked, struggling to remain calm. This whole thing was starting to get ridiculous. "It's got the size you want, it's got the speed—"

"It's a freighter," Tarkosa said flatly.

"It's a bulk cruiser, not a freighter," Jinzler corrected. "It's armed, it's armored, it's got the range, it's got the capacity—"

"It's unacceptable," Uliar cut in. "Show us something else."

Jinzler reached over and snagged the datapad, swallowing the retort he so very much wanted to say. Uliar and the two councilors had shot down every single suggestion he'd made, and he was becoming extremely irritated with the whole bunch of them. "Fine," he said, keying for Mon Cal ship designs. Maybe there would be something *here* that the crotchety old Survivors could live with.

Of course, there would then be the whole question of persuading either the Chiss to buy such a ship or the New Republic to donate it to the cause. But that would be a crisis for another day.

From his comlink came another chirp. "What *is* that noise you people keep making on our comlinks?" he demanded.

"What are you talking about?" Uliar asked.

"That little chirping sound," Jinzler said. "Do all your comlinks have frequency bleed-through or something?"

"I repeat, what are you talking about?" Uliar countered. "*You're* doing that, not us."

Jinzler frowned. "What are *you* talking about? We're not—"

"Ah, yes," Bearsh murmured, standing up. "As was the beginning, so is the end."

Jinzler shifted his frown to the Geroon. "What?"

"As was the beginning, so is the end," Bearsh repeated. Ducking his head forward, he slid the limp wolvkil body off his shoulders and let it thump onto the table in front of him. Against the wall behind him, his three compatriots had also taken off their wolvkils, laying them on the floor, and Jinzler had the sudden irrational thought that they were about to present the dead animals to Uliar as a gift to try to get him to cooperate. "Once, victims," Bearsh went on. "Now, victors." Reaching to the wolvkil's neck, he broke off its decorative blue-and-gold collar.

And with a sudden, brief shudder, the wolvkil came to life.

Someone gasped as the animal scrambled to its feet; one of the Survivors, Jinzler thought dimly as the wolvkil shook itself like a wet karfler. Or maybe it had been Jinzler himself. For the moment, his brain was too frozen with shock to process anything but the impossibility that was now staring him in the eye along its long, tooth-filled muzzle. At the far wall, he was vaguely aware that the other three wolvkils had similarly and inexplicably revived.

For a stretched-out second no one moved. Bearsh murmured something reverent sounding in that melodious, two-toned language of theirs; from the Survivors' end of the table came another soft gasp. "No," he heard Uliar breathe. "It can't—"

The four wolvkils leapt.

Instinctively, Jinzler shoved himself back from the table as the nearest animal jumped toward him, fully expecting a terrible stab of pain as its jaws closed around his neck. But the furry missile shot past without even grazing him with its outstretched claws. The momentum of Jinzler's push sent his chair tipping over backward, and as his shoulder and head slammed against the deck a brief burst of stars blurred his vision. Through the sound of the blood roaring in his ears he heard screams and shouts and the sputter of blasterfire. There was a ululating roar, another scream; and suddenly he found himself being hauled to his feet.

It was Tarkosa, his eyes wild, his age-lined face etched with fear and rage. "Get back, you fool," he snarled, giving Jinzler's arm a single tug toward the back of the room and then letting go and backing up hastily himself. Blinking once to clear his eyes, Jinzler looked behind him.

The calm scene of a few seconds before had dissolved into chaos. The three Chiss warriors were bent over or on their knees, wrestling with the snarling wolvkils, clearly fighting for their lives. The Peacekeeper who had been standing guard over them was already down, lying motionless in a widening pool of blood, his blaster lying on the deck beside his limp hand. Even as Jinzler stared in horror one of the Chiss managed to twist his charric far enough around in the grip of his attacker's jaws and fire point-blank into its torso. But the wolvkil shrugged off the shot without even a snarl, its teeth and claws continuing to tear at the warrior's arm and chest. Across the room by the other side wall, the remaining Peacekeeper had been knocked prone by the three Geroons whom he had been guarding. Two of them were pinning down his gun hand as the third sat on his chest, rhythmically beating his head against the deck.

From behind Jinzler came a sizzling hiss, and a streak of blue fire shot past his shoulder to impact squarely in the center of the third Geroon's back. The Geroon screamed something vicious sounding and rolled forward off the Peacekeeper's chest. A second shot struck his shoulder, blackening his robe and eliciting another scream—

And once again Jinzler ducked reflexively away as one of

the wolvkils abandoned the injured Chiss he'd been attacking and leapt past him. He spun around—

To see the wolvkil slam into Formbi, its snarling jaws snapping shut around the Aristocra's gun arm.

The impact staggered Formbi backward, but he managed to stay on his feet. Ignoring the blood suddenly flowing onto his sleeve, he twisted his arm around and tossed the charric to his free hand. Pressing the muzzle to the wolvkil's head, he fired.

That one at least wrenched a howl from the animal. But if the injury affected either its strength or resolve, it didn't show. Formbi fired a second time; and then the wolvkil seemed to realize it was no longer holding on to the proper arm. With one last tearing bite, it let go and reached out for Formbi's other arm.

It never had a chance to connect. Even as its jaws opened, Feesa appeared out of nowhere, a streak of yellow-clad blue that slammed into the wolvkil's side, tearing it off Formbi and sprawling both of them onto the deck.

The wolvkil howled in fury, twisting like a snake as it tried to buck her away. Feesa was faster, throwing her arms around its sides and burying her face in the fur of its back. The creature howled again, twisting its head back and forth as it tried to reach her. But Feesa held on, shouting in the Chiss language as Formbi fired round after round of blue fire into the wolvkil's body.

And with that, the paralysis holding Jinzler rooted to the floor abruptly snapped.

Bearsh was standing by himself in a little bubble of calmness, his hands on his hips as he coolly surveyed the carnage going on around him. "Call them off," Jinzler snapped, a sudden fury blazing inside him as he strode toward the Geroon. "You hear me? Call them *off*."

"I hear you, human," Bearsh said. The nervous, self-effacing voice Jinzler had become accustomed to aboard ship had suddenly changed to something harsh and arrogant. "You are as big a fool as they are. Stay back, or die now in agony instead of later in cold and darkness."

"*You're* the one who's going to die," Jinzler bit out, feeling his hands curling into fists. Bearsh might be younger, but Jinzler was a good head taller and at least fifteen kilos heavier, and the Geroon wouldn't have the element of surprise they'd had against the young Peacekeeper getting his brains beaten in. He would hammer the Geroon until he called off the attack. Would hammer him all the way to death, if that was what it took.

Perhaps Bearsh saw that in his eyes as he approached. His expression changed, and with a speed Jinzler wouldn't have expected he lifted his hands from his hips and grabbed for the end of his left sleeve. Jinzler tensed, lengthening his stride, trying to beat the Geroon to whatever weapon he was reaching for.

Bearsh's hand reached the sleeve; but instead of drawing a weapon, he merely ripped the outer layer of cloth away. Jinzler had just enough time to see that the arm was covered with what appeared to be lumpy packing material, half black and yellow, half translucent—

And abruptly the arm exploded into a hundred angrily buzzing insects.

He was barely able to wrench himself to a halt in time. For a second or two the insects swarmed aimlessly before coalescing into a spherical pattern swirling around Bearsh. "Careful, human," the Geroon warned softly. "Be very careful. I don't know what schostri stings would do to a human, but they're quickly fatal to most other life-forms we've used them against."

His mouths curved in a sardonic double smile. "Of course, if you wish to serve as a test case, come ahead."

Casually, he turned his back on Jinzler, crossing toward the Geroon whom Formbi had shot and the two uninjured ones still beating on the Peacekeeper. The swarm moved with him, as if genetically programmed to recognize him as their hive or queen.

Jinzler took a cautious step forward, keeping a wary eye on the insects. Another few steps, and Bearsh would be within reach of the injured Peacekeeper's dropped blaster. If he got to the weapon first, any hope of stopping them and the wolvkils would be gone.

But the Geroon had apparently forgotten there was another spare weapon lying loose on the deck, the one dropped by the other Peacekeeper. Or maybe he simply didn't think it was relevant, since the only ones close enough to reach it were already fighting for their lives against the wolvkils.

Everyone except Dean Jinzler.

He eased his way toward the gun, striving to be as invisible as possible. Even if he shot Bearsh, he knew, the swarm of insects might well take vengeance on him. But it would be worth it to watch Bearsh's smile turn to pain and then to death.

Still no one seemed to have noticed him. Another few steps . . .

"Ambassador!" Formbi called.

Jinzler twisted his head back around. Uliar and the two councilors had flipped the long conference table onto its side and were dragging it toward one of the room's back corners. Formbi and Feesa were with them, the Aristocra staggering slightly as blood continued to pour from his mangled arm. The wolvkil he had been fighting lay still on the deck, its fur almost uniformly black from multiple charric burns. Rosemari and Evlyn were already back in the corner, Rosemari's arms visibly trembling as she clutched her daughter close to her. "Ambassador!" Formbi called again. "Come. Quickly."

"Shh!" Jinzler hissed at him. Didn't they see what he was trying to do?

"Yes, Ambassador, go," Bearsh agreed.

Jinzler turned back. Bearsh was standing beside the now motionless second Peacekeeper, the boy's blaster pointed casually in Jinzler's direction. "Or would you prefer to die now in agony?"

Jinzler hesitated. But if the Geroons wanted them all dead, there was nothing and no one left to stop them anyway. Clenching his hands one last time, this time into fists of impotent rage and defeat, he backed away.

"Bring chairs," Uliar called. "Quickly."

With his full attention still on the blaster in Bearsh's hand, Jinzler groped blindly for some of the fallen chairs and came up with two of them. All the Chiss warriors were lying broken and bloody on the deck now, he noted distantly, their own battles over. The wolvkils who had killed them stood panting, watching Jinzler with unblinking eyes as they licked their bloody muzzles and paws.

The Survivors had the table in position by the time he arrived, set on its edge across the back corner to form a low barrier. What they wanted with the chairs was quickly evident as Uliar and Tarkosa stacked them like sections of a roof over the top of the triangle-shaped gap they'd created behind the table, using the back walls and the sculpture pedestals for support. The Geroons had gathered together now as well, watching in silence as they completed their task. "Now get inside," Bearsh instructed as the last roofing chair was set in place. "Quickly."

Silently, the prisoners complied, crawling through a gap that had been left between one end of the table and the bulkhead. Uliar, the last one in, pulled a final chair into the gap behind him.

And there they were, Jinzler thought bitterly. Caged animals, in a cage of their own construction.

There was the sound of footsteps, and Bearsh's face appeared through the latticework of chairs above them. "There, now, you see?" the Geroon said sardonically. He had his left arm stretched out to the side, and the swarming insects were beginning to settle back into their places there. "Even humans are capable of following orders."

No one replied. "All right, you've got us," Jinzler said, deciding that *someone* should find out what was going on. "What do you want?"

Bearsh's mouths twisted crookedly. "I want you all dead, of course," he said. "The only question remaining is the method."

He gestured behind him, to where the other Geroons were slathering some kind of salve on the one Formbi had shot. "Purpsh, for instance, would very much like to gun you all down right here so that he can enjoy your screams. Especially yours, Aristocra Formbi. But I've decided to let you choose exactly how you will die."

"You won't get away with this," Uliar said. The words were defiant, but to Jinzler his voice merely sounded old.

"Oh, I think we will," Bearsh said calmly as he rewrapped his sleeve over the now quiescent insects. "Your precious Jedi and Imperial stormtroopers should all be dead by now—our sabotage of the turbolift cars they were trapped in will have taken care of that problem. Who else is there to stop us?"

"*We* will," Uliar growled. "We've been ready for trouble for fifty years. You don't think we can take you?"

"I doubt it," Bearsh said. "At any rate, we're not likely to find out. With your communications jamming still in place, you won't be able to summon your pitiful little colony to the attack. By the time they wake up to what's happened, we'll be long gone." He smiled. "And *you* will be well on the road to a dark and icy death."

He reached down and shook his robe. There was a soft clatter as some small objects fell to the deck. "A small present for the survivors of Outbound Flight," he said. "We have used some already on the turbolifts; these should take care of this particular area."

Frowning, Jinzler turned his head sideways, pressing his cheek against the chair above him to try to see over the edge of the table. There were half a dozen threadlike objects on the deck, he saw, spreading out as they skittered their way toward the walls.

He caught his breath. "Line creepers."

"Very good, Ambassador," Bearsh said approvingly. "After all, I promised that you would die in cold and darkness, didn't I?"

"What are line creepers?" Uliar asked.

"They're like conduit worms," Jinzler told him, feeling his stomach tightening. "Only worse. Bearsh slipped a few into the control lines aboard the *Chaf Envoy* and nearly shut it down." He lifted his eyebrows. "That *was* you, wasn't it?"

"We'll be traveling through your vessel for a while longer, distributing the rest of our little pets for maximum effect," Bearsh said to Uliar, ignoring the question. "After that, we'll leave you to your doom."

"There's no need to destroy these people or their home, Bearsh," Formbi said. His voice was deadly calm, with only a hint of the agony he must be feeling from his torn arm. "If you want the *Chaf Envoy*, take it."

Bearsh snorted. "You underestimate us, Aristocra. We have bigger game in mind than a simple Chiss diplomatic vessel."

He waved toward the wolvkils. "And speaking of game, we'll be leaving our pets behind to make sure you stay here quietly until we are finished. I trust you noticed how difficult they are to kill. If not, or if some of you decide you'd prefer a quicker death than the one we'll be leaving you, I'm certain they'll enjoy the exercise."

"Bearsh—" Formbi said again.

But Bearsh merely turned his back on them and strode away. Again peering out through the chairs, Jinzler saw the other Geroons fall into step behind him, the two uninjured ones supporting the third. The door wheezed open, and Bearsh looked briefly out into the corridor. A moment later they were gone, the door sliding shut behind them.

Jinzler shifted his attention to the three remaining wolvkils. They were padding around now, continuing to clean themselves, occasionally sniffing at their fallen victims. But it was clear they were also keeping an eye on the prisoners behind their barrier.

"I don't understand," Rosemari said, her shaking voice barely above a whisper. "What do they want from us?"

Uliar sighed. "Vengeance, Instructor," he said. "Vengeance for crimes real and crimes imagined."

"What crimes?" Rosemari asked. "What did we ever do to the Geroons?"

"We did nothing to the Geroons," Uliar said bitterly. "That's the problem."

Jinzler turned around to stare at him. "What?"

"Didn't you know, Ambassador?" Uliar bit out, his eyes dark as he glared past Rosemari's shoulder. "Bearsh and his friends aren't Geroons.

"They're Vagaari."

CHAPTER 19

JINZLER BLINKED AT HIM, THE COLLECTED IMAGES OF THE VOYage flashing through his mind. How could Uliar even *think* that such excruciatingly humble travel companions could possibly be members of a race of pirates and slavers?

But even before the question formed in his mind, that last vivid image of Bearsh settled like a heavy curtain over all the rest: Bearsh standing placidly by as his wolvkils slaughtered their way across the meeting chamber. "How did you know?" he asked.

"Their voices," Uliar said as he stared into space, a distant agony reflected in his eyes. "Or rather, their speech, when they spoke in their own language just before their attack. I only heard it once, but it's something I'll never forget." The eyes came back to a hard focus. "You genuinely didn't know who they were?"

"Of course not," Jinzler said. "You think we would have let them aboard Outbound Flight if we had?"

"I don't know," Uliar said darkly. "Some of you might have." He turned his gaze toward Formbi. "Possibly the heirs of those who tried to destroy Outbound Flight in the first place."

"Ridiculous," Formbi said, his voice taut with suppressed pain. He was lying on his side along the back wall, his head cradled in Feesa's lap, the bloodstains on his sleeve growing steadily larger. "I've told you before: the Chiss Ascendancy had nothing to do with your destruction. Thrawn acted totally on his own."

"Perhaps," Uliar said. "But what about *you*, Aristocra? On whose behalf are *you* acting?"

"Why do we waste time with unimportant matters?" Feesa cut in angrily. "We must get medical attention for Aristocra Chaf'orm'bintrano. Where is your medical center?"

"What difference does it make?" Uliar growled. "Those things will kill anyone who tries to leave."

"No," Feesa said. "During the battle they attacked only those who carried weapons. As long as we leave unarmed and make no threatening movements, I believe we may pass safely among them."

"Interesting theory," Tarkosa said scornfully. "Are you prepared to risk all our lives on it?"

"It need be no one's risk but mine," Feesa shot back, starting to shift position in the cramped space. "I will go."

"No, don't," Evlyn said. "I saw one of them talking to the animals. I think he told it not to let any of us leave."

"Really," Uliar said, his tone suddenly subtly different. "And how would you know that?"

"I don't *know*," Evlyn said. "I said I *think*."

"I am willing to take the risk," Feesa insisted.

"I'm not," Formbi told her, reaching up to touch her arm with his fingertips. "You'll stay here."

"But—"

"That's an order, Feesa," Formbi said, his breathing starting to sound heavy as the loss of blood began to take its toll. "We will all stay here."

"Is that how Blue Ones face hard choices?" Tarkosa said scornfully. "To simply sit and do nothing until they die?"

"Maybe that's what they're hoping," Keely muttered. "Maybe their line creepers aren't as bad as they want us to think. Maybe they hope we'll go charging out there and get torn to bits."

"So instead we sit here and die?" Tarkosa shot back.

"No one's going anywhere," Jinzler said firmly. "There's no need. The Jedi and Imperials are still free. They'll find us."

Keely snorted. "Jedi," he said, biting out the name like a curse.

"There aren't any Jedi," Uliar said. "You heard Bearsh. They're already dead."

"I'll believe that when I see it," Jinzler said, turning around to peer through the chairs. The wolvkils had finished their postslaughter grooming and had moved closer to the makeshift refuge, probably drawn by the voices. They were prowling at arm's length away from the table barrier, their ears straight up, their jaws half open.

"We need a weapon," Uliar murmured. "That's what we need. A weapon."

"Those men and Chiss had weapons, too," Jinzler reminded him, looking past the wolvkils to the dead bodies scattered about the far end of the room. "What we really need is help . . ."

He trailed off, his eyes focusing on the nearest of the dead Peacekeepers and the comlink hooked to his belt.

The comlink the boy had reached for when Uliar had ordered the jamming to be shut off.

"Director," he said, trying to keep the sudden excitement out of his voice. "If we had one of the Peacekeepers' comlinks, could we shut off the jamming?"

"*If* we had one, yes," Uliar said. "There's a special twist-frequency command line built into those comlinks that allows for communication with other Peacekeepers and the command system."

"Do you know how to operate it?"

"Of course," the director growled. "I served my share of Peacekeeper duty."

"Except that the nearest comlink is ten meters away," Tarkosa pointed out. "Were you hoping to convince one of the animals to bring it to you?"

"No." Jinzler looked at Evlyn. "Not one of the animals."

The girl looked back at him; and for the first time since they'd met he saw an edge of fear in her eyes. "No," she whispered. "I can't."

"Yes, you can," Jinzler told her firmly. "You must."

"No," Rosemari cut in emphatically. "You heard her. She can't."

"Can't what?" Uliar demanded, his voice suddenly watchful.

"There's nothing special about her," Rosemari insisted, glaring warningly at Jinzler.

"Yes, there is," Jinzler said, just as firmly. "You know that as well as I do. Rosemari, it's our best chance."

"No!" Rosemari bit out, clutching her daughter tightly to her.

"So I was right," Uliar said softly.

Rosemari whirled on him. "Leave her alone," she flared at him, her voice trembling. "You're not going to send her to Three to die. You're *not*."

"Do you dare defy the law?" Uliar thundered.

"She hasn't *done* anything!" Rosemari shot back. "How can you condemn her when she hasn't even done anything?"

"She's a *Jedi*!" Tarkosa snarled. "That's all the law requires."

"Then the law is a fool," Jinzler said.

The three Survivors turned furious eyes on him. "Keep out of this, outlander," Tarkosa ordered. "What do you know about us, or what we went through?"

"Is that your reason for denying your children their birthright?" Jinzler demanded. "For keeping them from using and developing the talents they were born with? Is *that* your excuse—something that happened fifty years ago? Before any of them were even *born*?"

"No," Evlyn said, her face pleading, her eyes shimmering with tears. "Please, Ambassador. I don't want to do this. I don't want to be a Jedi."

Jinzler shook his head. "You don't have a choice," he told her quietly. "None of us gets to choose which talents and abilities we're born with. Our only choice is whether we take those gifts and use them to live and grow and serve, or whether we bury them in the ground and try to pretend they were never there."

Awkwardly, he shifted around in the cramped space and

took the girl's hand. It was shaking, and the skin was icy cold. "You can use the Force, Evlyn," he said. "It's one of the greatest and rarest gifts that anyone can ever be given. You can't simply throw it away."

She looked up at him, blinking back tears. Her face was so tight, he saw, and yet so controlled . . .

And suddenly, it was as if he were four years old again, gazing across the distance at his sister Lorana's eyes for the first time. Watching the wariness and uncertainty in her own face as she turned away; feeling himself seething with confusion and resentment at the special place she clearly held in his parents' hearts.

Or *was* that as clear as he'd thought?

He felt his hand tighten around Evlyn's as memories he'd spent years pushing away rushed in, washing over his carefully constructed view of himself and his life like a mountain stream cutting through loose mud. An image of his mother praising him for his near-perfect grade evaluation in fourth tier. Another image, this one of his father, complimenting him on his ingenuity as they worked together to rewire a section of the family holoviewer. More images—dozens of them—all showing that his long-held belief in parental neglect hadn't been true at all.

It fact, it had been an out-and-out lie. A lie he'd created and repeated to himself over and over until he'd genuinely believed it. A lie he'd created for one reason, and one reason only.

Jealousy.

He hadn't hated Lorana at all, he saw now. He'd simply hated what she'd become, because it was what he had longed to be but never could.

He closed his eyes. So simple . . . and yet it had taken him most of his life to finally recognize the truth.

Or perhaps it had simply taken that long for him to admit it to himself. Perhaps, down deep, he'd known it all along.

He opened his eyes; and as he did so, the image of Lorana's face vanished back into the mists of memory, leaving him once again sitting inside a ruined starship, huddled behind a makeshift barrier, holding a little girl's hand.

He turned to Uliar. "She has the power of the Jedi, Director Uliar," he said. "She always will. You should be honored to know her."

The other's eyes bored into him like a pair of hungry duracrete slugs. But there was apparently something in Jinzler's expression that warned against further argument. The director merely gave a contemptuous snort and turned his face away without speaking.

Jinzler looked at Tarkosa and Keely in turn, silently daring each of them to object. But whatever it was Uliar had seen, they saw it, too. Neither of them spoke.

And finally, he turned back to Rosemari. "There's one last thing," he said. "She needs the approval of the people she loves. More importantly, she deserves it."

Rosemari swallowed visibly. She didn't like this—that was abundantly clear in the lines etched across her face. But beneath the fear and pain, he could see some of the same toughness he remembered in his own mother. "It's all right, Evlyn," she said softly. "It's all right. Go ahead and . . . and use what you have."

Evlyn looked up into her mother's face, as if mentally testing her sincerity. Then she lowered her gaze to Jinzler. "What do you want me to do?"

Jinzler took a deep breath. "The Peacekeeper over there by the wall has a comlink on his belt," he told her. "Do you see it?"

Evlyn wiggled around to where she could peer through the mesh of the chair plugging the gap between table and bulkhead. "Yes."

"It's the only thing that can shut off the jamming and let us call to our friends for help," Jinzler said. "We need you to bring it to us."

"Your friends are dead," Keely murmured.

"No," Jinzler said. "Not these Jedi. I've heard of stories about them, Councilor. They can't be killed nearly as easily as Bearsh thinks."

"And there are still Chiss warriors aboard our ship," Feesa added. "Many of them. They can help us, too."

"But only if we can call them," Jinzler said, gazing into Evlyn's eyes. "Only if *you* can bring us that comlink."

Evlyn set her jaw. "All right," she said. "I'll try."

Jinzler felt his throat ache with an old, old pain. *Do or do not. There is no try.* His father had quoted that Jedi dictum to him over and over again as he was growing up. But never before now had he been able to get past his own resentment and see the encouragement embedded in those words. Pressing his cheek against the chairs above him, wincing as one of the wolvkils snorted a breath of fetid air practically in his face, he looked across the room.

At the Peacekeeper's side, the comlink twitched.

Uliar grunted something under his breath. The comlink twitched again, harder this time; and then, suddenly, it popped free of its clip and clattered onto the deck.

The wolvkils paused in their pacing, all three shaggy heads turning toward the sound. "Steady," Jinzler murmured. "Let it sit there a minute."

Evlyn nodded silently. A few seconds later, with nothing more to draw their attention, the wolvkils resumed their pacing. "All right," Jinzler said. "Now start it toward us. Slowly, and as steady as you can."

Slowly, though not at all steadily, the comlink began to move across the deck. One of the wolvkils paused again as it jerked its way to within three meters of the table, the animal's dark eyes watching the small cylinder with obvious curiosity. But none of its enemies was making any of the threatening moves it had been taught to react to, and its trainers clearly hadn't anticipated a situation quite like this. The wolvkil watched for a moment longer as the comlink rolled and bumped its way along, then lost interest and returned its attention to the creatures cowering behind their barrier. Again, Jinzler found himself holding his breath.

Then, almost anticlimactically, the comlink was at the chair. Reaching out carefully, Evlyn plucked the device in through one of the gaps in the mesh.

And an instant later jerked backward with a gasp as a snarling wolvkil slammed his snout into the chair, nearly knocking it out of position.

"Give it to me," Jinzler snapped, snatching the comlink out of the startled girl's hand. If a loose comlink rolling across the floor wasn't on the wolvkils' list of threats, something being held in an enemy's hand obviously was. "Here," he added, tossing it to Uliar as he swung his legs over and braced his feet against the chair. The wolvkil hit it again, but he'd gotten to it in time and it held steady. "Shut off the jamming."

Uliar's reply, if he made one, was lost as a set of snarling jaws and a clawed paw abruptly slapped into the chair directly above Jinzler's head. "Brace the chairs," Formbi called, struggling to sit upright and getting a one-handed grip on the back of the nearest one. Just in time; the third wolvkil leapt up onto the array of chairs above them, howling furiously as it bit and shoved its snout at them, trying to find a way through. One of its hind legs slipped down between two of them, and the animal howled even more furiously as it flailed around trying to extricate itself. The clawed paw slashed with random viciousness in the enclosed space, and Feesa gasped as it caught her across the shoulder, spilling a line of blood onto the bright yellow of her tunic.

"It's off!" Uliar called over the noise.

Holding grimly onto one of the chair backs with one hand, Jinzler thumbed on his comlink with the other, keying for general broadcast. "Luke—Mara—Commander Fel," he called. They couldn't be dead. They *couldn't*. "Emergency!"

BENEATH HER, LUKE GAVE ONE FINAL TUG ON THE CABLES, bringing Mara's eyes level with the lower edge of the turbo-lift door. "How's that?" he called.

"Good," Mara called back, running her fingertips along the corroded metal at the side of the door. In actual fact, another pull or two might have been a little better for what she needed. But it had been a long climb, and even with all the strength he'd been able to draw from the Force Luke's shoulders beneath her legs had been trembling with muscle fatigue for the past five minutes. Better that she strain a little herself and let him conserve what he had left for whatever lay ahead.

Because if they were right about that soundless cry they'd both sensed a minute ago, there was serious trouble up here.

Ah—there it was. "Got it," she announced. Wrapping her fingertips around the manual release, she gave it a careful tug. There was a click as it came loose; stretching out to the Force, she pried the door open.

But instead of opening to the cheery or at least adequate light of a standard turbolift lobby, it opened into almost total darkness.

"How come it's so dark?" Luke asked.

"Probably because there aren't any lights," Mara told him, looking around as she got a grip on the edge of the opening and pulled herself up and through. Strangely, even most of the permlights that should have been in the area seemed to be out. "We may have been wrong about this being the main living area. Wait a second," she added, peering down the corridor. "I can see some lights way aft. Maybe everybody's back there."

"Or maybe they're not," a voice came from the darkness to her right. "Just stay where you are."

Mara turned toward the sound—

And flinched back as the beam of a glow rod blazed to life in her face.

She reacted instantly, dropping and throwing herself to her left in a flat half roll that brought her back up into a squatting position with her lightsaber ready in her hand. The man with the glow rod tried to track the beam to her motion, but the half roll fooled him and the beam overshot her. For a fraction of a second she was able to see past the light to the shadowy figure behind it, and to the weapon he was holding in his other hand.

First things first. Reaching out with the Force, she got a grip on the weapon and twisted its muzzle away from her.

To her surprise, instead of fighting against the push as

most people instinctively did, the figure continued rolling his hand in the same direction, rotating at wrist and elbow and twisting out of her Force grip as he would have from a normal combat wrist lock. He swung the arm back around in a tight circle, and was bringing it back to bear when the glow rod beam came back to her face. "I said *stay put*," he snapped.

"Nice move," Mara complimented him, shielding her eyes from the light. This time, she recognized the voice. "Guardian Pressor, I presume?"

"Put down the lightsaber," Pressor ordered. "Then move away—"

He broke off with a gasp of pain, his glow rod twisting wildly in his grip and coming to rest pointed at the ceiling. Mara blinked away the last remnants of the sparkles in her eyes in time to see his blaster wrench itself out of his hand and go flying toward the turbolift. "Sorry," Luke apologized, pulling himself the rest of the way out of the shaft and catching the weapon in his outstretched hand. "But I don't think we've got time for a debate. Something's gone wrong up here."

"Obviously," Pressor growled, rubbing his wrist. "What did you do to the power?"

"It wasn't us," Mara said. "All we did was ungimmick the car you left us in—"

She broke off as a beep came from her belt. "The jamming seems to be stopped, too," she added, pulling out her comlink and touching the switch.

"—ara—Commander Fel," Jinzler's voice came urgently. "Emergency!"

"We're here," Mara said, throwing a sharp look at Luke. There were panicky voices and the sounds of serious commotion in the background. "Report."

"We're in the council meeting chamber," Jinzler said, clearly fighting to keep his voice steady. "Bearsh has us trapped by those wolvkils of theirs—"

"Wait a minute," Luke said into his own comlink. "The *wolvkils*? What wolvkils?"

"The ones they've been wearing everywhere," Jinzler ground out. "They weren't dead, just in some kind of suspended animation—very slick, very advanced. And they're not Geroons, either. They're Vagaari."

Pressor hissed something under his breath. "Vagaari?"

There was a muffled crash from the background. "What's happening?" Luke asked.

"The wolvkils are trying to get to us," Jinzler said. "We've got them blocked, but I don't know how much longer we can keep them out."

Mara looked at Pressor. "Which way?"

"There," Pressor said, pointing back toward the lighted area Mara had spotted earlier.

"Show us," Luke told Pressor, handing him back his blaster. "Jinzler? We're on our way."

"Watch out for Bearsh and the others," Jinzler warned as they followed Pressor down the corridor. "They left all the wolvkils in here with us, but they've got some nasty-looking stinging insects they use for personal protection. They might have other weapons, too."

"Got it," Luke said. "Any idea where they were heading?"

"They just said they'd be wandering around," Jinzler said. "It seems they also brought a supply of line creepers."

"Terrific," Luke muttered, glancing into a darkened doorway as they passed. "Fel? You there?"

"Right here, Luke," Fel's voice came promptly. "We caught the gist. What do you want us to do?"

"We're on D-Five," Luke said. "Where are you?"

"D-Six, about midway back along the starboard corridor," Fel told him. "You want us to head back to the turbolifts and join you up there?"

"The forward group isn't working," Luke told him. "From the way the lights and power have gone out, I'd say Bearsh has been here already with his line creepers. Guardian, are the aft turbolifts operational?"

"They should be," Pressor said. "I've got everything locked down between Four and Five, but from Six up to here they should still work."

"You copy that?" Luke called.

"Copy," Fel confirmed. "General Drask's calling the *Chaf Envoy* for the rest of his warriors. If we hurry, maybe we can catch Bearsh and his friends in a pincer."

"Except that Pressor's locked down all the turbolifts from D-Four," Mara interjected. "That *was* what you said, wasn't it?"

"It was," Pressor confirmed, punching keys on his own comlink. "Maybe I'd better confirm that was actually done. Trilli?"

Someone answered in a voice too quiet for Mara to hear. Pressor lowered his own voice, half turning away and speaking rapidly as he brought the person on the other end up to date.

Luke caught Mara's eye. "What do you think?" he asked.

"We don't have time to be creative," Mara said. "Not with Jinzler and the others under attack. Straight in is about all we've got to work with."

"Agreed," Luke said. "Unless we want to layer the attack, with us leading the charge and the Five-Oh-First, the Chiss, and Pressor's Peacekeepers coming in backup waves."

"We may not have any choice on the layering part," Mara pointed out. They'd reached a section of the ship where most of the permlights were functioning, she noted, as well as the majority of the regular lights. The line creepers must not have gotten a stranglehold on this area yet. "The Chiss in particular are going to have to gear up from stage zero. Who knows how long that'll take?"

"Let's find out," Luke said, lifting the comlink to his lips again. "Fel, did you hear the question?"

"Yes, but it appears to be a moot point," Fel said grimly. "Drask can't make contact with the ship. No answer, on any channel, from anyone."

Mara looked at Luke, her heart suddenly tight in her chest. He was staring back at her, a haunted expression on his face. The flurry of deaths they'd both sensed while they were down on D-1 . . .

"Luke?"

"Yes, we heard," Luke said. "Better get your team up here on the double. There's a good chance they may already have taken out the *Chaf Envoy*."

"Understood," Fel said grimly. "We're on our way."

Luke clicked off the comlink. "Guardian?"

"Looks like you can scratch most of our help, too," Pressor said darkly as he jammed his comlink back onto his belt. "Six of my Peacekeepers are missing."

"Six out of how many?" Mara asked.

Pressor snorted gently. "Eleven, including me. We weren't exactly a serious fighting force to begin with." He waved his blaster. "But they were *here* the whole time, either in the turbolift or with my people. When could any of them have slipped away, either back to your ship or to hit my men?"

"The key is that they *weren't* all here," Luke told him. "We had to leave one of them behind."

"Because of injuries sustained in a mysterious sneak attack," Mara added sourly. "What do you think, Luke? They shot Estosh themselves?"

"It's starting to look that way," Luke agreed, pausing to look down a cross-corridor before passing it by. "But at least they don't have the element of surprise anymore."

"They apparently had it long enough," Pressor said bitterly.

"Don't worry, we'll get them," Mara said. "What did you tell your people?"

"I told the ones who are left to hold position, observe, and stand ready to defend those around them if attacked," Pressor said, his jaw set belligerently. "Two of them were in that room with your people, and I'm not going to risk the others on some bantha-brained attack until I have a better idea what we're up against."

If he was expecting an argument, he was disappointed. "I agree," Luke said. "Actually, right now we need their eyes and ears around the ship more than we need the extra firepower."

"Absolutely," Mara agreed. "After all, how much trouble can four or five Vagaari make?"

She would remember that rhetorical question for a long time afterward. With Pressor in the lead, they rounded a jog in the corridor and ran straight into the Vagaari.

But not four Vagaari. Not even five Vagaari.

There were eight of them, Bearsh and seven others, striding down the corridor toward them about ten meters away. Bearsh was still dressed in his usual robe and tunic, minus his wolvkil, but the others were outfitted like soldiers, with helmets and full combat armor, armed with an eclectic mix of Chiss charrics and Old Republic blasters and carbines. Two wolvkils prowled ahead of them like advance scouts, while five more wove in and out of their formation like a fighter escort.

The two groups spotted each other at the same moment. "Halt!" Pressor ordered, snapping his blaster up to point at Bearsh.

The Vagaari halted, all right, in exactly the way Mara would have expected trained soldiers to. The four in front dropped instantly to one knee, giving the ones behind them a clear shot as all seven raised their weapons in silent warning. The wolvkils halted more reluctantly, their eyes glaring balefully at the humans, their tails swishing restlessly.

"Easy," Luke murmured, reaching out a hand to gently push Pressor's blaster out of line. At the same time, he subtly eased a shoulder in front of the other where he would be in a position to protect him if and when the Vagaari decided to start shooting. His lightsaber was ready in his hand, Mara noted, but as yet unignited. "Hello, Bearsh," he called to the Vagaari. "I see you've brought some friends."

"Ah—the Jedi," Bearsh said. If he was at all worried by their sudden appearance, it didn't show in his face. "So you survived the turbolift, after all. I'm very sorry for you."

"Why?" Mara asked, a part of her mind studying the Vagaari soldiers and trying to work through the unexpected numbers. Only five Vagaari had been invited aboard the *Chaf Envoy*; that much she was sure of. So where had the rest been hidden?

"Because it would have meant a quicker and less painful death for you," Bearsh said. "Now it will involve much more suffering."

"Why does anyone have to die?" Mara asked reasonably. "Why don't you tell us what you want? Maybe we can work something out."

Bearsh's eyes flashed. "You fool," he bit out. "You think the Vagaari can be bought off like trinket dealers in the marketplace?"

"Well, you came on this mission for *some* reason," Mara pointed out. "What was it?"

Bearsh snorted. "The avenging of fifty years of Vagaari humiliation," he said. "The achieving of fifty years of Vagaari desire. Does that tell you anything?"

"More than you'd think," Mara assured him. It did nothing of the sort, of course, at least not yet. But one of the first rules she'd been taught about interrogation technique was that every bit of information that could be coaxed out of an unwary or talkative subject was a piece that might later prove important to the overall puzzle. "And have you achieved those noble goals?"

Bearsh's twin mouths curved in a bitter smile. "Beyond our most optimistic hopes," he said. "The human remnant we leave behind will spend their last hours cursing themselves for how they have unwittingly served us."

"Sounds intriguing," Mara said encouragingly. "How about letting us in on the secret? We're all going to die soon anyway, right?"

Bearsh's eyes shifted to Luke. "Is this Jedi heroism?" he asked contemptuously. "To let your *female* speak while you cower in silence?"

Luke stirred. "I'm hardly cowering," he said mildly. "I let Mara do the talking because she's better at this sort of thing than I am. Comes of being trained to interrogate prisoners."

The Vagaari's smile turned smug. "You have it upside down, Jedi," he said softly. "And we have wasted enough time with you. Now, die."

He murmured something, and abruptly the two wolvkils in the lead leapt forward. Mara caught a flicker in Luke's sense as he prepared for combat— "No," she told him, brushing his chest with her fingertips as she took a long step to put herself between him and Pressor and the charging animals. "You did all the climbing. This one's mine."

Before he could argue the point she took another long step forward, stretching out to the Force as she gauged the distance and timing. Ears laid back, salivating jaws wide open, the wolvkils' paws hit the deck one final time and leapt straight for her throat—

With a quick sidestep, Mara ignited her lightsaber and cut both of them in half.

She turned to the Vagaari as the remains of the animals hit the deck behind her with sickening multiple *thuds*. "Now," she said conversationally, holding her lightsaber in ready position. "What was that about someone dying?"

Bearsh's eyes were wide, his face rigid with shock. The smug smile had vanished completely. His mouths worked a moment, and with a sort of strangled gasp he spat something in his own language.

In answer, seven alien weapons opened fire.

Mara was ready. Her lightsaber flashed as she opened her mind to the Force, letting it guide her hands, slashing the brilliant blue blade across the mixture of red and blue bolts. Her sharp focus on the threat in front of her gave her a sort of tunnel vision, but though she couldn't see him she could sense that Luke was at her side with his own lightsaber deflecting the bolts into bulkheads and deck and ceiling. Dimly, she sensed someone else firing nearby, and noticed one of the Vagaari stagger in his armor, his weapon twisted to fire uselessly into the ceiling. Pressor, she realized in a distant sort of way, firing through the defensive barrier she and Luke had set up in front of him. There was another shout of alien language, ringed by a sense of rage and desperation—

The remaining wolvkils leapt forward, apparently oblivious to the blaster bolts scorching the air around them as they

charged toward the defenders. Mara took a step forward as
Luke took one backward, her lightsaber never missing a beat
of their defense as Luke closed down his weapon and
dropped to one knee behind her. She might be better than he
was at detailed lightsaber work, but even after a long climb
he was far and away the best she'd ever seen at this kind of
focused accuracy with the Force. If the Vagaari weren't already sufficiently impressed, she thought as she continued to
deflect their shots, this ought to do it. The wolvkils reached
their jumping-off spot and started to leap straight at her—

They squealed like small lap dokriks, coming to an abrupt
and simultaneous halt as Luke stretched out with the Force to
momentarily scramble their nervous systems. As they stood
stunned, he sent a second, more precise mental jolt into their
systems, his mind searching out and focusing on their sleep
centers.

With a group sigh, the animals' legs collapsed beneath
them and they dropped unconscious to the deck.

Luke got back to his feet. "Well?" he challenged.

Farmboy—the word ran affectionately through Mara's
mind. She herself had been trained in ruthlessness, taught
never to risk herself for those who threatened her and who,
by definition, had therefore forfeited their right to live.

But Luke didn't see things that way. Even as the years had
grown and matured and hardened him, the inner core of ide-
alism and mercy he'd brought with him out of that moisture
farm on Tatooine had never faltered. Others might sneer at
that, she knew, or use his farming background as an insult.

But for her, the title was an acknowledgment of his moral
high ground, a large part of what she loved and admired most
about her husband. And at the end of the day, she slept better
for knowing that even their deadliest opponents had been
given every chance they could possibly hope to receive.

But in this case, the chance was wasted. Bearsh's only
response was to scream another order. His soldiers' only response was to intensify their rate of fire.

And as the shots began to come perilously close to her

face, Mara knew that this particular battle had come to an end.

That end came in the form of a lightsaber whipping through the air beside her, deftly slipping between the frenetic slicing movements of her own weapon. It flashed down the corridor, spinning like a blazing crop harvester disk, slicing through the Vagaari weapons and armor and bodies.

Two seconds later, it was over.

Mara straightened from her combat stance, breathing hard as she studied the fallen soldiers, stretching out with the Force for signs of any surprises still lurking nearby. But Luke had done what was necessary with his usual efficiency.

It was only then that she saw that Bearsh wasn't among the fallen.

"Where did he go?" she demanded, taking another look.

"Who?" Luke asked, looking up from the wolvkil he had knelt to examine.

"Bearsh," Mara said. "He's gone." She turned to look at Pressor. "Guardian?"

Pressor didn't answer. He was staring at the crumpled Vagaari bodies, his jaw hanging open in disbelief. "Pressor?" Mara tried again.

With an effort, he raised his eyes to her. "What?"

"Bearsh," Mara repeated, trying to stifle her impatience. After fifty years without Jedi, these people had apparently forgotten what they were capable of.

"Right," Pressor said, visibly pulling himself together. "He, uh, he took off right after"—he shot Luke a furtive glance—"after you put the animals to sleep. Or whatever you did to them. The rest cranked up their rate of fire, and he took off back down the corridor."

"We'd better get after him," Mara said grimly. "Luke?"

"Go ahead," he told her, moving to the next wolvkil. "I want to make sure they won't wake up until we're ready to deal with them. Go on—I'll catch up."

"Okay," Mara said, starting down the corridor. "Come on, Pressor—you have to show me where this meeting room is," she added, pulling out her comlink and flicking it on. "Fel, stay on your toes," she called. "It looks like we've got more Vagaari to deal with than we were expecting."

There was no answer. "Fel?" she tried again.

Still nothing. "I would say," Pressor said quietly, "that they've probably already figured that out."

CHAPTER 20

THE AFT SECTIONS OF D-6 WEREN'T AS WELL MAINTAINED AS the corridor between the nursery and the Jedi Quarantine had been. But the aft turbolift tubes weren't very far, the area was passable enough, and the 501st was what the training manuals would have called "inspired." They made it to the turbolift lobby without further incident, and in probably record time.

Fel had keyed the call button, and they were waiting for the car to arrive, when they got their first hint of imminent trouble.

"It doesn't sound right, Commander," Grappler insisted, the side of his helmet pressed against the turbolift door. "It sounds . . . it just sounds *wrong*."

"Wrong how?" Fel demanded impatiently. He was all for caution, but at the same time he didn't want to start jumping at moss creakings, either. Not with Formbi and the others in danger up there. "Does it sound old, rusty, cranky—what?"

"It's too heavy," Watchman decided suddenly, his helmet pressed to the door alongside Grappler's. "There's too much weight there for an empty car."

Fel shot a glance at Drask. "Could it be a problem with the repulsorlift generators?"

"No," Watchman said. "There's some of that, too, but not enough. The car is definitely loaded."

"And we must assume it is loaded with enemies," Drask said. "I suggest, Commander, that we take cover."

Fel grimaced. To run and hide felt cowardly somehow, especially since he still wasn't convinced there was anything but an empty turbolift car on the way. Still, it wouldn't do Jinzler and Formbi any good if he and the 501st got themselves slaughtered like amateurs. And since it was Drask who had suggested it and not he himself, he wouldn't have to put up with any of the general's criticism later. "Defensive positions," he ordered. Glancing around, he located a likely doorway a few meters back down the corridor and headed to it.

The room appeared to be a small duty galley for the engine crews, with dust and broken serving crockery everywhere. Settling himself into a position half straddling the doorway where he could see without exposing more of himself than necessary, he braced his blaster hand against the door controls and waited. The turbolift's hum changed subtly as the car settled into position . . .

And with a brilliant flash of white, the door exploded outward.

Reflexively, Fel ducked back as shrapnel and pieces of burning plastic clattered down the corridor. Apparently, Watchman and Grappler had been right. The sound of the explosion faded away, and he swung his eye and blaster back around the jamb.

Two armored figures charged out through the ragged opening, firing red blaster bolts in a scatter pattern as they came.

Fel inhaled sharply. After Jinzler's warning he had naturally expected the intruders to be some of Bearsh's disguised Vagaari cronies. But he'd expected the short robe-and-dead-animal-clothed beings they'd gotten used to seeing aboard the *Chaf Envoy*, not a fully equipped war party. Another pair of Vagaari charged out on the heels of the first two, four snarling and definitely not dead wolvkils emerging with them.

So far, the Imperials hadn't returned fire. It was, Fel decided, about time to change that. Wincing back slightly as one of the random shots sizzled off the bulkhead near him, he filled his lungs. "Halt!" he bellowed.

He hadn't expected any response except possibly better-directed enemy fire, and he wasn't disappointed. All four enemy helmets swung toward the sound of his voice, all four weapons still spitting fire as they tracked him. Coolly, centering his muzzle on the nearest Vagaari's chest, Fel squeezed the firing stud.

The alien staggered back as the blaster bolt blew a cloud of dust and partially vaporized armor from his chestplate. A fraction of a second later Fel had to dodge back around the door controls again as a hail of fire scorched the air where he'd been standing. He ducked down lower and swung his arm around the corner to fire a couple of blind shots in their direction. Out in the corridor, the sounds of the Vagaari weapons had been joined by the BlasTechs' distinctive nasal stutter, and a different sound he assumed was Drask's charric. Still firing, he eased an eye cautiously around the doorway to refine his aim—

Just in time to see one of the wolvkils leaping directly for him.

He dodged backward into the galley. The wolvkil's charge overshot the doorway, and Fel got a clean shot into the animal's flank as it passed.

But the wolvkil merely hit the deck and skidded to a stop, its claws scrabbling for purchase. Without any sign that it had just taken what should have been a killing shot, it turned back toward him. With a roar, it opened its jaws and leapt.

Fel backed up, firing another pair of ineffective shots into the wolvkil's head and shoulders, then dodged to his right, trying to avoid the animal's charge. But the wolvkil wasn't going to be taken in by the same maneuver twice. It hit the ground and instantly made a right-angle turn. Before Fel could do more than fire one last time, it was on him.

More by luck than by skill he managed to deflect the clawed forelegs from his face as he dropped his blaster and thrust his arms forward in a desperate attempt to grab the wolvkil's neck before its teeth could reach him. The animal twisted its head to the side in midair, its jaws clamping hard around Fel's right forearm.

Fel gasped as a stab of pain shocked through him. The animal's momentum shoved him backward, knocking him off his balance and toppling them both toward the deck. His flailing left hand caught a handful of neck fur; tugging hard as he twisted the rest of his body, he managed to turn the animal far enough that they hit the deck side by side instead of with the wolvkil landing on top of him.

Another thud of pain shot through Fel's side from the impact, a jolt punctuated by several sharper, more localized jabs from the bits of broken servingware beneath them. Again, the wolvkil didn't even seem to notice.

Fel tightened his grip on the animal's fur, trying desperately to come up with a plan. His knees and feet were too hemmed in by the wolvkil's body for him to try kicking it, even if he'd had some idea where its vulnerable areas were. His right arm was trapped and useless, and his left hand was effectively immobilized by the need to keep holding on to the wolvkil's neck.

But the animal's eyes were within reach. Maybe.

Fel stared at the dark eyes, trying to push back the agony long enough to think. Letting go of the wolvkil's neck would be dangerous, possibly even fatal. But it seemed to be the only chance he had. If he didn't do something fast, he could lose his right arm entirely, and with only one functioning arm the end would come very quickly. Bracing himself, mentally crossing his fingers, he let go with his left hand and grabbed for the wolvkil's eyes.

That had apparently been precisely the move the animal had been waiting for. With a triumphant growl, it instantly let loose of Fel's right arm; with its head and neck free, it arched its back, its bloody jaws aiming straight at Fel's throat. Fel had just enough time to jerk back, knowing that he'd gambled and lost—

As a white armored hand abruptly appeared in front of the darting jaws.

The wolvkil snarled as it clamped down on rigid plastoid-alloy composite instead of a soft human neck. The snarl quickly turned into a startled yip as it was hauled straight off the deck by its jaws and the scruff of its neck. "Ready?" the stormtrooper called, holding the wiggling animal at arm's length.

"Ready," another voice called back. With a grunt, the first stormtrooper heaved the animal over his head toward the far corner of the room. There was a sputter of multiple blaster-fire, and then silence.

"Nice job," Fel said, breathing hard as he started to get shakily to his feet. The stormtrooper still standing over him—Shadow, he was able to identify him now—grabbed his uninjured arm and helped him the rest of the way up. "Perfect timing and everything. Thanks."

"Don't mention it, sir," Shadow said. "How bad is it?"

"I'll live," Fel assured him, studying his arm. It looked terrible, he had to admit, but it didn't feel too bad. Though that could be the effect of the adrenaline still filling his bloodstream. It would probably hurt a lot more in a minute or two. "What happened out there?"

"We got them all," Cloud said, stepping to his side with a bandage and synthflesh tube from his medpac. "Seems their armor wasn't designed with BlasTechs in mind."

"What about General Drask?" Fel asked, trying to look past the two stormtroopers to the door.

"I am unhurt," Drask said, moving into view around Cloud. "I am sorry your rescue was delayed."

"As long as it got here eventually," Fel said, wincing as Shadow tore back his sleeve. "I shot it a couple of times, but it didn't seem to do any good. Look, Cloud, just stop the bleeding and kill the pain, all right? As long as I can use it, everything else can wait until later. So where are the vital spots on these things, anyway?"

"I'm not sure there *are* any vital spots," Watchman said as Cloud put away the synthflesh tube and concentrated on the bandage. "They look like normal animals, but their internal structure seems to be highly decentralized, with their nervous systems and vital organs distributed throughout their bodies. You have to basically turn the whole animal into chopped meat to stop it."

"I'll remember that," Fel said, eyeing the handful of fresh scorch marks on Watchman's armor. "Anyone hurt?"

"A few nicks," Watchman said, displaying a section of his left forearm where a tiny hole had been punched completely through. "They can wait until we get back to the ship."

Fel looked at Drask. "Assuming there's still a ship to go back to."

"There will be," Drask assured him darkly. "There are still Chiss warriors aboard the vessel. It, and they, will be waiting when we return."

"I hope you're right," Fel said. "Okay, that's good enough," he added as Cloud finished the first layer of bandage and started in on a second. "Is that turbolift car still operational, or did that little entrance of theirs wreck it?"

"It looked all right," Watchman said. "Grappler's doing a more complete check on it now."

"Oh, and the Jedi tried to reach us during the battle," Shadow added.

Fel hadn't even heard the call signal from his comlink. "What did they want?"

"They were warning us there were more Vagaari than we might expect," Watchman said.

"I think we got the message," Fel said, starting for the door. "Did anyone answer them?"

"I don't believe so," Watchman said. "I think we were all too busy at the time."

"Understandable," Fel said, retrieving his blaster from the deck where he'd dropped it. "We'll check in with them on the way up."

Grappler was waiting by the shattered turbolift door, his helmet swiveling back and forth as he kept watch along the various corridors for any other surprises the Vagaari might decide to throw at them. "The turbolift is operational," he confirmed.

"Good," Fel said, leading the way inside. "Let's go."

"What then is the plan?" Drask asked as the car began its slightly tentative rise toward D-5.

Fel braced himself. This went against everything he'd been

taught, and was going to be embarrassing besides. But he'd already concluded it was the only way. "The plan, General Drask," he said quietly, "is that I'm requesting you to take command of the Five-Oh-First for the duration of this battle."

It was, he reflected, possibly the most surprised he'd ever seen Drask get. "You are asking . . . *command*?"

"As you yourself pointed out, you're a ground officer," Fel reminded him evenly. "I'm a flight officer. This is your area of expertise, not mine."

"Yet they are your command," Drask said. "Do you so easily surrender them to another?"

"Not easily at all," Fel admitted. "But it would be the height of arrogance and pride to risk their lives, not to mention the lives of our companions, by insisting on amateur leadership when a professional is standing by. Don't you agree?"

For a moment Drask just gazed at him, his glowing red eyes narrowed. Then, to Fel's surprise, the general actually smiled. The first genuine smile, to the best of Fel's recollection, that any of the Chiss had given any of the Imperials since their arrival aboard the *Chaf Envoy*. "Well and artfully spoken, Commander Fel," Drask said. "I hereby accept command of this unit."

He lifted a finger. "But," he added, "whereas I know ground combat, you are far more versed in the design and layout of the particular battleground we find ourselves in. It will therefore be a joint command."

Fel inclined his head. In practice, he knew, joint commands were usually a disaster, spawning conflicting orders, dueling egos, and general chaos. But in this case, he also knew that none of those problems was going to arise. He would be content to feed Drask tactical data and let the general direct the action.

Drask obviously knew that, too. Which meant that the offer of joint command had been made solely as a face-saving gesture for Fel himself, to protect his position and his status among his men.

There were some aspects of the Chiss warrior philosophy that still drove Fel crazy. But clearly, there were other aspects he could learn to live with. "Very well, General," he said. "I accept."

"Good." Drask's eyes glittered as he lifted his charric. "Then let us show the Vagaari what it means to wage war on the Chiss Ascendancy and the Empire of the Hand."

Fel smiled, looking at his stormtroopers. "Yes," he said softly. "Let's."

THEY ATTACKED MARA TOGETHER, ALL THREE WOLVKILS CHARG-ing across the council meeting room like furry proton torpe-does. They leapt to the attack, their primary target clearly the hands holding the strange blue-bladed weapon.

Dodging coolly to the side, she cut them down with three quick slashes.

Across the room, Jinzler and the others in the makeshift refuge were already pushing aside the chairs that had made up the roof. "Hurry, please," Feesa pleaded, pushing away one of the chairs and then bending back down to take Formbi's arm. "Aristocra Chaf'orm'bintrano is badly hurt."

Mara closed down her lightsaber and hurried over, throw-ing a quick look at the three Chiss warriors and two young men sprawled on the floor as she passed them. Pressor was already kneeling beside one of the men, but it was clear to her that all five of them were beyond help.

They had pushed over the table and Feesa was helping a shaky and blood-soaked Formbi out when Mara arrived. "Everyone else all right?" she said, glancing around for other signs of injury as she refastened her lightsaber to her belt.

"No one else is hurt," Feesa confirmed, apparently ignor-ing the line of blood across her own shoulder. "Please, help him."

"Just relax," Mara soothed her, taking a moment to study the three old men who had left the refuge and gathered to-gether against the back wall, as if trying to stay as far away from her as they could. Probably some of the original sur-vivors of the Outbound Flight's destruction, she decided.

"Luke? Mara?"

She lifted Formbi's arm with one hand for a closer look as she pulled out her comlink with the other. "Right here, Fel. You all right?"

"We had a brief tussle with some of the Vagaari and their furry little pets," Fel said. "Watch out for those wolvkils—they're extremely hard to kill."

"Not if you have a lightsaber," Mara told him.

"I'll make a note to start issuing them to the troops," Fel said dryly. "Anyway, we're clear, and heading to D-Five in one of the aft turbolifts. Any new instructions?"

"For the moment, just take out any Vagaari you run into," Mara told him. "We still don't know how many there are, though, so make sure you don't get trapped in an attrition zone. And if you run into any colonists, try to move them somewhere safe."

"Copy. We're on our way."

"We'll be pushing our way back toward you soon," Mara said. "Luke?"

"Right here," his voice came back. "I've put all the wolvkils to sleep, and I'm on my way. What's your situation?"

"Under control," Mara told him. "You might as well not even stop here. Keep going and see if you can drive the Vagaari back toward the Five-Oh-First. I'll finish here and catch up with you."

"Right."

Mara returned her comlink to its pouch and gently let Formbi's arm down. "It's bad, all right," she agreed. "I think you're going to need more than our medpacs can handle. Pressor?"

Pressor looked up from his examination of the other young Peacekeeper, his eyes smoldering. "What?"

"Aristocra Formbi needs medical attention," she told him, wondering at his sudden change in attitude. "Where are your facilities?"

"You mean our medical facilities?" Pressor growled. "For the wounded?"

Mara frowned; and then, belatedly, she got it. Pressor,

kneeling beside one of his dead Peacekeepers . . . "I'm sorry about your friend," she said gently. "But there's nothing we can do for him now."

"So we should instead give our supplies to help an alien?" one of the older men by the wall demanded bitterly. "The very alien who was responsible for bringing these murderers aboard our ship?"

Mara turned to face him. "Look," she said, fighting to keep her voice and temper under control. "I understand your anger. But there's a time for analysis and blame setting, and this isn't it. You've lost two men—"

"Six," Pressor corrected harshly.

"You've lost *six* men," Mara snapped, resisting the temptation to remind him that none of them would have died at all if Pressor hadn't locked her and Luke away in that turbolift car. "That's the way warfare goes. They were armed, and they at least had a fighting chance."

She nodded back at the door. "That's more than you can say for the rest of the people out there. Unless we move, and move fast, they're *all* going to die. Is *that* what you want?"

"So go help them, Jedi," the old man bit out. "Who's stopping you?"

Mara shook her head. "We're not going to do this piecemeal, running around at cross-purposes and getting in each other's way," she said. "We do this together, or we don't do it at all. Our part is to fight. Pressor's part is to tell us where the enemy is, and to assist us."

She leveled a finger at the three of them. "*Your* part is to stay behind the battle line, treat the wounded, and protect our civilians until we get back. If that's unacceptable, we can leave right now."

"So nothing has changed," one of the other old men murmured.

"Apparently not," the spokesman agreed, his voice edged in bitterness. "Very well, Jedi. We'll heal your wounded. As you command." He drew himself up. "But when this is over, you *will* leave us. Is that understood?"

"Perfectly," Mara said, turning her back on him in disgust.

"All right, Feesa, you and the Aristocra can go with them. You, too, Ambassador."

"A moment, if I may?" Jinzler asked, stepping up to her. "I'd like to ask you a favor," he added, lowering his voice.

Mara stared at him in disbelief. A *favor*? "Jinzler, we don't have time for this."

"It's a very small favor," he assured her. "I want you to take Evlyn with you."

Mara frowned past his shoulder at the woman and the girl huddling together uncertainly behind Feesa and Formbi. "You must be joking."

"Not at all," Jinzler insisted. "She has rudimentary Force abilities. And you've already seen how Director Uliar and the other Survivors feel about Jedi. I think she'll be safer with you than with them."

"She'll be safer in a war zone?" Mara countered pointedly.

Jinzler's eyes were steady on her. "Please?"

Mara shook her head in exasperation. But even in her annoyance, she could sense that Jinzler was deadly serious.

And now that she was focusing her attention on the woman and girl, she could feel the gnawing fear within them, as well. A fear that seemed more personal than just the fact that there were armed Vagaari running loose aboard their ship. "Fine," she said with a sigh. "But she stays way behind me where it'll be at least halfway safe."

"Thank you," Jinzler said, beckoning to the girl. "Evlyn? Come on."

Mara shook her head again as the girl hurried toward her. *How to make a difficult situation even harder, in one easy lesson.* She just hoped it would be worth it.

"Mara?"

She turned to see Pressor coming toward her. "Yes?" she asked in a tone designed to warn him away from any further arguments.

But to her mild surprise, he hadn't come to argue. "Here— you might need these," he muttered, thrusting a pair of comlinks toward her. "Like you said, we have to work together here. These will connect you directly to me and to the other Peacekeepers."

"And there's a channel that cuts through jamming, too," Jinzler added. "Just in case Bearsh finds those controls and turns it on again."

"It's here," Pressor said, pointing out the setting.

"Thanks," Mara said, stuffing the comlinks into her belt.

"Be careful." Pressor glanced at his niece, then over at the old men glaring at them from across the room. "And," he added, lowering his voice, "may the Force be with you."

THERE WERE THREE ARMORED VAGAARI STANDING GUARD IN THE turbolift lobby when Fel, Drask, and the 501st arrived. They weren't standing guard for long.

"Power levels seem fine," Watchman said, glancing around. "Their line creepers must not have gotten this far aft yet."

"This will be the last place they will spread them," Drask said. "The Jedi said that the forward turbolifts have already been compromised. The Vagaari must make certain these remain operational if they hope to escape again to the surface."

"Makes sense," Fel agreed, visualizing the ship's layout in his mind. "To be specific, they need the turbolift that connects to the starboard side. That's the only one left that'll get them to D-Four."

"Which means they will have committed a large number of troops to its defense," Drask said thoughtfully. "What do you think, Commander? Would that be a good place for an ambush?"

"Maybe," Fel said doubtfully. "Of course, it's also the most likely place for them to be *expecting* an attack."

"I did not say an *attack*," Drask said, his eyes glittering maliciously. "I said an *ambush*. The aft turbolift cluster consists of six cars, does it not, operated singly or in groups?"

"Should be the same setup as the forward ones, yes," Fel said, nodding.

"And the starboard tube connects with D-Four, D-Five, and the storage core?"

Fel smiled tightly as he finally understood. "Yes, sir, it does," he said. "How do you want to proceed?"

Drask looked at the stormtroopers. "We will assign two to each mission, I think," he said. "Normally I would prefer three or more for the ambush unit, but the Five-Oh-First has shown itself capable of handling unusual odds."

"And if we don't have at least two of them here with us, the Vagaari may notice and get suspicious," Fel agreed. "Watch-man and Shadow, how would you like to take a walk?"

"Ready and willing, sir," Watchman said. "Once we've reached the turbolift pylon, what exactly do you want us to do?"

"You will take up position at the point where the tube from the storage core connects with the tube running between D-Four and D-Five," Drask told him. "We will attempt to drive the Vagaari back into the cars. As they lift toward D-Four, we will alert you, and you will destroy them in transit. Can that be done?"

"I think so," Watchman said. "It should be easy enough to lock down one of the cars just below the intersection point and climb the rest of the way into position."

"And as long as you have that one car tucked away out of the line of fire, you can shoot up any of the others that you need to," Fel added. "But make sure that one car *stays* tucked away, or we won't be able to get back to the surface our-selves."

"And watch out for the same kind of trap Pressor had set in the forward cars," Grappler warned. "They are likely to have wired this group, as well."

"No problem," Watchman assured him. "Now that we know how it works, we should be able to get up onto the roof of the car and either bypass or reroute the wiring."

"Good," Fel said. "Everyone clear on their job?"

There were four nods. "Then carry out your orders," Drask said. "Maintain comm silence unless absolutely necessary—the enemy may be able to locate your transmissions and thereby anticipate your movements. May warriors' fortune smile on your efforts."

Stiffening briefly to attention, Watchman and Shadow returned to the turbolift car. "Now," Fel said as the car's creakings faded into the distance. "What are your plans for the rest of us?"

"First, we borrow these." Stooping, Drask relieved one of the dead Vagaari of his blaster carbine and helmet. "The armor, unfortunately, is too small for us. Still, the weapons may be enough. Choose a weapon for yourself, Commander, and let us plot out our best approach to the enemy."

CAUTIOUSLY, LUKE EASED AN EYE AROUND THE JOG IN THE CORridor just ahead of him. Somewhere nearby he could sense a pair of vaguely hostile alien minds . . .

There was a flicker of warning from the Force, and he ducked back just as a pair of red bolts blew pieces of the corner past his face.

"Okay," he murmured aloud to himself. So they were closer than he'd realized, and more than just vaguely hostile. That was handy to know.

"Anyone ever tell you that talking out loud when you're alone is a bad sign?" Mara murmured from behind him.

"When the Force is your ally, you're never truly alone," Luke said gravely, turning around and blinking in mild surprise as he caught sight of the girl trailing silently behind his wife. "We have company?"

"So it would seem." Mara gestured to the girl. "You remember Evlyn, don't you?"

"Quite well," Luke said. "Hello, Evlyn."

"Hello," the girl said, a bit timidly. "I'm sorry about . . . earlier."

"That's all right." Luke looked at Mara, lifting his eyebrows questioningly.

"It's a long story," she said, "and I only have half of it myself. The short version is that Jinzler thinks she'll be safer with us right now than with her own people."

"All right," Luke said, setting his curiosity aside in favor of more pressing business. "Did you get the message from Fel?"

"The one about us pushing the Vagaari back toward the turbolifts?" She nodded. "Pressor's also heard from one of his people back there. It appears that as long as the Colonists stay out of their way, the Vagaari aren't bothering to shoot them."

"Rather have them die slowly, I guess," Luke said.

Mara nodded. "And to that end, they're also apparently scattering line creepers by the bucketful." She hesitated. "We may not be able to save this place, Luke."

He'd already come to that conclusion. "We'll just have to do what we can," he said. "And the faster we finish off the Vagaari, the less of a problem we'll have. Are any of Pressor's people going to be in a position to help when we start our push?"

"Not really," Mara said. "Four of them are inside current Vagaari territory, but I doubt their antiquated blasters have enough power to punch through that armor. Oh, and it turns out that two of the missing Peacekeepers had only been stunned by the Five-Oh-First as they passed through D-Six and are up and functional again. That helped Pressor's mood a little."

"Happy allies are good to have," Luke said. "Let's keep him that way by telling his people to stay put. Outnumbered and undergunned is a bad combination."

"Already done," Mara confirmed. "Though one bright side is that they're probably not as undergunned as they might have been. The fact that the Vagaari are using charrics and old Republic blasters against us implies they didn't bring any real weapons of their own, but had to loot the *Chaf Envoy* and D-Four's armory for what they needed."

"Makes sense," Luke said. "They couldn't risk the Chiss picking up odd power readings when they went through scanning their shuttle for line creepers. And of course, that leaves them with the same overage Tibanna gas problem the Peacekeepers have."

"Right," Mara said. "Even so, the outnumbering remains." She hefted her lightsaber. "So I guess it's up to us."

"And the Five-Oh-First." Luke paused, frowning as a distant sound caught his attention. "You hear that?"

"Sounds like blasterfire," Mara said, her forehead wrinkled in concentration. "And lots of it."

"Maybe they've decided some of the Colonists need to die right now after all," Luke said grimly.

"Or else one of Pressor's people decided to be a hero," Mara agreed. "Either way, I think that's our cue."

"Right." Luke ignited his lightsaber. The two Vagaari were still there, he knew, but it was unlikely they would be expecting a straight-out charge. "Ready?"

"Ready."

"AGAIN," DRASK ORDERED.

Fel nodded and fired again, sending a short burst from his borrowed carbine into the corridor wall a few meters in front of him, listening to the slightly wheezy and very distinctive sound of the ancient weapon. "Anything?"

"They sound agitated," the general said, holding his appropriated Vagaari helmet up to his ear. "Ah—there is an order."

Fel frowned. "How can you possibly know that?" he asked. "You don't even speak their language."

"There is a tone of command that is the same in all languages," Drask said. "Now we need only wait and see if it is the command we are hoping for."

"They're coming," Grappler murmured, cocking his head toward the corner he and Cloud were waiting beside.

"Stand ready." Drask gestured to Fel. "Fire again."

Fel did so, trying to watch both ends of the corridor at once. Between bursts he could hear rapid footsteps approaching . . .

Suddenly, with a clatter of armor, they were there: five armored Vagaari, charging to what they thought was their comrades' aid. They got off a single, startled volley before the two stormtroopers cut them down.

"Good," Drask said, surveying their handiwork with satisfaction. "That diminishes the enemy somewhat. Where do you recommend we go next?"

"There's a series of emergency battery rooms back that way," Fel said dubiously. "You aren't really intending to try this same trick twice, are you?"

"Not at all," Drask assured him. "It is time to take the battle to the enemy. The other stormtroopers should be in position by now; let us see if we can drive the Vagaari into reach of their weapons."

"Ah," Fel said. "In that case, we probably want the fluid systems service corridor instead of the battery rooms. There are two access panels in particular we might find useful: one opening into one of the cross-corridors on this side of the starboard turbolift lobby, the other door opening into the lobby itself."

"How likely are the Vagaari to have set up pickets at the entrance to this corridor?"

"Not very," Fel said. "It's narrow and probably not well marked."

"And it offers an avenue of retreat?"

"It has doors to both the main engine room and the secondary command complex," Fel told him. "We could hold off a small army from either place."

"Excellent," Drask said. "Take us there."

Cautiously, keeping an eye out for stray Vagaari, Fel led the way through a series of small utility rooms. They reached the entrance to the service corridor, only to find it jammed shut.

"What I don't understand is where they're all coming from," Fel said, stroking his bandaged right arm restlessly as he watched Grappler and Cloud work on the door. "That ship of theirs couldn't have followed us here, could it?"

"It could not, and did not," Drask told him. "But surely now that we know about their suspended animation technology the answer is obvious."

"But if they didn't—oh." Fel broke off, embarrassed. It *was* obvious. "Those three sealed rooms aboard their shuttle, the ones they claimed were open to vacuum."

"Yes," Drask confirmed. "Though undoubtedly a small portion of each *was* indeed open to space."

"Right—the part by the door sensor and access port," Fel said, nodding. "Otherwise, a secondary test by your people would have shown that the readings were fake."

"They would have had a secret way to reseal the rooms, of course," Drask said. "That was why they pretended Estosh had been attacked, to give him an excuse to stay behind."

"Only it wasn't just pretending—they really *did* shoot him," Fel reminded him. "These people are seriously out for revenge."

"Perhaps," Drask murmured. "Or perhaps they are motivated by something more practical."

There was a hollow popping sound from the door. "Got it," Cloud announced.

"Good," Drask said. "Proceed."

Cloud led the way, followed by Grappler, Drask, and Fel. The corridor was narrower than it had looked on the blueprints, Fel realized with a twinge of apprehension, with barely enough room for the stormtroopers to get through without scraping their shoulders on the piping and access manifolds lining the walls. Far too narrow for any of them to pass any of the others.

Which meant that if they had to retreat, it would be Fel and his injured gun arm who would be running point.

But at least the Vagaari did seem to have missed this particular back door. There were no sentries or other signs of enemy presence in the corridor. In fact, from all appearances, the place might not have been visited in years, and several times Fel had to fight back a reaction to the drifting dust being kicked up by their passage. It would be a shame to put this much effort into sneaking up on the enemy only to announce their presence with a coughing fit.

They made it to their target panel without incident. Drask motioned the stormtroopers to take up side-to-side positions in front of it, BlasTechs at the ready. Then, reaching around past them, he punched the release.

This door, fortunately, opened without any difficulty at all. The stormtroopers were ready, opening fire the instant the sliding panel was clear of their muzzles. "Can you see anything?" Fel shouted to Drask over the BlasTechs' stuttering screams.

"Vagaari," Drask shouted back succinctly. Return fire was starting to come now, and Fel winced as burst after burst slammed into his men, leaving blackened marks on the clean white armor. The targets were clearly plentiful—Fel could see both stormtroopers rhythmically swinging their weapons back and forth—but at the same time the return fire seemed to be increasing rather than decreasing. However many troops Bearsh had brought along, it was starting to look like a large percentage of them were right here.

And even the legendary 501st had a limit to what it could handle.

It took only a few more seconds for Drask to come to the same conclusion. Again reaching past the stormtroopers, he punched the control. The door slid shut, the metal ringing with the impact of belated Vagaari fire. "We have done what we can to encourage their retreat," he said, nudging Fel back toward the direction they'd come from. "It is time to make our own."

"Right." Fel turned around—

And froze. Moving stealthily through the passage toward them was a line of Vagaari warriors.

Apparently, the enemy hadn't missed this bet after all.

CHAPTER 21

GATHERING HIS FEET BENEATH HIM, LUKE DUCKED OUT OF THE doorway he'd been hiding in and sprinted ahead and down the corridor toward the next room in line. As he ran, a hail of blaster bolts scorched the air around him, scattering from his lightsaber blade. He made it to the doorway without getting hit and ducked inside the room.

It was another bunkroom, he saw, this one having been converted into a game area. In the back corner four young couples sat huddled together on the floor, their fear radiating toward him like a set of permlights. "It's all right," he assured them. "Don't worry, you're safe now."

None of them replied. With a sigh, he leaned back out into the corridor for another cautious look. He had hoped this strange aversion to Jedi was confined to the original group of Outbound Flight survivors. But whatever the reason for their hatred, they'd clearly done a good job of passing it on to successive generations.

Unfortunately, if Jinzler was to be believed, it also meant this was yet another place where it might not be safe to leave Evlyn alone. It was starting to look like they were going to have to drag her all the way back to the turbolifts.

Behind him, Mara signaled that they were ready. Raising his lightsaber again, he stepped back into the corridor.

Again, the Vagaari opened fire. But this time, the shots were coming from a set of doorways farther down the corridor. He and Mara might not be taking down many of the enemy with this maneuver, Luke reflected as he took a step toward them, but they were definitely pushing them back.

There was the sound of running feet behind him, and Mara and Evlyn ducked into the room he'd just left. "Clear!" Mara called.

Stepping back again, Luke joined them. "Everyone still okay?" he asked.

"Yes," Mara said. Evlyn looked a little winded, but seemed all right otherwise. "By the way, did you notice the Vagaari have their own jamming system up and running?"

"No, I hadn't," Luke said, frowning. "When did this happen?"

"Sometime in the past few minutes, I think," Mara said. "I tried to call Fel while you were clearing this last section and could get only static."

"Terrific," Luke muttered.

"Not as terrific as they think," Mara said, pulling one of the Old Republic comlinks out of her belt and handing it to him. "We can still keep in touch with Pressor and the Peace-keepers with these."

"That's something, anyway," Luke agreed, sliding the comlink onto his belt beside his own. "What do you suppose they're up to?"

"I don't know," Mara said. "It might not be anything more sinister than Bearsh deciding he was tired of coordinated attacks."

"Then again, it might," Luke pointed out grimly. "And Fel and the Five-Oh-First are back there all alone."

He caught the flicker of concern from his wife. Apparently, she'd grown fond of the Imperials. "We'd better pick up our pace a little," she said.

"Right," Luke said, stepping back to the doorway. "Here goes . . ."

THE VAGAARI IN THE FRONT OF THE LINE JERKED BACK AS A blaster bolt found a gap in his armor; he toppled over backward, his weapon blazing madly away as he fell. One of the shots sizzled past Fel's head as he crouched down in the corridor, and he winced away as he slammed a fresh Tibanna gas cartridge into his blaster. One more Vagaari down; a whole line of the aliens standing ready to take his place. "Report!" he shouted as he took another waddling step backward, trying to keep his head clear of his allies' fire.

"We're . . . still good, sir," Grappler called. But all the confidence in the galaxy couldn't hide the fact that the stormtrooper was hurting, and hurting badly. Too many enemies, too much blasterfire, and even the tough composite that made up stormtrooper armor was starting to disintegrate under the assault. Cloud had stopped replying entirely to questions and orders, though he was still on his feet, still firing, and still retreating in an orderly fashion. Grappler, Fel suspected, wasn't in much better shape.

Fel and Drask were still largely unscathed, crouched down as they were in order to give the stormtroopers a clear field of fire. But that couldn't last, either, and unarmored as they were, a single well-placed shot could easily put either of them out of action.

It would have been nice if they could have used their grenades. The stormtroopers had a complete set of them, along with gas-powered launchers built into their BlasTechs to speed them on their way. The problem was that an explosion among pipes filled with coolant and other working fluids would probably kill the attackers, the defenders, and half of Outbound Flight's remaining populace. The blasters were risky enough in here.

And on top of all that, the Vagaari had finally begun jamming their comlinks. The only mystery was why they hadn't gotten around to it earlier.

So here they were, trapped in a narrow corridor with enemies on all sides and no way to call for assistance.

And as Fel opened fire on the next Vagaari in line, it occurred to him that he was probably going to die.

It was an odd sensation, that. The possibility of death was always present in combat, of course, and there had been many times when he'd gazed out his clawcraft's canopy at the enemy ships rising to meet him and wondered if this would be the time. But in space combat there was always a chance of survival, even if your ship was blown completely out from under you.

Here, there would be no such chance. If the Vagaari blasters found him, he would be dead.

Dead.

"Where is this second access door?" Drask shouted into his ear.

Fel glanced around, getting his bearings. "Another two or three meters," he said. "Same side of the corridor as the last one."

"Understood."

Fel resumed firing, wondering at the Chiss's composure. The exit into the engine room that Fel had so confidently told him about was all the way at the other end of the corridor, too far away for them to reasonably expect to make before the Vagaari numerical superiority finally took them down.

But the access door into the turbolift lobby itself was only a few meters along the corridor. And so that was where Drask had ordered them to go.

The lobby would be full of Vagaari, of course. But anyplace they could reach would likely have that same problem. At least in the lobby they would have a little more room to maneuver.

And maybe the Jedi would come in time. Maybe.

THE MEDIC STRAIGHTENED UP, SHAKING HER HEAD. "I'M SORRY, Ambassador, but that's all I can do."

Jinzler nodded silently, gazing down at the treatment table. Formbi was lying still, his eyes closed, his breathing labored. The medic had mostly gotten the bleeding stopped, though Jinzler could see traces still seeping out through the bandages. But the Chiss had already lost a lot of blood, and there was no way to replace it.

At least not now. Not until they could get back to the *Chaf Envoy* and its medical supplies, or else find a Chiss crewer with the same blood type.

Assuming any of the crewers aboard the *Chaf Envoy* were still alive.

"What about bacta?" he asked, looking up at the medic again. "Is there any available?"

The medic looked at him in astonishment. "You must be joking," she said. "Most of the bacta we had was lost or corrupted in the battle and aftermath. We used up what was left probably twenty years ago."

"The ambassador isn't joking," a dark voice came from the corner. "He's most serious."

Jinzler turned around. Councilor Keely was sitting there, holding a salve bandage to his elbow where he'd somehow scraped it raw during the battle in the meeting room. "Ambassador Jinzler is a friend of all," Keely continued, staring at the deck. "Didn't you know? He's a friend to Blue Ones, to Jedi, even to murdering Vagaari. Yes, Ambassador Jinzler likes everyone."

He lifted a baleful glare to Jinzler. "This Blue One is the real reason your Jedi friends are so anxious to get to the turbolifts, isn't it?" he demanded, nodding at the table. "So that you can get him to his ship to be patched up. Once that happens, you'll all just fly away and leave us here to die."

"That's not true," Jinzler said, keeping his voice steady. He'd had doubts about Keely's mental stability even before the Vagaari had unleashed their wolvkils on him and the rest of the Council. Now he was even less sure about it. "There are also people aboard the Chiss ship who can get rid of the line creepers the Vagaari are leaving behind. The faster we get them down here, the sooner we can restore your ship to full power."

Keely snorted. "Oh, yes. It sounds so reasonable." Abruptly, he stood up. "But then, your entire profession is based around your ability to lie to people, isn't it?"

"Sit down, Keely."

Jinzler looked over at the room's waiting area, where Uliar and Tarkosa had been talking together in low tones. The conversation had ceased, and both men were gazing at Keely, their expressions unreadable. "Sit down," Uliar repeated. "Better yet, go back to your rooms."

"But he's a liar, Chas," Keely insisted. "By definition, that means he's been lying to us."

"Very possibly," Uliar agreed coldly. "But you will still sit down."

For a moment the two men locked gazes. Then, with a noisy huff, Keely dropped back into his chair. "Liar," he muttered, turning his gaze back to the deck.

The medic looked back at Jinzler, and he thought he could detect a hint of fresh strain in her face. "I'm going to run a sample of his blood," she told him. "It might be possible to synthesize at least some of the basic plasma for him. It wouldn't be whole blood, but it would be better than nothing."

"It would certainly help," Jinzler acknowledged. "Thank you."

The medic gave him a flicker of a smile and walked away. Feesa moved into the spot by the table where the woman had been standing, her face etched with worry as she gazed down at Formbi. "He'll make it," Jinzler assured her, knowing even as he said it that it was probably a lie. Maybe Keely was right about him. "He's strong, and they've got the bleeding stopped. He'll make it."

"I know," Feesa said, and Jinzler could hear in her voice that she knew she was speaking a lie, too. "It's just . . ."

"He's a relative of yours, isn't he?" Jinzler asked, searching for something less painful to talk about. "You know, I don't think I ever heard how Chiss families are set up. Especially those who make up the Ruling Families."

She looked at him blankly. "The Nine Ruling Families are like any other families," she said. "Blood and merit create siblings and cousins and ranking distants. Some are released, others are rematched, others are born to trial. The same as any other family."

She lowered her eyes to Formbi again. "This wasn't supposed to happen. None of this was supposed to happen."

On the table, Formbi's eyes fluttered partway open. "Feesa," he murmured. "No more."

"What do you mean?" Jinzler said, frowning. "No more what?"

Feesa turned her face away. "Nothing," she said, her voice suddenly sounding oddly muffled.

The back of Jinzler's neck began to tingle. "Feesa?" he prompted. "Feesa, what's going on?"

"Peace, Ambassador," Formbi murmured. "I will tell you . . . everything . . . later. But not . . . now." His head turned slightly to the side.

Toward where Keely was still staring at the deck, muttering to himself.

Jinzler felt his breath catch in his throat, a part of that conversation behind their wolvkil barrier flashing suddenly to mind. *You genuinely didn't know who they were?* Uliar had asked. *Of course not,* Jinzler had replied, angry and frightened and indignant. *You think we would have let them aboard Outbound Flight if we had? Some of you might have,* Uliar had countered. *Possibly the heirs of those who tried to destroy Outbound Flight in the first place.*

And then, suddenly, Feesa had broken in and changed the subject.

You really didn't know who they were? You really didn't know who they were? "Yes, Aristocra," he said quietly, feeling cold all over. "Later will do fine."

"THERE!" DRASK'S VOICE SHOUTED IN FEL'S EAR. "THERE!"

Fel glanced to his right in mild surprise. Preoccupied with defense, he hadn't even noticed that they'd reached the access door. He fired two more quick shots down the service corridor, then risked another sideways glance to locate the release control. There it was, half a meter above his head. "Grappler!" he shouted. "Stun grenade!"

"Shak," the stormtrooper muttered back, his voice strained.

The Eickarie word for *ready,* Fel recalled uneasily. Apparently, Grappler was too far gone to even be able to translate into Basic. Fel could only hope he was alert enough to remember to arm the stun grenade before he threw it. "Ready—" He lunged up and slapped the release "—go!"

The door creaked slightly as it began to slide open. Fel got a glimpse through the opening of armored Vagaari turning their weapons toward the noise; and then Grappler lobbed the grenade through the opening. Fel hit the release again, reversing the door's direction. There were sounds of sudden consternation outside as the panel slid closed—

And then the whole service corridor bulkhead seemed to bow inward toward them as the grenade went off.

"Now!" Fel shouted, hitting the release again as he switched his blaster to rapid fire and emptied it into the Vagaari at the other end of the corridor. The door slid open again, all the way this time, and he dived sideways through it.

He landed on the deck of the turbolift lobby between two groggy Vagaari who lay twitching where the force of the concussion had thrown them. Scrambling to his feet, ignoring the protest of cramping leg muscles, he turned and helped pull Drask through the opening. "What was that?" the Chiss asked, taking a stumbling step over the nearest Vagaari.

"Concussion grenade," Fel said, looking around as he slid his last Tibanna cartridge into his blaster. "Knocks everyone flat for a couple of minutes."

"And then allows them to awaken?" Drask demanded as Grappler staggered through the opening. Fel grabbed the stormtrooper's arm to steady him, grimacing at the dozens of pits and scorch marks discoloring his armor. "What sort of weapon is that for a warrior?"

"The sort a warrior uses when he doesn't know whether or not the enemy has hostages," Fel snapped. Cloud seemed to be having trouble with the door; reaching in, Fel grabbed his arm and pulled him bodily through. "Come on, we need to get out of here."

But it was too late. Even as he turned Cloud toward the turbolift doors and the corridor leading out of the lobby, he saw that the Vagaari in that direction were starting to stagger to their feet, their weapons tracking unsteadily toward the intruders. At the speed Cloud and Grappler were probably capable of, the enemy would be back to full strength long before they could run that gauntlet. The same went for the corridor leading aft and the cross-corridor leading portside.

Which basically left only the option of standing here and taking out as many Vagaari as they could before they were killed.

"Listen!" Drask murmured urgently. "I hear a turbolift car approaching."

Fel grimaced as he caught the telltale sound, too. Approaching full of enemies, no doubt, but he didn't have anything better to offer. If they could clear the car before those inside knew what was happening, they would at least have bought themselves a little cover.

In fact, if the Vagaari in the lobby stayed groggy long enough, they might even have a chance of using the car to get away. "Go," he told Drask, giving a tug on Cloud's arm to get him moving.

They picked their way through the maze of stunned Vagaari, the stormtroopers stumbling drunkenly, Fel doing his best to help and hurry them along. Drask, unencumbered with injured comrades, made the trip considerably faster and was standing ready at the door when it slid open. He swung around the edge to lean into the car, his charric spitting blue fire as he laid down a killing pattern.

The pattern broke off almost before it started. "Empty," he called, swinging back around again to cover the Vagaari still getting to their feet. A shot blistered past his head; shifting his aim, he fired once to silence the gunner. "Hurry!"

The Chiss had shot three more Vagaari, and the room was starting to fill with blaster bolts by the time Fel and the stormtroopers stumbled through the open door. "We're in," Fel shouted as he guided his charges to the rear of the car. The enemy fire was still highly random, but the Vagaari would be getting both their balance and their aim back any minute. "Hit the control—there."

"Storage core?" Drask asked, still firing as he ducked inside.

"Yes," Fel said. Whatever reinforcements Bearsh had

would undoubtedly be up on D-4, and Fel had no interest in taking them on just now. "Come on, hit it."

Drask did so.

Nothing happened.

Drask hit it again, and again, then tried the switch to D-4. Still nothing. "What's wrong?" Fel demanded, hurrying to his side.

"It does not function," Drask snarled. "The Vagaari have locked it down."

A burst of enemy fire splattered off the edge of the door. "Come on," Fel said, grabbing Drask's arm and dragging him to the back of the car. So that was it. The enemy had anticipated their final move, and they were now well and truly trapped. Fel had failed his men, failed Admiral Parck, failed Aristocra Formbi and the rest of the Chiss.

But if the Vagaari expected them to die quietly, they were in for a rude shock. Cloud and Grappler had sunk to the floor, semiconscious, their BlasTechs hanging loosely from their hands. Fel grabbed Cloud's weapon, checked the power indicator, and swung it around to point at the door. Outside, he could see the Vagaari starting to move purposefully around, fully in control now and probably setting up their pattern for a rush on the car. Leveling the BlasTech toward the opening, Fel braced himself . . .

And with a sudden shattering of metal and plastic, the front part of the car's ceiling exploded inward.

Instinctively, Fel twisted his head away, squeezing his eyes shut against the flying debris. The roar of the blast faded and he turned back, blinking open his eyes.

At the front of the car, barely visible through the roiling dust, stood a pair of Imperial stormtroopers.

Watchman and Shadow had arrived.

There were, Fel had estimated, about thirty Vagaari in the turbolift lobby. They never had a chance. The two stormtroopers stood shoulder to shoulder in the doorway, fresh and uninjured, taking the enemy's attack unflinchingly as they systematically raked the lobby with blasterfire.

Fel sank down onto the floor beside Cloud and Grappler,

the BlasTech falling loose in his hands as he listened to the firefight, the combat tension finally beginning to drain out of him.

And as it did, he slowly became aware of pain digging into his body from a dozen different places on arms, legs, and torso. Apparently, he wasn't as uninjured as he'd thought.

By the time the battle was over, he needed Drask's help to even stand up.

THE TWO VAGAARI FIRED ANOTHER BURST, THEIR BLASTER bolts scattering from Luke's lightsaber blade. He pressed forward grimly, letting the Force manipulate his defense, shortening the gap between him and the attackers. In the distance, the sounds of multiple blasterfire from a minute earlier had gone ominously quiet. Wrapped in the tunnel vision of combat, he couldn't tell what the outcome had been, but it was beginning to look as if he and Mara were already too late to be of any help there.

The Vagaari intensified their fire. Setting his teeth, he struggled to keep up with the attack—

And suddenly, the screaming of their weapons was joined by blasterfire of a more modern pitch and rhythm. For a handful of seconds the two sounds played a deadly duet, and then all weapons fell abruptly silent.

"Luke? Mara?"

Luke let his lightsaber slow to a halt in ready position, his lungs heaving as he relaxed his tight focus and began opening up his mind again. The voice and the sense accompanying it had been very familiar . . .

"We're here, Fel," Mara called out as she and Evlyn came up behind him. "Come on, Luke, they're hurt."

Luke blinked sweat out of his eyes as he closed down his lightsaber and joined the other two hurrying down the corridor. He could sense the pain now: waves of it, sweeping toward him.

The two groups met around the next jog in the corridor, beside the bodies of the three Vagaari Luke had been slowly pushing back. "These the last of them?" one of the storm-troopers asked, gesturing at them with his BlasTech.

"As far as I know, yes," Luke said, eyeing him and the others with concern and a bit of awe. All four stormtroopers had been through the wars, all right, with blaster burns scattered and clustered all across their once-sleek armor. On two of them, the white color of their breastplates had been almost completely obliterated, with at least a dozen spots on each where the armor had been burned clean through. It was hard to believe they were even alive, let alone more or less on their feet. Fel didn't look to be in terrific shape, either, and though he seemed to be walking on his own Luke could see that Drask was standing ready to offer him a helping hand. "I see you've been busy," he said. The words sounded rather bland, but somehow seemed to fit the casual dignity and bravery he could sense from all six of the group. "I'm sorry we weren't able to get to you faster."

"We managed," Fel said, his voice rigid with the strain of someone fighting back pain and determined not to show it. "Afraid we left a mess by the turbolifts that someone's going to have to clean up."

"Don't worry about it," Luke assured him. "What about Bearsh? Did you see him?"

"I didn't, no," Fel said, glancing around at the others. There was a general murmur of agreement. "He must have made it to D-Four before we were able to deal with their rear guard."

"Rear guard?" Mara asked. "You saying there are still more of them up there?"

"Definitely," one of the stormtroopers said. "We could hear them working in the turbolift pylon while we were bringing the car in."

"I don't suppose you got a head count," Luke said.

The stormtrooper shook his head. "We were too busy getting the car moving and laying out the flash paste to give them much attention."

"I have done a rough calculation, however," Drask said. "From the size of the three inaccessible rooms aboard the

Vagaari vessel, I estimate Bearsh could have brought as many as three hundred troops with him."

Luke whistled. "Three *hundred*? They must have been stacked like data cards in there."

"With their hibernation technology, that would be entirely possible," Drask agreed.

"What were they doing in the pylon?" Evlyn asked.

They all looked at her. "What?" Fel asked.

"You said they were working in the turbolift pylon," the girl reminded them. "You said you didn't count them, but didn't you at least look to see what they were doing?"

The two slightly-less-injured stormtroopers looked at each other. "Not really," one of them confessed. "We could see the lights, and they were definitely working on the tube and not on any of the cars. But that was all we got."

"We had more pressing things to think about at the time," the other stormtrooper added.

"Well, let's think about it now," Luke said. "What could Bearsh be up to?"

"Maybe there's a quick way to find out," Mara said, stooping beside one of the Vagaari bodies and pulling off his helmet. "Let's ask him."

She glanced over the controls, then keyed on the built-in comlink. "Hello, Bearsh," she called toward the voice pickup. "This is Mara Jade Skywalker. How's it going up there?"

There was a long pause. "Bearsh?" she called again. "Come on, Vagaari, look alive."

"I'm sorry, but General Bearsh is unavailable at this time," a voice replied, sounding distant and oddly hollow as it came from the helmet's headphones. "So you still live, Jedi?"

Luke grimaced. *General* Bearsh, no less. "That's right, Estosh," Mara said. "We still live, you're up and around again—it's just a glorious day for us all."

"Not for all, Jedi," Estosh said, an edge of malicious pleasure in his voice. "But for the Vagaari, this is indeed a day of satisfaction. Where precisely are you?"

"We're standing around on a Vagaari-free Dreadnaught," Mara told him. "You want something more precise?"

"No need," Estosh said. "I see you now, there in the corridor beside the Number Two Turbolaser Coolant Room."

Luke glanced at the marker beside the nearest door in mild surprise. Apparently, the Vagaari had very precise locators built into their troops' helmets. "What do you mean, *Vagaari-free?*" Estosh went on.

"Oh, didn't you know?" Mara said. "Your rear guard's dead. All of them."

"Really," Estosh said. "Interesting. You Jedi are more effective warriors than we realized. Our mistake."

"A mistake others paid for," Mara pointed out. "But I suppose that's typical. I don't suppose you're brave enough to come down here and take any of the risks yourself?"

Estosh chuckled melodiously. "Thank you for your invitation, but no. The Supreme Commander never takes the same risks as the common soldiers. I have my duty, and they have theirs."

"Supreme Commander, you say," Mara said. "I'm impressed. Speaking of duty, you surely didn't sacrifice forty-odd troops just to kill off a couple of hundred humans and a few Chiss, did you?"

"Of course not," Estosh said. "Tell me, is Master Skywalker there with you?"

Luke hesitated, sensing the trap lying beneath the question. Estosh was willing to talk, but only if he knew he didn't have a Jedi running loose and unaccounted for.

On the other hand, if Luke confirmed he was here listening, his own freedom of movement would be severely limited, at least for the length of the conversation. With Fel and the stormtroopers largely out of commission, it would be a bad idea to let the Vagaari pin both him and Mara down to this one particular spot.

Mara, he could sense, had come to the same conclusion. Fortunately, she'd also come up with the answer. Smiling wickedly at Luke, she pulled out the comlink Pressor had given her and lifted her eyebrows.

He nodded understanding, taking a rapid couple of steps aft down the corridor as he pulled the matching device from his own belt. Clicking hers on, Mara held it near the helmet's voice pickup and nodded. "Yes, I'm here, Estosh," Luke said into his comlink. "What do you want?"

"Nothing in particular," Estosh said offhandedly, his voice coming more faintly now from the comlink as Luke continued down the corridor toward the aft turbolift lobby. It was time, he decided, to see what exactly was going on up there. "I merely didn't want to have to repeat all of this for you later. You're right, we did indeed come here for revenge. But certainly not for the few ragged handfuls of humans who will soon be dying alongside you. No, our revenge will be against the entire Chiss race."

The colonists, Luke saw, were beginning to emerge now from the various nooks and crannies they'd been hiding in. Most of them shied back again at their first sight of him. "Nice to have goals in life," Mara commented. "But I find it hard to believe there's anything aboard Outbound Flight that's going to help you take down the Chiss Ascendancy. Or are the Vagaari in the habit of using high-flying words that don't really mean anything?"

"Mock me all you wish, Jedi," Estosh snarled. "But *I* am up here, and *you* are down there."

Luke had reached the turbolift lobby now. There was a single car waiting there behind the piles of Vagaari bodies, a car with an oddly shaped hole blown in the front part of the roof. He stepped inside and turned back toward the control panel.

It was only then that he saw that Evlyn had followed him.

He blinked at her in surprise, cutting off his comlink's voice pickup. "What are you doing here?" he demanded.

"I want to help," she said. "What can I do?"

His first instinct was to tell her to get back to Mara where she'd be safe. The only way he was going to be able to find out what the Vagaari were up to would be to go up to D-4 and take a look for himself. If they'd left a reception committee watching that approach, it could get messy.

But there was something about the expression on the girl's face that was stirring old memories . . .

"And up there is about as far as you're going to get,"

Mara's voice scoffed over the comlink, the tone carefully designed to draw Estosh out still further. "Or had you forgotten we're in the middle of the Chiss Redoubt?"

"I want to go with you," Evlyn said. "Please?"

Luke smiled as the memory clicked. *I want to go with you.* He could still remember his eagerness and frustration as he'd said those same words to Ben Kenobi, way back on the first Death Star. But Ben had refused him, going alone to shut down the tractor beam that was preventing the *Millennium Falcon* from escaping.

And thereby going to his death.

Would things have been different if he'd allowed Luke to go along? Of course they would. Leia might never have been found and rescued, for one thing. Han certainly wouldn't have gone out on a limb for her back then, at least not alone.

Still, there had been many times over the years when he'd lain awake in the dark hours of the night, visualizing how he and Ben together might have been able to defeat or at least neutralize Vader, then go on to free Leia from her cell, then take R2-D2 and the precious Death Star data to Yavin 4.

"Ah, so there are things even the great Jedi don't know," Estosh scoffed back. "Perhaps it was merely your basic combat skills I underestimated."

There was really no question as to what the logical, practical decision should be. Evlyn would be at risk up there, as well as being a possibly crucial distraction for Luke himself.

And yet, despite all the logic, his instincts were whispering the exact opposite.

Trust your instincts, Luke . . .

"Get ready to stop the turbolift," he told her. Bending his knees, stretching to the Force for strength, he jumped through the ragged opening up onto the car's roof. The reason for the odd shape of the hole became clear the instant he saw the multicolored wires crisscrossing the roof. Like the forward turbolifts, this one had been wired as a trap. The stormtroopers who had made the hole had rearranged and extended some of the lines, then shaped their explosive ribbon to avoid damaging the rest of them. "And if I tell you to get out of here, you *immediately* take the car back down and get Mara and the Imperials, without question or argument. Understood?"

Evlyn nodded. Stretching to the Force again, Luke reached down through the opening and keyed the switch.

The car began to lumber its way toward D-4, "downward" from where Luke was currently sitting. Pulling out his glow rod, he adjusted it to tight beam and waited.

"That's a little unfair, Estosh," Fel's voice came from the comlink. "Even Jedi can't be expected to know everything. That's why they have allies like us. You see, we know all about the recorder you tapped into the navigational repeater lines."

Luke frowned at the comlink. A recorder in the navigational lines, that Fel and the 501st had known about?

And that they hadn't mentioned to anyone else?

"Ah, so that's what the diversion with the line creepers was all about," Mara said. Even at this distance, Luke could sense her own surprise and annoyance that Fel hadn't let them in on the secret. But nothing but interested professionalism was coming out in her voice. "You knew you might be leaving this party early, so you made sure you'd have a recording of the route back to the Brask Oto Command Station. And your little chat with Jinzler in the forward observation lounge was because he happened to be too close to the action?"

"Yes," Estosh said, sounding grudgingly impressed that she'd caught on so quickly. "If he'd left at the wrong moment, he would have seen Purpsh installing the device. Master Skywalker, are you still there?"

Luke clicked the comlink voice pickup back on. "Still here, Estosh," he assured the other. "But even that recording isn't going to get you all the way out of the Redoubt, you know. We were half an hour into the flight before you got it tied in."

"That last part will be easy enough," Estosh said offhandedly. "Leaving the edge of a star cluster is not nearly as difficult as navigating one's way inside."

The turbolift car had hit the main gravity eddy field now and was rotating around in the darkness. A moment later it finished its turn, leaving Luke with a clear line of sight all the way to the curve where the pylon entered the underside of D-4.

He frowned. Even though he couldn't see the far end of the tube, he ought to be able to hear the sounds of any activity going on around the curve. But all was silence. Whatever the Vagaari had been doing, they were apparently finished.

That was probably a bad sign. Flicking on his glow rod, he shined it upward.

And caught his breath. There, packed around the tube a few meters out from the curve, he could see a solid ring of flat gray boxes.

Boxes like the ones he and Mara had run into on their initial trip through D-4. Boxes Mara had identified as being full of explosives.

The Vagaari had mined the pylon.

CHAPTER 22

LUKE GAZED UPWARD, FEELING HIS THROAT TIGHTEN. THERE was undoubtedly an orderly and systematic method for detaching Dreadnaught-4 from the rest of Outbound Flight. Clearly, the Vagaari weren't interested in finding out what that procedure was.

The car was approaching the ring now. "One thing that puzzles me, Estosh," Luke said into his comlink, holding his free hand horizontally over the hole in the ceiling where Evlyn could see it. "You couldn't have known any of the Dreadnaughts would even be in one piece when we set off on this trip, let alone ready to fly. And you certainly didn't need all these troops just to track the *Chaf Envoy*'s path into the Redoubt." The car reached the explosives, and he jabbed at the air with his finger. Evlyn was ready, and the car settled tentatively to a midair halt.

"That's right," Mara said. Luke could sense her concern as she picked up on his sudden tension, but again all of it was carefully filtered out of her voice. "So what *was* the original plan? Just out of curiosity, of course."

"You humans are strange creatures," Estosh said, his melodious voice starting to pick up an edge of suspicion. "Here you are, about to die, and yet instead of struggling to postpone your fate, you sit quietly and ask about things that cannot possibly help you."

Slowly, Luke ran the light from his glow rod along the explosives. The detonator wiring seemed straightforward enough, the kind of arrangement he'd seen demolitions techs use during the Rebellion. In theory, he should be able to simply pull it out of all the packages within reach.

The problem was that the detonator box itself was a quarter of the way around the tube from him.

There is no emotion; there is peace. Taking a careful breath, Luke tried to think. He could, of course, easily use the Force to maneuver his lightsaber over to the box and cut it away from the boxes of explosives. But the Vagaari might have wired it with a collapsing release to prevent any last-minute tampering. If it was rigged that way, cutting it free would instantly trigger a detonation.

In addition, there was something else pressed up against the metal beneath the boxes, something he could see but couldn't get to without disassembling everything on top of it. Unknowns were always to be considered dangerous, especially in explosives work.

"The thing is, you see, we Jedi don't die nearly as easily as you might like," Mara told Estosh calmly. "There's a good chance we'll be seeing you again, and the more we know about you, the easier it'll be for us to peel your epaulets back for good when we do."

Still, Luke decided, unknowns or not, if he could get over to the box he stood a good chance of figuring out how to disarm it. The problem was that the turbolift pylon was perfectly smooth, with no protrusions anywhere nearby that would hold his weight. The cluster of buried cables he and Mara had used for their climb up the forward pylon weren't situated close enough to the box, either. He probably could have rigged up something out of liquid cable, but he'd used up most of his supply when he and Mara had sealed off the edges of that first turbolift car.

But if his particular car was too far away, one of the *other* cars in the cluster should be positioned to pass right next to it. All he and Evlyn had to do was continue up to D-4, where the Vagaari had presumably locked the rest of the cars, transfer to the correct one, and ride it back down again. He wouldn't even have to expose them to enemy fire by going into the lobby; he could use his lightsaber to cut through the sides of the cars until they reached the one they needed.

He looked down into the car and gestured upward. Evlyn nodded and touched the switch, and the car began to rise again. They lifted past the explosives, around the curve—

"How very confident of you," Estosh said, his voice suddenly silky smooth. "My only regret is that I will not actually witness your deaths. Farewell, Jedi." There was a click from Luke's comlink as the Vagaari broke the connection—

And suddenly, below him, the turbolift pylon erupted in an eerie, flickering greenish-blue light and the sound of metallic hissing.

"Luke!" Mara called over the comlink. "What's going on?"

"I think they're about to blow the pylons," Luke said grimly, gesturing Evlyn to stop the car. The other five cars of the cluster were visible now directly above him, along with the gap the car they were riding would normally slip into. "You know any type of detonator that hisses and gives off blue-green light?"

"Sounds like a scorch stick," Mara said. "It's an acid-based, high-temperature paste used to burn a score mark in something to help the explosives crack it more cleanly."

"How long until it burns around a pylon this size?"

"Half a minute," Mara said. "Maybe a little more. If you're anywhere near it, get out now."

Luke listened to his heart thudding in his throat as he weighed his options. If he could just get to the detonator before the scorch stick finished its burn . . .

But no. Not in half a minute. Certainly not with Evlyn along to slow him down.

He shouldn't have brought her with him. For the first time in a long time, his instincts had played him false.

But this wasn't the time for questions or recriminations. "Right," he said, jabbing downward. "We're on our way."

Evlyn didn't need to be told twice. She hit the switch, and the car headed down again. On sudden impulse, Luke snatched his lightsaber from his belt and ignited it. If the Vagaari were going to get away, at least they weren't going to get away clean. Using the Force to hold down the switch, he hurled the weapon upward toward the gap in the cluster of cars. It hit the upper part of the turbolift lobby, and he had just enough time to see the wobbling blade carve out a large hole in the metal before the curve in the tube blocked it from his sight. The car dropped past the ring of explosives—

And with a jolt, he saw that Mara had overestimated how much time they would have. The scorched section already extended over more than half the circle, with the flickering fire seeming to pick up speed as it worked its way around toward the detonator.

They had maybe five more seconds before it finished.

"On the floor," Luke shouted to Evlyn, jumping in through the hole in the roof. The car wouldn't be nearly enough protection from the explosive power about to be unleashed, he knew, but it was all they had. "Come on, get on the floor," he repeated.

But to his surprise, Evlyn ignored him, remaining by the control panel as she punched keys on a command stick she'd plugged into the droid socket. He reached out a hand for her, wondering if she didn't understand or if she'd simply frozen in fear.

But even as his hand closed on her arm, he caught the sense of desperate determination in the girl. As he started to pull her down, she touched one last key on the command stick—

And Luke found the two of them abruptly floating in midair as the floor dropped out from under them. The car hit the main gravity eddy and began its turn, blocking his view of the explosives and the fiery blue-green glow.

An instant later, the pylon blew up.

The car floor seemed to leap up at him, slamming hard into his face and body, the impact knocking most of the air out of his lungs. He was still holding Evlyn's arm; reflexively, he pulled her close beside him as the shock wave from the explosion washed over them.

He was still holding her that way, ears ringing from the shock wave, when the car's side wall disintegrated.

He gasped as the pieces slammed into him, some of them hitting like clubs, others digging into his back and arms and legs like knife blades. Beside him he heard Evlyn cry out and let the Force flow into her, trying to suppress some of her pain. The rain of shrapnel stopped, the buffeting faded away, and Luke risked a look upward through what was left of the ceiling. The lower curve in the pylon was visible above them, with the safety of D-5's turbolift lobby just beyond it. Shakily but steadily, the car continued upward.

It was then he suddenly noticed that he couldn't breathe.

He expanded his chest, trying to fill his lungs. But there was nothing there. With the car shredded and the far end of the tube blown open, he and Evlyn had only the planetoid's thin atmosphere available to them.

Steady, Luke told himself sternly, forcing himself to relax. His body's cells contained enough oxygen for at least another half minute, he knew, and Jedi techniques could stretch it to triple that time. He shifted his hand to the back of Evlyn's neck, trying to let his own trust in the Force ease into her and slow her breathing. A few seconds later, the car settled into its place in the turbolift lobby.

The door remained closed.

Luke set his teeth, glaring up at it. But of course it wouldn't open on its own, not with a near vacuum on one side. It would have to be pried past its safety interlocks. Stretching out to the Force, he got a grip on the panel and pulled.

The door quivered once, but remained closed.

Luke tried again, trying to gather more strength. But between the effects of the concussive blast, the pain from the shrapnel still throbbing through his body, and the oxygen deprivation, he couldn't focus the necessary power.

His vision was starting to go hazy. Another few seconds and he would sink into unconsciousness. He stretched out one final time—

And with a thud that shook the whole car, the door

slammed open. Luke opened his eyes, squinting through the rush of air blowing suddenly in his face.

Mara, her eyes blazing with fear, concern, and, yes, anger at him, grabbed his arms and pulled him through the door. Pressor was right beside her, lifting his niece through to safety.

The door slammed shut as Mara released her grip on it. "Hi, sweetheart," Luke said, managing a smile. "I'm home."

She shook her head. "Skywalker—"

"I know," Luke said. Still smiling, he let the darkness take him.

THE MEDICAL BAY RECOVERY ROOM DOOR SLID OPEN, AND MARA stepped inside. "How are they?" Jinzler asked, looking up from his chair by the side wall. "I heard one of the medics say they were in pretty bad shape."

"It looked worse than it really was," Mara assured him. Jinzler's face looked calm enough, she noted, but his hands in his lap were opening and closing restlessly. "Most of Evlyn's injuries were superficial and should heal pretty quickly," she went on. "Luke had some deeper cuts, but they caught it all before he lost too much blood. He's gone into a Jedi healing trance while they finish patching him up."

Fel grunted. "Must be a nice thing to be able to do."

"It can be handy," Mara agreed, looking around the room. They were, she decided, about as sorry a lot as she'd seen in a long time. Formbi was lying on one of the recovery tables, his eyes only occasionally fluttering open, his breathing deep and slow. Beside him on opposite sides of the table sat Drask and Feesa, the former looking drained above his own collection of bandages, the latter merely looking exhausted and apprehensive. Fel and the stormtroopers had gathered together in a back corner beside stacks of their mangled armor and were working their way through their own list of injuries. The alien stormtrooper, Su-mil, she noted with interest, had pale orange blood.

"So," Mara went on, raising her voice a little. "As long as we seem to have some time on our hands, why don't we all have a nice long talk together?" She looked at Fel. "You can start, Commander. Did I hear you say earlier that you caught the Vagaari wiring a recorder into the *Chaf Envoy*'s navigational lines?"

"We didn't actually catch them in the act," Fel said. "Sumil found the recorder after it had already been planted."

"I stand corrected," Mara said. "So why didn't you say anything to anyone?"

"To be perfectly honest, because we didn't know whom it was safe to tell," Fel said evenly. "We didn't know whether Bearsh had put it there, or General Drask, or Aristocra Formbi, Ambassador Jinzler—" He looked Mara straight in the eye. "—or you."

"I see," Mara said, accepting his gaze and sending it straight back at him. "All right, then, let's try this one. You told us once that you didn't know why Parck had sent you on this mission. You lied. Then you changed your story and said you'd been sent to protect us. I think you lied that time, too. You want to take one more stab at it?"

Fel's lip twitched. "Admiral Parck told us the mission would be going into great danger. We were sent to give added protection to Aristocra Formbi. And that was *all* we were told," he added firmly. "We didn't even know what direction the danger was going to be coming from." He grimaced. "If we had, I guarantee Bearsh and his friends would be locked up in binders right now."

"Yes," Mara murmured, stretching out with the Force. It did indeed seem to be the truth this time. Or at least, the truth as Fel knew it, which might not be the same thing. "I suppose this clears up the mystery of your missing operational manual, too."

Fel nodded. "Apparently the Vagaari wanted to know everything they could about Outbound Flight before we arrived."

"Right," Mara agreed. "All of which brings up an even more interesting point."

She turned to face the three Chiss. "As I think about it, Aristocra Formbi, you asked for an amazing amount of muscle to accompany you on this trip. First you called Parck and asked for Luke and me, only the message got waylaid. Then, when it looked like we weren't going to show, you called him back and got him to send a unit of the best stormtroopers he had available."

"And it was indeed fortunate all of you were here," Drask said, nodding his head gravely. "We owe you our lives."

"Yes, you do," Mara agreed. "But here's the question. How exactly did you know you were going to need all this help?"

"I do not understand what you are asking," Drask said evenly. But there was a new tightness at the corners of his eyes. "You were invited to take possession of Outbound Flight. That is all."

Mara shook her head. "Sorry, General, but that won't fly. After that incident with the line creepers, the Aristocra gave us specific orders not to use our lightsabers aboard the ship. Even when we couldn't get into the Dreadnaught's docking bay, neither of you asked us to just cut it open, which we could have done in a fraction of the time it took the techs with their torches."

"Yes," Jinzler put in, sounding suddenly thoughtful. "I remember thinking about that myself at the time, wondering if it was some form of stiff-necked Chiss pride."

"That was what I thought, too," Mara said, smiling tightly. "In fact, I thought it right up to the minute Bearsh told me to die and casually sent his wolvkils charging at me . . . and I cut them in half."

Jinzler inhaled sharply. "Your lightsaber," he said in sudden understanding. *"He'd never seen a lightsaber."*

"That's right, he hadn't," Mara agreed. "Because Formbi made *very* sure they never saw us in action. That, plus our Jedi abilities in general—which they also never really saw—gave us an edge they were completely unprepared for."

She looked back at the three Chiss. "So again: how did you know we'd need that edge?"

"I do not appreciate the tone of your words," Drask said stiffly. "You may not make such unsupported accusations against a senior member of the Fifth Ruling Family."

"Feesa," Jinzler murmured suddenly.

Mara looked at him. "What?"

"Feesa," Jinzler repeated, nodding as if an odd puzzle piece had suddenly fallen into place. "In the turbolift, right after Pressor sprang his trap, she was frightened far more than seemed reasonable. It was because we were all alone in there with Bearsh and another Vagaari, wasn't it?"

Feesa didn't answer. "I see," Mara said, eyeing Formbi closely. "So I was wrong. It wasn't the Aristocra running this scam at all. It was Feesa."

The Aristocra's closed eyelids twitched. "And since she's obviously too young to be a senior member of a Ruling Family or anything else," Mara went on, "I guess it's perfectly all right for me to make such accusations against—"

"Enough," Formbi said quietly.

"Please, Aristocra Chaf'orm'bintrano," Feesa said, an edge of urgency in her voice. "It's all right. I'm not afraid to admit my part in this."

"Your loyalty honors me, second niece," Formbi said, reaching over to touch her hand. "But it was my plan, and my decision. I cannot and will not allow others to take the responsibility for my actions."

He turned his head slightly. "Jedi Skywalker: approach where I may see you, and ask what you will."

Mara stepped up beside Feesa. "You knew they were Vagaari, didn't you?" she said, determined not to let his drawn face or the oozing blood on his arm influence her. "You knew it right from the start."

Formbi nodded. "Yes."

"But you told me you'd never seen one before," Jinzler objected.

"That was true," Formbi acknowledged. "But I had received a detailed description from one who *had* seen them." He smiled at Jinzler. "You, of all of us, should understand."

Mara stared at Formbi as it suddenly hit her. "You mean . . . *Car'das*?"

Again, the Aristocra nodded. "He and I spoke briefly when he brought the ambassador to the *Chaf Envoy*," he said.

"When the Vagaari then appeared, I knew it was indeed them."

"Car'das gets around more than I'd realized," Mara commented. "Is he also the one who clued the Vagaari in on this in the first place?"

"No," Formbi said. "When I sent the message to Admiral Parck requesting Master Skywalker's presence, I made sure the transmission had enough edge leakage to be intercepted in the regions where we suspected the Vagaari were gathering their strength."

"And even knowing who they were, you let them aboard your ship?" Jinzler demanded, sounding more surprised than angry.

Formbi closed his eyes again. "The Vagaari are a violent people, Ambassador," he said wearily. "They have killed many, enslaved many others, and driven all who know them to terror and despair. Worse, they may already have made alliances with powers even more dangerous than they are. If Bearsh succeeds in escaping with even a partial route into the Redoubt, I have no doubt that knowledge will be used against us to terrible advantage."

"So the Vagaari need to be slapped down hard," Mara said, frowning. "So what's the problem?"

Formbi smiled wanly. "The problem is Chiss military doctrine, Jedi Skywalker," he said. "Specifically, the decree that no potential adversaries may be attacked until and unless they first act against Chiss interests within Chiss space."

Mara stared at him. "You *wanted* them to make a move against you," she said, not quite sure she believed it. "You invited them aboard one of your ships and into your most critical military base, hoping they'd pull this exact stunt."

Drask snorted. "This *exact* stunt? That had better *not* be the case."

"Of course I didn't expect what actually occurred," Formbi assured him. "My expectation was that the five Vagaari we permitted aboard would attempt to take control of the *Chaf Envoy* at some point after we reached Outbound

Flight. That would have been sufficient provocation for us to act."

"Especially when you add in the slaughter of a few un-armed crewers?" Fel put in.

"Loss of life was neither necessary nor expected," Formbi insisted, some heat seeping through the fatigue into his voice. "My ship had been specially prepared for this mission. All crewers had been provided with hidden areas near their duty stations where they could protect themselves from attack as they watched for the Vagaari to betray themselves. With a squad of warriors in the Dreadnaught docking bay, I also expected there to be ample warning if Bearsh and the others attempted to return to the vessel. We expected to merely catch them in the act of attempted theft or sabotage, which would have satisfied the rules of engagement."

He closed his eyes. "I did not expect such a massive attack to come from the other direction," he said, the heat fading away. "The warriors whom I stationed in the Dreadnaught are certainly dead. So perhaps are all who we left aboard. Their blood now lies on my hands."

"It's hardly your fault that you didn't know about the Vagaari suspended animation trick," Jinzler pointed out. "Car'das must have missed that one."

"He merely met them," Formbi said. "He wasn't given a tour of their technical facilities."

"He'll have to do better next time," Mara said. "What about the others? Feesa and General Drask and your other aides?"

"Feesa knew the entire plan," Formbi said. "That was why I insisted she come along, so that if anything happened to me she could direct the operation. No one else knew more than you yourself were told."

He smiled slightly. "Though I believe General Drask was able to deduce much of the truth."

"Much, but not all," Drask rumbled. "It would have been better if you had taken me into your full confidence."

"If I had, you would have been as guilty as I of manipulating events to bring about this end." Formbi shook his head. "No. On my hands, and mine alone, must this rest."

"You can sort all that out when you get home," Mara said. "Can we assume the rules of engagement have been satisfied?"

"They have been more than satisfied, Jedi Skywalker," Drask said darkly. "We have been attacked without justification or mercy. A state of war now exists between the Chiss Ascendancy and the Vagaari."

"Good," Mara said. "I'd hate to have to go through this again just because we'd missed something in the fine print. In that case, there's just one little loose end left. That falling cable that nearly knocked Luke across the room when we first came aboard the *Chaf Envoy*. I trust you're not going to try to blame *that* one on the Vagaari?"

Drask cleared his throat self-consciously. "I am afraid I am to blame for that incident, Jedi Skywalker," he confessed. "When Aristocra Chaf'orm'bintrano asked Admiral Parck who of the New Republic would be the best warriors to have at hand against possible trouble, he recommended you and Master Skywalker."

"He seemed to have firsthand knowledge of your fighting skill," Formbi murmured.

"Yes," Drask said. "However, I did not entirely trust his tales of Jedi abilities."

"So you arranged a demonstration," Mara said. "Did we meet with your approval?"

"Let us simply say that you did not disappoint." Drask smiled slightly. "The demonstration arranged today by the Vagaari gave you a far better opportunity to prove yourselves."

"Yes," Mara murmured. "I should hope so."

Behind her, the door slid open and Evlyn and Rosemari stepped in, Pressor close behind them. "There you are," Mara said. "How are you feeling?"

"I'm all right," the girl said, looking around at the others as the door slid shut again. Possibly comparing bandage counts, Mara thought with a brief flicker of amusement. "Is

Luke all right?" she asked. "I mean, Master Skywalker? He saved my life, pulling me down and protecting me when the pylon exploded."

"He's fine," Mara assured her as her mother steered her to one of the other recovery tables. "And as far as saving lives goes, I think the two of you come out pretty even on that scoring."

"What do you mean?" Rosemari asked, an odd edge to her voice. "Evlyn didn't do anything."

"She most certainly did," Mara insisted. "Evlyn reactivated that turbolift trap at exactly the right moment to shoot the car down the tube and into the eddy rotation just before the explosives detonated. If she hadn't done that, it would have been the fractured ceiling that took the brunt of the explosion instead of the wall, and a lot more high-speed debris would have gotten through. That kind of prescient timing can only come from the Force."

"But you won't tell them, will you?" Rosemari pleaded. "Please?"

"They don't like Jedi here, Mara," Fel said quietly. "I don't know exactly why, but they don't."

"We don't just not like them, Commander," Pressor said grimly. "If the council sticks the Jedi label on someone, they get immediately sent over to Three."

"You mean D-Three?" Jinzler asked. "The Number Three Dreadnaught?"

"That's the one," Pressor said. "The pylons between it and the rest of Outbound Flight were destroyed or collapsed during the attack and crash, leaving it isolated from everything else. So Uliar and the other Survivors set it up as a place where anyone with Jedi traits could be safely banished."

"I thought that was what the Quarantine on D-Six was for," Fel said.

Pressor shook his head. "Quarantine is for people they *suspect* of using the Force," he said. "Three is where they get sent once they're pretty sure."

"*Pretty sure,* you say?" Su-mil asked softly, his alien expression very still. In some ways, Mara reflected, he looked even more dangerous without his armor. "And how certain exactly is that?"

Pressor looked away from him. "*They're* completely sure," he said. "The Managing Council is. I can't speak for the rest of us."

He looked at Mara. "And it's not a death sentence, really," he added with an odd combination of earnestness and embarrassment. "The place has been set up with plenty of food and power. A person could live there for a lifetime in reasonable comfort."

"But in complete isolation," Su-mil said darkly. "You sentence these people to a life of loneliness."

Pressor sighed. "We've only done it twice," he said. "At least, up to now."

"They're not going to send her there, Jorad," Rosemari said. "They can't."

She looked suddenly at Mara. "You can take her with you, can't you?" she asked. "You can take her when you leave."

"The plan was to take *all* of you with us," Mara told her. "Unfortunately, unless we can get out of here and back to the *Chaf Envoy*, neither option has much of a future."

"I spoke to the techs a few minutes ago," Pressor said. "Most of the blast doors stopped working years ago, and most of the ones that *did* work have now been locked open by those cursed conduit worms. Unless we can get a few of them working again, we're not going to be able to get either the turbolift doors or any of the outer hatchways open without losing all our air."

He looked at Drask. "I take it there's still no word from your own ship?"

The general shook his head. "No," he said. "And I no longer believe they will be coming."

"You think they're all dead?" Pressor asked.

Drask closed his eyes. "Including crew members, there were thirty-seven warriors aboard the *Chaf Envoy*," he said. "The Vagaari may have had as many as three hundred." He opened his eyes into slender cracks of glowing red. "They would not have been prepared for such a devastating assault."

Mara felt her stomach tighten. The sudden multiple deaths she and Luke had sensed aboard D-1 could have been all the Chiss, or a sizable fraction of them, or just the squad of warriors Drask had left in the D-4 docking bay. There hadn't been any way to tell at the time, and there still wasn't.

Though if there *were* surviving Chiss, it might not make any difference. Even if the Vagaari hadn't bothered to hunt down and kill everyone aboard, they would certainly have made a point of wrecking the ship on their way out. "So in other words, we should assume we're on our own," she concluded. "All right. Pressor, you said D-Three was isolated from the rest of Outbound Flight. That means you must have vac suits to get back and forth. Any of them still in working condition?"

"A couple dozen of them are," he said. "But as I told you, we can't get the hatches open."

"We don't have to," Mara told him. "All you need to do is build a small caisson around one of the turbolift doors with me in it. I can cut through the hull, climb up the pylon, and make my way cross-country to the *Chaf Envoy*."

"And how do you get back in?" Drask asked.

"I'll figure that out later," Mara told him. "What do you think?"

Above them, the lights flickered. "Terrific," Pressor muttered, glancing up. "They must be getting to the generator."

"What, we're running on generator power already?" Mara asked.

"We are in this part of the ship," Pressor said. "They've already gotten into the main power conduits."

"Wait a minute," Jinzler said, frowning. "You have portable generators? How many?"

"Probably ten that still work," Pressor said. The lights flickered again—"Better make that nine."

"I never even thought to ask," Jinzler said, sounding disgusted with himself. "Get them together as quickly as you can—all of them—and set them out along the corridors."

"Connected to what?" Pressor asked, sounding confused.

"Connected to anything you want," Jinzler said. "Lights, heaters—anything. Just crank them up to full power and then shut down the main reactors."

"It will not work," Drask declared. "Even if the generators succeed in drawing the line creepers out, there are too many of them. They will quickly overload and destroy the generators' wiring, then return to the larger sources of power."

"That's right," Jinzler said, smiling tightly. "*If* the worms actually get to them."

He turned back to Pressor. "But they won't, because around each generator you're going to create a moat of salt water. The worms will crawl in, short out their organic capacitors, and die."

"You're kidding," Pressor said. "I've never even heard of that."

Jinzler shrugged. "It's a trick we came up with when I was bumming around Hadar sector after the Clone Wars. It's fairly disgusting, but it works."

"I'll get the techs on it right away," Pressor said, pulling out his comlink. "You've certainly had a varied career, Ambassador."

Jinzler's answer, if he made one, was lost as a sudden surge of distant emotion yanked at Mara's attention. "Something's wrong," she said, pulling her lightsaber from her belt and heading for the door. Pressor got there ahead of her, slapping the release and ducking through.

It was then that they heard the shouting in the distance ahead.

"Come on," Pressor growled, drawing his blaster as he and Mara sprinted down the corridor.

They rounded a turn and nearly collided with a dozen techs and civilians running in the other direction. "They're back!" one of the techs gasped, jabbing a finger behind him as he dodged around Pressor. "In the turbolift. They're trying to break in."

Pressor swore under his breath, thumbing on his comlink.

"All Peacekeepers to the forward starboard pylon," he ordered. "The Vagaari are back."

"This doesn't make sense," Mara objected, trying to stretch out to the Force as she ran. But the flavor of the alien minds was too faint to sort out against the clamor of civilian panic throbbing in the air around her. "Why would they have come back?"

"Maybe they decided they wanted to watch us die after all," Pressor said grimly. "If so, they're going to pay heavily for the privilege."

One of the other Peacekeepers was waiting in the darkness when they arrived at the turbolift lobby, the beam from his glow rod twitching back and forth as he fidgeted with apprehension. "They're coming through," he hissed, turning the beam on one of the doors. "I can hear them working on it. What do we do?"

Pressor never had a chance to answer. Almost before the words were out of the other's mouth, the door suddenly gave a violent creak and cracked a centimeter open. Three pry bars were in place before it could close again; and with another series of creaks the door was forced open. Pressor and the Peacekeeper leveled their blasters at the opening, and suddenly two combat-armored figures leapt out of the gloom, their own glow rods swinging back and forth. Behind the lights, Mara could see hand weapons tracking as they searched for targets—

"No," she snapped, reaching out to the Force and twisting all four muzzles to point into opposite corners of the lobby. "Don't shoot. They're friends."

She stepped into the middle of the standoff as a third armored figure emerged into the room. "Welcome to Outbound Flight, Captain Brast'alshi'barku," she said, bowing slightly to the newcomer. "I thought you'd never get here."

CHAPTER 23

"WE NEVER EVEN HEARD THE VAGAARI LEAVE," CAPTAIN TAL-shib said disgustedly, his red eyes blazing even more brilliantly in the dim glow of the recovery room permlights. "We were sitting like fools in concealment in the command center, waiting for them to make their move. But they simply exited their own vessel, scattering line creepers along the way, and left. Apparently they had already decided to take the Old Republic vessel and had no time to waste with us."

"Yes, Bearsh would have informed Estosh of the new plan by that time," Drask agreed. "They had had the foresight to appropriate a set of special operations communicators before traveling to Outbound Flight and were able to send pulse messages through the humans' jamming."

"I wish I had known," Talshib rumbled. "We could have deployed to intercept them."

"It's just as well you didn't," Mara commented from the other side of Formbi's recovery table. "You saw what happened to the squad we left in the Dreadnaught's docking bay. They never even had a chance."

"Perhaps," Talshib said reluctantly. Warriors' pride, Jinzler thought as he leaned against the wall by the open doorway watching the discussion. Or perhaps just pride in general. Talshib would probably have preferred an overwhelming enemy attack, even if it had meant dying in combat, to the situation he currently found himself in.

Mara must have sensed that, too. "No *perhaps* about it, Captain," she said firmly. "If you hadn't been around to rig that sealant tent across the broken pylon, we'd still be trying to figure out how we were going to get out of here."

Talshib snorted. "Thus permitting you to travel freely from one dead vessel to another."

"Neither of them will be dead for long," Drask put in firmly. "If Ambassador Jinzler's technique works, both vessels should be functional within a matter of days."

Talshib snorted again. That was probably a good deal of his attitude problem, Jinzler had already decided. The Vagaari line creepers had wiped out the *Chaf Envoy's* communications with the landing party and otherwise crippled the ship before the crew, lurking in their hidey-holes, had even realized they were under attack.

And then, as if that weren't embarrassment enough, it was human ingenuity that was going to clear out his ship for him. *That* had to really gall him, and Jinzler was a little surprised that Drask had gone out of his way to mention where the plan had come from.

Unless Drask had done it on purpose, a not-so-subtle reminder to his subordinate that even the Chiss could learn from other species on occasion. Certainly the general's politely unfriendly attitude toward humans seemed to have warmed perceptively over the past few hours. Jinzler could only wonder what had happened to cause that change.

"Here comes another one," Evlyn stage-whispered from a few paces down the corridor. "No; two of them. No; it's a whole crowd."

Jinzler moved away from the wall and the discussion and crossed to her side. In the much brighter light blazing away from a rack above the portable generator, he could see a group of perhaps twenty line creepers wriggling their way across the deck toward the enticing aroma of electric current.

"Careful," he warned as Evlyn started toward them. "If you get too close your own bioelectrical energy might distract them."

"Okay," she said, backing up again. Together they watched as the fragile-looking creatures climbed briskly up over the lip of the wide, flat basin the generator's stubby legs were resting in. One by one, they dropped into the salt water, twitched a few times, and went still. "That's really cool," she commented.

"Effective, too," Jinzler agreed absently, most of his attention still back on the snatches of conversation he was able to hear of Formbi's war council. Drask and Talshib were discussing their options now, with Mara, Formbi, and Fel occasionally putting in a comment or suggestion. Luke, still in his Jedi trance, was across the corridor in the operating room where they'd finished patching him up.

Unfortunately, none of the options being batted around sounded particularly hopeful, at least not from where he was standing. Borrowing extra generators from Outbound Flight might speed up the decontamination process aboard the *Chaf Envoy*, but even so the best possible projected completion point was at least three days away. Unless the Vagaari had mechanical trouble along the way, the stolen Dreadnaught would have far too much of a head start for the *Chaf Envoy* to catch up with it before it reached the Brask Oto Command Station and escaped from the cluster.

"You'll be leaving soon, won't you?"

Jinzler shifted his full attention back to Evlyn. "We all will," he told her. "You, your mother—all of us."

"I mean as soon as the Blue—I mean the Chiss ship is fixed, you and Mara and Luke will be leaving."

"But we'll be back," Jinzler promised. "Or at least, some Chiss transports will be. They'll take you anywhere you want to go."

She shook her head. "It won't make any difference," she said quietly. "No matter where we go, Uliar will find some kind of Three to put me in."

"They're not going to do that," Jinzler insisted. "Surely they learned a lesson from this whole thing. If it wasn't for you, a good many more people might have died."

"That won't make any difference," she said again. "Not to them." She sighed. "I wish you'd never come here. If you hadn't . . ." She trailed off.

"If we hadn't, what?" Jinzler prompted. "You would have gone on living a lie?"

"I could have pretended," she said. "Lots of people pretend." She looked squarely up into his eyes. "Even you do."

An edge of guilt dug up under Jinzler's rib cage. "That's different," he said. "If I hadn't told them I was an ambassador, the Chiss might not have let me come along."

"But you're here now," she reminded him. "You could have stopped pretending a long time ago."

"Yes, well, we're not talking about me, young lady," he reminded her firmly. "We're talking about you. And the point is, you shouldn't be ashamed of what you can do."

"Maybe not." Pressor's voice came from behind them. "But that doesn't mean she should announce it from the command deck, either."

Jinzler turned. Pressor and Rosemari were coming down the corridor toward them, Pressor with a pile of sacks across one forearm. "I brought you a new collection bag," he said, peeling one off the stack and handing it to Evlyn. "These are plasticized, so they won't get as soggy."

"Thanks," she said, taking it and handing him her partially full one in return.

"I really think you ought to go join the rest of the people down on Six, Evlyn," Rosemari said, eyeing her daughter's bandages. "Don't you think you'd be more comfortable there?"

"Would *you* be?" Evlyn said pointedly.

The corners of Rosemari's mouth tightened. "I suppose not," she conceded. "Director Uliar's probably been talking to people already."

"I'm sure he has," Pressor said. "But I've been thinking, and there may still be a way to backtrack on this."

"What do you mean?" Rosemari asked.

"Well, think about it," Pressor said. "Besides the stuff in the turbolift, which no one else saw, the only thing Evlyn did was pull that comlink across the meeting room deck. We could easily churn the water by saying it was actually Ambassador Jinzler who did that."

"Except that I'm not a Jedi," Jinzler pointed out.

"Maybe you lied about that," Pressor countered. "Or maybe you didn't even know yourself that you had the power."

"And you *are* the brother of a known Jedi," Rosemari added thoughtfully. "That has to count for something. Maybe your pep talk in the meeting room actually stimulated *your* powers, not Evlyn's."

"Are you suggesting I lie for your daughter?" Jinzler asked.

Rosemari held his gaze without flinching. "Why not?" she said. "It was you and your people who got her into this mess."

"It's not a mess," Jinzler insisted. "It's an opportunity."

Beside him, Evlyn stirred. "Ambassador Jinzler says I shouldn't be ashamed of who I am."

"Ambassador Jinzler doesn't have to live among these people," Pressor retorted, glaring at Jinzler.

"I do for the moment," Jinzler pointed out ruefully. "A moment that could stretch out considerably, I might add. We won't know until the line creepers have all been cleaned out whether or not they caused any permanent damage. We could conceivably find out that the *Chaf Envoy* will never fly again."

"That could be a problem, all right," Pressor grunted. "I don't suppose it occurred to you to bring a spare hypercapable vehicle with you?"

"We brought three, actually," Jinzler said with a grimace. "The commander's glider, the transport the Imperials came in, and Luke and Mara's ship. The Vagaari hit all three on their way out. Talshib says they even took the time to sabotage their own shuttle, and it wasn't even hypercapable."

Pressor shook his head. "They're thorough, you have to give them that. So how long until the rest of the Chiss come hunting for you?"

"That's just it," Jinzler said. "Formbi was playing this so close to the table that I'm not sure the rest of the Chiss even know we're out here. There are some aboard the command station we passed on our way into the cluster, of course, but the Vagaari might well be planning to destroy that on their way out. If they succeed, it might be months before anyone comes back out this way."

"That would solve the problem, wouldn't it?" Evlyn murmured.

They all looked at her. "What?" Pressor asked.

"That would solve the problem," Evlyn repeated. "Because if you stay, they'd have to put Luke and Mara in Three if they put me there. And they couldn't do that, could they?"

"I doubt it seriously," Jinzler agreed hesitantly. That hadn't even occurred to him.

"And then they could teach me how to be a real Jedi," Evlyn continued, looking up at her mother. "Then we wouldn't have to be afraid anymore about what they might do to me, because they couldn't."

Rosemari reached up to stroke her daughter's hair, an oddly pinched expression on her face. "Evlyn . . ."

"That's what you want, isn't it?" Evlyn pressed. She turned back to Jinzler. "It's what you want, too, isn't it?"

"Certainly, I want you to develop your gift," Jinzler agreed. "But we're the only ones who know about the Vagaari and what they've found out about the Redoubt. If we get stuck here, it may mean the deaths of many more Chiss."

"Is that important?" Evlyn said, a strange edge of challenge in her voice.

"Of course it's important," Rosemari said. Her voice seemed sad, almost resigned, yet at the same time had a sense of peace to it. "Ambassador . . . there may be another hypercapable transport available. We have a Delta-Twelve Skysprite sitting in one of the docking bays over on Three."

Pressor turned to his sister, his jaw dropping in astonishment. "We've got a *what*?"

"A Delta-Twelve Skysprite," she repeated. "It's a two-passenger sublight transport with a connecting hyperdrive ring. Dad showed it to me once when we were working over there together."

"I didn't know there was anything like that aboard Outbound Flight," Pressor said.

"Not many people do," Rosemari said. "And I don't think anyone knows why it was even aboard. Dad certainly didn't."

She looked at Jinzler. "The problem is that the Managing Council made Dad disassemble the hyperdrive. They knew they'd never be able to find a way out of the cluster, and they didn't want one of their exiled Jedi to figure it out and get away."

Jinzler took a careful breath. A hypercapable ship . . . "You say the ring was disassembled, not destroyed? Are all the parts still there?"

"I'm sure Dad didn't break anything," Rosemari said. "He was being very careful. And when he was done, he put everything into a storage locker. If you could get it to work, someone might at least be able to go for help."

"So you'd just let us go?" Jinzler asked, eyeing her closely. "Even though keeping us here might help your daughter?"

"Against your will?" Rosemari asked quietly. "And at the cost of all those Chiss lives?" She shook her head. "Not for me. Not even for my daughter. *Jedi serve others rather than ruling over them, for the good of the galaxy.*"

She looked down at her daughter, a bittersweet smile on her lips. "You see?" she said. "I even know the Code."

Evlyn wrapped her arms around her mother. "I knew you'd do the right thing," she murmured.

Jinzler took a deep breath. "Mara?" he called.

Three seconds later Mara appeared at the recovery room doorway, Captain Talshib right behind her. "What is it?" she demanded, glancing around for trouble.

"Rosemari says there's a Delta-Twelve tucked away over in D-Three," he told her. "You ever hear of that particular model?"

"Sounds vaguely familiar," Mara said, frowning in concentration. "Remind me."

"It was from Kuat Systems," he told her. "They manufactured the entire Delta line, including the Delta-Seven Aethersprite the Jedi used as starfighters during the early days of the Clone Wars. None of the Deltas had an internal hyperdrive, but TransGalMeg Industries made a hyperdrive ring for it to dock into. The Twelve was basically a larger, two-person version of the Seven that had its weapons stripped off for the civilian market."

"I'll take your word for it," Mara said. "So what's the question?"

"The question is whether you or Luke could fly it," Jinzler said.

"But the hyperdrive doesn't work," Pressor reminded him.

"I'll fix the hyperdrive," Jinzler said tartly. "Can you fly it?"

"Don't worry," she assured him grimly. "If you can fix it, we can fly it."

"You can fix it?" Evlyn asked, her voice sounding awed.

Jinzler looked at her. She was gazing up at him, her eyes as awed as her voice. A girl who had the power of the Jedi . . . and yet she was awed and impressed that he could fix a hyperdrive.

Suddenly he was staring at his sister again, all those years ago.

"Pretty exotic training for an ambassador," Pressor murmured.

Jinzler turned to face him; and as he did so, he felt himself drawing up to his full height. "I'm not an ambassador, Guardian," he said, his voice ringing clearly down the corridor with a pride and self-respect he'd never, ever felt before. "I'm an electronics technician."

He looked down at Evlyn and smiled. "Like my father before me."

As if from deep inside a well, a familiar voice called their standard code phrase. "I love you."

Luke blinked his eyes open, fighting the equally standard surge of disorientation. It was dark in the operating room, with only a dim permlight glowing off to one side, but he had no trouble recognizing the face leaning over him. "Hi, Mara," he said, working moisture into his mouth. "How's it going?"

"Better than I would have thought when you went under," she told him. "First things first. How do you feel?"

Experimentally, Luke took a deep breath. "Mostly healed, I think," he told her. "Muscles and skin seem fine." He wiggled his shoulders. "Except for my left shoulder blade."

"You took a big piece of shrapnel there," Mara said, rolling him half up onto his right side and probing the half-healed injury with her fingertips. "That one'll take a little more work."

"We seem to have time," Luke pointed out, glancing around the darkened room. Apparently, Bearsh's line creepers had gotten a solid grip on Outbound Flight's electrical systems. "Your turn."

"The Vagaari didn't bother to kill any of the Chiss when they left the *Chaf Envoy* except the squad we'd left in the Dreadnaught docking bay," Mara said. "That ambush is apparently what we felt while we were poking around D-One. They did dump a whole bunch of line creepers, though, which have pretty well incapacitated everything over there." She made a face. "Including the *Sabre*, of course."

"Of course," Luke agreed, eyeing her face and wincing for Estosh's chances if Mara ever caught up with him again. Messing with his wife's ship was not a healthy thing to do. "So we're basically stuck here?"

"Not as stuck as Bearsh was hoping," Mara said. "Jinzler taught us a little trick to draw the line creepers out of the conduits and kill them. Another three or four days and we should have all the ships cleaned out."

She smiled tightly. "Even more interesting is that Outbound Flight had a small starship tucked away. A Delta-Twelve Skysprite."

"Never heard of it," Luke said. "Is it functional?"

"They're running the final diagnostics on it now," Mara said. "Jinzler's stopped being an ambassador, by the way, and gone back to being a lowly hyperdrive tech."

"Sounds like a more useful profession at the moment," Luke said. "What about the others? Did everyone make it out of the battle all right?"

"Yes, though no one's going to be doing any strenuous dancing for a while," Mara assured him. "The Five-Oh-First took the most damage, but Fel says they should be fine. The big question right now is whether you feel up to a little trip."

Luke had already figured out where the conversation was heading. "You mean to try to whistle up an alert on the Vagaari before they get out of Chiss space?"

"Preferably before they even get out of the Redoubt," Mara said. "Don't forget they've got a whole bunch of disguised fighters waiting for them at that command station."

"Right." Luke had forgotten that, actually. "You figure they'll try to destroy the station on their way out?"

"*I* would, if I were trying to sneak out with a stolen warship," Mara said. "But right now they've only got a six-hour head start on us. They're also flying a Dreadnaught, which weren't exactly known for their speed even under the best of circumstances. *And* we know the course they're on. If we can get out of here in the next hour or two, there's a good chance we can beat them to the station."

"Yes," Luke murmured.

Mara cocked her head slightly. "You don't sound convinced."

"Just thinking," he said. "What about food and air? I seem to remember Deltas not having a lot of range."

"It has enough," Mara assured him. "Anyway, we only have to make it out of the cluster."

"Right," Luke said, still considering. "How about recognition signals? I presume that the Chiss on Brask Oto aren't just going to take our word for any of this."

"Hardly," Mara agreed. "Formbi's already given me a recorded message to transmit to them, with Drask and Captain Talshib cosigning on it. Drask's also given me his private emergency prefix signal, or rather the one that'll be current on the day we reach Brask Oto: two-space-one-space-two."

"Sounds reasonable," Luke grunted, easing himself up into a sitting position. "Do we have time to eat before we take off?"

"They've packed us a lunch," Mara said. "We need to get going as soon as Jinzler gives the okay."

"Then that time is here," Jinzler said, stepping through the doorway. "The Skysprite checks out just—"

He broke off. "What is it?" Luke asked, frowning at the sudden surge of emotion in Jinzler's face and sense.

"That lightsaber," Jinzler said, his voice suddenly stiff. "May I see it?"

"Sure," Luke said, pulling the relic from his belt. "We found it down on D-One, in what was left of the bridge."

"We think it might have been Jorus C'baoth's," Mara added.

"No," Jinzler said quietly as he carefully turned the old weapon over in his hands. "It was Lorana's."

Luke felt his heart tighten. "I'm sorry" was all he could think of to say.

Jinzler shrugged, a fractional lifting of his shoulders. "I knew she hadn't made it," he said. "All this hatred and prejudice would have disappeared years ago if they'd had a true Jedi living and working in their midst. Do you know how she died?"

Luke shook his head. "The bridge was pretty well wrecked, and of course any evidence that might have been there is half a century old. There was no way for us to tell whether she died in the crash or before." He hesitated. "We did find some alien bones in the same area, though. They may or may not be connected with her."

"They probably were," Jinzler murmured. "She would have died trying to protect her people."

"I'm sorry," Luke said again. "Would you like to have it?"

For a moment Jinzler continued to gaze at the lightsaber, and Luke could sense the struggle going on within him. Something that had been his sister's; possibly his last link to that part of his own life . . .

He took a deep breath. "Yes, I would," he said, handing it back to Luke. "But not now. You might need it; and I rather like the idea of Lorana's lightsaber being used against those who helped destroy her. You can bring it back to me when this is all over."

"I will," Luke promised, taking the weapon back with a new reverence.

"And you'd better get going," Jinzler added. "The ship's still over in D-Three, so you'll need vac suits to get to it. I'll take you to where Pressor's got a pair laid out for you."

LUKE HAD EXPECTED TO SEE MOST OF THEIR COMPANIONS ON the way out, with the opportunity for both a proper farewell and also a quick assessment of their individual injuries.

It didn't work out that way. Fel and the stormtroopers had been moved down to D-6 with most of the rest of the colony, where they would be more comfortable while they recovered from their battle wounds. Drask and Formbi had been similarly transferred back to the *Chaf Envoy* for more specialized treatment than the Outbound Flight medics could provide, with Feesa as always staying at the Aristocra's side. Director Uliar and the rest of the council had rather pointedly retired to D-6 as well, leaving behind an unspoken but distinct impression that they wouldn't be returning to D-5 until it was free again from the taint of the Jedi and their influence.

Which meant that aside from a couple of silent techs and a pair of Chiss warriors guarding the turbolifts, the only ones there to see them off were Jinzler, Pressor, Rosemari, and Evlyn. Only Evlyn seemed to have anything to say, and she seemed too shy or troubled to say very much of it.

Under other circumstances, Luke would probably have taken the time to try to draw the girl out a little. Mara, he knew, would definitely have done so. But with the Vagaari already hours ahead of them, personal and social considerations would have to wait.

Ten minutes after arriving at the turbolift lobby they were suited up and ready to go. One of the Chiss guided them up the broken turbolift tube to the sealant tent and field air lock that the *Chaf Envoy*'s crew had installed, then escorted them over the rough terrain of the planetoid's surface to the docking bay where the Delta-12 was waiting.

Thirty minutes later, after a quick test of the control systems and a final diagnostic check, Luke eased the Skysprite out of the docking bay and turned its nose upward.

"You ever ride in anything like this?" he asked as they drove toward the brilliant starscape.

"No," Mara said, unsealing one of the self-heating food packets Jinzler and the Outbound Flight techs had put aboard for them. "According to Jinzler, Kuat sold the Delta line around forty years ago to Sienar Systems. They got most of the starfighter contracts under Palpatine, and they either built the hyperdrive into the hull or left it out completely."

"Like with the old TIE fighters," Luke said, his stomach growling as he sniffed at the aromas rising from the packet. Karkan ribenes with tomo-spice; one of his favorite meals. Mara must have had a hand in the menu arrangements. "I never thought the TIE design made much sense."

Mara shrugged as she laid out the tray of ribenes, set a golden plaitfruit beside it, and pulled out two bottles of flavored water. "They were cheap to make, and Palpatine didn't mind spending pilots. Lunch is served. Dig in."

Luke set at the meal with enthusiasm, tearing the ribenes off the slab and devouring them right down to the bone, alternating with bites of the plaitfruit. It had been a long time since he'd eaten, and healing trances were always hard on energy reserves. Mara took a couple of the smaller ribenes, but from the way she nibbled at them it was clear she must have already eaten aboard Outbound Flight and was simply being companionable.

Midway through the meal the control board pinged with the announcement that the Skysprite had reached the edge of the planetoid's gravity well. Mara keyed in the hyperdrive, and with a flash of starlines they were off.

They chatted about inconsequential things as they ate, mostly just enjoying the chance to spend a few minutes of tranquillity together. Luke finished off the ribenes and plaitfruit, and Mara produced a pair of choclime twists for dessert. "So," she commented as Luke bit into his. "When are you going to tell me about that deep revelation back in the recovery room?"

"Nothing deep or surprising," he told her, savoring the sweet tang. "It was just a random thought."

"Such as?" she asked, taking a bite of her twist.

"Such as, why should we settle for just warning the Brask Oto station?" he said. "Dreadnaughts might not have been known for speed, but they *were* known for toughness, and I doubt Thrawn took out *all* the weapons in his attack. Even if the station is alerted, it's going to have a hard time taking both a Dreadnaught *and* a Vagaari battle carrier."

"Agreed," Mara said. "So option two is?"

He smiled at her. "We intercept the Dreadnaught en route, get aboard, and take it back ourselves."

"Uh-*huh*," she said. "Just the two of us?"

Luke shrugged. "They won't be expecting it, that's for sure."

"No, it sounds too crazy even for us," Mara agreed dryly. "Any particular ideas on how we would get aboard without them noticing and massing fire against us?"

"Already taken care of," Luke assured her. "Back when Evlyn and I were retreating down the pylon, I threw my lightsaber into one of the D-Four turbolift doors, opening it to space. Assuming the local blast doors are working, that should have isolated the whole lobby area from the rest of the ship. We maneuver this thing into what's left of the pylon, go inside, reseal the hole I cut, repressurize, and we're in."

"Great," Mara said. "Then all we have to do is cut our way through two hundred Vagaari soldiers and take over the ship."

"Something like that," Luke agreed. "You game?"

Mara shrugged. "Sure, why not? I didn't have anything else planned for after lunch."

"Good," Luke said, wiping his fingers and mouth with his napkin and dropping it into the empty ribene container. "Then all we have to do is plot out our intercept point, maybe use some Jedi navigation technique to make up a little more time, and we'll be in."

"Right," Mara said, slipping the last half of her choclime twist back into its wrapper and resealing it. "Except that *I'll* be doing all that. *Your* job right now is to finish healing."

Luke grimaced. But she was right. "Fine," he said with a theatrical sigh as he adjusted his chair to horizontal position. "You always get all the fun stuff."

"I know," Mara said sweetly. "And I appreciate you indulging me that way. Now, go to sleep."

"Okay." Luke took a deep breath and stretched out to the Force. "Just don't forget to wake me when we get there."

"You'll be the first to know," she promised. "Pleasant dreams."

His last view before the darkness of the healing trance folded over him was of her red-gold hair shimmering in the light as she bent over the navigation console.

CHAPTER 24

"I LOVE YOU."

Luke jerked slightly as he came out of his healing trance. "Are we there?" he asked, working moisture into his mouth.

"We're there," she confirmed. "More importantly, so is our wayward Dreadnaught. It came into the system about fifteen minutes ago and is angling around the star to get into position for the next jump. It should be crossing our bow in about half an hour."

Luke peered out the canopy at the asteroid Mara had settled the Skysprite beside. "Nice location," he complimented her. "How'd you manage to sneak in without them spotting you?"

"Actually, we were a little ahead of them," Mara told him. "They weren't anywhere in sight, so I gambled that they hadn't picked up an hour or two somewhere along the way and settled in to wait."

"Good," Luke said, stretching again and bringing his seat back to a sitting position. "Where exactly are we?"

"Well, that's the bad news," Mara admitted. "We're only another hour or two outside the Brask Oto Command Station. If we let them get back into hyperspace, we're going to be pushing it to take back the ship in time."

"Okay, so it'll be a challenge," Luke said, offhandedly. "I think we can handle it."

Mara frowned suspiciously at him. "You're not going all super-Jedi on me, are you?"

Luke gave her an innocent look. "Me?"

"Skywalker—" she said warningly.

He grinned once, then sobered. "No, of course not," he assured her. "I just don't think they're going to put up that much resistance, that's all. We pretty well proved aboard Outbound Flight that we can take them."

"We proved it to the ones who didn't survive," Mara pointed out. "I'm not convinced Bearsh and Estosh will have gotten the message. You're not really expecting them to just surrender, are you?"

"No, not really," Luke said regretfully. "But I don't think their troops will just stand there and get themselves slaughtered, either. If we can push them back to the bridge, I'm going to offer Estosh a deal: we'll let him and his people leave the Dreadnaught, get back into their carrier, and leave in peace."

"Under Chiss escort, of course," Mara said. "And if he doesn't go for it?"

Luke grimaced. "Then we'll just have to take them out."

"Sounds reasonable," Mara said. "Come on; you've got just enough time for a quick snack before we have to get ready."

They were in their vac suits and back at their chosen control boards when the Dreadnaught appeared around the side of the asteroid. It was, Luke noted, nearly five minutes ahead of Mara's estimate. Estosh was apparently pushing the ancient ship for all it was worth.

"Okay," he muttered, watching the huge mass of metal lumber past and trying to gauge the best moment to swing out of their partial concealment. The massive sublight engines blazed into view—

He threw power to the Skysprite's drive, blasting them away from the asteroid on a vector paralleling the Dreadnaught's course. Keeping them clear of the larger ship's ion emissions, he swung them around the starboard side and underneath. The stumps of the four broken turbolift pylons looked like sections of a model maker's mounting stand in the light from the distant star. "Anything?" he asked as he swung toward the aft-portside tube.

"No course twitching; nothing tracking us," Mara reported.

"Of course, the aft sensors *are* the ones the Colonists would probably have skipped if they hadn't felt like fixing everything."

"Or they may just have skipped the point-defense weaponry back here," Luke reminded her, easing up to the shattered end of the pylon for a closer look. It didn't look like there was going to be enough room for him to lift the Skysprite straight upward, canopy-first, as he would into a standard docking bay.

But if he rotated the ship ninety degrees, standing it on its drive nozzles and taking it in nose-first . . .

"I hope," Mara said, "that you're not thinking what I think you're thinking."

"I am," Luke said. "Hang on."

He gave the engines a burst of power, pushing the small craft ahead a dozen meters along the Dreadnaught's underside. Then, shutting down the main drive, he shifted power to the forward-ventral maneuvering jets, pitching the Skysprite's nose upward. The pylon stump slid past, and he fired one final burst from the main drive, running them straight upward into the tube.

To the accompaniment of a horrendous screech of torn metal.

Luke fought back a wince as he activated the forward landing claw, firing it past the turbolift cars to a more solid connection with the wall. "Was that the hyperdrive ring?" he asked as he took in the cable slack, winching the Skysprite another couple of meters into the pylon.

"Let's just say we'd better not need a quick exit," Mara said. "Aside from that, it was a classy maneuver."

"Thanks," Luke said, shutting the Skysprite's systems back to standby and making sure his vac suit was sealed. "At least we don't have to wonder whether or not they heard us coming. Grab the sealant kit and let's go."

The Skysprite's canopy was, fortunately, reasonably flat, and they were able to get it open in the cramped space without having to cut their way out. Working his way up the landing claw cable, Luke maneuvered between the parked turbolift cars to that last-second gash he'd carved with his thrown lightsaber and squeezed through it.

The damage turned out to be even more impressive than he'd expected. The lightsaber handle had apparently bumped the top of the door a fraction of a second before the blade had closed down, swinging it up and nicking a small hole in the lobby ceiling.

"Nice," Mara said, nodding to the latter as she handed Luke the sealant kit through the opening and then eased her own way through it. "You cut off not only the turbolift lobby, but a section of the next deck up, too. Anything up there they would have particularly missed?"

"Just the next turbolift lobby up," Luke said, looking around. His lightsaber was lying over in a corner beside four dead Vagaari who had been in the wrong place when the Dreadnaught broke free and the lobby depressurized. The blast doors that had reacted to the emergency were about five meters away down each of the three corridors leading away from the lobby. "I think one of the aft electronics supply rooms is just down the corridor from it, though, and a droid maintenance facility is off in the other direction," he added, starting across the lobby. "Depending on which blast doors reacted up there, either or both of those might have been locked away from them, too."

Mara grunted. "It would have been a lot simpler if *none* of them had worked," she pointed out, taking the sealant kit back from him and opening it. "Then the whole ship would have depressurized, and they'd all have died right then and there."

"Which they obviously didn't, since the ship is still under power," Luke pointed out, retrieving his lightsaber and taking a quick look at the alien bodies.

"I didn't say I believed it," Mara said. "I just said it would have been simpler. Anyone we know?"

"Nope," Luke said, experimentally igniting the lightsaber. The green-white blade flashed to existence with gratifying strength. "Good," he said, closing it down again and hooking it onto his belt next to Lorana's. "I was afraid the activator might have stuck on and drained all the power. You need any help?"

"No, I've got it," Mara said, unfolding the patch to the proper size and starting to seal its edges around the gash. "You just stand there and be ready for trouble. They may try to pull something cute even before we get the lobby repressurized."

"Right." Moving to the blast door blocking the corridor leading forward, he stretched out to the Force. There were alien minds in that direction, he could tell, and a high degree of maliciousness. But that was all he could read. Holding his lightsaber ready, he waited.

No attack had come by the time Mara finished laying out the patch and checking its integrity. "Ready?" Luke asked as she packed the kit away.

"Ready," Mara confirmed. "You sure you don't want to use the emergency oxygen tanks to repressurize? It would let us get out of these suits before we have to do any serious fighting."

Luke looked over at the red-rimmed emergency cabinet fastened to the side wall with its collection of oxygen tanks, sealant kits, and medpacs. "I'd rather leave that in reserve," he told her. "Depending on how much of a fight the Vagaari put up, we may wind up needing extra oxygen somewhere else along the line."

"Okay." Igniting her own lightsaber, she took up a ready stance a couple of meters in front of the blast doors. "Remember, just nick it. Enough to let the air in but not enough to trigger anything they might have on the other side."

"Right." Standing as far off to the side as he could, feeling awkward in the confines of his vac suit, Luke jabbed the end of the green-white blade through one corner of the thick door.

There was a sudden hissing noise, and a stream of air began to blow in through the opening, its edges swirling white as water vapor condensed and froze in the vacuum. He glanced at the atmosphere tester on his vac suit, wondering if the Vagaari might have tried poisoning the air on this deck.

But there was nothing. A minute later the whistling faded away as the pressures equalized.

"Anything?" Mara asked.

Luke checked the tester again. "Looks clear," he said.

"Good." Laying her lightsaber on the deck, Mara popped her helmet and started stripping off the vac suit. "I hate trying to move in these things. Watch for company, will you?"

A minute later she was finished. A minute after that, both vac suits were off and piled neatly back near the turbolift doors. "Here we go," Luke commented as Mara took up a stance a couple of meters back from the blast door, her lightsaber humming in front of her. "Let's see what the Vagaari have come up with."

Reaching out with the Force, he keyed the control. Ponderously, the blast doors began to slide back into the walls.

And from a dozen standing and kneeling Vagaari five meters back came a withering hail of blasterfire.

Luke was ready, keying the doors instantly closed again as Mara scattered away the shots that had made it in. "Well, that answers *that* question," she commented.

"Partially, anyway," Luke corrected. "Did you happen to notice the little flat boxes lying along the sides of the walls?"

She shook her head. "Observation was *your* job," she reminded him. "*My* job was staying alive."

"Right," Luke said. "Anyway, they were just like the little gray boxes they used to mine the turbolift, except that these were white."

"White?" Mara frowned, then nodded. "Of course—repainted to blend in with the corridor walls. How many were there?"

"I didn't get an actual count," Luke said, studying the image in his memory. "But they were spaced a meter or two apart and ran all the way down to where the corridor jogs to the right."

"Cute," Mara said. "So the next time we open the blast doors, we'll probably see the Vagaari in full retreat. We'll chase them, watching for blaster shots, and whoever's handling the detonators will have his choice of when to blow us to bits."

"Something like that," Luke said, looking at the ceiling above them. "What do you think? We go up?"

"They'll probably have something ready up there, too," Mara said, her voice and sense suddenly thoughtful. "After all, they've seen what lightsabers can do."

"You have an idea?" Luke prompted.

She favored him with an evil smile. "What they *haven't* seen is this," she said. Letting go of her lightsaber, she levitated it in front of her.

"Okay," Luke said. "So?"

Mara's reply was a twitch of her head back toward the turbolift lobby. Frowning, Luke followed. She stepped to the Vagaari bodies in the corner and, stretching out to the Force, levitated one of them upright. Focusing her control, she moved its arms and legs, keeping it a couple of centimeters above the floor, making it stride rather shakily across the lobby as if it was still alive.

Or, rather, as if he and Mara had put on their enemies' armor as a disguise.

She lifted her eyebrows questioningly. "Doesn't look all that realistic," he pointed out doubtfully, levitating one of the other bodies for himself and sending it across the deck. His didn't look any more alive than hers did. "But if we keep them moving, the Vagaari may not notice."

"I think it's worth a try, anyway," Mara said.

"Definitely," he agreed. "Let's do it."

Moving their puppets to the blast doors, they settled them into standing position. "Quickly, now," Mara said, crouching down beside the wall where her presence wouldn't be immediately obvious. "We don't want anyone getting a clear look."

Luke nodded. Stretching out to the Force, he keyed open the doors.

Mara's prediction had hit it exactly. The Vagaari who had been firing from just outside the doors were already halfway down the corridor, firing wildly behind them in full retreat.

Mara sent her puppet charging after them, its arms and legs pumping madly. Luke's was right behind it. The apparently terrified retreating Vagaari disappeared around the distant corner—

And with an earsplitting blast, the entire corridor exploded in a burst of fire and smoke.

Luke winced, feeling his puppet twist around as it was buffeted violently by the blast before sprawling out of his control onto the deck. His ears ringing, he caught Mara's eye and nodded. She nodded back, and together they sprinted ahead through the smoke and heat.

They met the returning Vagaari just around the corner as the aliens headed back to check the results of their handiwork. The battle was over very quickly.

"Twelve down," Luke commented as he looked down the corridor. There were no signs of trouble or activity, at least not up to the next jog some ten meters ahead. "Plus the four from the turbolift lobby makes sixteen."

"Which might actually be a significant number if we knew how many there were to begin with." Mara nudged one of the bodies with her boot. "Recognize anyone?"

Luke frowned at the alien face. "Is that Bearsh?"

"Sure looks like him," she said. "These guys are a lot more impressive in combat armor than in those silly robes, aren't they?"

"Most species are," Luke said. "Looks like he was leading this particular charge personally. That's a good sign."

"How so?"

"Estosh called him a general," he reminded her. "If he's sending generals to handle field operations, it might imply he hasn't got all that many warriors left."

"Good point," Mara agreed. "Between the dent we made in his troops on Outbound Flight and the people he absolutely *has* to have crewing the Dreadnaught's duty stations, he may very well be hurting for bodies to throw at us right now."

"Right," Luke said. "Either that, or Bearsh was simply being overconfident."

"You are so very helpful sometimes," Mara said, shaking her head in mock annoyance. "I'm surprised you didn't go into politics. Come on, let's get moving before they come up with something else."

They reached the corridor jog Luke had noted without further incident and paused there, looking carefully around the bend. Still no signs of enemies, but twenty meters ahead another set of blast doors had been closed across their path. "Looks clear," he murmured.

"There are three sets of doors leading off each side of the corridor, though," Mara pointed out. "Perfect place to hide while you're waiting to pounce."

Luke closed his eyes, stretching out his senses. He could feel the malevolent, brooding presence of Vagaari all over the Dreadnaught, scattered through his mind like vaguely defined bubbles of heat in a cold room. But none seemed to be very close. "I'm not picking up anyone in there," he said.

"Neither am I," Mara confirmed reluctantly. "I still don't like it."

"Then let's get through it quickly." Throwing a last look at the empty corridor behind them, he rounded the corner and headed forward.

He was just passing the middle set of doors when the left-hand door ahead of him slid open, and five growling wolvkils padded into the corridor.

He braked to a halt, lifting his lightsaber warningly toward the animals. From behind Mara came the sound of another door opening, and he glanced back as four more of the predators filed in from one of the aft set of doors to block their retreat.

"Well, this is cute," Mara murmured. "You see what the stylish wolvkil is wearing this season?"

Luke hadn't; but now his jaw tightened as he spotted the fragmentation grenade slung under each wolvkil's belly. "I was wondering what they thought this was going to accomplish," he commented, adjusting his grip on his lightsaber as he tried to think. So far the wolvkils didn't seem inclined to attack, but were contenting themselves with growling from a distance. But that could change at any moment.

Mara had come to the same conclusion. "Let's try a strategic withdrawal while we think this out," she suggested, easing up to Luke's right and tapping the release on the door beside him. It slid open, and Luke sensed her concentration as she gave the interior a quick check. "Clear," she said. "Come on."

Together, they eased into the room, lightsabers ready. The wolvkils made no move to follow. Mara touched the inner door control, and the panel slid shut. In the glow from his lightsaber Luke found the light pad, flicked it on, and closed down his weapon.

They were in what appeared to be one of the many pumping stations that were by necessity scattered around any ship this size. Sets of conduits snaked along the walls and high ceiling, most of them running into one or the other of two huge and silently chugging rectangular boxes with rounded corners set against the bulkhead across from the door. "Cozy," Luke commented, looking around. There were no other exits from the room, but of course that didn't mean anything to a Jedi with a lightsaber. "Let's see if we can carve ourselves a back door," he suggested. Stepping to the forward wall, he ignited his lightsaber—

"Wait," Mara said.

Luke paused, looking over his shoulder at her. "What?" he asked.

She was gazing at the wall in front of him, her sense tight and suspicious. "Luke, what's the usual procedure for sealing a hull breach?"

He frowned. "You send some repair droids to the vicinity, close the blast doors behind them, pump out the air to equalize pressures, then open the inner doors to give them access to the leak."

"Right," Mara said, nodding. "The Vagaari have had four days to seal the gash you cut in the turbolift lobby. We know there are housekeeping droids still working, and we know there *were* enough repair droids rolling around at one time to fix all the damage Thrawn did to the hull. And anyway, even if none of them works anymore, Estosh surely brought a pressure suit or two along they could have used to go in themselves and fix it."

"But they didn't," Luke said thoughtfully. "Why not?"

"Because if we'd come up the pylon and found your gash all sewn up, we might have decided to come aboard somewhere else," Mara concluded grimly. "This way, they could reasonably predict where we'd come in, and could concentrate on making this one corridor as much of a death trap as they could."

She nodded toward the wall in front of him. "So why should this part of it be any different?"

"Good question," Luke agreed, closing down his lightsaber and stepping aside. "In that case, you'd better do this."

It took three delicate strokes for her to tease a scratch all the way through the bulkhead. And it was indeed a very good thing he'd let her go first.

"Terrific," she said darkly, sniffing at the liquid trickling down the wall. "Secondary reactant fuel, which most certainly wouldn't normally be stored next to a pump room. Estosh is kindly offering us the opportunity of immolating ourselves."

"How generous of him," Luke said, looking up at the ceiling. "I wonder if they've ever seen how high a Jedi can jump."

"I don't think so," she said. "But it wouldn't take a Jedi to climb that maze of pipes fastened to the wall. If they were being thorough, they'd certainly have booby-trapped the ceiling, too."

"Right," he conceded. "What about down? Any idea what's below us?"

"Usually it would be substructure, environmental equipment, and other bulk stuff," Mara said. "Not a place you want to go randomly swinging lightsabers."

"So we can't go down, up, or sideways, and outside the

door there's nothing but wolvkils and fragmentation grenades," Luke concluded, looking around for inspiration.

"*And* we've got a reactant fuel leak going," Mara reminded him. "Any ideas?"

Luke's gaze paused on the two humming pumps. Each of them was nearly two meters tall and a meter wide, with a casing built of heavy metal and a front access cover shaped like a rectangular, flat-bottomed bowl with rounded corners and edges. "Actually, yes," he told her, popping the release on one of the covers and swinging it open. The cover was as strongly built as the rest of the casing, with a ten-centimeter lip all the way around the perimeter. "Let's get these doors off."

Igniting his lightsaber, he sliced off the hinges, catching the cover in a Force grip as it started to fall ponderously toward him. "I hope you're not planning to use these things as shields," Mara warned as she cut the other cover free. "There are an awful lot of grenades out there."

"No, I've got something else in mind," Luke assured her, leaning the cover up against the wall by the door and closing down his lightsaber. "Time to go for the high ground." Getting a grip on two of the pipes fastened to the wall, he started to climb.

Mara followed silently, clearly puzzled but willing to give him the benefit of the doubt. Midway through their climb, he could sense when she suddenly caught on. "Okay," he said when they were about two meters off the deck. Looking down over his shoulder, he stretched out to the Force and lifted the two covers to hover in the air just beneath him and Mara, their bowl sides up. "You ready?" he said.

Her answer was the *snap-hiss* of her lightsaber. Reaching over to the dripping bulkhead, she slashed the blade through it.

With a sudden gurgle, the trickle became a flood, the aromatic fuel flowing down the wall and running across the floor. "Watch your timing," Luke warned as the sloshing pool began to fill the small room. "Remember, the lips on these things are only about ten centimeters high."

"I know," Mara assured him. She had her lightsaber closed

down and back on her belt now, with her sleeve gun drawn. "Get ready . . . *now*."

Abruptly, the door slid open at her Force command, the pool of fuel flowing out into the corridor. There was a surprised yelp from one of the wolvkils—

And Mara fired a single shot from her blaster into the liquid.

It ignited with a tremendous roar, the flames shooting nearly a meter off the deck. Even with the hovering covers protecting them, Luke found himself wincing at the rush of heat that washed over and past him. The yelp outside had become a howl of pain and fear, and he could hear startled Vagaari voices mixed in with those of the wolvkils. The height of the flames diminished as the blazing liquid continued to flow out into the corridor, settling down to perhaps thirty centimeters.

It was time to go. "Take the right one," he called to Mara over the noise of the flames, pointing to the hovering cover nearest her. He felt her take its weight. Then, focusing all his attention on the other one, he maneuvered it into the center of the doorway and settled it down onto the deck. Bracing himself, he jumped.

He hit the cover dead center, dropping into a crouch as he landed. The flames crackled all around him, flowing nearly to the level of the cover's lip, giving him the sudden feeling of being in a boat floating on a river of fire. Recovering his balance, he straightened up and looked around.

The entire corridor was filled with fire and smoke and the screams and howls of the injured. Through the shimmering heat haze to his left he could see flame-sheathed Vagaari writhing in agony as they staggered around trying to find a way out of the rolling river of fire. To his right, the blast doors reflected back the light of the flames, making metallic pinging noises as the sudden heat created uneven expansion in the metal.

Surprisingly, he saw only a couple of wolvkil bodies lying burning in the inferno. Apparently, the animals' speed was as good for escape as it was for attack.

Turning back to the room, he again stretched out to the Force, taking the second cover from Mara's grip. Sliding it over his head through the blocked doorway, he maneuvered it along the corridor and set it down in the flames just in front of the blast doors. "Okay," he called to Mara. "Let's go."

Bending his knees, he leapt over the fire to land in the center of this second metal boat. He glanced back to see Mara land safely in the cover he'd just vacated, then turned and slapped the blast door release.

There were no Vagaari waiting on the other side, though if there had been the flaming liquid now streaming out along the floor toward them would probably have sent them running anyway. Luke made another jump to get past the edge of the expanding fire and turned back around, ready in case Mara needed assistance.

She didn't. Without having to pause to open the blast doors as Luke had had to, she did the final part of the trip in two quick back-to-back leaps, landing on the deck beside him. Even before she was down, he stretched back out to the control and closed the blast doors again.

"Well, that was fun," she said, breathing hard after her trip through the smoke. With its source of new fuel now blocked, the fire on this side of the blast doors had settled into a small pool that was busily burning itself out. "Uliar's going to have a fit when he sees what we've done to his Dreadnaught."

"He can bill us," Luke said, looking around. "I vote we get out of this corridor. The command deck's another four decks up anyway."

"Seconded and approved," Mara said. "I take it you'll want to avoid the turbolifts?"

"Absolutely," Luke said, looking up at the high ceiling. "But as you pointed out, they haven't yet seen how high we can jump."

Igniting his lightsaber, he locked the switch on and hurled it spinning into the ceiling, carving out a neat hole just wide enough to pass comfortably through. "There we go," he said, catching the weapon and closing it down as Mara fielded the circle of deck metal as it tumbled toward them. "Let's go."

* * *

THEY MADE IT TO THE COMMAND DECK'S LEVEL WITHOUT FUR-
ther trouble. Either the Vagaari had been thrown into disarray
by the turning of their firetrap against them, or else Mara had
been right about their defenses being focused on that single
corridor.

Still, there was a lot of distance yet to cover before they
reached the command deck, and a potentially large number
of Vagaari still available for Estosh to throw at them. Senses
alert, lightsabers held at the ready, they started forward.

But for a while, Luke began to wonder if the aliens had indeed given up. As they'd already discovered on the lower
decks, the damage was greatest in the Dreadnaught's midsection, where Thrawn's attack had methodically taken out
the turbolaser blisters and shield projectors. The debris and
twisted bulkheads made for ideal ambush points, yet the Vagaari made no attempt to use them. There were occasional
stacks or lines of explosives, but laid out hurriedly and with
no attempt at subtlety or camouflage, almost as if simply
dropped there by Vagaari trying desperately to get out of the
path of the approaching Jedi. The two clusters that couldn't
be bypassed were quickly disarmed.

They made it through the midsection and continued on
into the forward operations and crew areas. Here the resistance was slightly better organized: teams of three to five Vagaari would lurk in doorways or curves in the corridor, firing
concerted volleys of blasterfire as Luke and Mara came into
view. But again, Jedi senses and reflexes were more than adequate to the task, and it usually took only a few seconds of
fire for the aliens to realize that their surprise had failed and
to break off, scattering away into the shadows. From all appearances, it would seem Estosh was in the last stages of
helpless desperation.

Mara didn't believe it, either. "He's up to something," she
muttered as they passed the site of the latest would-be ambush, stepping over the bodies of the two Vagaari who had
been unlucky enough to have their shots reflected straight
back at them.

"Of course he is," Luke said, glancing in both directions as they reached yet another cross-corridor. No one lying in wait in this one. "The question is, what? What else could Outbound Flight's organizers have brought aboard that he could use against us?"

"We'll find out soon enough," Mara said. "Another couple of cross-corridors and we should be there."

They moved ahead cautiously. Three minutes later, they reached the command deck.

It was the same setup as they'd seen earlier on D-1, minus the extensive damage that the impact with the planetoid's gravel pit had created down there. A wide cross-corridor ran across the width of the ship just aft of the command deck, with an archway and sealed blast door set into the bulkhead directly in front of their portside corridor. Thirty meters to their right was a similar entryway, this one set in front of the main starboard corridor. Beyond the two blast doors would be the monitor anteroom with its long rows of consoles; from the far side of the anteroom, a single archway and even heavier blast door would lead onto the bridge proper.

"They're in there, all right," Luke said, stretching out toward the thick bulkhead with his mind. "Quite a few of them. I get the feeling they're expecting us."

"They got that part right, anyway," Mara said. "How do you want to work this?"

Luke looked down the cross-corridor toward the starboard entryway, considering their options. The fact that the Vagaari had sealed the anteroom blast doors implied they weren't going to give up their territory quite so easily. "We go straight in," he decided. "Whatever they've got planned, they've either got a duplicate trap at each of the two doors, or else they've saved everything for the bridge proper. Either way—"

"Hold it," Mara cut him off, her head cocked. "You hear something?"

Luke frowned. A new sound had been added to the background noises of a capital ship in flight, a metallic rumbling coming from their right. He looked again down the cross-corridor toward the other anteroom door—

And suddenly, a giant wheel-like machine rolled into view from the starboard corridor. It braked to a halt and began to open like a strange metal flower.

"Oh, no," Mara breathed, tossing her lightsaber to her left hand and snatching out her sleeve gun.

But she was too late. Even as she fired, the machine finished unfolding, its curved head rearing up over its tripod legs, its jointed forearms settling themselves into horizontal position, the hazy sphere of its deflector shield flickering to life and spattering Mara's shot into the ceiling. The head shifted slightly toward them, as if noticing the intruders for the first time, the arms swiveling their permanently mounted blasters to point in their direction.

It was a droideka. But unlike the one they'd so recently faced in Jerf Huxley's cantina, this one appeared to be fully functional.

And it was hunting them.

CHAPTER 25

MARA STILL HAD HER LIGHTSABER IN HER LEFT HAND AS THE droideka opened fire. She swung it around, trying to get it to guard position—

Just as the green blade of Luke's lightsaber cut in front of her, deflecting the shots that had been aimed at her torso. "Come on!" he shouted.

She didn't need to be told twice. Moving as quickly as they could while still defending against the sudden hail of fire, they ducked back into the portside corridor they'd just left. "Well, that's just—"

"Later," Luke snapped. "I hear it folding up again."

Mara swore under her breath, jamming her sleeve blaster back into its holster as she took off down the corridor. "Wait a second," she said as a thought suddenly occurred to her. "Keep going," she added, ducking into an open doorway to her right.

Luke broke stride. "What—?"

"I'm playing a hunch," she hissed back. "Get going before it sees you talking to an empty room."

She could tell he didn't understand and that he furthermore wasn't at all happy about leaving her alone like this. But as she could sense his doubts, he could also sense her confidence that it was a gamble worth taking. Giving her a quick nod, he resumed his sprint away from the command deck. Listening closely, Mara heard the droideka's rumbling change pitch as it made a tight turn around the corner and rolled into the corridor behind her husband. The pitch changed again as it spotted Luke in the distance and headed in pursuit. Taking a couple of steps backward into the room, hope-fully putting herself out of range of the droideka's sensors, Mara pulled out her blaster again and leveled it at the door-way. She could very literally have only one shot . . .

Abruptly, a blur of shiny metal flashed into view. Letting the Force guide her hand, she fired.

The droideka was gone again almost before it registered in her vision, and from the direction it had disappeared came an abrupt cacophony of metal on metal as it scrabbled to a sud-den halt to deal with this unexpected menace on its flank. Mara jumped to her feet and charged for the doorway, hop-ing she might get in a follow-up shot before it could recover its balance.

But the machine was too fast. By the time she emerged into the corridor, it had already started to wheel around toward her. Aiming for the sensor cluster in its head, she fired.

Too late. The droideka again got its shield up in time, ricocheting the shot away. It finished its unrolling and rose again, weapons tracking toward her. Mara dropped her blaster, igniting her lightsaber and bringing it back up in front of her. The droideka's blasters lifted slightly—

And suddenly the machine staggered as something big and dark came flying down the corridor and slammed into its shield from behind, sending its first volley into the deck. Mara backed away down the corridor, blocking the droideka's shots as it waddled awkwardly after her. A moment later, she'd made it back to the cross-corridor outside the command deck. A second object slammed into the droideka, and she took ad-vantage of the distraction to dodge to her left and run full-speed toward the starboard corridor. Hoping fervently that the droideka didn't have a friend waiting in ambush, she rounded the corner.

No one was waiting, droideka or Vagaari. She'd made it two cross-corridors back when Luke stepped out in front of her, palm upraised. "It's all right," he said. "It's not follow-ing."

"You'd better be right," she said, breathing hard as she

slowed to a halt. "Thanks for the assist. What were you throwing at it, anyway?"

"Whatever odds and ends were handy," he told her, glancing around and pointing her to a nearby electronics repair room. "The first one was a power converter, I think, and the second was a two-meter piece of structural bracing girder that had been broken off and was lying around."

"Neither of which is exactly a lightweight," Mara pointed out grimly as they stepped inside the room. "If hitting it that hard didn't do anything but spoil its aim for a couple of shots, we can forget about that as a way to take it down."

"I think you're right," Luke agreed. "What about you? Any luck with that sucker shot?"

Mara shrugged. "I'm pretty sure I hit the sensor head, but I don't know what kind of damage I did. Probably not very much—it sure didn't have any trouble lining up its blasters on me afterward."

"So they can't keep their shields up while they're rolling?"

"Right," Mara said. "About all they can do with their shields up is that little waddle thing. Problem is, in wheel form they're just too fast for a good killing shot."

"Certainly not from a blaster that small," Luke said. "Maybe we should see if we can find something with a little more power and try it again."

"Maybe," Mara said doubtfully. "But then you're going to run into a different limitation. With blasters, the more power it's got, the bigger and heavier it is. Even with the Force I had enough trouble hitting it with my sleeve gun. It would be that much harder to move even a carbine fast enough to keep up with a droideka's speed and maneuverability."

"How about if it wasn't moving?" Luke asked. "Could that same carbine punch through the shield?"

Mara shook her head. "I've never seen the specs, but from what I've heard it sounds like it would take something a lot bigger than that to do the trick."

"So we're back to hitting it when it's on the move," Luke concluded. "Maybe you should have tried that ambush trick with your lightsaber instead of your blaster."

"Wouldn't have worked," Mara said. "I would have had to stand right at the doorway to reach it, and it would have picked me up long before it got within range."

"How about now that its sensors are damaged?"

"I'd hate to try it," Mara said hesitantly. "There are several different types of sensors grouped there—composite radiation, vibration, and I think one or two more. It can aim and fire using any combination of them."

"Terrific," Luke said, starting to sound a little frustrated. "We can't use blasters, and we can't use lightsabers. So how *did* the Jedi of that era deal with them?"

Mara felt her lips tighten. "Mostly, they ran away," she said. "I can't remember a single story of a Jedi taking out a shielded one on his own."

Luke seemed taken aback. "Oh."

"*Oh,* indeed." Mara leaned her head back out of the room to peer down the corridor. "You *did* say it had stopped, right?"

Luke nodded. "I heard it unroll. From the direction of the sound, I'd guess it's sitting midway between the two command deck doors."

"Like a big metal vornskr on guard duty."

"Exactly," Luke said, starting to sound back on track again. "At least now we know what else Outbound Flight's organizers packed aboard. Where in the worlds did they get a droideka, anyway? I thought only the Trade Federation had them back then."

"They did, but you forget that the Trade Federation had been allegedly rehabilitated after the Naboo incident," Mara pointed out. "They were all sweetness and light—well, they were all grudging cooperation, anyway—until the Separatists dropped the hammer at Geonosis and the Clone Wars began. Someone probably persuaded them to donate a few to Outbound Flight with an eye toward sentry use on any new colonies they might set up." She gestured. "Fortunately, it looks like the Vagaari only have one of them working."

"One is plenty for me," Luke assured her dryly. "I'm surprised they got even that far."

"I'm not," Mara said sourly. "Or at least, I shouldn't have been. The more I think about it, the more I think droid technology was what Estosh came here looking for in the first place."

"What makes you say that?" Luke asked, frowning.

"It was right after that first cleaner droid appeared on D-Four and you slipped away to scout out our path," Mara said, feeling yet another twinge of professional embarrassment. Like the fake Geroon refugee ship, this was something she should have instantly caught on to. "We got to talking about droids in general, and one of the Vagaari asked specifically about droidekas. There's no place he could have picked up that term except from Fel's operational manual."

"Okay," Luke said slowly. "But we already know they're the ones who stole it."

"Right," Mara said. "But there were four densely packed data cards in that set. What are the odds they would have stumbled across a list of droid designations unless they were specifically looking for them?"

"Even less than the odds they'd find the maintenance and activation procedures," Luke said, nodding. "So this whole fuss is over nothing but a few droids?"

"They're only a few droids to us because we're so used to having them around," Mara pointed out. "Remember what Fel said about the Chiss not having droid technology? If the Chiss don't, probably no one else out here does, either. If the Vagaari can learn how to build and field a droid army, they're going to have a huge advantage, especially among the less developed cultures who seem to be their preferred prey."

"I guess you're right," Luke said. "So the original plan was probably to kill everyone aboard the *Chaf Envoy*, spread out through Outbound Flight to collect all the droids they could find, then sneak back through the Redoubt before we were gone long enough to have raised any alarms."

"That's my guess," Mara said. "It was just pure luck they got a working Dreadnaught as a bonus."

Luke grimaced. "Some bonus. The chief Vagaari's going to be *really* pleased to have this show up on his doorstep."

"Not if we can help it," Mara declared. "Come on, you're the Jedi Master. Think of something."

"Maybe we don't actually have to destroy it," Luke said. "All we really want to do is to get onto the command deck and take control of the ship."

"And, what, we just persuade the droideka to turn its head for a minute?"

Luke smiled tightly. "As a matter of fact," he said, "I think we can do exactly that."

CAREFULLY, LUKE EASED HIS WAY TO THE END OF THE STARboard corridor. Directly in front of him was the archway and access door into the command deck, while somewhere out of sight to his left the droideka was standing guard.

He stretched out his mind to Mara, sensed that she was in mirror-image position thirty meters away in the portside corridor. The droideka was now directly between them . . . and the way its arms were hinged, it could only fire in one direction at a time. Bracing himself, he ignited his lightsaber and stepped out into the cross-corridor.

The droideka was, as he'd surmised earlier, standing with its back to the command deck wall midway between the two access doors. Its shield popped on as its sensors detected Luke's movement, its guns swiveling as it tracked toward him. "Yes, it's me," Luke called, lifting his lightsaber to guard position as he took another two steps toward the machine. "Come on; have at it."

The droideka obliged with a burst of blasterfire. Luke's lightsaber flashed back and forth, deflecting the shots as he slowly reversed direction back the way he'd come. He made it back to the corner and ducked back to safety. Closing down his lightsaber, he turned aft and started running down the corridor, listening between the thudding of his footsteps for the sounds of the droideka giving chase.

The sounds didn't come. Frowning, he slowed to a halt, listening more closely. Still no pursuit. Reversing direction again, he returned to the corner and eased an eye around it.

The droideka's response was another round of blasterfire

that gouged a fresh set of pits in the metal walls. But in that single brief glimpse Luke had seen that the droideka hadn't budged from the spot where he'd left it.

Retreating a few paces down the corridor, he pulled out his comlink and thumbed it on. "Mara?"

"It doesn't seem to want to come out and play, does it?" her voice answered.

"No, it's apparently happy right where it is," Luke said. "You want to give it a try?"

"Not worth the effort," Mara said. "It's already seen that there are two of us, and it's smart enough not to get suckered into chasing one of us when the other one's unaccounted for. I was afraid we were going to run into that problem."

"It was still worth a try," Luke said. "On to Plan Two, I guess. You ready?"

"Ready," she answered. "Watch yourself."

"Right." Luke shut off the comlink and returned it to his belt. Stepping back to the corner, he lifted his lightsaber, braced himself—

And spun 180 degrees around a fraction of a second before the burst of blasterfire erupted toward him from far down the corridor. Another Vagaari hit squad had launched its assault, apparently hoping to sneak up on him while he was concentrating on the droideka.

Like the previous attacks, this one was over quickly. Luke could sense the pain that indicated one of the deflected bolts had returned to its source, then sensed the distance change as the aliens retreated, dragging their wounded comrade with them.

He took a deep breath. With the combat tunnel vision fading, he could sense Mara's sudden anxiety. He sent her a quick mental assurance, plus a wordless warning to watch her own back. Stepping to the corner again, lightsaber held ready, he charged suddenly toward the archway in front of him.

The droideka must have expected a repeat of Luke's earlier, more cautious appearance. Its first spatter of fire passed harmlessly behind him as he sprinted across the cross-corridor and skidded to a halt in front of the anteroom door. The droideka's second volley found the range, and Luke set his teeth firmly together as he swung his lightsaber across the multiple shots coming at him. He didn't dare split away enough of his attention to look behind his attacker; but if Mara was on schedule, she was even now moving stealthily from her corridor to the portside anteroom door . . .

Abruptly, the fire coming at Luke broke off as the droideka pivoted around. Luke had just enough time to see Mara in the distance, stabbing her lightsaber into the edge of the blast door, as the droideka opened fire.

He felt his breath catch in his throat. But Mara had been expecting that move, and had her lightsaber back up in time to defend herself.

And now, with the droideka's attack pointed in the other direction, it was Luke's turn. Lifting his lightsaber to point horizontally, keeping a wary eye on the droideka, he jabbed the blade into the blast door beside him.

Again, the droideka reacted, swiveling back around toward him. Luke brought his lightsaber up, dropping into combat focus again as the quadruple blasters began laying down their withering rain of fire. Behind the droideka, he knew, Mara would have returned to her own assault on the command deck. If the droideka continued to play this game, eventually both of them would make it through.

The droideka had apparently figured that out, too. Firing one last volley at Luke, it dropped its shield, folded back into wheel shape, and charged down the cross-corridor toward Mara. Luke set off in pursuit—

And barely got his lightsaber back up in time as the droideka's blasters fired a twin burst at him.

He managed to block the shots, his stride faltering with the sheer unexpectedness of it. He hadn't realized it was possible for droidekas to shoot while in wheel shape. The machine fired a rolling burst at Mara, then another at Luke as the positioning of its blasters came back to the right spot in its rotation. It fired another shot at Mara—

Luke inhaled sharply, breaking into an all-out run as the

droideka's strategy suddenly became clear. It was going to roll right up to Mara, moving so close that even Jedi reflexes wouldn't be fast enough to handle the shots. *Run,* he thought desperately toward her. *Get away. Now.*

Mara didn't move. She'd figured out the droideka's plan, too, he could sense; but instead of trying to get away, she was waiting for it, lightsaber ready, preparing to meet the destroyer head-on. Luke breathed a curse that was half anger and half fear and leaned into his sprint, driving himself desperately toward his wife. The droideka was nearly on her now—

Then, even as it fired one final time from the wheel position and screeched to a halt a bare two meters away, Mara finally moved. She leapt forward and to the side, moving out of its line of rolling fire and lunging toward it with her lightsaber.

Once again, the droideka's mechanical reflexes were too fast. It had its shield up even before it finished unrolling, bouncing her lightsaber blade uselessly off the hazy surface. The droideka continued uncurling, its blasters swinging up and out into full maneuverability again as Mara tried to bring her lightsaber up in time. The blasters spat fire—

And with a final desperate lunge, Luke hurled his lightsaber forward directly in front of the blasters, blocking the shots. "Come on!" he shouted.

Mara needed no encouragement. She jumped past the droideka, plucking Luke's lightsaber out of midair as she passed it, and hit the deck running. Luke braked to a halt, snatching back his weapon from her as she shot past him. A second later, they were sprinting together toward the safety of the starboard corridor.

Only it might not be as safe as Luke had expected. Behind them, he could hear the sounds as the droideka once again folded up and set itself in motion. Now that it had both of them in sight, it had apparently decided to go on the offensive.

They reached the starboard corridor and ducked around the corner. "It's following us," Mara panted.

"I know," Luke panted back. "Keep going. We may have to try that lightsaber ambush after all."

Mara didn't reply. Maybe she was thinking about pointing out that the droideka's sensors were obviously still functional enough to make that gesture useless. More likely, she was conserving her air.

Again, he caught the sounds behind him just in time. "Watch it," he snapped, skidding to a halt and spinning around. The droideka had stopped a couple of meters into the corridor and was in the process of unfolding. "In there," Luke ordered, nodding to a cross-corridor cutting across their path a couple of meters behind them.

The droideka opened fire as they backed toward it, but at this distance Jedi reflexes were more than adequate to handle the attack. A few seconds later, they were into the corridor and out of its sight.

For a moment they leaned side by side against the cool metal wall, panting hard. In the distance, Luke could hear the droideka starting to fold up again, and risked a quick look around the corner. If it thought it could bottle them up . . .

But with the enemy temporarily out of its sight, the machine had apparently decided to go back to guard duty. Luke watched it finish its reconfiguration and roll almost leisurely back around the corner into the command deck corridor. "This isn't working," he commented.

"No kidding," Mara growled back. "Thanks for getting me out of that, by the way. I thought I might have a chance to get in a killing thrust before its shield went up."

"I guess it saw you coming," Luke said. "Did you know it could shoot while rolling that way?"

"No," Mara said. "Either that was a very well-kept secret, or else it's something new that someone built into this particular model. It's not all that effective—you saw it could only fire straight along its path, and only at the spot in its rotation when the blasters were turned to the right spot."

Luke grunted. "It was effective enough for me."

"No argument there." Mara shook her head. "We need a

new approach, Luke. We keep playing this game, and eventually it's going to wear us down."

"Or a Vagaari sniper squad will get us while we're being distracted," Luke agreed. "Let's think it through. We know we can't get it with the shield up. That means we have to get it before then, either while it's still rolling or else right as it stops and starts to unfold."

"And as we just saw, it can put its shield up before it finishes unfolding if it senses an attacker nearby," Mara pointed out.

"Which means we can't let it see the attack coming," Luke agreed. "Which brings us back to some kind of ambush."

"Right," Mara agreed. "Problem: the only place around here to hide is inside one of the rooms off the corridor."

"Which we already tried."

"Right," Mara said. "What we need is for it to follow us someplace more promising. Maybe aft to the turbolaser blisters, where we've got all that wreckage to set up in."

Luke shook his head. "It's not going to let us do that," he said. "You saw what it did just now. With both of us clearly in sight, it still stopped two meters in from the command deck corridor, fired a few times, then went back to guard duty."

"It did, didn't it?" Mara commented, her expression changing subtly as she stared at the wall across from them. "You think you could pick out the exact spot where it stopped?"

Luke pulled up the memory. "Easily," he said. "Both times it stopped about two meters in, right in the center of the corridor where it's as safe from possible ambush as it can get. Of course, there's no guarantee it'll go to the same spot the next time."

"Oh, I think there is," Mara said, smiling a sudden, private smile. "Even if this is one of the models with an autonomous brain, the Vagaari can't possibly have the skill to have programmed anything fancy into it. I'm guessing it's been given its patrol parameters and is going to stick with them down to the half centimeter."

"Okay," Luke said, eyeing her suspiciously. He knew that

look, and it generally meant trouble. "But there's still no cover anywhere nearby for an ambush."

"That's okay," she said. "For this one, we're not going to need cover. Here's the plan . . ."

GETTING A FIRM GRIP ON HIS LIGHTSABER, LUKE ONCE AGAIN stepped out into the command deck corridor.

The droideka's head swiveled toward him, as if not believing he was actually going to try this again. Luke took another step; the droideka responded by tracking its blasters toward him. "Get ready," Luke murmured. He took a third step, sensing Mara stepping into the corridor directly behind him—

And suddenly all other sensations and awareness vanished as the droideka opened fire.

Luke's lightsaber flashed back and forth, deflecting the blasts as he continued to sidle toward the starboard anteroom door. He reached it, dimly hearing the *snap-hiss* behind him as Mara ignited her own weapon.

The droideka reacted instantly. Even as Mara stabbed her lightsaber blade into the blast door, it ceased fire, folded up, and began rolling full-speed toward them. Luke watched its approach, trying to judge the timing— "Go!" he snapped at Mara. He deflected a burst of rolling fire as he heard her close down her weapon and take off back to the relative safety of the corridor. He held position another half second, then broke out of combat stance and charged after her.

The droideka kept coming. Luke heard the subtle changes in pitch as it altered direction to continue the chase, and put some extra speed into his running. If he hadn't been right about the droideka's positioning the last time, or if the machine wasn't as precisely programmed as Mara was hoping, this wasn't going to work.

The sound of the rolling wheel abruptly halted. "There it goes!" Mara called, braking to a halt in front of him.

Luke stopped and spun around, lightsaber ignited and ready. The droideka was standing in the center of the corridor, exactly where it had been the last two times it had chased them in this direction, its hazy deflector shield up as it finished the process of unfolding into attack position.

And beneath it, lying on the deck beside one of its tripod feet where Mara had carefully placed it before they'd launched their little feint, was their secret weapon.

Lorana Jinzler's old lightsaber.

Lying *inside* the droideka's deflector shield.

Luke lifted his lightsaber; but in salute, not defense. Even as the droideka's blasters settled into firing position, he felt Mara stretch out to the Force, twitching Lorana's lightsaber off the deck and rotating it to point upward toward the large bronzium-armor bulb at the base of the droideka's abdomen. With an asthmatic *snap-hiss* the green blade blazed to life, slicing into the droideka's heavy alloy body—

Luke had just a fraction of a second of premonition. "Down!" he snapped, grabbing Mara in a Force grip and pulling her down onto the deck beside him with their backs to the doomed machine.

And with a thundering explosion, the droideka disintegrated.

Luke squeezed his eyes shut, wincing as the blast washed over him like a desert sandstorm, the heat singeing the back of his neck, the concussion lifting him up off the deck and slamming him back down again, the tiny bits of shattered metal whipping across his back and legs and arms like maddened stingflies. A wave of acrid smoke followed behind the blast, curling his nostrils. A second later cooler air flowed across him in the opposite direction toward the partial vacuum, causing a brief moment of turbulence.

And then, everything was once again still. Cautiously, he opened his eyes and looked back over his shoulder.

The droideka was gone. So was Lorana's lightsaber, he noted with a twinge of guilt.

So was most of the portside blast door.

"Come on," he said to Mara, dragging himself upright. He felt a little woozy, but otherwise he seemed all right. "Let's get in there before they recover."

"What?" Mara asked vaguely, rubbing at her cheek as she

got shakily to her feet and turned around. "Oh. That could be useful."

"Right." Luke looked around for his lightsaber, which had somehow ended up another three meters down the corridor, and stretched out to the Force to call it to his hand. "I take it that bulb thing with all the bronzium armor was the droideka's mini-reactor?"

"You got it," Mara said, stooping and retrieving her own lightsaber. "I was just trying to shut it down. I didn't mean to shut it down quite that violently."

"You must have hit one of the power regulators," Luke said, taking a couple of deep breaths as he looked her over. Her clothing was badly scorched, but aside from a few minor cuts and burns she seemed uninjured. She still had some of the same blast-induced fogginess he himself was fighting, but it was rapidly fading away. "Come on—we have to get in there," he repeated.

"Right," Mara said, her voice firmer this time. Taking a deep breath, she started forward. "Let's do it."

The left side of the blast door had been collapsed inward, crumpling the thick metal and leaving a gap big enough for two people to step through together. He and Mara did just that, lightsabers ready in front of them.

There was, as it turned out, no need for caution. Outside, the concussion shock wave from the exploding droideka had had a long, wide corridor to spread out into as it dissipated its energy. Here, however, it had had only the relatively con-fined space of the monitor anteroom to bounce around in. From the looks of the twenty or so Vagaari sprawled over their consoles or lying twitching on the deck, the wave must have done some fairly serious bouncing.

"They'll keep," Luke decided, looking across the rows of chairs and monitor consoles toward the archway and blast door leading into the bridge. "Let's see if we can get inside before Estosh realizes we're here."

"Go ahead," Mara said, nodding to the left where one of the consoles had suddenly started beeping. "I want to see what's coming through over there."

Luke nodded, threading his way through the rows of consoles toward the door. He was nearly there when there was a hollow metallic clank, and with a ponderous rumble the door began to slide open.

"Sss!" Luke hissed a warning to Mara as he jumped to a group of consoles a couple of meters to the right of the door. Closing down his lightsaber, he dropped into concealment behind one of the cabinets and peered cautiously around the side.

Behind the opening door were a pair of nervous-looking Vagaari pointing heavy blaster carbines out into the monitor anteroom. At their feet, growling deep in their throats, were a pair of wolvkils.

Luke held his breath, recognizing the opportunity that had just been handed to them. Protected by thick bulkheads from any damage from the exploding droideka, the Vagaari in the bridge had nevertheless certainly noticed the blast. Estosh had apparently decided it was worth the risk of sending someone out to see what was going on.

Which meant the bridge now lay wide open to them, with only a couple of soldiers and their pet wolvkils standing in their way.

The question was how best to take advantage of that.

One of the soldiers said something back over his shoulder. Another voice replied from inside the bridge. Reluctantly, Luke thought, the two Vagaari stepped through the doorway and started across the room toward the wrecked blast door, their weapons clutched tightly in their hands.

And as they did so, one of the wolvkils turned its head and looked straight at Luke.

Luke looked back, stretching out to the Force. Back aboard Outbound Flight, he'd touched the nerve centers of a group of the predators, searching out the pathways that would let him put them harmlessly to sleep. Now, though, he needed something subtler, something that would suppress their curiosity or their aggressive instincts without doing anything as obvious as dropping them like a couple of soft-dolls. Carefully, quickly, he traced along a wolvkil's nervous system . . .

And then, across the room, someone moaned.

The two Vagaari jerked in unison toward the noise, their weapons jerking with them. The moan came again, more gurgling this time. One of the aliens murmured something to the wolvkils, and Luke was suddenly forgotten as the two animals headed in that direction. The Vagaari followed, weapons held ready. Behind them, the door to the bridge reversed its direction and began to slide closed.

And with a tight smile, Luke rose from his concealment, took two quick steps behind the oblivious soldiers, and slipped through the closing door.

CHAPTER 26

THE MOVE WAS SO SMOOTH AND QUIET THAT FOR THAT FIRST half second no one in the bridge even seemed to notice him. Luke took that moment for a quick assessment of the situation: ten Vagaari dressed in brown uniforms standing or sitting at various of the multitude of control consoles, the huge transparisteel viewport in front of them still showing the mottled sky of hyperspace, the big status board curving around the starboard bulkhead showing three more minutes to breakout.

And then the Vagaari who had been working the blast door controls suddenly focused on him and managed a strangled gasp.

The aliens at the consoles spun in their seats, goggling. Luke lifted his lightsaber and ignited it; and abruptly, every one of them hauled out a blaster and opened fire.

Most of that first panicky volley went wide. Luke easily blocked the three shots that had been accurately aimed and, mindful of the critical equipment filling the room, took care to send the deflected shots directly back to their sources. The next volley was even more poorly aimed as the surviving Vagaari, suddenly recognizing the danger they were in, scrambled for some semblance of cover. Luke took advantage of the unintended lull to send the Vagaari operating the blast door controls sprawling to the deck, reaching out to the Force to key the door open again. The rest of the Vagaari, now crouched beside consoles or behind chairs, opened fire again; a flurry of shots later, two more of them lay sprawled on the deck. Behind him, Luke sensed Mara sprinting to the archway to assist—

"Amacrisier!"

Abruptly, the firing ceased. Luke held his stance, senses alert. "You are remarkable warriors indeed, you Jedi," one of the Vagaari said calmly from midway across the room as he holstered his weapon. "Had I not witnessed it myself, I would not have believed it."

"Everyone needs a little amazement in their lives, Estosh," Luke commented. "You look good in that uniform."

"I appear now as I truly am," Estosh countered, straightening up proudly. "Not the pathetically eager drone I made myself to be."

"It was a nice performance," Mara commented as she slipped in through the doorway to stand beside Luke. "I do think you overplayed it a little, though."

"No matter," Estosh said, starting to stroll casually across the bridge. "It fooled you all into thinking we were harmless. That was all that mattered."

"Actually, you didn't fool everyone," Mara corrected him. "Aristocra Formbi was on to you right from the start."

Estosh stopped short. "You lie."

Mara shook her head. "No, but go ahead and believe whatever you want. So. You've got your droids, and you've even got yourself a Dreadnaught to carry them in. What's the rest of the plan?"

Estosh's mouths twisted. "Again you choose to let your female carry out your interrogation?" he sneered at Luke as he resumed his pacing.

"She's just making conversation," Luke said, feeling his forehead creasing. Estosh wasn't just pacing aimlessly, he realized suddenly. He was heading somewhere specific.

"Speech is for drones and prey," Estosh said contemptuously. "The conversation of warriors is in their actions."

"We like to think we're pretty good at both," Luke said, wondering what the other was up to. One of the Vagaari who'd been killed in that first volley was sprawled across a console in Estosh's path; the helm, he tentatively identified it. Could the dead Vagaari be carrying a special weapon Estosh was hoping to get hold of? Or was there an important course change he wanted to make?

Alternatively, there were two live Vagaari glaring silently at the Jedi from twin consoles a little farther along the same projected path. Could Estosh be hoping to drop down behind them, using them as living shields while he did something clever?

Either way, it was time to put a stop to it. Luke shifted his weight, preparing to head off on an intercept path—

"Let him go," Mara murmured from beside him.

Frowning, Luke glanced at her. There was a gleam in those brilliant green eyes, a microscopic smile creasing the corners of her mouth. She flicked her eyes briefly toward his, and crinkled her nose significantly.

"True warriors do not care if they talk well," Estosh said scornfully.

Luke turned back to Estosh, running through his Jedi sensory-enhancement techniques. The Vagaari's meaningless tirade grew painfully loud in his ears, but Luke wasn't interested in sounds right now. Inhaling slowly, he sorted though the drifting aromas of age and dust, human and Vagaari, searching for whatever it was Mara had already spotted.

There it was; very faint and distant. He inhaled again, trying to identify it . . .

And stiffened. It wasn't the distinctive tang of explosives, as he'd expected, but something far more virulent.

Poison.

Not just any poison, either. The acidity of the scent betrayed this as a corrosive poison, one designed to burn straight through the protection of a breath mask or atmosphere filter and then do the same to the victims' lungs. It was a last-ditch weapon, lethal to defender and attacker alike, used only when defeat was inevitable but allowing an opponent victory was unthinkable.

He sent a quick, furtive look around the room. There were Jedi techniques for detoxifying poisons, techniques he had successfully used a number of times in the past. Problem was, they generally didn't work against corrosive poisons like this one. The acidic matrix meant that both detoxification and healing techniques had to be used simultaneously, something that was nearly impossible for even an experienced Jedi to do without losing control of one or the other procedure.

And the poison could be concealed virtually anywhere on the bridge, remote-triggered by any of the Vagaari. With the traces he and Mara had detected already filling the air, there was no way for them to track it down to its source.

He looked questioningly at Mara. She nodded, that gleam still in her eye, and for an instant their minds touched, possibilities and contingencies and plans swirling wordlessly between them.

"—who have no strength or cunning of their own," Estosh continued, still strolling along on his random-looking walk.

"Oh, I don't know," Mara said. "I'll grant you have a fair amount of brute strength, but your level of cunning is pretty pathetic. Aristocra Formbi knew about you from the start; and Luke and I know all about the fighter carrier you left at the Brask Oto Command Station."

"The point being that you're outgunned and outmaneuvered," Luke said, picking up on Mara's cue. If they tried to negotiate with him, he would be less likely to suspect they were also on to this last-ditch effort of his.

And if he could actually be persuaded to surrender, so much the better. "So you might as well give up now," Luke went on. "If you do, we'll promise you and your people safe passage outside Chiss territory."

"Your *remaining* people, that is," Mara added. "Take too much time arguing the point, and that number's likely to shrink some more."

"Perhaps," Estosh said, coming to a casual stop in front of the helm console. "But perhaps none of us expect to leave this vessel alive anymore."

He leaned forward with his forearms resting on the front edge of the console, his hands dangling casually a couple of centimeters above the controls. "Perhaps the future glory of the Vagaari Empire will be a sufficient payment for our efforts."

"No," Luke said quietly. "You won't even get that."

"We shall see," Estosh said. He took a deep breath, straightening up to his full height. As he did so, his fingers dipped suddenly to the controls beneath them. There was a quiet beep; and a second later, the hyperspace sky flowing past the viewport turned into starlines and then into stars.

In the distance, Luke could see the lights of the Brask Oto Command Station directly ahead. The station, and the faint glow of a hundred starfighter drives spiraling around it. Even as he felt his throat tighten, he spotted the multiple flash of laserfire.

"The victory is ours," Estosh said calmly. He lifted his arms toward them. "And now," he added, "you will die."

He clenched his hands into fists; and from each of his sleeves a thin spray of pale green mist shot outward.

"Go!" Mara snapped, jumping sideways toward the red-rimmed emergency cabinet fastened to the wall beside the blast door.

Luke took a deep breath, holding it as he charged through the maze of control consoles toward Estosh. The two Vagaari nearest their commander, he noted, had already slumped over, twitching violently with the effects of the poison. He angled to the side; Estosh responded by shifting his arms to aim the spray more directly toward Luke's face. Clearly, he too was holding his breath, hoping to live long enough to watch his enemies die.

With a suddenness that startled even Luke, Mara's lightsaber flashed past overhead, spinning its way across the bridge. Reflexively, Estosh ducked, his head turning to follow the weapon's motion.

And as he looked away, Luke took a long step toward him, ducking low to stay beneath the poison spray. With two quick slashes of his lightsaber, he sliced open Estosh's sleeves and the gas canisters strapped to his forearms.

With an explosive *poof!* the directional spray became a billowing green cloud as the entire contents of the canisters were dumped at once. The fog enveloped Estosh's head, roiling outward as Luke took a long step backward. Estosh spun back toward him, his face nearly invisible behind the cloud, his body starting to twitch and contort as the acid burned his skin and the poison worked its way into his lungs despite his efforts to keep it out. For a moment his eyes locked with Luke's—

And then, across the bridge, Mara's thrown lightsaber hit the transparisteel viewport, slicing it open.

In an instant the bridge became the center of a windstorm as the air streamed violently out into space. The expanding poison cloud swirling around Estosh was whipped away with the rest of the atmosphere, turning into thin green tendrils as it was sucked toward the gap. Behind Luke, reacting to the sudden loss of pressure, the bridge blast doors slammed shut.

The twisting vortex blew Estosh off his feet, dumping him to sprawl onto the deck. He turned around to face Luke, hands scrabbling desperately and uselessly across the metal, his face a mask of pain and hatred. "Jedi!" he spat out hoarsely, his last breath a curse.

But Luke was already gone. Even as the windstorm erupted around him he began leaping over and around the control consoles, letting the wind at his back add to his speed as he raced across the bridge toward the hole Mara had cut. Her lightsaber was bouncing precariously along the edge; reaching out with the Force, he closed down the weapon and drew it back to him, jamming it into his belt alongside his. His lungs were starting to ache as the air pressure dropped nearly to zero, and he again stretched out to the Force for strength. Reaching the viewport, he skidded to a halt beside the crack and spun around.

Across the room, Mara had the emergency cabinet open, one hand poised on the oxygen lever, the other holding a patch kit. At Luke's nod she pulled down on the lever and sent the kit spinning through the air into his outstretched hand.

The gale, which had subsided to a faint whisper, began to pick up again as the oxygen tanks across the room flooded more air into the escaping flow. Luke counted out a few more seconds to make sure all of the poison gas had been flushed out, then pulled open the patch and slapped it across the hole.

There was a sizzling sound, more felt than really heard in the painfully thin atmosphere. The swirling wind subsided, and he felt the air pressure returning to normal. He exhaled the rest of the air he'd been holding in reserve and took a cautious breath. There was just a residual hint of the poison, drifting through the bridge like a bad memory, far too dilute to pose any danger.

He looked around the bridge. The Vagaari lay across their consoles or in contorted poses on the deck. All were dead.

He sighed. *Jedi respect all life, in any form . . .*

"Snap out of it, Luke," Mara called. "We've still got work to do."

Luke focused on her. She was leaning over the helm console, the one Estosh had made such an effort to reach before he died, working feverishly at the controls. "Right," he said, coming toward her. "What did he do there?"

"Exactly what I thought he would," Mara told him, and he sensed her grim satisfaction as she straightened up. "Okay, I caught it in time." She nodded at the viewport. "Now we just have to figure out what we're going to do about *that.*"

Luke turned and looked. During the past few minutes, Estosh's final helm command had continued to drive them toward the Chiss command station.

And from their new vantage point he could see that the defenders were in desperate straits. The Vagaari fighters swarming around it were as maneuverable as X-wings, but with considerably more firepower, and they whipped around the base in a complex dancelike pattern that made them nearly impossible to hit. So far the base's shields were holding, but from the methodical way the fighters were hammering at it he knew it wouldn't be long before they'd battered the defenses down far enough to begin causing serious damage. Off to one side, drifting along outside of the attack pattern, was the Vagaari colony ship, looking like a strange spherical skeleton now that its brood of fighters had been launched.

"And that's after only a few minutes of combat," Mara murmured. "These guys are good."

"The beeping console in the anteroom?" Luke asked.

She nodded. "It was the comm monitor, indicating a signal being sent out from the bridge," she confirmed. "It had to have been Estosh's attack order." She shook her head. "No wonder Formbi wanted an excuse to launch a campaign against these people."

"I don't think they'll need more of an excuse than they've already got," Luke declared, crossing to one of the weapons stations. "Can this thing still fight?"

"What, against ships that small?" Mara countered. "Not a chance. Certainly not with just the two of us to run it. Besides, all we're likely to have are the anti-meteor laser cannon and maybe one or two of the smaller point-defense stuff. Thrawn demolished all the heavy weaponry fifty years ago."

Across the bridge, one of the consoles pinged, and a Vagaari voice began speaking faintly from its speakers. "They've spotted us," Mara said, stepping toward it. "You have anything you want to say to them?"

"Just a second," Luke said, an idea popping into the back of his mind. "No, don't answer. Find me a sensor station and tell me what's happening with the Vagaari carrier."

He sensed Mara's puzzlement, but she headed off across the bridge without comment. Luke went the other direction, toward where the weapons consoles were located. Maybe Thrawn's attack had missed something.

But no. All the turbolaser and ion cannon status boards showed red. "Got it," Mara called, and he looked over to see her leaning over another console. "The carrier's in pretty bad shape, actually. Power output minimal; life support systems minimal; serious damage to its north and south poles."

"Probably where its own heavy weapons were," Luke said with satisfaction. "I was hoping the Chiss had gotten in some good shots before they were surrounded."

"Fine, but that still leaves the fighters," Mara pointed out. "And us with no weapons."

"We won't need any," Luke assured her. "Get back to the helm—"

He broke off as a stutter of laserfire raked suddenly across the hull just below and forward of the bridge. "What the—?"

"Chiss fighters," Mara snapped, grabbing the console for balance as the deck shook with another set of impacts. "At least twenty of them, coming in from behind."

Luke bit down hard on his lip. He'd had a perfect plan; only now here came the Chiss threatening to ruin it.

And maybe to blow the Dreadnaught out from under them in the process. "I'll transmit Formbi's message," Mara shouted as another volley stuttered across the hull. "If they believe it—"

"No!" Luke cut her off, looking around him. It *had* to be on this side of the bridge somewhere. "No communications, to anyone. Get back to the helm and get us an evasive course toward the station."

"What? Luke—"

"Don't argue," Luke snapped, crossing back to the turbolaser control console and looking at the consoles near it. "If we say anything to the Chiss, the Vagaari will know we can transmit."

"And that's a problem?"

"*Yes,* that's a problem." Beneath him, the deck started to sway slightly as Mara keyed in the evasive maneuvers he'd called for. "We need to look like a ship that can't communicate, where Estosh is still in command—ah," he interrupted himself. There it was, nestled between the ion cannon and forward deflector shield consoles: the anti-meteor laser cannon. "Keep us evasive," he ordered, keying the activation switches. The board shifted to green with gratifying speed. "Okay. What was Drask's emergency prefix code again?"

"Two-space-one-space-two," Mara told him. "And you've lost me completely."

"Just cross your fingers." The Chiss fighters were swinging around for another pass. Mentally crossing his own,

Luke aimed the laser cannon just astern of the group and fired: pulse-pulse; pulse; pulse-pulse.

For a long moment nothing happened. The fighters completed their turn and regrouped, heading back for another strafing run. Luke fired the pattern a second time, again aiming just wide of the group. They kept coming; he fired a third time—

And then they were on him, flashing over the Dreadnaught's surface, pouring volleys of laserfire into the hull.

Only this time there were no thuds as sections of hull metal vaporized explosively away. No impacts; no shaking of the ship; no nothing.

"I'll be a roasted nerf," Mara breathed. "They've cranked their lasers down to minimal power. They figured out the message."

"And at the same time were smart enough not to give the game away to the Vagaari," Luke said, abandoning the laser console and heading off across the bridge in a search pattern again. "I could learn to like working with these people."

"They're coming around for another pass," Mara reported. "You want to keep it evasive?"

"Right," Luke confirmed. The console he was looking for . . . *there*. "Where are the Chiss fighters?" he called as he keyed for activation.

"Off our portside stern."

"Good," Luke said. "Bring our flank around to portside, as if we're running interference for the Vagaari."

"Got it."

The view ahead turned as the huge ship began rotating sluggishly to the left, and Luke shifted his attention to the attacking Vagaari. If they reacted the way every other squadron he'd ever served with would react under these circumstances . . .

He caught his breath. In twos and threes, the Vagaari were beginning to break off their attack on the station. "Keep going," he ordered, hearing the excitement in his voice. "Keep us between the Chiss and the Vagaari."

"The Chiss are firing again," Mara reported. "Again, just for show."

"Perfect," Luke said, his full attention on the Vagaari. They were definitely abandoning the station now, pulling away in an orderly fashion and forming up again as they headed away at full attack speed.

Moving straight for the Dreadnaught.

Mara had spotted the new maneuver, too. "Uh . . . Luke?" she said hesitantly.

"Trust me," he said. Reaching down to his console, he keyed a switch.

And deep beneath them, he heard the faint sound of metal grinding against metal as the forward starboard hangar deck doors slid reluctantly open.

Across the room, he heard Mara's huff. "You're not serious," she said. "You really think they'll just—? No."

"Of course they will," Luke said. "Remember, their own carrier is wrecked. What else are they going to do?"

He looked up as she stepped to his side. "You have got to be the most brazen con artist I've ever met," she said, shaking her head.

"Better even than Han?" Luke asked innocently. "Why, thank you."

"It wasn't necessarily meant as a compliment," Mara said. "That was a pretty serious risk you took."

"Not really," Luke said. "Remember, I know how starfighter pilots think. The rule is, any friendly port in a battle." He smiled lopsidedly. "And as far as they know, we're as friendly as they get."

Together they stood and watched until the last of the Vagaari fighters had come aboard. "There we go," Luke said, keying the massive docking bay door closed again. "*Now* we can send that message of Formbi's off to the station. I'm sure they'll want to be aboard to help us give the Vagaari pilots the bad news."

STATION COMMANDER PRARD'ENC'IFLAR WAS A TALL CHISS with a generous helping of white in his blue-black hair and a highly intimidating look in his glowing red eyes. He was also, if Mara was reading the name and facial structures correctly, a relative of General Drask.

"We are grateful for your assistance in this matter," he said rather stiffly, his eyes mostly following his own people as they moved around the Dreadnaught's bridge inspecting the equipment. "It is evident now that Aristocra Chaf'orm'bintrano's counsel was well thought."

"Though I daresay you didn't think so at the time?" Mara suggested.

The glowing red eyes flicked briefly to her. "Past thoughts are irrelevant to the realities of the present," he said, looking away again. "You have aided us in the protection of our people and of our military secrets. That is high service from those who are not Chiss." He looked suddenly back at them again. "The secrets *are* safe, are they not?"

"Almost certainly," Luke assured him. "We had a chance to look at the communications log while you were coming aboard. Estosh made only that one transmission, and that was a short-range signal to his carrier here at Brask Oto."

"And he couldn't have sent anything earlier," Mara added. "Not from inside the Redoubt's natural interference."

"I see," Prard'enc'iflar murmured. "We will hope you are reading the data correctly."

Mara caught Luke's eye, sensing his wry amusement. For all his official gratitude, it was clear the commander privately wasn't all that impressed by humans and their abilities. Much the way Drask himself had been, in fact, early on in the mission.

It was time to give that attitude a little nudge.

"So what happens now?" she asked. "I mean, as far as the Vagaari are concerned?"

"They have committed multiple acts of war against the Chiss Ascendancy," he said flatly. "Even as we speak a strike force is being assembled, and scout ships are being sent to search for the enemy's location."

"That'll take time," Mara pointed out. "There's a lot of territory out there for the Vagaari to hide in. By the time you find them, there's a good chance they'll realize Estosh's team is overdue and fade back into the background hum."

"Have you an alternative to suggest?" Prard'enc'iflar demanded. "Or do the mind tricks Aristocra Chaf'orm'bintrano speaks of allow you to pull the location of the Vagaari base from dead minds?"

"Actually, we can't even do it with live minds," Mara said. "But we don't have to."

She pointed to the helm console. "The location is right in there."

"So *that's* what he was doing at the helm," Luke said, and Mara could sense his sudden understanding. "I thought he was just bringing the ship out of hyperspace."

"No, he was going for something more long range," Mara said, studying the confusion in Prard'enc'iflar's face. "You see, Commander, Estosh knew it was over as soon as we reached the bridge. He had a last-ditch weapon that he thought would kill all of us, so he figured that at least we wouldn't win. But even if he died in the process, he still wanted to get this ship to his people."

"So we let him key in an automatic course heading to take the ship to wherever their rendezvous point was," Luke said.

"Which is probably also where most of their heavy warships are waiting." Mara gestured again to the helm console. "Would you like me to pull the coordinates for you?"

For a long moment Prard'enc'iflar just stood there gazing at her. Then, with the twitch of a lip, he gave her a small bow. "Thank you," he said softly. "I would like that very much."

CHAPTER 27

"So there was nothing left at all?" Jinzler asked, just to be sure.

Luke shook his head, his expression pained. "No," he said. "We searched the debris pretty thoroughly afterward. We couldn't even find a piece of the amethyst to bring back to you. I'm sorry. I know how much it meant to you."

"It's all right," Jinzler told him. And for a wonder, it really was. That lightsaber had been the last thing that had belonged to his sister. His last link to her life.

And yet, the loss wasn't hurting nearly as much as he would have expected it to. Perhaps because he no longer needed objects to remember her by. Perhaps because all those painful memories were finally beginning to heal themselves.

And to heal him.

"Actually, it's rather fitting," he added. "Lorana came aboard Outbound Flight dedicating herself to protect and nurture the people here. It's only fitting that her lightsaber be sacrificed for them, just as she herself was."

Luke and Mara exchanged glances, and he could see the caution in their expressions. As far as they were concerned, there was still no way of knowing how Lorana had died, or what she had been doing at the time of her death.

But Jinzler didn't care. *He* knew she'd died defending Outbound Flight. That was all that mattered.

From somewhere down the corridor came a multiple thump of dropped boxes, and a strangled curse. "Moving day is such fun, isn't it?" Mara commented, peering down the corridor in the direction of the noise.

"Especially when half the tenants are convinced they're being evicted," Jinzler agreed ruefully.

"Uliar and the Managing Council still don't want to leave?" Luke asked.

"The Chiss are practically having to drag them out by their heels," Jinzler said. "I know; it's crazy."

"Not that crazy," Mara said, her eyes thoughtful. "Even if there's nothing here for them anymore, it's still been their home for fifty years."

"It's all about familiarity," Luke agreed soberly. "No matter how unpleasant or dreary a place might have become, it's always hard to give up something you've become so used to."

Jinzler nodded, remembering back to his childhood. "Coruscant."

"Tatooine," Luke said.

"The Empire," Mara added quietly.

Luke threw her an odd look, but turned back to Jinzler without commenting. "Speaking of empires, I understand you're going to the Empire of the Hand with them?"

"I'm going with Rosemari and Evlyn," he corrected. "Since they insist on staying with the rest of the Colonists, I guess that's where I'm going, too."

"I wish you'd talk to them," Luke said. "Nothing against the Empire of the Hand, but they don't have any way to give her proper Jedi training."

Jinzler lifted his hands, palms upward. "The Colonists don't want to go to the New Republic," he reminded Luke. "It's got the word *Republic* in its name, and it's got Jedi. End of argument."

"I understand," Luke said. "I just don't like letting Evlyn go off without a proper instructor, that's all. Keep working on them, will you?"

"For whatever good it'll do." Jinzler smiled lopsidedly. "Actually, I suspect that Commander Fel's going to be working the opposite direction, hoping that Evlyn's presence will induce *you* to come over to his side and set up an academy there."

"Did he say that?" Luke asked, frowning.

"Not in so many words," Jinzler said. "But he *did* ask me to tell you that Admiral Parck's offer of a job is still open."

"Right," Luke said, throwing another sideways look at Mara. "Be sure to thank him the next time you see him."

"That may be a while," Jinzler warned. "I understand he and the Five-Oh-First have already left with General Drask."

"Probably gone to join up with the Vagaari attack force," Luke said.

"Probably," Jinzler agreed. "Both Drask and Fel strike me as the sort of people who like to see things through to their conclusion."

"Rather like you?" Mara suggested.

"Hardly," Jinzler admitted, glancing around the ancient metal corridor. "I may have come here to see the end of Outbound Flight, but I didn't do a very good job of being there for the middle. Or the beginning, for that matter."

"I was referring to your decision to stick with Rosemari and Evlyn," Mara said.

Jinzler blinked. "Oh. Well . . . maybe. I guess we'll see how I do."

"Anyway, keep in touch," Luke said, taking Mara's arm. "The *Chaf Envoy*'s taking Formbi out of here in about an hour, and we need to say a few quick good-byes before we take off."

"I'll try," Jinzler said dubiously. "I don't know how well any messages would get through, though."

"They'll do fine," Luke assured him. "I know Parck has some contact with Bastion these days, and after this I think the Nine Ruling Families may be willing to discuss diplomatic relations with Coruscant. We should get anything you send."

"Provided some hotshot in a relay station doesn't intercept it along the way," Mara added.

Jinzler felt his face redden. "There's that, of course," he conceded. "Another good reason for me to sit out in the Empire of the Hand for a while."

"Don't worry, we'll square things with Karrde," Luke assured him. "You just take care of Rosemari and Evlyn."

"I will." Jinzler held out his hand. "Good-bye. And thank you. For everything."

THE TRIP BACK THROUGH THE REDOUBT WAS, THANKFULLY, uneventful. By the time the *Chaf Envoy* emerged at the Brask Oto station, the news was waiting that the Chiss strike force had successfully located and attacked the Vagaari warships gathered together for their anticipated rendezvous with Estosh's team. General Drask reported that the enemy had been taken by surprise and destroyed.

Of course, Luke reminded himself privately, that was probably what Thrawn had reported fifty years ago, too. Whether the Vagaari would still be a threat somewhere down the line would remain to be seen.

He and Mara took their leave of their hosts, accepting one final thanks from the still bedridden Formbi, and headed for home.

The *Jade Sabre* was cruising through hyperspace, and they were lying together in bed in their stateroom, when Luke finally asked the question he knew his wife had been expecting for days. "So," he said, deciding on the casual approach. "Have you made your decision yet?"

"Decision?" Mara asked, apparently deciding to play it coy.

"You know what decision," Luke growled, not really in the mood for coy. "About whether you're going to take Parck up on his offer to join the Empire of the Hand."

"That would certainly be something, wouldn't it?" Mara commented thoughtfully. "All those people on Coruscant who never really liked or trusted me would have a Harvest Day special with that one."

"I'm being serious," Luke said.

"Hey, relax," she soothed. "I'm joking. You know I'm staying with you."

"I know that." He braced himself. "What I meant was . . . if you really need to be there, I'm willing to go with you."

"I know," she said quietly, reaching over and taking his hand. "And you don't know how much it means to me that you are."

She hesitated. "I won't deny that the idea has some attraction," she admitted. "Ever since this whole thing started, I've been fighting some strange survivor's guilt over the fact that I lived through the Empire's destruction when so many other people didn't. I kept wondering if I was just lucky, or whether there was some other reason behind that."

"Of course there was," Luke said.

He felt the subtle muscle movements as she smiled. "I meant some reason besides completing your life and making you happier than you ever thought possible."

"Ah," he said dryly. "And what did you conclude?"

"I don't know," she conceded. "All I know is that I was given about as clear a choice as anyone could hope to have. On one side was the chance to again serve an empire, this time an empire that had all the strengths I'd always admired but none of the evil. A chance to give back some of my time and ability to the heirs of the people who'd spent so much time and energy teaching me those skills in the first place."

"And on the other side, you have the New Republic," Luke murmured. "Squabbling, political brushfires, Bothan backblading, and an occasional diehard who *still* doesn't trust you."

"That was the choice, all right," Mara said. "But no matter how nice and ordered and comfortable the Empire of the Hand might look, I've decided that my place right now is with the New Republic."

"You're sure?" Luke asked, one last time.

"I'm positive," she said. "Besides, how could I drag you away from your sister and everything you fought so hard for?"

"It would have been tricky," he admitted. "But I could have adapted. I guess I'm just surprised that after all this time you would still even have to make such a decision."

"I wondered about that myself," Mara agreed. "But I could feel the Force in this, right from the very beginning. Maybe it was that lingering survivor's guilt that had to be dealt with. Or maybe the New Republic is in for some rough times and I needed to be clear in my own mind exactly where I stood before it happened. Good enough reasons for the Force to send us out here."

"Not to mention the fact that we were needed to keep Formbi and everyone else alive?"

"There's that, too," Mara agreed. "I always like it when I get to accomplish three things at the same time. It makes life so much more efficient."

"Yes," Luke murmured. "And I'd be the first to say that the New Republic is certainly where you're needed the most. So is that finally settled?"

"It's settled," she confirmed. "We're in for the duration, dear." She squeezed his hand. "I'm just sorry your own quest didn't turn out so well."

He shrugged. "No, but it's not really over yet. I still think there must be useful records of the old Jedi *somewhere* aboard Outbound Flight. We're just going to have to wait until we get hold of the entire thing and can go through it console by console."

"Which could be a while," Mara warned. "It could take the Chiss years to dig it out of that rock pile, especially with the shape it's in."

"That's okay," Luke said. "We've lived this long without it. We can wait a few more years if necessary. Patience is a virtue."

"Never had much use for it myself," Mara said lightly.

"Yes, I've noticed." Luke paused. "You want to tell me the rest of it now?"

"What rest of it?"

"The other thing that's had you walking around like a kid in a cemetery at midnight," he said. "The thing you've been trying to bury where you hope I won't notice it."

He could sense her sudden discomfort. Clearly, she had indeed been hoping he wouldn't notice. "It's nothing, really," she hedged. "Just a weird thought from my overly suspicious imagination that I can't quite get rid of."

"Origin and caveats noted," Luke said. "Quit stalling and let's have it."

"Okay," she said reluctantly. "Did it ever occur to you—I mean, did you ever *really* think about it—just how sneaky and convoluted this whole scheme of Formbi's was?"

"You forgot to add *underhanded*."

"Oh, absolutely underhanded," Mara agreed. "The idea of dangling Outbound Flight and the Redoubt in front of the Vagaari precisely so they could push the Chiss just that little bit too far is about as devious as you can get. Especially when you add the extra touch of bringing us aboard as the ultimate wild card for Formbi to play against them."

"Devious and a half," Luke agreed. "So?"

She took a deep breath. "So who do we know who specialized in exactly that kind of convoluted plan?"

"I don't know," Luke said, his voice frowning. "Car'das, maybe? You said he used to work with Karrde, who's always been pretty good at the devious approach himself. And we already know he was the one who maneuvered Jinzler aboard."

"I suppose it could have been him," Mara said. "Though from what Shada said it sounded like he mostly keeps out of galactic affairs these days. I was thinking more about someone with a proven record for strategic and tactical finesse."

Luke tensed as he suddenly saw where she was going. "No," he insisted reflexively. "It couldn't be. We destroyed that clone, remember?"

"We destroyed *a* clone," Mara corrected him. "But who's to say he didn't have another one stashed away somewhere?"

"No," Luke said firmly. "It's impossible. If there was another clone of Thrawn running around, we would have heard about it by now."

"Would we?" Mara countered. "Remember, according to Parck, the only reason Thrawn came back to attack the New Republic in the first place was to whip us into fighting shape for some danger looming out there at the edge of the galaxy. Maybe he figures we're as ready as we're going to be and has decided to concentrate on clearing out some of the local troublemakers from his own backyard."

"Or maybe the Vagaari were more than just locals," Luke said, feeling his stomach tighten. This was making far more sense than he cared for. "Maybe they've already been in contact with the threat Parck and Fel mentioned to you."

"Could be," Mara agreed. "Of course, that would just give the Chiss one more reason to squash the Vagaari as quickly as possible. Not only would it eliminate part of the threat, but they might also learn something about possible new enemies when they sifted through the rubble."

Luke shook his head. "I wish you'd mentioned this while we were still aboard the *Chaf Envoy*," he said. "We could have asked Formbi about it."

"That's exactly why I *didn't* mention it then," Mara told him. "Because we probably *would* have asked, and frankly I don't want to know. If Thrawn's back, I think we can assume he's more or less on our side."

She exhaled between her teeth. "If he's *not* back, I guess we'll all just have to make do on our own."

"Yes," Luke murmured. "But we'll do all right."

"I know." Mara rolled onto her side to press herself closer against her husband, and Luke felt the warmth of her body and spirit flowing into his. "Because whatever it is we wind up facing, we'll be facing it together."

He reached his arm around to stroke her cheek. Yes, they would indeed. Because whatever prohibitions and restrictions the Jedi Order had imposed on its members during the Old Republic, he knew now in the core of his being that, somehow, those restrictions no longer applied to him and his fellow Jedi. This was the New Jedi Order, and he and Mara were walking together in as perfect a harmony with each other and with the Force as he could ever expect. "The Force will be with you always, Mara," he murmured in her ear. "And so will I."

"Yes," she murmured back. "Whatever the future brings."

They were still holding on to each other as they fell asleep.

FOOL'S
BARGAIN

by

Timothy Zahn

IT HAD BEEN DRIZZLING AS THE STORMTROOPERS OF THE IMPE-
rial 501st Legion assembled at their various jump points for
what all hoped would be the final battle of this latest war. By
the time the orders had been given and the individual companies began to make their way to their parts of the assault line,
the drizzle had widened into a full-scale storm, complete
with driving winds and a sky nearly black enough to turn the
twilight of the city and surrounding countryside into full
night.

"Looks like something out of a bad legend," Choral of Unit
Aurek-Four murmured from the right-hand line of stormtroopers seated on the rack benches against the wall as the
disguised troop carrier rolled cautiously along the quiet city
streets.

"What does?" Dropkick of Aurek-Three asked from half a dozen men down the line.

"What do you think?" Choral countered, nodding toward the viewscreens showing the scene out the transport's nose.

Behind his helmet faceplate, Twister, unit commander of the four-man group designated Aurek-Seven, frowned slightly as he studied the image. Choral had a point, he had to admit. The fortress rising out of the ground at the edge of the city had always had something of a ghostly, unreal air about it. Now, as brief glimpses of the gray-and-red towers came to them between the city's buildings, the whole scene lashed by winds and surrounded by sporadic flashes of lightning, that sense of otherworldliness seemed even sharper.

On Twister's left, his unit-mate Watchman gave a soft snort. "Personally, I've always liked tackling legends," he said. "It's so much fun to let the air out of them." He gestured toward the viewscreen. "*I* just hope the son of a lizard is actually in there."

"Well, if he isn't, this is going to be a serious waste of effort," Cloud grumbled from Watchman's far side. "Especially with the Eickaries finally on the move. If it were up to me, I'd give them another month to chase the Lakra back into these reinforced beetle holes of theirs, then drop all two hundred of 'em into piles of rubble and go home."

"And how many more Eickaries would die in another month of fighting?" Shadow, Aurek-Seven's fourth man, asked from Twister's right. "If we're going to arm a people and then turn them loose against oppressors, we have a certain obligation to see they don't just go charging into a meat grinder."

"I understand that," Cloud agreed. "But Kariek is *their* world, after all, not ours. After putting up with the Warlord and his thugs all these years, it seems to me they should have the honor of kicking them out."

"Kicking them out or executing them," Watchman said. "I imagine Eickarie common law will demand a particularly gruesome death for the Warlord."

"*I'd* buy a ticket," Cloud said dryly. "That still doesn't explain why we don't just blast the whole fortress to rubble.

Getting buried by a few tons of rock ought to be a gruesome enough death to satisfy even the Eickaries."

"I'm sure the generals have their reasons," Twister said, putting just enough edge to his voice to warn the other three to drop the subject.

"I know," Cloud muttered, apparently not yet quite ready to let it go. "I just don't think this guy is worth any more Imperial lives than he's already cost."

Twister didn't answer. The others took the hint, and the conversation finally subsided.

But the question, he could tell, was still weighing on them. It was weighing on everyone in the transport, for that matter.

It wasn't just the forty men of Aurek Company who were involved in this. Not by a long shot. There were hundreds of Imperial troops setting up for battle, including three more companies of the 501st. Most of them were out in the woods and plains on the other side of the fortress, preparing for a straight-in assault with massive air and ground support. The Empire of the Hand was making a serious effort to capture the tyrant who had oppressed this world and its people for the past fifty standard years.

But why?

Cloud had a point. Strong though these ancient Eickarie fortresses were, they hadn't been designed to withstand the kind of firepower the Empire of the Hand could bring to bear. If Intelligence thought he was in there, a couple of hours of serious bombardment would turn the fortress into a heap of charred rock, dead Lakran mercenaries, and an equally dead Warlord. Once the leader himself was out of the way, the remaining pockets of resistance would be easy enough to deal with, especially with the whole planet finally united against the mercenaries. It would be quick, efficient, and a lot easier on the stormtroopers and other ground soldiers.

Obviously there was some very important reason why the Empire of the Hand wanted or needed the Warlord alive. The question was: what was that reason?

Mentally, Twister shook his head. The typical soldier, he knew, wouldn't even be having these thoughts, or at the very

least would be keeping them to himself. Soldiers were uniformly taught to accept orders without question and to carry
them out without hesitation.

To a certain point, of course, that was true of Imperial
stormtroopers as well. But only to a point. This wasn't Palpatine's Empire, and the stormtroopers lining the transport's armored sides weren't simply the unfeeling, unthinking killing
machines he had once unleashed on the Republic. The elite
troopers of the Empire of the Hand were selected for intelligence as well as combat skill, trained to walk that fine line
between obedience and initiative, between honest question
and unquestioning trust.

Slowly, Twister sent his gaze across the forty armored men
seated silently around him. He'd been with Aurek Company
for nearly six years now, two of them as Aurek-Seven's commander, and in that time he'd learned that there was very little Imperial stormtroopers couldn't accomplish once they set
their minds to it. They had been ordered to go in and capture
the Warlord, and he had no doubt they would succeed. None
of them, certainly not Twister himself, needed to know the
reasons behind the order.

But the questions remained.

"One minute," the driver called.

There was a soft flurry of activity as the stormtroopers
made one final check of their BlasTech E-11 blaster rifles
and other equipment. The transport slowed to a crawl, and
the rear doors swung open. Silently, in groups of four, the
stormtroopers began to drop out into the downpour, slipping
away to their assigned positions through the deserted streets.

Aurek-Seven was the last unit out. Twister hit the ground
in a jog, taking a couple of steps to brake himself to a halt as
he gave the area a quick scan. The buildings rising around
them showed only a few lights, and were as silent as the
streets themselves. "Looks like the Eickaries have figured
out that the Warlord's vicinity isn't a healthy place to be,"
Cloud commented from beside him.

"Let's hope so, for their sake," Twister said, finishing his
visual scan and checking his bearings. "Move out."

Their designated position was two streets away, in a narrow alley between a five-story apartment house and one of the city's many grimy, low-class cantinas. From that location, according to the surveillance holos, they should have a view of the eastern approach to the building designated Watchtower Two.

The two watchtowers were a peculiarly Eickarie military concept, one that most of the stormtroopers didn't think very highly of. Disguised as ordinary apartment or office buildings, they were in fact high-tech sentry and spy stations for the fortress two kilometers away at the edge of town, connected to it by armored underground passageways. In the not-too-distant past, when vicious tribal warfare had been a part of Kariek's everyday life, the watchtowers had allowed whoever was currently occupying the fortress to keep an eye on members of opposing tribes in the city for trade or social calls or possibly a sneak attack. When the Warlord had taken possession of all the fortresses, he and his mercenaries had used the watchtowers in much the same way, except that to them every Eickarie was a potential member of the opposition. Many a dissatisfied citizen, complaining privately with a friend in the street about the Warlord's cold-handed rule, discovered too late that he had been observed, recorded, convicted, and sentenced, sometimes before the conversation was even over.

The watchtowers themselves were of no particular strategic value, given that the recently formed United Tribes Command already had control of the city itself. Their importance, and the reason most of the stormtroopers considered them a bad strategic concept, lay in the tunnels connecting them to the fortress. If Aurek Company could capture either or both watchtowers, they would have a vector into the Warlord's refuge that wouldn't involve running the gauntlet of heavy defenses arrayed against the rest of the Imperial forces gathered outside the city.

Of course, the Warlord wasn't stupid, either. He would certainly have rigged as strong a set of defenses in those tunnels as he could manage, including mines, booby traps, and as many blasters and Lakran mercenaries as he could squeeze in. But this was the 501st Legion, the legendary "Vader's Fist." They'd handled worse in their long history. They would handle this, too.

Aurek-Seven reached their target alley, and Twister gave it a quick look. Spaced out along the base of the apartment building were half a dozen stairways leading down to garden apartments or small shops, all dark, while the cantina was showing only the normal security lights of a closed business. No one was visible anywhere. Holding his blaster rifle high across his chest, Twister slipped into the alley, the others fanning out behind him.

They were nearly to the cantina door when a flicker from his helmet's sensor display strip caught Twister's eye. "Watch it—someone's in there," he warned the others, shifting his BlasTech to point in that direction as he gave the display another look. Unfortunately, with the pouring rain skewing the infrared data and wiping out any chance of a gas-spectrum analysis, there was no way to distinguish between a harmless Eickarie and a seriously hostile Lakra. "Stay sharp."

He'd barely finished the warning when the cantina door swung open and a young Eickarie male stepped out into the alley, the rain cascading off the glistening band of black scales that curved over the top and sides of his otherwise mostly green face. He was dressed not in the usual brightly colored layered evening robes but dark, close-fitting slacks, low boots, and a loose serape jacket. "Good evening, Imperials," he said in passable Basic. "May your tribe find joy."

"May your tribe find wealth." Twister gave the traditional reply, frowning as he notched up his helmet's vision enhancers. It was hard to tell in the gloom, but he couldn't see any of the color fluctuations in the orange facial highlights that conveyed most of the Eickaries' emotional information. The young alien was calm and composed—not the usual reaction of a simple citizen suddenly and unexpectedly coming face to face with four Imperial stormtroopers.

Which implied either that the Eickarie was drunker than he had any right to be this early in the evening, or else that the encounter wasn't as unexpected as it appeared. "May I ask what you're doing here?" he asked the native.

The orange highlights turned a dark pink, the equivalent of an ironic smile. "Odd," he said. "I was about to ask you the same question."

He lifted a hand before Twister could answer. "But this is no place for a conversation," he went on. "I am certain you would be more comfortable inside."

"We appreciate your concern," Twister said, making a subtle hand signal. Around him, he could sense the movements as the others casually turned into an outward-facing defensive square. Despite his fifty-year record of brutal tyranny, and despite the recent alliance of all of Kariek's major tribal leaders, the Warlord still enjoyed a small but not insignificant degree of support among ordinary Eickaries. Some were collaborators, whose profits and lives would be at risk if he was finally overthrown, but most were simply people who feared and resisted change of any sort, even change for the better. If this was a trap . . .

"Apartment building," Watchman murmured from behind him. "Slow and casual."

Twister cautiously turned to look.

The empty stairways leading down to the shops had stopped being empty. Each of them had sprouted three or four Eickaries, all dressed in the same dark clothing, all armed with blasters or antique tribal projectile weapons or grenade launchers.

All the weapons, of course, were pointed at the storm-troopers.

"As I said," the first Eickarie repeated calmly. "This is no place for a conversation. Please: the first stairway?"

Twister pursed his lips, his mind sifting rapidly through his options. Under normal circumstances, he would already have used the tongue switch to click on his comlink headset and call for backup. Aurek-Four and Aurek-Nine were one alley away and could be here in ninety seconds.

But in this case, the entire Imperial attack force was under strict comlink silence. The Warlord had a highly sophisticated comm-detection system, and even with the Imperials' encryption rendering their communications unreadable he would likely be able to triangulate on any signals and so deduce his opponents' locations. If he hadn't already been tipped off about tonight's attack, that would pretty much do the trick.

Alternatively, Twister could order his men to open fire, trusting their armor to withstand the Eickarie assault long enough for the threat to be neutralized. But the sound of weapons fire coming from the shadow of his watchtowers would be far more compromising than even triangulated transmissions.

Besides, the Imperials were here to free these people, not kill them.

"As you wish," he said, hand-signaling his men to stand easy.

"You sure we want to do this?" Cloud asked quietly.

"If they were on the Warlord's side, they wouldn't have invited us in for a chat," Twister pointed out. "They'd have opened fire and been done with it."

"Just because they're not on his side doesn't mean they're on *our* side," Watchman reminded him warily. "And I don't like the fact that our sensors didn't pick them up skulking around in there."

"The rain might have interfered," Twister said, looking at the display strip. The Eickaries were registering just fine now.

"It didn't interfere with *him*," Watchman reminded him, nodding toward the lone Eickarie still waiting calmly in the downpour for his captives to make their decision.

"We can ask them about it inside," Twister said, making it an order. Cloud was right, he had to admit; he *wasn't* at all sure he wanted to do this. But at the moment, there didn't seem to be a lot of other options. "Lower your weapons and let's go."

THE STAIRWAY LED DOWN A DOZEN STEPS INTO A SMALL TAILOR'S shop that looked as if it had been abandoned years ago. Inside, a dozen more Eickaries were waiting in a circle against the walls, all of them as heavily armed as the ones outside. The young spokesman circled around the four stormtroopers as they filed into the room, crossing to a rusty seam-sealing table and hopping up to sit on it. "I ask again," he said, looking at each of them in turn. "What are you and your fellows doing in our city tonight?"

"Is this the hospitality of the Eickarie people?" Twister countered, trying to remember everything he'd read about the local culture on the flight here two months ago. Up to now Aurek Company hadn't had much direct interaction with the natives, but he had a feeling that the next few minutes were more than going to make up for it. "To ask questions before we have even exchanged names?"

"Do not reply!" an older Eickarie along the wall warned sharply, his orange highlights shifting to red and then purple. "He speaks left-handed, seeking your name to offer in trade to the Warlord."

Twister frowned; and then it clicked. *Left-handed* was Eickarie slang for a lie; *right-handed* the corresponding term for the truth. "I do not speak left-handed," he insisted. "If there's a question I'm not permitted to answer, I'll tell you that. But I will never speak left-handed to you."

The older Eickarie sniffed. "And would not a left-handed speaker also say he would never—?"

"Peace, Ha-ran," the Eickarie seated on the table cut him off. "His question about our hospitality, at least, is right-handed." He looked back at the stormtroopers. "I am Sumil," he said. "And you?"

"I am called Twister," Twister told him. "These are my unit-mates Shadow, Cloud, and Watchman."

He turned to look at Ha-ran. "And with respect to your tribe and its princes," he added, "if you believe we're here to make any trades with the Warlord, you haven't been paying attention to the events of your world over the past eight months. Our people have been fighting tirelessly at the side of the Eickaries, working to tear the Warlord's grip from your throat."

"Then why do you physically assault his stronghold?" Ha-ran spat. "Why not simply destroy it with him inside? Why do you risk your lives to meet him face to face?"

Twister grimaced behind his helmet. Everyone on the planet seemed to be wondering the same thing tonight. "Why did you risk your lives to meet *us* face to face?" he stalled.

It was not, as it turned out, the best thing he might have said. "We called you here to learn what you are doing," Ha-ran said, his highlights turning nearly black. "And to perhaps seek an accommodation with you. Is that what *you* seek with the Warlord?"

"What sort of accommodation could we possibly want with him?" Watchman objected. "We came to this world to destroy him."

"Did you?" the old Eickarie retorted. "Or did you merely seek to conquer him?"

"For what reason?" Watchman persisted. "What could he possibly have—?"

"Watchman," Twister said quietly.

The other broke off. "We don't know why we're here tonight," Twister told Ha-ran honestly. "None of us is high enough in the counsels of our tribe's princes to be given such answers."

"They are called 'generals,' not princes," Su-mil put in. "And you have no tribes, but only the single Empire of the Hand. Do not patronize us, stormtrooper."

Twister turned back to face him. There was something vaguely comical about the Eickarie's stance, a small part of his mind noted, sitting up there on the sealing table with his feet dangling half a meter off the floor.

But at the same time, there was a strength and resolve in his eyes and posture that silenced any inclination toward laughter. "You're right," Twister acknowledged. "I was merely attempting to speak in terms your people would be familiar with."

"We are familiar with many terms," Su-mil said.

"As I now understand," Twister said. "I ask your forgiveness for my unintended offense."

For a moment the other studied him. Then, his orange highlights faded to amber. "My forgiveness is given," he said. "You admit, then, that you seek to meet the Warlord face to face?"

"Our orders are to penetrate the fortress and take him alive," Twister told him. "As I said, I haven't been told the reason behind those orders."

"Then let me tell you what *we* think," Su-mil said. "We think your Empire of the Hand is hoping to make a bargain with the Warlord—a fool's bargain, which will bring ruin on all who raise a hand to it. We think you have united the Eickarie people this way solely to obtain a stronger bartering position for yourselves."

"That's ridiculous," Twister insisted reflexively. "I can't believe my prin—my generals would do such a thing."

"Why not?" Ha-ran demanded. "Are the plundered relics and treasures of the Eickarie people worth nothing to you who travel the stars?"

"Or perhaps the Warlord is already an ally of yours," Su-mil added. "None of the Eickaries has ever seen him outside his armor. For all the evidence we have, he could even be a human like yourselves."

Twister took a deep breath. Unfortunately, that was another very good point. As far as he knew, none of the Imperials knew what kind of being was walking around inside the Warlord's fancy armor, either.

But the possibility that it could be a renegade Imperial had never even occurred to him. "I don't know the reasons for my orders," he said. "But this is my third campaign for the Empire of the Hand, and I've studied the histories of many others. Certainly my leaders have made mistakes, but I have never known them to betray those who trusted them."

"So for you it comes down to a matter of trust?" Su-mil asked.

"Ultimately, that's what it comes down to for any of us," Twister told him. "Trust in your leaders and allies, and loyalty to those who have put their trust in you."

He gestured toward the door. "And right now, there are

soldiers out there who have put their trust in us, relying on us to protect their flank from attack. I would humbly request that you allow us to leave and fulfill that trust."

For a long moment the room was silent. Su-mil eyed him, his highlights subtly changing shade as he considered. Then, suddenly, they returned to their original orange. "I offer a bargain of my own," he said. "In the dungeons of this fortress you seek to penetrate are hundreds of Eickaries who have been imprisoned over the years by the Warlord and his soldiers. Most committed no offense but to resist his tyranny. Will you commit yourself and your fellow stormtroopers to releasing them before you carry your battle to the Warlord's inner stronghold?"

Twister felt an unpleasant shiver run through him. He wasn't trained to negotiate with these people. He certainly wasn't authorized to make tactical arrangements with them.

Trained to walk that fine line between obedience and initiative . . .

"I'm not sure I can commit to such a promise," he said carefully. "My orders are very clear, and the lives of my fellow soldiers lie in the balance. Most of the fortress's outer defenses are controlled from the Warlord's inner stronghold; the sooner we can capture it, the sooner the battle will be over."

"We will certainly release the Eickarie prisoners," Shadow added. "We just may not be able to do so before we face the Warlord."

"I understand your conflict," Su-mil said. "Let me perhaps make the bargain sweeter to your lips. If you will right-handedly make to me this promise, I will lead you inside the fortress along a path the Warlord knows nothing about."

A murmur rippled through the assembled Eickaries, an echo of the stir Twister could sense going through his own men. Apparently, Su-mil's offer had taken everyone by surprise. "What kind of path are we talking about?" he asked. "Is it nearby? Surface, aerial, underground?"

"Do not tell him!" Ha-ran snarled. "This is *our* fight, not theirs. *Our* responsibility, not theirs."

"It is nearby," Su-mil said, his large eyes unblinkingly on Twister.

"This is a fool's bargain, Su-mil—"

"Be silent, Ha-ran," Su-mil said calmly, cutting him off. "For here, and for now, I command. What say you, Imperial? I will not tell you more until you have agreed."

Twister took a careful breath. *Obedience and initiative* . . . "I have no authority to bind anyone but myself and my unit," he told the Eickarie. "But if you can indeed get us in past the Warlord's defenses, I pledge that Unit Aurek-Seven of the Five-oh-First Stormtrooper Legion will do whatever we can to assist in the release of your prisoners."

"And I'll bet we won't be helping you alone, either," Shadow put in. "The commander will definitely want to know about this."

"Yes," Twister said. "We can't risk using comlinks, but I'll send one of my men back to contact Aurek Company's commander and report on our situation and your offer."

"We cannot accept more delay," Su-mil warned. "Already this discussion has devoured precious time."

"Three of us can go with you right now," Twister offered. "If the commander decides to send in more forces, they can catch up." He gestured to Cloud. "Get back and report the situation, and strongly urge that he send in backup. Su-mil, can they come here to get directions to this secret back door?"

"I will leave two of my soldiers behind to guide them," Su-mil said.

My soldiers. Twister felt a new shiver run up his back. This wasn't just some group of vigilantes or gang of would-be plunderers, then. That could be good, or it could be very dangerous.

But at the moment, he had more important things to worry about. "Go," he told Cloud, giving the proper hand signal to confirm the order. Cloud nodded acceptance; crossing the room, he stepped through the circle of Eickaries and headed out again into the rain.

Twister looked back at Su-mil. "I have made the best bargain that I can," he said. "The decision to accept or reject it is now yours."

Again, Su-mil seemed to study him, as if there were anything he could learn by staring at stormtrooper armor. "I accept," he declared, lifting his right hand and tracing out a complicated pattern in the air. "I, Su-mil of the Family Meen-tris, Clan Sav-ro, Tribe Hu-shi-crive, do make this bargain with you."

"And I, Jorm Whistler Mackenni of Unit Aurek-Seven of the Five-oh-First Legion of the Imperial Stormtroopers of the Empire of the Hand, make this bargain with you," Twister replied in turn. It felt strange to speak his real name while in full armor, but the situation clearly demanded it. "Where exactly *is* this back door?"

Su-mil's highlights went pink in another Eickarie smile. "It is directly behind you," he said. "Unknown to the Warlord, this particular fortress had *three* watchtowers."

"FOUR CENTURIES AGO, THE CRO-SAL-TREI TRIBAL CHIEF COMmanding the fortress found himself attacked by two other tribes," Su-mil explained as the three stormtroopers and twenty of the Eickaries made their way down the dark tunnel. "When it was clear that the battle was lost, he and his family and supporters attempted to flee. Unfortunately for them, the attacking tribes knew about the third watchtower and were able to trap them inside the tunnel."

Twister winced as his foot crunched something underfoot. Another bone, probably. The floor was littered with the things, along with rusted twists of metal and occasional scraps of brightly colored clothing. "It would seem they lost that battle, too."

"There was no battle," Su-mil said. "The attackers merely sealed both ends of the tunnel and left them here to die."

Behind Twister, Watchman muttered something. "Would you have preferred many have died in unneeded combat?" Su-mil demanded, half turning to glare at the other.

"Please keep your voice down," Twister said, throwing Watchman a warning hand signal. Confined inside a narrow tunnel, outnumbered seven to one by a group of Eickarie paramilitaries with the Warlord's mercenaries not all that far away, was not the time to have a discussion on military ethics. "There might be listening devices at the other end."

"They will hear nothing," Su-mil said, still glowering. "The tunnel is heavily protected against detection and attack. We may seem primitive to you of the Empire of the Hand, but we are not savages."

"I never believed that you were," Twister assured him. That explained why they hadn't picked up Su-mil's soldiers until they'd emerged onto the stairways. The entire watchtower building probably incorporated the same sensor-blocking materials as the tunnel itself. "Why didn't the next owner unseal it and put it back in operation?"

"It was not known what survival equipment the trapped enemies might have taken inside with them," Su-mil said. "It was therefore thought prudent to leave the tunnel sealed for at least a year. Unfortunately, before that year ended the victors were overthrown in a sudden attack by yet another tribe."

Twister nodded his understanding. "Who didn't know anything about the third watchtower."

"Correct," Su-mil said. "And they could not learn otherwise because their victims had already altered the floor plans. This newest group of occupants unwittingly repeated the omission with their own diagrams, and the truth has been hidden ever since."

"How come *you* know about it?" Shadow asked.

"The family who had the honor of the first tribal leader's final defeat was mine," Su-mil said, an unmistakable note of pride in his voice. "It is a history that has been passed down among us."

With an eye toward holding it as a trump card against some future enemy, no doubt, Twister decided. Little could they have anticipated what sort of enemy that would turn out to be.

"Air vent coming up on the right," Watchman murmured.

"We need to be extra quiet now, Su-mil," Twister warned.

"Vents are good at piping sound places where you don't want it to go."

"I see no vent," Su-mil said, craning his neck forward.

"It's recessed," Watchman told him. "But I can see the eddy pattern in the dust."

"You see remarkably well," Su-mil said, lifting a hand over his head and tracing out a pattern with his fingers. Abruptly, the muffled noises of Eickarie footsteps and the softer sounds of weapons rubbing against clothing ceased completely. The aliens became shadows moving in the darkness, quieter even than the stormtroopers.

The vent was there, all right, its grille recessed just as Watchman had predicted. Twister gave it a quick check as the group filed past, but didn't spot any evidence of the warning sensors any reasonable tyrant ought to have installed there. Apparently, the Warlord really *didn't* know about this tunnel.

They were twenty meters past the vent before Su-mil spoke again. "Your companion has remarkable eyesight," he murmured. "I could not see the vent myself until we were within three arms' reach of it."

"Our helmets incorporate various types of sensors," Twister explained. "Watchman is the unit's tech specialist, which among other things means he has a more advanced set."

"Tech specialist," Su-mil repeated as he looked more closely at Watchman. "I have heard the term, but always assumed it merely meant one who dealt with weapon and vehicle maintenance."

"Not at all," Twister assured him. "You'd be amazed at some of the things they can do."

"We're getting close," Watchman warned.

Twister took the hint and stopped talking. A hundred meters of silence later, they reached the end of the tunnel, blocked by a heavy-looking metal door, gritty with the corrosion of age. For a few minutes the others stood by as Watchman and Shadow examined it, consulting between themselves in clipped technical phrases. Their consultation complete, Shadow pulled out his tube of flash paste and began stuffing it carefully into the cracks around the door.

Twister touched Su-mil's arm and motioned him and his soldiers back to a safe distance.

The paste worked with its usual gratifying speed and efficiency, burning the door's edges far enough back for the two stormtroopers to pry the panel free and drag it out of the way. Beyond the door was a second barrier, this one composed of stone blocks cemented together by slabs of grayish mortar a good centimeter thick. "I don't suppose you and your friends had a plan for getting through this one, did you?" Twister murmured to Su-mil as Watchman ran his fingers experimentally over the mortar.

"Of course," Su-mil said, reaching beneath his serape jacket and pulling out a tube of his own. "Catalytic mortar solvent. Of no use against modern structures, but it should be effective against materials of this era."

"We'll find out in a minute," Twister said, passing the tube to Watchman. The other unsealed it and began laying out a thin bead along the grayish lines, and a soft sizzling sound wafted its way into the silence. A minute later the blocks began to sink slowly downward as the mortar separating them softened and trickled down the sides of the stone like melted candle wax. Two minutes after that, the process was complete, with the wall reduced to nothing more than a simple stack of discolored blocks.

The vertical compression following the loss of the mortar had left a small gap right at the tunnel ceiling. Twister checked his sensors, confirmed that the air flowing in on them wasn't poisoned, and gave Watchman a hand signal. The other nodded back, already pulling out the fiber-op spyscope from its compartment on his belt. He plugged one end into the jack on his helmet and slid the other up through the opening. For a few seconds he moved it back and forth, examining whatever was beyond. "Looks like an old torture chamber," he said quietly. "Probably unused—lots of dust."

"Keep it quiet anyway," Twister said, nodding. "Go ahead and—"

He broke off as a handful of the Eickarie soldiers brushed past him, politely but firmly shouldering the stormtroopers aside. Reaching up through the gap, they got a grip on the topmost blocks and started pulling them inside.

Watchman looked at Twister, his stance one of silent protest. Twister sent him an equally silent calming gesture; reluctantly, the other stepped out of the aliens' way.

The Eickaries had removed the first tier of stones and were starting on the second when the comlink activation ping sounded in Twister's headset. "All units: *attack*!" a voice ordered.

"Better snap it up, Su-mil," Twister said as a flow of orders and tactical reports and the faint sounds of weapons fire began to come from his headset. "Aurek Company's started its attack."

"They are working as quickly as possible," Su-mil replied, his orange spots going a little darker with a sudden emotional intensity. "Does this mean they will send no reinforcements to us?"

"I don't know," Twister said, touching the tongue switch that shut off his comlink again and motioning the others to do the same. They couldn't afford to get distracted by the sounds of a battle they weren't a part of. "I could call the commander and ask, but that might compromise our position."

"Then do not do so," Su-mil said, the orange going darker yet. "If we must do this alone, we will."

Three minutes later, the Eickaries had cleared away enough of the stones to allow passage. Shadow and Watchman went first, darting one at a time through the gap with their Blas-Techs held ready. Su-mil was right behind them, the rest of his soldiers filing through with him before Twister could find a gap in the flow.

He finally got inside and nudged his way through the circle of Eickaries to the door. Shadow and Watchman were listening at the panel, Su-mil standing close behind them. "Report," he ordered, trying hard to keep his annoyance at the Eickaries out of his voice. The three stormtroopers were clearly the best equipped of the group to lead the way into possible danger, and Su-mil surely knew it.

Still, as Cloud had pointed out earlier, Kariek *was* their world. He supposed that gave them the right to go rushing foolishly forward in its defense.

Watchman lifted his helmet away from the door. "Lots of activity out there," he reported. "All of it a fair distance away, though. From the echo pattern, I'm guessing there's a fairly wide corridor leading straight out from us for five to fifteen meters and then intersecting with a cross corridor."

"The noise is probably reinforcements heading to the watchtowers," Shadow added. "I can't see any other reason for so many people to be this far underground, especially with a major attack under way above."

Twister turned to Su-mil. "You know where the dungeons are?"

"To the right," Su-mil said, gesturing with that hand. "They should not be far."

Twister nodded. If they could avoid the mercenaries and keep the element of surprise, there was a chance they could spring the prisoners and be on their way to the Warlord's inner stronghold before the Lakra tumbled to the fact that they had intruders in their midst. "Is that door locked?"

"It was," Shadow said, swinging the panel open a couple of centimeters.

Twister got a firm grip on his BlasTech. "Go."

Shadow opened the door another couple of centimeters, peered out, then pulled it wide and ducked into the corridor, Watchman and Su-mil right behind him. This time, Twister managed to get ahead of the rest of the pack.

The corridor was wide, low-ceilinged, and dimly lit, with the cross corridor Watchman had deduced about eight meters ahead. The sounds of thudding Lakran feet filled the air, echoing off the stone walls and making it difficult to get a fix on direction or distance. Still, Twister thought as they hurried toward the cross corridor, the entrances to the other watchtowers ought to be at least a couple of corridors away from their current position, and both of them somewhere off to their left. If the infiltrators could make it to the cross corridor undetected, they would then be moving away from the main focus of activity as they headed for the dungeons.

They were nearly to the cross corridor when their luck ran out.

The six armored mercenaries who came thundering along down the cross corridor nearly ran down Shadow as he started to ease his helmet around the corner. There was a screech of surprise from one of them as they skidded to an uneven halt that left them spread out in a line across the intersection. They fumbled with their blasters, trying to bring them to bear on the unexpected intruders.

Watchman and Shadow were already firing, their Blas-Techs sending a rapid-fire stutter of blaster bolts into the torso plates of the two Lakra at their end of the line. Automatically, Twister focused his attention on the other end of the shooting gallery, sending a multiple burst of fire across that mercenary's chest. Beside him, Su-mil was firing at the Lakra beside Twister's opponent, the heavy thuds of his projectile weapon forming a counterpoint to the high-pitched whine of the Imperial blasters.

It was only as his target Lakra began to stagger under his assault that Twister realized that none of the other Eickaries was firing.

Which left two of the Lakra completely unopposed as they brought their weapons around.

The first salvo caught Twister squarely across the chest. But with their weapons still in motion only a small number of the energy bolts actually connected with his armor, the rest under- or overshooting him. There was a sudden gurgle from behind him as one of the Eickaries apparently caught some of the wild shots—

Then Su-mil shifted his aim, abandoning his original target and booming a pair of rounds into each of the as-yet-untouched Lakra.

It wasn't nearly enough to stop them, not as fully armored as they were. But unlike the BlasTechs, the projectile weapon packed a heavy punch. The impact sent the two Lakra staggering, deflecting their own fire into the ceiling for perhaps half a second.

Half a second was enough. Watchman and Shadow had finished off their opponents and now opened fire on the two Su-mil had just rocked back on their heels. Twister shifted his fire back to his original and not-quite-silenced enemy, noticing Su-mil do the same with his.

Three seconds later, it was all over.

Shadow and Watchman were out in the cross corridor straddling the smoking Lakran bodies as they checked both ends of the hall. "Clear," Watchman announced. "But it won't be for long."

"Acknowledged," Twister said, looking behind him at the Eickaries.

They were just standing there, some of them twitching a little, others fingering their weapons uncertainly, all of them staring at the dead enemies.

Enemies they themselves hadn't lifted a finger to help kill.

Twister let his gaze linger another second, then turned to Su-mil. "You called them soldiers?" he asked pointedly.

Su-mil's orange highlights had gone a dusky brown. "They froze with surprise," he said, his voice unreadable. Explanation or excuse, Twister couldn't tell which. "I apologize for their failure. It will not happen again."

"I'd really like to believe that," Twister told him. "Unfortunately, I don't think I can take that chance."

"Do you mean to go back on your promise?" Su-mil asked bluntly.

Twister hesitated. The Eickaries placed great store in promises made between those who had exchanged full names. But at the same time, he had a mission and orders of his own to deal with. "We'll still free your prisoners," he said. "But only *after* we've captured the Warlord."

Su-mil didn't answer. Twister eyed him another second, giving him every opportunity to argue his case. "Then you had best depart," the Eickarie said at last.

"Footsteps," Watchman snapped, he and Shadow stepping back into the partial cover of the corner.

"Direction?" Twister demanded, a sinking feeling in the pit of his stomach as he moved forward to join them.

"Could be either," Watchman told him, swiveling his head back and forth. "All these echoes—"

"Never mind." Twister cut him off, coming to a sudden decision. The bulk of the Lakra would still be congregating off to their left to oppose Aurek Company's attack. Therefore, he and his unit would go right. "Head right. Maybe we can skulk our way past them."

He stepped around the corner and hurried down the corridor, the other two stormtroopers forming up behind him. Ten meters ahead, another corridor cut across theirs at an angle. They could hear more thudding footsteps, some of them definitely coming closer—

"Halt!" Su-mil's voice barked suddenly from behind him. "Lower your weapons!"

Twister turned, sheer surprise bringing him to a stop. Su-mil and his soldiers had poured into the corridor behind the Imperials and assembled themselves into a classic two-tier firing wall. "What do you think you're doing?" he demanded.

And then, ten meters behind the Eickaries, a dozen Lakra suddenly appeared around a corner, surging down the passageway toward them like a bad-tempered river. There was another burst of noise from behind him, and Twister turned back to see another mercenary squad appear from the angled corridor ahead.

Unit Aurek-Seven of the 501st had been trapped.

"Lower your weapons to the ground," Su-mil repeated, lifting his rifle to point squarely at Twister's face. "Do it now, or you will die."

There didn't seem to be many options. "Do it," Twister growled to Shadow and Watchman, crouching down and setting his BlasTech onto the floor.

Shifting his rifle to a one-handed grip, Su-mil lifted the other hand above the heads of his soldiers and gestured toward the approaching Lakra. "Fellow servants of our Glorious Majesty!" he shouted. "We have captured them!"

* * *

THE FIRST WAVE OF LAKRA PICKED THEIR WAY PAST THE BODIES of their comrades at the intersection and came to a halt behind the Eickaries, their weapons trained warily on the natives' backs. Leaving the rest of his squad on guard, the mercenary leader strode through the group to Su-mil's side, shoving aside anyone not quick enough to get out of his way. "What have we here?" he growled in a voice that sounded like rocks being run through a fruit blender, the heavy blaster in his massive hand holding steady on Twister's chest. "Imperial stormtroopers. An interesting catch."

He looked sideways at Su-mil. "*If* they were indeed caught," he added pointedly. "Who are you, and what are you doing uninvited in His Glorious Majesty's home?"

"I am Su-mil." Su-mil's aim shifted slightly, as if he no longer needed to keep as close a watch on the Imperials now that the Lakra had arrived. "I am a loyal subject of His Glorious Majesty, who finds heartache in the invasion of my home by Imperial intruders."

"That may be as it may be," the squad leader said. "Why are you here?"

"Ah, that is a tale of extreme Eickarie courage," Su-mil said proudly. "We found them on the street, clearly intent on attacking our Glorious Majesty's home. They pointed their weapons at us and demanded we lead them inside."

Twister frowned. That wasn't at all the way it had been. What was Su-mil trying to do, make himself and his friends look more heroic?

"And you did so?" the Lakra prompted.

Again, Su-mil's aim twitched fractionally to the side. "We showed them where the tunnel was hidden and brought them through it," he said.

"How?" the Lakra asked. "Both towers were guarded."

"There is an unguarded entrance."

"You will take us to this entrance as soon as these enemies have been secured," the squad leader said ominously. "Did more of them come in?"

"No," Su-mil said. "These three were all we brought in."

"Yet others may follow," the Lakra said, turning halfway

around and giving a brief order in his own language. One of the mercenaries grunted a response, and a third of them turned and hurried back the way they'd come. Again stepping carefully over the bodies of their fallen comrades, they returned to the corner where they'd first appeared and set up a defensive position. "And these?" the leader continued, gesturing back toward the dead Lakra. "What happened to them?"

"The Imperials shot them down," Su-mil said, his voice contemptuous. Again, his weapon shifted. "I and my people played no part in the slaughter."

"Despite these weapons you carry?" the squad leader snapped, his voice suddenly heavy with suspicion. "And how do you come by them, if the invaders merely stopped you on the street?"

Su-mil's weapon shifted aim again. "The weapons are ours," he conceded. "We told the Imperials we would agree to assist them." Once more, his aim shifted. "But we would never use such weapons against our Glorious Majesty and our fellow servants."

Twister grimaced. He was a traitor, all right, a traitor to his own people as well as to the Imperials who were bleeding and dying to try to help them. And a shameless smooth-talker on top of it, standing there looking calmly at his victims as he pointed his weapon at Twister's left eye.

His *left* eye?

Twister stiffened as it suddenly clicked. The weapon's apparently arbitrary movement wasn't arbitrary at all. It was, instead, Su-mil carefully alternating his aim between Twister's left and right eyes.

Left-handed: a lie. Right-handed: the truth.

Quickly, he ran back through the conversation, this time paying attention to where the weapon had been pointed at each exchange. *We have captured them*—a lie. *I am Su-mil*—the truth. *I am a loyal subject of His Glorious Majesty*—a lie. *We found them on the street, clearly intent on attacking our Glorious Majesty's home*—the truth. *They pointed their weapons at us and demanded we lead them inside*—a lie. *We showed them where the tunnel was hidden*—the truth. *I and my people played no part in the slaughter*—a lie. *We told the Imperials we would agree to assist them*—the truth.

We would never use such weapons against our Glorious Majesty and our fellow servants—a lie.

And for the first time since Aurek-Seven had run into Su-mil and his soldiers, Twister felt a tight smile creasing his face. A clever and resourceful fellow, this Su-mil. And he was obviously hoping Twister and his fellow Imperials were the same.

Because it was suddenly clear what the Eickarie had in mind. He'd told the truth about an unguarded entrance into the fortress, but the Lakran squad leader had jumped to the conclusion that that entrance was connected to one of the two known tunnels. The fact that he'd sent some of his troops back to guard against any further intrusion from that direction was proof.

Which meant that if Aurek Company *had* sent reinforcements, they might be emerging any moment now into the middle of a split enemy force.

Both parts of which were facing the wrong direction.

Reaching out with his tongue, he touched his comlink switch. "Cloud: report," he murmured, pitching his voice low enough to be inaudible outside his helmet.

Cloud's voice in his ear was the most welcome thing he'd heard for days. "We're in the room beyond the wall," Cloud's voice came promptly in his ears. "Situation?"

"Pinned to right of first cross," Twister said, sensing Shadow and Watchman stir slightly as their comlinks came on and they picked up the news of the approaching reinforcements. "Enemy split: four-eight. Friendlies pinned with us to right."

"Acknowledged," Cloud said. "On our way."

"It's good to know the Glorious Majesty has such loyal supporters," the Lakran squad leader rumbled to Su-mil with only a hint of sarcasm. "You will put your weapons on the floor now."

"But we face very dangerous enemies," Su-mil protested,

his weapon shifting to Twister's right eye. "We cannot know when it will be necessary to fire."

"The Lakra will do any firing that is necessary," the squad leader assured him, turning his blaster away from Twister and pressing the muzzle against the side of Su-mil's neck. "Now. Put down your weapons."

"You'll have no trouble on that score anyway," Twister said, lifting his right hand and pointing his forefinger straight at Su-mil's right eye. "When you see your friends falling in front of you, you'll know the time of death has arrived."

"Silence!" the squad leader spat, sending a baleful glare at the stormtroopers. From Twister's headset came a pair of acknowledging double-clicks as Shadow and Watchman confirmed his veiled order. "Very soon now, you will be begging for the time of death to be allowed you."

"Countdown: three," Cloud's voice murmured in Twister's ear.

"Oh, I don't know," Twister said proudly, raising his voice to fill the corridor and help cover any inadvertent footfalls. "Somehow, I don't think so."

And as the last word rang through the air, a group of white-armored men boiled into the corridor behind the Eickaries.

Twister didn't wait to see any more. Even as the reinforcements began firing at both ends of the split Lakran force, he and the rest of Aurek-Seven threw themselves flat onto the floor.

Leaving a direct line of fire between the mercenaries behind them and the Eickarie firing wall.

Su-mil had promised that his soldiers wouldn't freeze the next time. He was right. Twister hadn't even gotten a grip on his dropped weapon when the hodgepodge of Eickarie weapons opened up, laying down a blaze of fire at the Lakran squad. By the time he had scooped up the BlasTech and rolled over ready to use it, the battle was over.

He scrambled hastily to his feet. "Report," he called into his comlink.

"Clear," Cloud's voice came back. "No casualties."

The same, unfortunately, couldn't be said for the Eickaries. Of the twenty soldiers Su-mil had brought in with them, six were on the floor, four writhing silently in pain, the other two already dead. Even outnumbered as they'd been, the Lakran squad had given a good account of themselves.

At least, he hoped all the casualties had been caused by the Lakra. It would be very unfortunate if some of the rescuers had accidentally overshot their targets.

"This way, Twister," Cloud called. Twister looked up from the Eickarie casualties to find the rest of the stormtrooper squad moving back along the corridor toward the intersection where the newly dead Lakra were lying. "The company's meeting heavy resistance in the tunnels," he went on. "New orders are to attack from this end and try to break up their defenses."

Twister looked at Su-mil. The Eickarie was standing over the body of the Lakran squad leader, his eyes on Twister, his orange highlights gone dark again. "I'm sorry, but we can't do that," he told Cloud. "I made a deal with Su-mil to clear the dungeons first."

Cloud stopped short, turning around to look back at his unit leader. "Twister, this was a direct order," he warned.

"Understood," Twister said. "Good luck. We'll join you when we can."

One of the other stormtroopers had paused beside Cloud. "Yet you said you would not help us," Su-mil reminded Twister quietly.

"That was when I wasn't sure I could rely on your soldiers," Twister told him. "You've now proven that I can." A movement caught his eye: Cloud and the other stormtrooper had finished their conversation, and Cloud was jogging back down the corridor toward them as the rest of the stormtroopers resumed their march in the other direction. "I hope you're not here to argue," he warned as Cloud came to a halt in front of him.

"Hardly," Cloud assured him. "I decided that if they can manage without three of us, they can probably manage without four."

"And whole-unit court-martials are so much more efficient?" Shadow said dryly.

"Something like that," Cloud agreed. "Let's move."

SU-MIL DETAILED THREE OF HIS SOLDIERS TO TAKE THEIR DEAD and wounded back into the relative safety of the tunnel. Then, with Su-mil and Twister in the lead, the twelve remaining Eickaries and four stormtroopers set off for the dungeons.

They met no further resistance. Apparently, the squad that had burst in on them from this direction had been the last Lakra who hadn't already been summoned to either the tunnel defenses or to the surface. Alternating his attention between the distant battle reports, his helmet sensors, and the hallways themselves, Twister wondered if he dared hope that even the dungeon guards might have been called away to active service.

No such luck. At Su-mil's murmured warning, he and Shadow swung out around the last corner to find two armored Lakra standing at attention beside a massive metal door, blaster carbines slung over their shoulders.

A direct assault on the dungeons was apparently the last thing anyone in the Warlord's command structure was expecting. The two stormtroopers got off a solid volley before the guards had time to do more than scramble madly for their weapons. As the blaster bolts shredded the mercenaries' armor, Su-mil stepped out of concealment and finished the job with a pair of shots from his projectile weapon. "We must hurry," the Eickarie said as the two Lakra thudded to the floor.

"Wait a second," Cloud said as Watchman headed for the door. "We agreed to get you to the dungeons—"

"You agreed to assist in freeing the prisoners," Su-mil cut him off. "Come. Now."

"Twister?" Cloud asked, his mind clearly on their comrades fighting in the tunnels a quarter of the fortress away.

"You heard him," Twister said, suppressing his own impatience. "Come on."

The outer door opened onto a wide landing from which a dozen steps led down to a large, circular cavern with more locked doors spaced around its circumference. "How fast can you open them?" Su-mil asked, looking around.

"Very," Watchman assured him, stepping to a desk at one side of the landing and picking up a knife-blade-shaped data card. "All it takes is the key."

"Go," Twister told him, turning the muzzle of his Blas-Tech toward the door they'd entered through. "We'll watch for trouble here."

With the key in hand, the release did indeed go quickly. But as the imprisoned Eickaries began to emerge, blinking, into the brighter light of the cavern, Twister could sense that something was wrong. Many of them, not surprisingly, cringed back at the sight of Watchman's armor as he opened their doors, staring with the same fascinated suspicion at the other three stormtroopers grouped together on the landing. More baffling was the fact that they seemed to be avoiding not only their fellow prisoners but Su-mil and his soldiers as well.

It was Shadow who caught on first. "They're all from different tribes," he murmured.

"And they were captured before the United Tribes Agreements were put together," Twister said, a sour taste in his mouth as he understood. "Which means they're still fighting their petty little tribal disputes."

He thought he'd been speaking quietly. Apparently, not quietly enough. "Our disputes are *not* petty," Ha-ran insisted, glowering up at the stormtroopers from his position at the foot of the stairs.

Twister frowned down at him. After his loud complaints in the tailor shop, the older Eickarie hadn't said a word during the trip through the tunnel. As Twister thought about it, though, he realized that, silent or not, Ha-ran had always been close at hand, hovering at Su-mil's elbow.

He was just wondering what that might mean when Ha-ran started up the steps, his gait suddenly stiff. "Move away," he ordered the stormtroopers, gesturing them back. "Su-mil?"

Su-mil was instantly at his side, taking his arm and assisting him up the steps. "Was he hit?" Shadow asked quietly.

"I didn't think so," Twister said, looking Ha-ran up and down. There certainly weren't any bloodstains or scorch marks on his clothing.

"He is merely old," Su-mil said, gesturing the stormtroopers back as he and Ha-ran reached the landing. "Older than you realize. Move back, please. Prince Ha-ran wishes to address the prisoners."

Twister felt his jaw drop. "*Prince* Ha-ran?"

Ha-ran ignored him, turning instead to face the mass of Eickaries below. *"Ha-ran mish-ra hee-sae sha-kae drof-si-shae-ral,"* he called, holding a hand out over the crowd.

Twister frowned in concentration. Aurek Company had gotten a two-day crash course in the main Eickarie trade language on the trip here, which had so far served him fairly well in his limited contacts with the natives. Unfortunately, Ha-ran was going way too fast for him to keep up.

Apparently, the others weren't doing any better. "Where's a protocol droid when you need one?" Cloud muttered as Ha-ran continued speaking.

"He said, 'I am Ha-ran of the Family Mish-ra, Clan Sha-kae, prince of the Tribe Si-shae-ral,'" Su-mil said softly from beside them. "'I am here to speak of the present and of the future.'"

Cloud stirred. "Twister, we don't have time for speeches."

"Quiet," Twister ordered, gazing at Ha-ran with new eyes. Eickarie princes rarely went into combat, and never without fifty thousand soldiers along for the ride. This was definitely one for the record lists. "Go on, Su-mil."

"'The present is that we are in our final battle against our oppressors,'" Su-mil continued, translating, as Ha-ran's proud voice echoed from the dingy stone. "'But unless you embrace the new future that we the United Tribes of Kariek have forged, we will be no better off than we were before they came.'"

"I don't get it," Shadow murmured. "Why do we even care what a bunch of shaggy prisoners think? Shouldn't they be grateful enough at being sprung that they'll do what they're told?"

"You do not understand," Su-mil said, his orange patches going a dark yellow. "These are not ordinary criminals or even ordinary opponents to the Warlord's tyranny. Many of these Eickaries are nobles and elders, taken as hostages to ensure the good behavior of their tribes."

"It didn't work very well, did it?" Watchman put in. "Hostages or not, pretty much the whole planet signed on to the United Tribes Agreements."

"The Warlord might still choose to execute them, or use them as living shields to ensure his own escape," Su-mil pointed out. "That was the reason we feared your unexpected attack, and why I insisted they be freed before the Warlord was routed from his inner sanctum."

"I understand," Twister said. "You couldn't just let them be slaughtered; but you also couldn't afford to let them come out and try to pick up their lives where they left off. If they did, you might slip right back into the old cycle of endless tribal warfare."

Su-mil looked closely at him. "That is indeed the danger," he confirmed. "You are more perceptive than I had realized."

"And you in turn are rather deeper than *I* realized," Twister returned. "Let me guess: none of these prisoners is from your own tribe?"

"That is correct," Su-mil said. "The most important are from Ha-ran's tribe and its allies, which is why he volunteered to come with us tonight. Of all those who might have spoken to them of peace, he has the greatest chance of convincing them."

"How's it working?" Shadow asked.

Su-mil gazed down at the crowd. "Not well, I fear," he conceded. "Those of the Tribe Si-shae-ral are listening closely, but many of the others seem impatient and closed-minded. They may believe it to be a deception."

"In the meantime we have a job of our own to do," Cloud said grimly. "And I don't think we can afford to hang around here any longer."

Twister nodded reluctant agreement. From the running dialogue of orders and reports streaming through his headset, it sounded like the rest of Aurek Company was in an uphill battle back in the two main tunnels. "He's right, Su-mil," he said. "We'll have to leave you to sort things out on your own."

He was starting to turn away when a sudden thought struck him. "Unless," he went on, "you'd like to invite them to come along and see what can be accomplished by people who don't fight among themselves."

Su-mil's highlights went to a shade of green only slightly lighter than the rest of his face, the Eickarie version of a frown. "You refer to the soldiers of your Empire of the Hand?"

"Of course," Watchman said, catching on. "We'll show them how we work together to defeat the Lakra who subjugated them."

"And maybe even capture the Warlord along with it," Shadow added.

Su-mil's highlights warmed from green to pink in a tight smile. "They might indeed find that instructive," he agreed. "Perhaps Ha-ran should invite his tribesmen to assist, as well."

"Why not?" Twister agreed casually. "I'm sure they'd enjoy watching history in the making as the Hu-shi-crive and Si-shae-ral tribes overthrow the Warlord."

"I will suggest it." His highlights fading back to orange, Su-mil turned and began speaking quietly to Ha-ran.

Twister gestured to Watchman and Shadow. "There has to be an armory around here somewhere for the guards," he said. "Go find it."

The others nodded acknowledgment and left. "This had better not take long," Cloud warned, his hands fingering his BlasTech restlessly.

"Understood," Twister said, gazing out on the crowd and trying to gauge their reaction to Ha-ran's new suggestion. "But if this works, I think it'll be worth the wait."

It worked, all right, and faster than Twister had expected.

Faced with the possibility that some other tribes would grab more than their share of the glory, the newly freed prisoners barely let Ha-ran finish his comments before they were clamoring to be allowed to assist. At Twister's suggestion, the prince split the new fighting force into three groups, with each group lining up along traditional tribal alliances as much as possible. By the time the squads were ready, Watchman and Shadow had the guards' armory open.

Five minutes later, they were ready. Two of the groups, under Shadow's and Cloud's command and bolstered by some of Su-mil's soldiers, headed toward the two tunnel exits where Aurek Company was still trying to break through the Lakran resistance. The third group, including Twister, Watchman, and the rest of Su-mil's force, headed inward toward the Warlord's central stronghold.

"I do not trust the apparent safety," Su-mil commented as the group slipped through the empty corridors. "Surely they must expect an attack in this direction."

"That depends on whether anyone's figured out yet how we got in," Twister told him, keeping a sharp eye out for trouble. "Remember, the first report from the two squads that had us pincered would have indicated the attack had come from a secret way in through one of the known tunnels."

"And since the first report was also the last," Watchman added, "we've got a fair chance of getting pretty far in before they figure out what's happening."

"But surely they will not assume that the attackers at those tunnels will not break through," Su-mil objected. "Surely they will be prepared for more fighting."

"Oh, they will," Watchman said, suddenly putting up a hand. "And I'd say they're prepared for it right about here."

Twister peered into the gloom as the group came to a halt. Three meters ahead, the corridor they were traveling along opened up into a large, high-ceilinged room whose stone walls were decorated with colorful flags and imprint shields. Probably those of the last tribe to own the fortress, Twister guessed, before the Warlord had come in and booted them out. There were several long and heavy-looking wooden tables laid out throughout the room, with equally heavy wooden chairs surrounding them. In the wall directly across from their corridor was a large metal door.

"It is the storm banquet chamber," Su-mil identified it, keeping his voice low. "A place for feasting in comfort and safety when the spring storms endanger the towers."

Twister nodded. According to the floor plans the Eickarie leaders had drawn for them, the fortress's inner stronghold was a round room completely surrounded by a larger circular area that was broken up into four segments. From the curve of the wall he could see from where they stood, it looked like this storm banquet chamber was one of those four circular segments. "We're almost there," he said. "Booby-trapped?"

"Not too seriously," Watchman said, his helmet moving back and forth as he examined the room. "There's a scent of explosives: grenades under some of the tables or chairs."

"Command frequencies?" Twister asked.

"Nope," Watchman said regretfully. "No carriers, either, so I'm guessing they're not remotes. Probably fused with proximity triggers."

"Too bad," Twister said. With remotes, the Imperials could often find and lock down the control frequencies, rendering such devices useless. There wasn't much they could do with proximity fuses except identify and locate them. "I guess they're learning. What else?"

"Two sniper hollows, one on each side of the door behind those long banners, with one Lakra hiding in each," Watchman said. "The door itself is running enough current to kill a bantha, and the Warlord probably has fifty Lakra inside the stronghold with him. Aside from that, it seems pretty clear."

Beside Twister, Su-mil stirred. "Do we simply stand here?" he demanded.

"Patience," Twister advised, frowning across the room at the electrified metal door. There was something about this whole thing that didn't feel quite right. "He's trying to locate the grenades."

One of the released prisoners growled something. "He says that is not possible," Su-mil translated.

"Tell him he'd be amazed at what's possible for the Empire of the Hand," Twister said, still studying the door.

Su-mil turned to the other Eickarie, murmuring in their trade language, and Watchman stirred. "All right," he said. "There are grenades beneath those chairs"—he pointed at two of the ones closest to them—"that end of that table"—he indicated one of the tables to the right—"and those chairs there and there," he finished, pointing to two chairs on opposite sides of the hidden sniper hollows. "Those last two are probably there to blast anyone trying to sneak up on the snipers from the side. There are a few more, but they're off to the sides, away from our optimal attack vectors."

"Okay," Twister said, running his eyes across the blast points and working out a sequence. The sniper and under-chair grenade combination was a trick they'd seen the Lakra use before: if an attacker came in high, the sniper would get him; if he came in low to avoid the sniper, he was right in position to take the full brunt of the grenade blast. "We'll send the Eickaries back a ways down the corridor and blow the two closest grenades. The blasts should give us enough cover to move in toward the door, avoiding the booby-trapped table. Once we're in front of the door, we'll use whipcords to grab the two chairs on the sides, pull them in front of the sniper hollows, and detonate their grenades. That should either take the snipers out of the game completely or at least slow them down long enough for us to get the door open."

"Sounds good," Watchman said, shifting his BlasTech to one hand and getting his whipcord thrower ready. "Su-mil, get them back."

Su-mil gave a brief order over his shoulder, and the rest of Eickaries backed up a few steps. "How do we detonate the grenades?" he asked, making no move to join the rest of his people. "It will not be easy to shoot through those chairs."

"Just watch," Twister said, wondering if he should insist Su-mil go back with the others. But the young Eickarie would probably refuse, and they didn't have time to argue. "Watchman?"

"Ready," the other said.

"Go."

With a faint hiss of compressed air, Watchman's whipcord snapped outward toward one of the two booby-trapped chairs. The grapple on the end caught the backrest just above the seat, and with a flick of his wrist Watchman pulled backward. The chair tipped sideways toward him and toppled onto the floor, putting the heavy wooden seat squarely between the stormtroopers and the hidden grenade.

As the room echoed with the thud, Twister lobbed a concussion grenade over the edge of the seat into the path of the other grenade's proximity sensor.

The double blast was deafening, or at least it would have been without the sonic cutoff protection of their helmets. The physical effect on the room was equally spectacular, the force of the blast rocking everything in its path and sending clouds of splinters and dust into the air. The sound of the blast had barely faded away before Watchman disengaged the grapple and fired the whipcord into the second of the nearest rigged chairs. Another yank, another toppled chair, and a second blast and cloud of debris joined the first.

Half a heartbeat later the two stormtroopers were on the move, cutting across the room at a sharp angle to avoid the booby-trapped table, then cutting back and braking to a halt directly in front of the electrified door. Twister had his whipcord thrower out, fumbling his BlasTech slightly as he tried to handle both devices at once.

"Pull the chair over," Su-mil's voice shouted in his ear. "I will detonate it."

Twister blinked in surprise. Su-mil had followed right behind them and was crouched between the two stormtroopers, his own weapon held ready. "Right," he shouted back, setting down his BlasTech and firing his whipcord. The grapple caught, and with both hands free it was a simple job to pull it over and drag it to just in front of the hidden sniper hollow. "Go!"

Su-mil fired, and Twister winced slightly as the edge of the explosion slammed into him, threatening to knock him off his feet. He glanced into his rear display, confirming that his armored body had shielded Su-mil, just as another blast rocked him from the other direction. "Clear," Watchman called. "Cover me, and I'll start on the door."

"Right," Twister said, scooping up his BlasTech again. The grenade's explosion had ripped the concealing banner from the wall, revealing a concave metal door with narrow viewing and firing slits in it. Nothing seemed to be stirring within; apparently the grenade had punched enough stuff through the openings to knock the sniper inside at least temporarily out of commission.

They hadn't been so lucky with the other sniper, though. Twister turned to see a heavy blaster poke its nose through the lower slit, swiveling toward the intruders by the door. "Get behind me!" he snapped to Su-mil, swinging up his own weapon and firing a burst across the viewing slit.

There was no effect. The blaster continued to track toward them—

And then, suddenly, a withering hail of fire erupted from the corridor. The Eickaries whom Su-mil had sent down the corridor for safety were on the move, targeting the Lakran sniper as they charged across the room.

The Lakran sniper reacted to the new threat exactly the way Twister would have expected a trained soldier to. Abandoning his attack on the stormtroopers, he shifted his aim to the advancing Eickaries, and several of them toppled over with grunts or shrieks of pain as his blaster began to take its toll.

But there were too many of them, and the Lakra had too little time. Even as Twister added his BlasTech's firepower to theirs, three of the former prisoners made it all the way across the shooting gallery. With their backs pressed against the wall to either side, they jammed the muzzles of their weapons into the slits and fired half a dozen bursts each. There was a single dying stutter from the sniper's weapon, and then the muzzle abruptly tipped upward and slipped back inside.

"Sha-mees craa shes-ayi," Su-mil called. "I have praised

their valor in your name," he added to Twister. "I trust that is acceptable."

"Absolutely," Twister assured him as another pair of Eickaries ran to the quiet sniper hollow, firing a few volleys into the slits to make sure it stayed quiet. "Add our thanks for the timely assist, and then tell them to spread out and stand guard while we get this door open."

Su-mil called out another order, and the Eickaries obediently spread out across the room, pushing over tables and chairs for cover and digging in for combat. Old rivalries or not, Twister thought wryly, there was nothing like a common enemy to draw people together.

He shifted his attention back to the door. Watchman was kneeling in front of it, his BlasTech on the floor beside him, nearly finished assembling the components he would need to safely short out the current. "Status?"

"Almost ready," Watchman reported.

Twister nodded and turned back to Su-mil. "Another minute—"

He broke off. Su-mil was staring at the door, his highlights a very dark green. "What's the matter?"

"This door," Su-mil said slowly. "There is something not right about it."

Twister felt a tingle at the back of his neck. One soldier with a bad feeling might be nerves or overreaction. Two soldiers with the same bad feeling was something worth paying attention to. "Can you tell what it is?"

"No," Su-mil said, his highlights going a shade darker as he frowned a little harder.

"Hold it a second, Watchman," Twister said, his eyes running methodically across the door. The sensors still read it as solid metal charged with a high-voltage current. The lock? No; that looked all right.

He looked around the room where the Eickaries were preparing for battle, painfully aware that precious seconds were ticking away. The Warlord would have to be both deaf and stupid not to realize his sanctum had been breached, and no matter how badly his mercenaries might be pinned down he would absolutely find a way to shake some of them loose to deal with this threat.

In fact, they were almost certainly on their way. Twister glanced back at the corridor they'd come in by, half expecting to find a mass of armored Lakra already marching toward them. But the corridor was still deserted, as far back as he could see.

As far back as he could see . . .

He snorted with exasperation. So simple, and so obvious. "Put it away," he told Watchman. "This isn't the door."

"What?" the other demanded, sounding stunned as he looked up.

"It's a decoy," Twister said, pointing behind him. "Would *you* put the door to *your* stronghold right at the end of a long hallway, where your enemies would have a fifty-meter running start to slam a battering ram into it?"

"Or a clear shot for a missile barrage," Su-mil added, his highlights fading again to dark orange. "Of course. The real door will be concealed, and offline with any of the hallways."

Twister nodded. "So let's find it."

It didn't take long. Now that he knew what to look for, he quickly spotted the subtle cracks in the mortar between the stones a couple of meters to the side of the rightmost sniper hollow. "Here it is," he announced, gesturing to the others with his BlasTech.

"We must hurry," Su-mil warned as the two stormtroopers started stuffing flash paste around the door. "There may be other ways through which they can escape."

"None that your people know about, anyway," Twister told him, focusing his attention for a moment on the streaming reports coming in through his headset. "Even if there are, it won't gain them anything. Aurek Company's just broken through both tunnels and are forming up now with Cloud and Shadow and the rest of your people. Another minute and they'll be on their way here."

"You think we should wait for them?" Watchman asked.

"No," Su-mil said firmly, his large eyes shining. "We have

come this far. Let us be the ones to present to them the prize."

"Besides, they're still controlling their main defenses from in there," Twister reminded him. "The sooner we take him, the sooner we can shut them down."

Thirty seconds later, they were ready. "Stand clear," Watchman cautioned the Eickaries, who had gathered together in front of the hidden door. "When it goes, it'll go hard."

"And tell them to let us go in first," Twister added as Su-mil translated Watchman's warning. "They'll still have plenty of firepower waiting in there, and we're the only ones in armor."

Su-mil gave another order. "Do not worry," he told Twister, switching back to Basic. "We will do what is necessary."

"Okay," Twister said, taking another step back himself. "Watchman: go."

The other squeezed the detonator, and the flash paste lit up with its usual destructive brilliance. Twister checked his sensors one final time, half expecting some of the Lakra inside to have slipped out through one of the stronghold's other doors and launch a last-minute sortie. But apparently the Warlord preferred to keep all his bodyguards between him and the attackers.

The flash paste hit its final crescendo, and Twister caught a glimpse of the sudden network of stress cracks in the stone before the entire door abruptly shattered into a spray of blackened gravel. Reflexively, he winced back as the shower of rocks washed over him—

And was nearly knocked off his feet as the Eickaries surged past him. Screaming in defiance, they charged through the opening.

"Wait!" Twister shouted. "Su-mil—"

But Su-mil had already joined the general rush through the door. "Our world!" he called back over his shoulder. "Our ways!"

With that he was gone, vanished into the stronghold and the heavy weapons fire now coming from inside. Snarling a curse, Twister regained his balance and tried to force his way through the rear of the Eickaries' formation, listening helplessly to the sounds of gunfire and the screams of the casualties.

Then, as abruptly as it had begun, the firing ceased. Shouldering his way past the last cluster of Eickaries, Twister finally made it inside.

The stronghold was a scene of carnage. Eickarie bodies were everywhere, some still twitching, others lying motionless with the heaviness of death. Another dozen were still standing, several of them clutching painfully at torsos or limbs. Sprawled on the floor beyond them were a dozen Lakra bodies, the last of the Warlord's bodyguard. None of those bodies were twitching.

And beyond them, still wearing his fancy full-body armor, was the Warlord himself.

He was lying on his back on the floor, his dark faceplate turned upward, his arms spread to the sides. Standing over him, his feet pinning the Warlord's wrists to the floor, his projectile weapon held ready for action, was Su-mil.

But his gun wasn't pointed at the Warlord, prepared to deliver the final killing shot that Eickarie honor demanded. It was pointed instead at the semicircle of Eickaries facing him.

His eyes turned to Twister as the stormtrooper stepped through the ring of Eickaries. "I have told them," he said, his voice wheezing; and only then did Twister notice the blackened section of clothing on his left side. "We made a bargain. You freed our people; I have left the Warlord alive."

"Thank you," Twister said, touching his comm tongue switch as he stepped to Su-mil's side and turned to face the other Eickaries. Over by the main status board, he noted peripherally, the thudding of heavy circuit breakers could be heard as Watchman began closing down the fortress's defenses. "Command; Aurek-Seven," he called. "We've penetrated the stronghold, and are shutting down the remotes."

"Acknowledged, Aurek-Seven," a crisp voice came back. "What about the Warlord?"

Twister felt Su-mil sag against his side. "We have him," he told the commander. "Thanks to the Eickaries."

SU-MIL WAS TAKING A REST BREAK AT THE REHAB ROOM'S RE-sistance machine when Twister finally tracked him down. "There you are," he said, coming up behind the Eickarie. "You may not have heard, but the doctors say you're healthy enough to leave here."

"I have heard, thank you," Su-mil replied. "But I have chosen to stay until my injury is completely healed." His highlights turned pale blue with curiosity as he looked Twister up and down. "Even in a hospital you wear your armor?"

"Orders," Twister said. "Your new leaders aren't very happy that the Warlord hasn't been turned over to them for trial and execution. Some of the people seem inclined to take out their frustration on anyone they catch wandering out in the open."

"It is not only you who are so affected," Su-mil said ruefully. "My role in those events has also been cast in an unflattering light." He gestured around him. "One reason why I remain here instead of returning to my own home."

"Your role was to help end the war and lift the oppression of your world," Twister reminded him.

"That aspect seems unimportant to many," Su-mil said. "All they see is that I made a fool's bargain that cost the Eickarie people their right of vengeance."

"If you ask me, it's this whole right of vengeance thing that's kept your tribes tangled in wars all these centuries," Twister pointed out. "Anyway, whether or not your people understand the bigger picture right now, history will vindicate your actions. *And* your bargain."

"Perhaps," Su-mil said. "But history is a long way off. Until it arrives, I must endure the looks and the whispers and the faded orange of my people."

"Oh, that future might arrive sooner than you think," Twister said thoughtfully. "Your newly formed InterTribal Council has been invited to a meeting this afternoon where they'll find out why exactly we wanted the Warlord taken alive."

"And that reason is?"

"Because, just like you, we had no idea who or what he was," Twister said. "The way he walked around encased in that armor, we couldn't tell whether he was another Lakra, a rogue Eickarie, or someone from a species we hadn't run into before. And if it was the latter, we needed to find out what he was, where he came from, and whether he was an aberration or whether his whole species liked to go off conquering other planets."

"And?" Su-mil prompted.

"Box Number Three," Twister said grimly. "Brand-new species, not in any of our files. He's been pretty blustery, but we've managed to pry the location of his home system out of him, and we're putting together a task force to head over there and make contact."

"I trust you will be careful."

"Don't worry," Twister assured him. "Even the cockiest people tend to go a little quiet when they find a couple of Star Destroyers cruising by overhead. If they're a threat, we'll find out and deal with them appropriately."

"I have never seen a Star Destroyer," Su-mil commented. "I hope to someday have that privilege."

"As a matter of fact, I think that can be arranged," Twister said, his voice studiously casual. "I've been instructed to ask whether you might be interested in applying for a commission in the Imperial Five-oh-First."

Su-mil's highlights turned dark red in surprise. "I?"

"Why not?" Twister countered. "You're intelligent, discerning, combat-skilled, and able to think on your feet. On top of that, you're willing to trust your leaders or comrades and obey orders even if you don't fully understand the reasons behind them. Put all those together and you've got a pretty rare package, one the Five-oh-First is always on the lookout for."

"And you accept nonhumans into your ranks?"

"Like I said, it's a rare combination," Twister said. "As long as your world is a member of the Empire of the Hand, you're eligible."

"You assume Kariek will join you."

Twister glanced around, making sure no one else was within earshot. "Actually, those negotiations have already started," he told Su-mil, lowering his voice. "I get the feeling your leaders would like to have a permanent Imperial presence in the system as soon as possible, just in case the Warlord's people turn out to be as unfriendly as he was."

Su-mil turned to gaze out the window. "Don't get me wrong," Twister warned. "An offer like this doesn't automatically entitle you to a commission. You'll have to work, and work hard, before you earn the right to wear the white armor."

"If I succeed, I will no doubt be perceived by some as having deserted my people," Su-mil pointed out quietly. "And if I fail, those perceptions will still be there."

"That's possible," Twister conceded. "Even if your leaders decide to join the Empire of the Hand, it may be a long time before the common people really accept that."

"And so you offer me yet another fool's bargain," Su-mil said, his highlights going pink with a wry smile.

Twister shrugged. "Sometimes those bargains work out in the end," he said. "Think about it, and let me know when you're ready."

"I am ready now," Su-mil said, standing up. "As you no doubt have already foreseen."

Twister smiled behind his faceplate. "As it happens, I have a transport waiting."

Read on for an excerpt
from the exciting prequel to
Star Wars: Episode III
Revenge of the Sith

LABYRINTH OF EVIL

by James Luceno

CAPTURING TRADE FEDERATION VICEROY—AND SEPARATIST
Councilmember—Nute Gunray is the mission that brings
Jedi Knights Obi-Wan Kenobi and Anakin Skywalker, with a
squad of clones in tow, to Neimoidia. But the treacherous
ally of the Sith proves as slippery as ever, evading his Jedi
pursuers even as they narrowly avoid deadly disaster. Still,
their daring efforts yield an unexpected prize: a unique holo-
transceiver that bears intelligence capable of leading the Republic forces to their ultimate quarry, the ever-elusive Darth
Sidious.

Swiftly taking up the chase, Anakin and Obi-Wan follow
clues from the droid factories of Charros IV to the far-flung
worlds of the Outer Rim . . . every step bringing them closer
to pinpointing the location of the Sith Lord—whom they
suspect has been manipulating every aspect of the Separatist

rebellion. Yet somehow, in the escalating galaxy-wide chess game of strikes, counterstrikes, ambushes, sabotage, and retaliations, Sidious stays constantly one move ahead.

Then the trail takes a shocking turn. For Sidious and his minions have set in motion a ruthlessly orchestrated campaign to divide and overwhelm the Jedi forces—and bring the Republic to its knees.

CHAPTER 1

DARKNESS WAS ENCROACHING ON CATO NEIMOIDIA'S WESTERN hemisphere, though exchanges of coherent light high above the beleaguered world ripped looming night to shreds. Well under the fractured sky, in an orchard of manax trees that studded the lower ramparts of Viceroy Gunray's majestic redoubt, companies of clone troopers and battle droids were slaughtering one another with bloodless precision.

A flashing fan of blue energy lit the undersides of a cluster of trees: the lightsaber of Obi-Wan Kenobi.

Attacked by two sentry droids, Obi-Wan stood his ground, twisting his upraised blade right and left to swat blaster bolts back at his enemies. Caught midsection by their own salvos, both droids came apart, with a scattering of alloy limbs.

Obi-Wan moved again.

Tumbling under the segmented thorax of a Neimoidian harvester beetle, he sprang to his feet and raced forward. Explosive light shunted from the citadel's deflector shield dappled the loamy ground between the trees, casting long shadows of their buttressed trunks. Oblivious to the chaos occurring in their midst, columns of the five-meter-long harvesters continued their stalwart march toward a mound that supported the fortress. In their cutting jaws or on their upsweeping backs they carried cargoes of pruned foliage. The crushing sounds of their ceaseless gnawing provided an eerie cadence to the rumbling detonations and the hiss and whine of blaster bolts.

From off to Obi-Wan's left came a sudden click of servos; to his right, a hushed cry of warning.

"Down, Master!"

He dropped into a crouch even before Anakin's lips formed the final word, lightsaber aimed to the ground to keep from impaling his onrushing former Padawan. A blur of thrumming blue energy sizzled through the humid air, followed by a sharp smell of cauterized circuitry, the tang of ozone. A blaster discharged into soft soil, then the stalked, elongated head of a battle droid struck the ground not a meter from Obi-Wan's feet, sparking as it bounced and rolled out of sight, repeating: *"Copy, copy . . . Copy, copy . . ."*

In a tuck, Obi-Wan pivoted on his right foot in time to see the droid's spindly body collapse. The fact that Anakin had saved his life was nothing new, but Anakin's blade had passed a little too close for comfort. Eyes somewhat wide with surprise, he came to feet.

"You nearly took my head off."

Anakin held his blade to one side. In the strobing light of battle his blue eyes shone with wry amusement. "Sorry, Master, but your head was where my lightsaber needed to go."

Master.

Anakin used the honorific not as learner to teacher, but as Jedi Knight to Jedi Council member. The braid that had defined his earlier status had been ritually severed after his audacious actions at Praesitlyn. His tunic, knee-high boots, and tight-fitting trousers were as black as the night. His face scarred from a contest with Dooku-trained Asajj Ventress. His mechanical right hand sheathed in a tight-fitting glove. He had let his hair grow long the past few months, falling almost to his shoulders now. His face he kept clean-shaven, unlike Obi-Wan's, whose strong jaw was defined by a short beard.

"I suppose I should be grateful your lightsaber *needed* to go there, rather than desired to."

Anakin's grin blossomed into a full-fledged smile. "Last time I checked we were on the same side, Master."

"Still, if I'd been a moment slower . . ."

Anakin booted the battle droid's blaster aside. "Your fears are only in your mind."

Obi-Wan scowled. "Without a head I wouldn't have much

mind left, now, would I?" He swept his lightsaber in a flourishing pass, nodding up the alley of manax trees. "After you."

They resumed their charge, moving with the supernatural speed and grace afforded by the Force, Obi-Wan's brown cloak swirling behind him. Victims of the initial bombardment, scores of battle droids lay sprawled on the ground. Others dangled like broken marionettes from the branches of the trees into which they had been hurled.

Areas of the leafy canopy were in flames.

Two scorched droids little more than arms and torsos lifted their weapons as the Jedi approached, but Anakin only raised his left hand in a Force push that shoved the droids flat onto their backs.

They jinked right, somersaulting under the wide bodies of two harvester beetles, then hurdling a tangle of barbed underbrush that had managed to anchor itself in the otherwise meticulously tended orchard. They emerged from the tree line at the shore of a broad irrigation canal, fed by a lake that delimited the Neimoidians' citadel on three sides. In the west a trio of wedge-shaped *Acclamator*-class assault cruisers hung in scudding clouds. North and east the sky was in turmoil, crosshatched with ion trails, turbolaser beams, hyphens of scarlet light streaming upward from weapons emplacements outside the citadel's energy shield. Rising from high ground at the end of the peninsula, the tiered fastness was reminiscent of the command towers of the Trade Federation core ships, and indeed had been the inspiration for them.

Somewhere inside, trapped by Republic forces, were the Trade Federation elite.

With his homeworld threatened and the purse worlds of Deko and Koru Neimoidia devastated, Viceroy Gunray would have been wiser to retreat to the Outer Rim, as other members of the Separatist Council were thought to be doing. But rational thinking had never been a Neimoidian strong suit, especially when possessions remained on Cato Neimoidia the viceroy apparently couldn't live without. Backed by a battle group of Federation warships, he had slipped onto Cato Neimoidia, intent on looting the citadel before it fell.

But Republic forces had been lying in wait, eager to capture him alive and bring him to justice—thirteen years late, in the judgment of many.

Cato Neimoidia was as close to Coruscant as Obi-Wan and Anakin had been in almost four standard months, and with the last remaining Separatist strongholds now cleared from the Core and Colonies, they expected to be back in the Outer Rim by week's end.

Obi-Wan heard movement on the far side of the irrigation canal.

An instant later, four clone troopers crept from the tree line on the opposite bank to take up firing positions amid the water-smoothed rocks that lined the ditch. Far behind them a crashed gunship was burning. Protruding from the canopy, the LAAT's blunt tail was stenciled with the eight-rayed battle standard of the Galactic Republic.

A gunboat glided into view from downstream, maneuvering to where the Jedi were waiting. Standing in the bow, a clone commander named Cody waved hand signals to the troopers on shore and to others in the gunboat, who immediately fanned out to create a safe perimeter.

Troopers could communicate with one another through the comlinks built into their T-visored helmets, but the Advanced Recon Commando teams had created an elaborate system of gestures meant to thwart enemy attempts at eavesdropping.

A few nimble leaps brought Cody face-to-face with Obi-Wan and Anakin.

"Sirs, I have the latest from airborne command."

"Show us," Anakin said.

Cody dropped to one knee, his right hand activating a device built into his left wrist gauntlet. A cone of blue light emanated from the device, and a hologram of task force commander Dodonna resolved.

"Generals Kenobi and Skywalker, provincial recon unit reports that Viceroy Gunray and his entourage are making their way to the north side of the redoubt. Our forces have been hammering at the shield from above and from points along the shore, but the shield generator is in a hardened site, and difficult to get at. Gunships are taking heavy fire from turbo-laser cannons in the lower ramparts. If your team is still committed to taking Gunray alive, you're going to have to skirt those defenses and find an alternative way into the palace. At this point we cannot reinforce, repeat, cannot reinforce."

Obi-Wan looked at Cody when the hologram had faded. "Suggestions, Commander?"

The ARC made an adjustment to the wrist projector, and a 3-D schematic of the redoubt formed in midair. "Assuming that Gunray's fortress is similar to what we found on Deko and Koru, the underground levels will contain fungus farms and processing and shipment areas. There will be access from the shipping areas into the midlevel grub hatcheries, and from the hatcheries we'll be able to infiltrate the upper reaches."

Cody carried a short-stocked DC-15 blaster rifle and wore the white armor and imaging system helmet that had come to symbolize the Grand Army of the Republic—grown, nurtured, and trained on the remote world of Kamino, three years earlier. Just now, though, areas of white showed only where there were no smears of mud or dried blood, no gouges, abrasions, or charred patches. Cody's position was designated by orange markings on his helmet crest and shoulder guards. His upper right arm bore stripes signifying campaigns in which he had participated: Aagonar, Praesitlyn, Paracelus Minor, Antar 4, Tibrin, Skor II, and dozens of other worlds from Core to Outer Rim.

Over the years Obi-Wan had formed battlefield partnerships with several Advanced Recon Commandos—Alpha, with whom he had been imprisoned on Rattatak, and Jango-tat, on Ord Cestus. Early-generation ARCs had received training by the Mandalorian clone template, Jango Fett. While the Kaminoans had managed to breed some of Fett out of the regulars, they had been more selective in the case of the ARCs. As a consequence, ARCs displayed more individual initiative and leadership abilities. In short, they were more like the late bounty hunter himself, which was to say, more *human*.

In the initial stages of the war, clone troopers were treated no differently from the war machines they piloted or the weapons they fired. To many they had more in common with battle droids poured by the tens of thousands from Baktoid Armor Workshops on a host of Separatist-held worlds. But attitudes began to shift as more and more troopers died. The clones' unfaltering dedication to the Republic, and to the Jedi, showed them to be true comrades in arms, and deserving of all the respect and compassion they were now afforded. It was the Jedi themselves, in addition to other progressive thinking officials in the Republic, who had urged that second- and third-generation ARCs be given names rather than numbers, to foster a growing fellowship.

"I agree that we can probably reach the upper levels, Commander," Obi-Wan said at last. "But how do you propose we reach the fungus farms to begin with?"

Cody stood to his full height and pointed toward the orchards. "We go in with the harvesters."

Obi-Wan glanced uncertainly at Anakin and motioned him off to one side.

"It's just the two of us. What do you think?"

"I think you worry too much, Master."

Obi-Wan folded his arms across his chest. "And who'll worry about you if I don't?"

Anakin canted his head and grinned. "There are others."

"You can only be referring to See-Threepio. And you had to *build* him."

"Think what you will."

Obi-Wan narrowed his eyes with purpose. "Oh, I see. But I would have thought Senator Amidala of greater interest to you than Supreme Chancellor Palpatine." Before Anakin could respond, he added: "Despite that she's a politician also."

"Don't think I haven't tried to attract her interest, Master."

Obi-Wan regarded Anakin for a moment. "What's more, if Chancellor Palpatine had genuine concern for your welfare, he would have kept you closer to Coruscant."

Anakin placed his artificial hand on Obi-Wan's left shoulder. "Perhaps, Master. But then, who would look after you?"